CAUGHT IN THE WEB
(INVISIBLE SPIDERS BOOK 2)
BY
JASON R. DAVIS

FoF PUBLISHING

Published by
FoF Publishing
1526 Kenilworth Ct.
Suite #1
Stoughton, WI 53589

Please visit us online at http://fofpublishing.com
Jason Davis website can be found at http://jasonrdavis.net

Edited by: Kim Young
Cover Illustration by
SnS-Photo (Jim Sorfleet)
Cover Model: Kat McGill Mayer
Zombies: James Caraway and Val Antuna
Special Effects Makeup: James Caraway
Set Design: James Caraway and Ken Spriggs
Copyright 2015

Dedicated to my mother

While there are similarities to her place of business, it is used as a reference only. None of the actions in this book or any actions that take place are meant to represent certain people. All people, actions, and accounts are fictional.

Except for Sullivan. He is a real person, and thank you for allowing me to use your name and personality in this piece of fiction.

PROLOGUE

That couldn't be what he thought it was. He heard them, the *pop-pop-pop*, and knew it must be firecrackers. It was the middle of the day in July. People had plenty left over from the Fourth, and it wasn't all that uncommon for them to be going off at any time of day. Kids running around, playing with M-80's or quarter sticks… That had to be what he heard, and they were probably doing it right outside the store. That's why he heard it all the way in the back room.

BJ picked the box up off the shelf, looking to make sure it had the right spark plug label. The room was dark, and he was back there in what seemed like the caverns of the store. It was bright outside, and he was back there in the depths, looking through their stock of auto parts, gathering what his customer was waiting for. He was in there while kids ran around outside, letting off fireworks. Damn, he wished he could be out there.

It had to be fireworks. There was just no way, no matter how much it sounded like it, that it could be gunshots. They were too close to the town. Gunshots, no matter what time, would ever fly in town. It didn't matter if the chief was on duty or not. He would still bring down harsh justice if someone was out there shooting.

Yeah, BJ thought to himself as he continued to walk up from the back of the store, carrying the boxes of spark plugs to cash register, *it has to be firecrackers. Kids are just playing around outside.*

He set the box down on the counter and looked up at the man waiting for them. Dog, a large man who wore a small, too tight shirt that may have been green at one time, stood there. As he started to ring up his purchase, BJ had to try not to look at the "spare tire" that Dog was itching.

"So what you doing after you get done tuning her up?" BJ said, trying not to look up at the hat, the old red "Budweiser" hat that had once also contained the numbers of Dale Earnhardt, Jr.…until someone had taken the time to work the numbers off. BJ still remembered when Dog, on a drunk summer night around a bonfire, had cut the numbers off after Earnhardt had switched companies and was no longer driving for the beer company. Dennis…or Dog, as he liked to be called…had used a knife he kept in his tackle box and had cut his hand open pretty good. He had been drunk enough to not realize it until the task had been done.

Dog really wasn't the brightest when it came to everyday tasks, but when it came to cars, the man could tear one down to its head gasket and put it back together again while he was still hung over.

"Planning on taking the party barge out over to Illini and dropping a few lines. You workin' tomorrow? I can hold off until you get outta here. Grab another case and you can pitch a tent."

It was a good thought. Get out of town and under the stars for the weekend. Occasionally, there would be some guys out there at Illini State Park that were known to play some bluegrass, and it wasn't uncommon to get everyone in the campground around one fire. Bluegrass wasn't BJ's music of choice, but when you're camping out and someone is playing live music, it is hard not to sit back and enjoy. And between songs, there would be the bullshit that would fly and laughs would be shared.

Then *they* would be the ones firing off the quarter sticks. He still had a box of Black Cats he had brought back from Indiana, as well as a few other good noise makers. Ha, there wasn't anything better than throwing a pack in the fire and watching as people scattered when they went off…unless it was when you lit a firecracker and let it go off right under someone's chair. It was a good time to sit back, nearly falling out of your own chair as you watched them jump out of theirs.

Of course, it was because of firecrackers that BJ knew he couldn't ask Dog if he had heard the kids outside. Dog could barely hear anything after the M-80 accident when they were kids. Thinking about it, putting Dog's head into a garbage can, then dropping an M-80 in there might not have been the best of ideas. Dog had lost a portion of his hearing, as well as more of what little sense he had to begin with.

"That does sound like a good idea. Anyone else you know gonna be out there?"

BJ rang up the items, adding in his discount and knocking the price down to cost. After all, BJ was the only one working in the store for the time being as Cindy was late, and he knew that no one would probably catch it.

"That'll be $10.80, Dog."

"Shit, Beej. Can't you do anything for me? Throw some shit in for free? Hook a brotha up."

"Man, I'm already hookin' you up. Now shut up before someone comes in here and catches on."

Dog was putting on a show of acting like he was having trouble finding his wallet. Of course this was a show as he wanted BJ to go ahead and outright pay for the damn things, but BJ had been through this many times before. He knew he just had to wait it out with this friend and, eventually, the old torn-up leather wallet would emerge and money would be produced.

BJ never knew why Dog did this every time. The man made more money than he did. Dog had a good job at the car dealership down the road because he was one hell of a mechanic, even on those damn foreign jobs he had to work on all day. Still, anytime they were anywhere, he always acted as though he never had any money and was always trying to get anyone else to pay for him.

It was another of the many reasons the man still had no woman. They never want to date someone who was always acting as though they were broke.

"Come on. I need to save up. Unless you're goin' to be bringin' the beer?"

Now he was bringing the beer when he hadn't even said he was coming out there yet? This was how the man always talked him into doing all that crap for which he was always getting into trouble. It always started out like this.

BJ heard it again. Louder and more distinct this time, and there was now no way he could say it was some kids or a car backfiring. Those were definitely gunshots, and from the look BJ saw on Dog's face, he knew that Dog *had* heard them.

He wasn't sure what he was doing, what he was even thinking he was going to do, but when he heard the little artificial bell from the door alarm, he realized he was moving, hurrying to see what was going on. He wished he could say it was to do something heroic, but he knew it had more to do with him wanting to see what was happening, rather than the possibility he was going out there to help someone.

BJ didn't have to look behind him to know Dog was on his heels. He could almost feel the large man's mass following behind him. When he wanted to, the big man could really move.

BJ reached the parking lot and slowed, looking around. The auto store faced the main street, but most of the strip mall was around the side where the larger part of the parking lot was. He could see the stoplight, as well as a fast food joint, a hotel, and a golf course. There wasn't a lot of traffic, especially for afternoon on a summer day, but he really didn't see many people out, either. There was nothing that seemed like it could have been the cause of the gunshots.

Dog hurried to his truck parked in the handicap spot in front of the store. *Yeah, Dog was handicapped all right. Handicapped in the head,* BJ thought.

Dog opened the door with a loud creak, then BJ noticed that he was still carrying the box of plugs. He tossed them on his passenger seat as he was bending over, reaching for something under the seat.

"Those were semi-automatics. Sounded pretty weak."

Hearing more gunshots, BJ spun. The echo off the stillness made it a little difficult to pinpoint exactly where they were coming from, but if he had to guess, he'd say they were coming from around the side of the building.

"Yeah, police issue," Dog said, standing back up and holding a double-barreled sawed-off shotgun. BJ knew that the thing wouldn't have a long range, but considering where Dog pulled it from, it wasn't meant to shoot too far. Oh, no. That was meant to decapitate anyone who ever tried to get into Dog's truck without permission.

"Which means Mandy might be in trouble," Dog said as he looked from the gun to BJ.

"Man, don't you think we should go check it out first?"

"Mandy might be in trouble."

"Yeah, and she's just as likely to bust your ass and put you in the drunk tank again."

Mandy was Dog's kid sister and was on the local police department. She was part-time, didn't do much and, for the most part, just went around handing out parking tickets. That made her the most hated young woman in town, which she didn't let bother her because she had plans to get out of this little shithole, backward ass, anthill of a town one day and go to Peoria, where she could be a real cop. BJ figured if that would ever happen, Dog would be right behind her, probably with his shotgun, ready to shoot anyone that even laid a hand on her.

Dog was already walking past BJ, nearly pushing him out of the way, no longer paying much attention to him. "I'm not drunk," Dog grunted to him as he stepped past.

BJ trailed behind him, and he had a bad feeling he wasn't going to like whatever they found when they went around the corner.

CHAPTER 1

Sarah felt the vibrations of the phone ringing in her suit jacket before she even heard the chirping sound of her cell. She reached for it and slid her finger across the screen, barely even watching as she made the motion. Her alarm had not gone off this morning and she was already running late. It wasn't her way. She was the tiger lady when it came to tardiness and being late was not in her DNA. It made her want to scream as these people. They just kept trying to step in her way as she crossed the lobby of the large building. Didn't they realize she was in a hurry?

"Speak."

"Where are you?" She recognized the voice. Morgan was calling, which meant things were not good. Why else would her lab assistant be calling her? There hadn't been a staff meeting scheduled that she had forgotten about, had there? She couldn't remember one and knew she would not have scheduled one before her office hours. She only did that in a crisis, and there hadn't been one when she had left the night before.

Sarah stepped around the corner of the security desk, barely looking over at the large security officer as she walked past. The machine made a little beep as she swiped her card, but even as her face popped up on the screen, she ignored the security guard. It didn't matter. Even though she didn't look up at him, he acknowledged her ID as she rushed through the metal detector. The bank of elevators was in sight just past the hallway.

She wasn't looking around. The office building she had been working in for nearly ten years was more familiar to her than her own home. Her lab was on the thirteenth floor. Well, she was one of many scientists and researchers who worked up there, but she only cared about her own.

The building was a well-designed, large building, windows surrounding the street-level entry. It was like so many of the other downtown office complexes, the only difference being the additional security as soon as you entered. Many probably only noticed that, which was good because then they wouldn't think about what else was different about the building. Such as that the hallway, decorated in a lavish marble finish, had two rows of elevators. Most would assume both sides were the same. At first glance, they did look a lot alike. Both sides had three gold doors, brightly polished and well-maintained so that nothing ever tarnished the beautiful sheen. Above the elevators on both sides, there was a little display that had a red number to count up or down, depending on which direction the elevator was going. Oh yes, they both looked very similar. They were supposed to.

It was only when someone looked at the call pad for the elevators that differences could be noticed. When a person would first go to the elevators on the right, they would see the typical call button…a round piece of white frosted plastic, which was a little nicer than many of the other downtown office buildings, with an arrow in the center pointing up.

It was when a person went to the elevators on the left that things changed. The pad didn't have a button. It had a black box much like the number counter above the elevators on the other side of the hallway.

Sarah walked up to it and positioned her thumb in its center, feeling the little tingle of electricity that came to life beneath her thumb. There was a brief sensation of heat, then a pricking feeling, then she pulled her thumb away.

In that brief second, her thumb had been scanned, and her fingerprint recorded and verified with a sample of her blood. Once the sample was done, the blood was discarded and the needle would be sanitized with fire and alcohol.

Once her identity and the fact that she was alive when the scan was made was verified, the door would open. It was just an extra level of security. With what was held in her labs, and what they had access to in her part of the building, there was never enough security. There would never be enough, but they still fought to do as much as they could. If what was up there was to ever get out, there was much to lose and many could die. There would never be enough security to keep that safe.

Finally, the scans finished, the center door opened. Sarah held back just a second, waiting as Morgan was still on the phone.

"You need to get to the airport," Morgan was saying.

"How soon?" It was uncommon for them to be told to get onto a flight. She didn't like when it happened but, typically, they would have called her while she was at home, tell her to get some things together, and they would have left that evening. Or she would get the call the night before and would meet her team at the airport in the morning.

"The team is already on its way to the airport. We leave in a half-hour. I'm on my way out of the lab right now."

Sarah was flabbergasted. There was no way they could get to the airport in a half-hour! It just wasn't feasible.

"I'll meet you down here," Sarah said. She watched as the door to the elevator closed in front of her. Something was happening, and it wasn't good.

"Meet me on the roof. The chopper will be here in five." Sarah could hear the larger woman already wheezing and knew she was already out of breath. It wasn't that Morgan was out of shape, but she was a terrible asthmatic. Between the stress of whatever was going on and having to rush around, it was probably making it near impossible for her to breathe. Sarah wanted to tell her to take a minute and calm down, but she didn't know what was going on, so she didn't think it would be a good idea for her to have the woman slow down.

She lowered the phone from her ear and looked at herself in the reflection of the elevator. On most days, she considered herself to be a decent-looking woman. She was older, her hair now had to be colored dark brown as, over the last few years, silver had started to intrude. She was still slim with a nice shape. At one time, she had been concerned about how small and pointed her nose had been, but she had grown to like its charm. After all, it made her think of Sarah Jessica Parker from *Sex in the City*. A show that, for a long time, had been one of her favorite guilty pleasures.

Parker had made her much happier about the way she looked. Change the hair color and she felt like she looked like her most days. For work, she would often wear a sensible business suit with a modest skirt…not too high to be seductive, but not too low to be Amish.

Sure, she wasn't a guy grabber, but she felt that had more do to with her not having time for them, and not for her lack of looks. She just never tried.

However, as she was looking at herself in the elevator doors, she seemed to look a lot more rugged now. Maybe it was the scared, dark look on her face, or maybe it was how her shoulders, often straight and confident, now slumped a little.

Get your shit together, Sarah, she thought to herself as she reached out her finger again, and was scanned for clearance one more.

Whatever was waiting for her up in that chopper, wherever they were taking her, she knew it wasn't good. Why hadn't they called her first? They had probably called her office, Eric expecting her normal early arrival. She had that "first person in the office" attitude, and it was known throughout the building. It went with the whole reputation that she carried. He had probably called there and when he had gotten Morgan, she probably didn't want to embarrass Sarah and had just told him that she was busy. It made sense, though she wished she knew more about what was going on. If she had talked to Eric herself, she could have made him tell her something about what they could expect. She wasn't used to being in the dark. She didn't like it.

Sarah was the leading researcher in the United States for what was classified as "Unknown Pathogens". That meant that whenever there was a new mutation or something that couldn't be diagnosed, she would often be called in for a consult. Most of the time, things happened over the phone, emails were sent through secure networks, and high definition pictures were often sent for her to make educated hypotheses as to what it was.

She had given a few briefs on field work, and had written up a few papers about how she felt certain things should be contained and investigated. However, going into the field…well, that typically only happened once, maybe twice a year, typically never in such a hurry, and she was almost always sent overseas.

This was being rushed. Someone needed her right away. This wasn't going to be a long flight overseas if there was that much of a rush on it. If that was the case, they would have sent her pictures and had her do the research virtually.

This was being rushed so that meant, more than likely, whatever was going on wasn't far away. It was going to be somewhere in the United States. Did that mean there had finally been a biological attack?

She could feel her heart starting to race as the doors for the elevator opened once again. This time, she hurried in, not allowing them to close.

* * * *

The gravel crunched beneath the tires of the large vehicle as it pulled off the road. It had been a half-hour drive from the armory to Hammond's city limits, but it would have been quicker if it hadn't been for road construction along the way. He would have to look at the map again to see if he could give the rest of his troops an alternate route to keep them from getting caught in the traffic. If he hadn't forced the driver of his caravan to go into the ditch and around the line of cars eight miles back, they would still be sitting there, trying to get around the now one-lane road.

The large troop carrier came to a stop with a jerk, making Sergeant Wade push against the restraint of his neon green seat belt. He gave a dark look to the private that was behind the wheel, but the man missed it, and the sergeant didn't push it. Instead, he quickly stepped out and took a brief look at the city limits sign just a few feet away from him.

Hammond, Pop. 9,903.

Ten thousand people and he had to keep them from leaving town.

Once they had left the armory, he put all his emotions aside. It would be deadly for him to think about what they were about to do. If he dwelled on it and thought about the action they were taking, he was afraid he wouldn't be able to do it. His stomach already burned and felt like it was eating away at him from the inside.

Dammit, now is not the time to be thinking about family, he thought. He couldn't let anything personal get in the way of doing his duty. He had a responsibility to his country. He swore an oath to God and country and, while he questioned the God, his country was his family.

No matter what damn color they put into the White House, he had a duty to his country, but this sure as hell never would have happened on anyone else's watch up there. Anyone else would never have let a mistake like this happen, allowing a town to be quarantined off. What was it, some kind of biological test gone wrong? What could have led this town, in the middle of nowhere, to get cut off from the rest of the world?

"Sergeant!" a uniformed soldier called out as he hurried up from the troop truck that had followed behind the one he rode in. The man was holding out a large radio receiver, and he reached for it. As he did, he looked around at the rest of his men, who were scrambling into the street with a series of barricades. He knew that once they set them up, they would move the trucks in front of them as reinforcement before pitching the tents to the side of the road.

Blocking the roads was going to be the easy part. As he put the large radio to his ear, he grimaced while looking at the large acres of farmland that stretched between the roads. Sure, he could block the roads, but there was a lot of space in between them and watching over it seemed like an impossible task, especially with the corn stalks high enough that a person could easily make their way through unnoticed.

It was a nightmare situation, a military action on United States soil, and he was at the "nothing he could do" end of it. If he was overseas and somewhere he felt like he could do more, could control his environment without as many legal implications, he would have sent out teams to torch the fields, making it possible for a clear line of sight.

"Mitch!" yelled a voice through the radio, and he turned his attention back to it.

"Yes, sir!" Damn, it was the colonel.

"You in position?" the voice barked at him with an angry, commanding voice.

"We just arrived at the first post. My men are positioning themselves at the other stations and securing them. We will be continuing on to the next location as soon as the first barricade is set up."

"How far out are you from the city limits?"

"We are *at* the city limits, sir."

There was a silence on the other end of the line, and he wasn't sure if the colonel had just disconnected or if he was planning his replacement. He didn't know what the hell the man wanted. He was told to secure and quarantine the town. He had never been told how far out to set the barricades, and he didn't think it really mattered. He figured as close to the town as possible would cause less questions and inconvenience.

"Okay, secure them. I'll be there within the hour, setting up secondary positions ten miles out. No one in or out, sergeant."

"Yes, sir!"

"Over and out."

"Over and out."

He knew this time that the colonel had disconnected. He handed the phone back to the soldier who was standing there, then turned back to the rest of his men. They were working quickly, and the camp would be set up within five minutes. Not bad, but that didn't mean he still couldn't yell at them. They needed to know he was still biting at their heels or they would get lazy.

"I want this camp set up and ready in two minutes! Five minutes, I want the line at attention! Last man to be in line will be digging latrines! Understood?!"

The men seemed to pick up their pace, but that could have been his imagination. He would like to think he got them to bust their ass, though. He would like to think a lot of things. He didn't want to think about what the hell would get the colonel off base and coming all the way up there to them. And if he would be there within an hour, that meant they mobilized even before he and his men.

So what in the hell was going on? He sure wished he knew.

"Pierce!" he called over to the man with the radio who had just started to walk away so he could set up his equipment in one of the tents. "Pierce! Get with the other units. I want everybody's status before we line up, make sure they are all in position. Then call the armory. I want to know how the remaining troops are coming, if the guard for the area has been called in and notified. Make sure they are also getting ahold of the guard inside the town. I want those soldiers to know the situation and get with the authorities to try and keep all those inside the city limits calm. The local law enforcement must help to keep people from trying to get to our lines. We have orders to shoot, but it must not come to that. Got it!"

"Yes, sergeant!" The man hurried to where four other men had just set up one of the tents. His equipment had already been brought to it and he quickly went to busting them out of the crates and onto the tables.

Get the perimeters secure, get the people locked down…lock in all the pigs and get them ready for the slaughter.

His stomach twisted into a knot as he thought about it. That's exactly what all this was. There were so many grisly possibilities of locking in all these people. He had friends and family in there. What was he going to do when he had his sister in his sights with an order to shoot? Would he be able to pull the trigger?

None of this was good, and he was sure this night wasn't going to end well. Pigs in a pen, and the pen is all fenced in. So many roads leading in and out, so many gates for the farmers to watch their livestock. If the pigs tried to run and get out, would they really be able to hold them? Oh no, this was not going to end well at all.

He thought back to the map he had seen. Back at the armory, he had pulled out a large map of the area, detailed with many of the roads. It would never have *all* the roads as there were always the small farm roads that never made it onto the maps, but it didn't matter. The map they used had been detailed enough, showing the crisscrossing patchwork. He had looked at it, thought about all those lines as they worked their way across the terrain. Taking out all the fields and the topography, it was all just a bunch of lines. Lines that all came to a centralized point…Hammond.

He knew what it looked like, the lines getting closer together as they merged to one point. He couldn't help but think about it. He didn't know why he had never seen it before, and why he didn't think it had anything to do on what was going on now. Why should it? He couldn't help but think with how all the roads came together, it had an eerie similarity to a spider web.

And now the townspeople, and even himself, were all the flies.

"Pierce, make sure to get a call in. Make sure they got the choppers in the air, and to keep their eyes on the corn."

CHAPTER 2

Rob couldn't think of a day he regretted leaving Chicago more than any other day. Sure, the crime was bad there and he had always been forced to be on his toes. A Chicago cop never knew when the next bullet might be shot, or when they would take a figurative knife in the back. In fact, he had seen that, just last year, Chicago had topped New York as the number one murder capital in the United States. Another statistic he didn't want to contribute to. He had been thankful when he got a job out of the city.

But at least when he was part of the Chicago PD, he wouldn't have found himself stuck out in the middle of nowhere. His bills, back when he had a steady full-time job, had always been paid, and he was able to put food on the table. He was able to survive and not have to work the odd jobs he was now having to do around the neighborhood just to earn a little extra income. He would have been making enough money to have had the spare on his car fixed so that when his tire had blown, he would not have been left stranded on the side of the road, stuck on what seemed like some forgotten back highway that no one used anymore. He wouldn't have been out there when the corn was so high, he had no clear way of seeing where there might be a farmhouse he could walk to, or some kind of help he could find.

Yeah, so why didn't he use his cell and call for help? That was why people had the damn things, so that they wouldn't be stranded in the middle of nowhere. Not that he had the best damn cell reception out there. He already learned that from experience. But to have to worry about reception, he would have had to remember to bring the phone with him, instead of leaving it sitting on his nightstand where he had been using it as his alarm clock that morning.

Thankfully, someone had finally shown up to help him. A truck driver, a larger man who looked to be in his mid-forties, had pulled off and picked Rob up, bringing him to the closest town. Of course, it didn't do him any good to get to the county courthouse to testify in the vandalism case he was supposed to be appearing at, but with most of the morning wasted on the side of the road, all he really wanted at this point was to get somewhere cool, sit down for a bit, and maybe get his hands to stop shaking from everything that had happened that damned morning.

He had never had a tire blow on him going sixty miles an hour. The front of the car had rocked up, coming crashing back down. The whole world around him started shaking as he fought to keep control of the car. It seemed odd that he really only had to fight for control for the first few seconds, when the car had crashed back down from the initial blow out. After that, the car seemed to stabilize itself, and he was able to ease it over to the side of the road. Sure, it seemed easy and, for a long time, he hadn't really thought about what he had done. The whole time he had been focused on just reacting. It had seemed so easy…until he had time to think about it afterwards and wonder just how he had actually done it.

Bruce, the truck driver, had picked him up, taken him to a little diner for some lunch, then had taken him to the garage he knew right across from a friend's bar. Rob appreciated it, and had enjoyed the meal. He hadn't thought too much about the whole experience and how he was lucky to be alive. Now though, as he watched the large man walking away from him and heading off to the little bar, he had time to think. His hands were shaking as he realized that his morning, his shitty morning from hell, could have been a lot worse. He could easily have lost control of the car, it could have flipped over, the rubber and metal from the tire could have ripped into the engine and done some damage or caught on fire, and he might not have walked away from it.

All in all, he was definitely lucky to be alive.

Rob watched and saw the little bar that Bruce was heading towards, making sure to make note that it was the building just across the railroad tracks, caddy-corner to the little garage he was at, and not the bar just across the street from him. They were so far off the main drag of town, he was surprised there were two bars, but he made sure that he would go to the correct one as soon as he was done talking to the mechanic.

He looked around the little garage. Back in Chicago, he would have thought it was a meth lab…the dirty windows, the clutter in corners, junk piled on top of junk. The place didn't look like it was open for business and looked like it wanted to stay off people's radar. Why would anyone choose to go there? It seemed like a place abandoned and forgotten. The cars that were parked in the lot along the side of the building were covered in dust that even the latest rain hadn't been able to wash clean. He doubted even the newest car was less than ten-years-old, and he questioned who would possibly pay the $700 that was crudely written on its windshield in large, washed-out soap numbers.

But Bruce had ensured him this guy would be okay. He wondered just how Bruce knew him, but Bruce was from the area, while Rob, living just thirty miles from there in a small town he had moved to just over a year ago, was still a stranger.

He didn't know if he would ever get over the differences between being a Chicago PD officer to being a small town deputy. It had been a big shock when they had moved down there, and it continued to always amaze him that it could get more unexpected. It wasn't like Mayberry, like the television shows he had seen growing up, but it wasn't much like those modern shows that teens watched, either. The sheriff didn't know everyone, didn't *care* to know everyone, and the police force wasn't always on duty. At least that's how it was in the small town in which he was a deputy. He wasn't sure how much different it would be in the town he was currently stranded in. In his town, the local law enforcement was on duty from 4 p.m. until 4 a.m., and anything after that required a call to county. The sheriff worked five days a week. That left only weekends for Rob to work and was the reason why he had to find various odd jobs around the town to make ends meet.

Why had they left the city and his full-time job again?

Oh, that's right. Because, on his last call as a CPD officer, he had been shot, set on fire, pushed down some stairs, and awoke weeks later in a hospital. That, and the fact there had been a rash of school shootings at his son's school, made him and his wife re-think the idea of living in the city. While he hadn't meant to do something as drastic as moving far out in the country, the job that was available and the house they had found made him jump at the chance.

Yes, he had jumped at the chance to have a house large enough that he could have his own man-cave. Pardon him for wanting to have his own space and have a room to sit back in, with a big screen television to watch the Sunday football games. Of course, when he found out the job wasn't full-time, the big screen television never reached his man-cave.

He walked over to the front door of the little place, noticing that he could just make out the flip sign through the dirty glass of the door…"through the dirty He pushed on the door, momentarily fighting as it was stuck, then cringing a little as it scraped the door frame before releasing and letting him step inside.

The smell of stale cardboard, old oil, and the heavy musty odor of dirt attacked him, and he was instantly reminded of what his garage had first smelled like when they had moved into his house. It had only been a year ago and it was huge. Coming from Chicago, and buying the house for only a fraction of what they had paid for their condo, they hadn't been ready for the amount of space they would have. He also hadn't been ready for the garage attached to the house. He had no idea what the previous owners had been like, although looking at the boring white walls throughout most of the house, he didn't think they had been too imaginative. The garage must have been the storage area for most of their shit, and the previous owners didn't believe in disposing of old oil. He had found jugs of the stuff, and the garage reeked of it. The smell seemed like it had infused itself into the cement floor and the wood beams, like it was a part of it.

It wasn't filling him with confidence that this mechanic's garage smelled much the same way. Did he really want to trust his car to this guy? Sure, he only needed to get a tire fixed, but something about that bothered him. He felt like he was forgetting something. He didn't know what it was, but there was a thought hiding in the corner of his mind. Something here wasn't going to go how he wanted it to. He wasn't sure how he knew, but he had that uneasiness telling him something was about to go wrong.

Once he had opened the door, there was a digital jingle that seemed off key, the batteries probably dying. He closed the door behind him, the metal again squealing in protest as it fought its frame.

"Can I help you?"

Rob turned to see a short, grease-covered man standing in the open doorway to the garage area. The man seemed to fit right in with the small front counter area, which was a dirt-covered mess. His shirt was covered in dark streaks, his weathered skin was darker in spots from where grease and other traces of God knows what were streaked across. His skin was tight, stretched like leather, his veins protruding from years of hard work and living on the hardships of the job. The man looked small and scrawny, but Rob had seen the type before. He was the kind of man who didn't look like much but was covered with tight muscle, the kind that was like iron in a pinch. It was a leanness that only came from hard work.

"Yeah, my car… I had a flat tire on the way into town and I'm without a spare. Was wondering if you could come out and put a new one on?"

"What size?" The man stepped the rest of the way into the room. Rob could see that the name on the shirt. "Mike". He walked over behind the counter and grabbed a piece of notebook paper from a pad that was next to the phone. The rest of the counter was covered in work orders, scattered into various piles.

"Excuse me?" Rob walked up to the counter.

Mike raised his eyebrow. "What size is the tire? I can take one out and change it, but I need to know the tire size."

Shit, that was what Rob had been forgetting. He needed to know the rim and tire size, *especially* the rim size. While it wasn't recommended, he could put a tire on that wasn't the same size as the others. He could do it. It would just really screw up the alignment and the car would pull in one direction. However, the rim size he would need to know for sure, or Mike wouldn't be able to put on a tire that fit. There was very little he could do about guessing the right rim size, and he didn't know it off the top his head.

"I…I don't know," Rob finally said as the man's glare hadn't softened. It grew more intense, and Rob thought he saw the man's shoulders sag a little. It didn't surprise him. Rob had just made himself one of the harder to deal with customers. He hadn't meant to, but that didn't matter. Mike looked like he had dealt with one too many hard cases that day.

Blowing out a breath, Mike asked, "Where's it at?"

"Well…"

* * * *

Jason knew he couldn't stay hidden in the kitchen for too long before the customers in the bar would get frustrated with him. While that didn't matter to him, as he really couldn't care less about any of them, he knew it would upset his mom. She would, of course, hear about it. He was sure that no matter what he did, she would hear about it so he didn't know why it really mattered. No matter what he did, these people would always complain about him because he wasn't her. He couldn't relate to them, or vice versa. He knew he should try and cause the least amount of complaints while she was on vacation. He was in charge of watching the bar and he didn't want to disappoint her. She deserved her time away and it would be good that she felt like she could take a vacation every once in awhile.

But his aunt was really upset. He was holding her at arm's length, and she was a wreck. Her body was trembling, her lower lip quivered, her eyes were puffy and red. She was on the brink of crying again. How had she been able to drive to the bar? He had found her like that out in her car just a few minutes ago, sitting behind the steering wheel and crying as she looked off into space. He didn't know how long she had been sitting like that before he had taken out the garbage. It couldn't have been too long; otherwise, one of the patrons probably would have said something to him. She had parked not too far from the door, so they definitely would have noticed her.

So how could he leave her? It was one thing to leave her and check on the patrons out there, but she wanted him to go to the house. He understood why. Bad things would happen if he didn't, but how could he? Right now, there was no way she could handle even just the couple of people that they had out there. The conversation they just had couldn't seem to sink in. Had his aunt really just confessed to killing someone?

When he had first brought her into the back, she had already stopped crying. He hadn't been too sure how long ago she had stopped, but it must have been just before he had found her. The corners of her eyes had still been wet, her cheeks were still red. He led her to the back of the bar, her head low so that none of the patrons could really see her face.

She stayed quiet the whole way. Even when he got her away from people, she stayed that way. It bothered him. Something had happened at the house, and his gut twisted at the possibility something had happened to Lisa.

Lisa was Jason's little sister. He didn't know why his parents had waited ten years after they had him before having another child. Maybe it had something to do with them just wanting another baby to squirm around the house and break things, or maybe they were just afraid of starting to get their freedom back because he would soon be able to take care of himself. Hell, who was he kidding? He knew the reason why. They were getting ready to get divorced. Lisa was that one last attempt to make everything right in so many ways.

So was that it? *Had* something happened to Lisa? Now that they were in the back and away from people, his insides twisting in aggravation because she didn't just say what had happened, he finally asked her. He looked down at her face in the crook of his shoulder as she was so much shorter than his six foot, one inch frame.

"Is Lisa okay?"

Tina seemed shocked. She pulled back and looked up at him. Then the moment passed and she was shaking her head. She rushed over to the sink, turned on the faucet, and started to splash cool water on her face.

"It's not Lisa. She's fine. She's at the game." Tina turned off the water, but she didn't turn to face him. She kept her head low and as he watched her fight to keep her body from shaking, he knew she was trying to keep the tears back. She was on the verge of losing it all over again.

It didn't feel right that he should be the one to console her. With how young his aunt was, only five years older than himself, he felt like he was acting like a boyfriend, not a nephew. It felt like what should be done, but he didn't feel like he should be the one to do it. It was inside that personal bubble, one that said he should always keep her at a distance, or else other feelings may develop. She was his aunt, dammit! Although she *was* cute, he couldn't think like that. It was just sick.

He stepped behind her, again keeping her at arm's length, and reached out to touch her shoulders. Her back stiffened, and he knew that it had been the wrong move. He quickly stepped back, dropping his arms and bowing his head.

Damn, he was no good at this. Why did this have to happen while his mom was away?

"She's at the game," Tina continued, "but she will be home soon."

Jason felt like there was something in how Tina said that. It seemed to drop the temperature in the room to freezing, making him shiver. What happened to that July heat outside?

She turned to face him, and he saw she was on the verge of releasing more tears. "You have to go back to the house. You need to. Lisa could be home anytime, and he's still there. You need to get there and take care of him. Lisa shouldn't have to see that."

"Take care of who? What's wrong?

The dam broke and the tears came again. Her hand quickly came up to try and hold them back but, as it shook there, it did little more than wipe away at the corners before falling back to her side. She leaned back against the counter and looked down at the floor.

"I killed him. At least I think I killed him. I don't know, but I think so. It doesn't matter. He can't be there when Lisa gets home."

"What? Who?"

"Vince."

"Vince? Who's Vince?"

"My boyfriend. The one who…"

Tina couldn't finish. She just bent over, quivering. She didn't have to finish, though. He had overheard the conversations she had with his mom. He knew Vince had beaten Tina, and she was staying with them to hide from him. So he had found her? Had he tried to hurt her and something happened? She was here, so she had gotten away from him, but she was convinced that he was dead? Maybe he was, and now she wanted him to…what? Hide the body? Why not call the police? That was probably what he was going to do.

It did mean he needed to get back to the house, especially if Lisa *did* come home to find a dead man there. His sister wouldn't take that too well, and it would probably give her nightmares for the rest of her life. He couldn't let her see that. Tina was right. He had to go to the house.

"Hey, kid?!" he heard someone call from the other room.

"I gotta go take care of some customers. Are you going to be okay for a minute or so?" he asked her. She nodded. He hoped so, but he had his doubts. She tried to sniffle back some of the tears and smile up at him, but he knew it wasn't real. Her eyes were still lost and pleading, still glinting with the threat of more tears as soon as he was gone.

He quickly hurried out of the kitchen and to the man that was sitting at the bar. Mr. Jones was still sitting at his end, and Jason was kind of surprised to still see him there. Usually, when he was getting ignored, he would just get up and leave. Not only was he still there, but he stayed past the time he normally did. He usually only stayed this late when there was someone just as annoying as he was that wouldn't stop talking to him.

Jason turned away from the old man who called him. He was surprised to see another person just a couple of stools down. The new man looked older with some stubble that showed he hadn't shaved for a couple days. He was a husky, rugged man who looked like he didn't miss too many meals and didn't get out much. Jason ignored him as it was hard not to because the other man was impatiently tapping his beer bottle against the bar.

"Sorry," he said as he hurried towards the impatient asshole. He could really wait as far as Jason was concerned. He didn't really like dealing with pushy pricks, and this guy seemed determined to push his buttons. He had already labeled the man as a dumb hillbilly redneck prick, and he had no tolerance for him. Maybe it was how they interacted with each other, but the feeling seemed to be mutual. The man wasn't anything great to look at, and his stained wife-beater, along with the well-worn "Lite" hat that looked like a dog had once thought it was a play toy, had Jason thinking of the man as something he didn't even want to wait on. Hell, he probably owed money on a tab his mom kept under the counter. Seeing that she wasn't there, he was spending the money he should have paid it off with on some more beer. Jason didn't know the man, so he couldn't check on it. It wouldn't surprise him, though.

He wanted to trick the man into giving him his name. Jason didn't think the stranger was smart enough to figure out what he was doing, but doubted he would be willing to talk long enough to get it to work. Jason didn't feel like putting forth the effort anyway. It would only piss off the maggot and make him leave. Then again, maybe that would be a good thing.

"Just hurry the fuck up."

Jason nodded to him and quickly turned back around, going down the side of the bar near Mr. Jones. He opened the cooler, momentarily relishing in the blast of cool air that escaped, and grabbed a brown bottle. He was already opening it as he hurried down to the man and put it in front of him. He took the money from the pile on the bar, then turned to the register and put it in the till.

Jason really did like many of the people who came into his mom's bar. Josh and a few others were good friends and he would occasionally flirt with a few of the girls that came in there, though none of them were really his type. There were also the assholes, and Jason did not have the tolerance his mom had in dealing with them. He just wished they would leave him the hell alone.

"I'm done with this," the man said.

Jason turned and saw the large bucket next to him full of tickets. Jason took it and put it below, then turned his attention to the other man sitting there.

"Really sorry about the wait. Had some issues in the back."

"Screwing around back there with the little missus?" he said, a mocking smirk working its way through his grease-stained face.

"Eew. That's my aunt," Jason said, making a face, and turned to look towards the new guy who was just a couple of stools down. "So, what can I get you?"

"Well, what I want is one of your mom's heavenly pre-mixed Bloody Marys, but..." The man hung on the word "but", stopping Jason as he had already been bending over to grab the jug of mix from the cooler. "I'm in the truck today so I'll have to settle for a Coke," Bruce finally said. "Yeah, I gotta be good."

Jason stood and walked back down to the cooler, grabbing a can of Coke. He had to get out of there, and more people coming in was not helping. He had to think of someone who could watch the bar. How could he leave? Just close it up? Yeah, his mom would love it when she heard about that, and she *would* hear about it.

"Better make it a diet," Bruce called down. Jason nodded and reached back into the cooler.

How could he leave the bar? Truth was, he didn't have too many people he could trust with it. Sure, he had grown up in the area, but he never had too many friends, and most of them he did have had already moved away to go to college, just like he did. He just happened to be home to help out his mom, but he normally wouldn't have even been there.

In fact, the only friend he did have that still lived around there was his best friend and the one he still kept in contact with pretty regularly. Hell, they did a show together every Wednesday night but, more often than not, that was done through Skype and long distance. That still didn't mean Jason would trust the bar to him.

As he walked past the hallway that led to the back, he could still hear Tina crying.

It was settled. He had to call Sullivan. He had already tried to call him a bunch of times earlier, just out of boredom. Hopefully, now he could get the lazy bastard out of his damn bed.

Jason put down the open Diet Coke and quickly filled a glass of ice to set next to it. He didn't even take the man's money as he quickly turned, went to the phone, and started dialing Sullivan's number.

Once again, he didn't answer. *Damn him! Come on, Sully. Answer the damn phone*, he thought to himself.

CHAPTER 3

Sullivan finally pulled himself out of bed, his head hanging as a thick fog, mixed with the weight of an anvil, kept away all waking thought. The spinning room and wobbling floor fought against his sense of what was up and down, and he had to struggle with it. He didn't want to get up, but knew if he didn't want to be in a piss-soaked bed, it was now or never.

"Ugh." He still didn't want to open his eyes. He wouldn't have, but his bladder was telling him that it was time to go…if not to the bathroom, then in his bed. He was obliged to listen to it, and he hadn't drunk enough the night before to accept waking up covered in his own urine. He needed two more beers and a bottle of Jack before that would be acceptable.

He opened his eyes and looked around the room. Yep, it was just how he left it. His own little slice of heaven stuffed into the silver bullet of a camper, was filled with piles of comic books, movies in a variety of genres, books, and video games. Nothing but the necessities were allowed in his mobile home because on the day the zombie apocalypse happened, he had to have all of it here and ready to move.

However, it didn't pack well, so it was scattered all over the place. The only part of his place that was organized was the trunk he had positioned right behind the driver's seat. It contained his collection of firearms, ammunition, arrows for the bow mounted on the ceiling, and his collection of porn. Oh yeah. He was ready.

Just because the place looked messy, didn't mean it was dirty. He didn't consider himself a slob. There was no food lying around, nothing that might attract bugs and ants. No, he picked up after himself. He considered himself to be clean, just not overly-organized.

Still, first thing in his morning, which was just a little before noon according to the clock, it did make things a little difficult when making his way from his couch bed to the bathroom hallway in the back of the camper. He didn't use his back bedroom because he had gutted that and had made it into his computer and radio studio. It was from there that he recorded his podcasts and broadcasted his pirate radio show. Even though he was ready for the day the zombie apocalypse happened, he wanted to make sure everyone else was, as well. If they listened to him, they would be.

He stood and looked around, his eyes adjusting to the daylight. He could feel the crust of sleep around his eyes and wiped it away. Sure, he kept his place clean, but towards the end of the night, the bottles got further and further away from the garbage, and he looked to see the amount of beer cans and bottles scattered around the room. He had one hell of a show last night, and it had gone on pretty late. The evidence was all around him, and he had to move carefully so he didn't step on any of the cans with his bare feet. There were also some papers scattered about that he figured he must have bumped into on his way to his couch last night.

Stepping past his counter and glancing at his cell phone, he saw that it glowed. Someone had just left him a voicemail.

He wondered if that was what had woken him. He really didn't feel ready to get up, his mind still lingering in the drunk from the night before. It just didn't feel right to be up this early. And who the hell was calling him? Must be a bill collector, as all his friends knew not to leave voicemails. Just call and hang up and, if he felt like it, he would call them back. Plus, most of them would know better than to call him before noon. They would know there was no chance he would be up that early.

He picked up the phone and glanced at the display, making sure to still keep one eye on the floor as he walked around the various heaps. Now that he was partially away from the disaster zone around his couch, there were smaller, less dangerous items to step on and he could focus more on the phone.

Jason had called him thirteen times? He should have known better than to leave a voicemail, but there it was. His screen showed three new messages, all of them from Jason. Then again, if anyone was likely to leave him a message, Jason sometimes did just because he knew how much it annoyed him, but three of them this morning?

Sullivan shrugged and put the phone back into his pocket. Maybe he'd call him back in an hour or so. First, he had to do his morning ritual. After all, he needed to piss, shit, and shower. Maybe he'd think about dealing with people after that. It was too early to think about it. Right now, he just wanted to get the day started so he could get it done. He was already looking forward to when he would be able to go back to bed.

He stepped around a pile of books and his toe clipped on the bookcase.

"Ow!" he hissed in pain as he crashed over into the door frame to the bathroom. Flashes of pain shooting from his toe, he lost feeling in the tip. His other foot stumbled, and he tried to keep from falling. His foot landed on something sharp, and he felt himself falling, the world around him rising up. Out of the corner of his eye, he saw the bathroom sink coming at him. Then his knees crashed down, and he was barely able to reach out and grab the sink, keeping himself from slamming into it.

"Fucking shit!" He flopped over, turning so he could sit in the small bathroom, which was barely big enough to stand in. Now he was sitting in the bathroom and the hallway at the same time. He had to fight with the slim door frame to pull his foot up and examine it. First the one that had stepped on something sharp, then the one he had stubbed. No blood. Good. At least he hadn't cut himself.

He hung his head. This was going to be a *great* day. The pounding in his head was getting worse, his feet were now sore and he could feel a little wetness, which meant he had pissed a little on himself. What the fuck? Could this shit get any worse?

The pounding in his head seemed to grow and shake, making the walls around him tremor in their wake. He felt it cave in on him. The pain clouded his thoughts, a vice grip tightening in on his attempt to think. It beat in time with…

Damn it! It wasn't his headache that was making the damn walls shake. Someone was pounding on his fucking door. Who the fuck could it be and, whoever it was, they weren't going to like what they were about to get.

Sullivan stood, wobbling a little. Whoever was there, it had better be good.

* * * *

Jason pounded on the door, the intensity shaking the cheap metal of the camper, and cursed his best friend. Why did the man insist on never growing up, making Jason's life so damn hard? It was like the podcast they did. Why did Jason always have to do all the work? Sullivan was never on time, he never did his research and, other than making obscene references, he was pretty much useless. Well, except for the fact that his laid back attitude and obscene humor probably made the show as entertaining as it was. It sure as hell wasn't Jason's dry wit.

How was he ever supposed to trust Sully watching his mom's bar? What was he thinking? There was no way he could trust him. Honestly, he only had to drive across town. He was probably going to be longer just trying to wake up Sully and get him over there.

The door crashed open, pulled so quickly that it slammed against something near it. He heard cursing from the other side, more things crashed to the floor, something sounded like glass hitting the fake linoleum on the floor, but he didn't hear it break. The door still wasn't open all the way, and he saw it continued to be jerked inward, probably slamming into more clutter until, finally, it could be opened enough for Sullivan to emerge.

"For fuck's sake, man!" Sullivan snarled at him. Jason noticed he didn't open the screen door or invite him in. Not that they had time. Jason couldn't let this become a snarling match, although his first instinct had been to retort back about how he had to come over there because the lazy ass wouldn't answer his phone or get himself out of bed. He was angry, frustrated and, with how his friend was standing there ready for a fight, he wanted to give it to him.

His blood burned with frustration. He hadn't realized just how pent up he had been getting, and having a willing partner for a verbal assault made him just want to lash out. Why was he having to take care of the bar? Why did he have to worry about his aunt and his sister? His aunt was supposed to be *their* watcher, *their* babysitter. Why was he having to take care of her? Why the hell did the whole damn world seem to always come down on his shoulders, leaving him to fix everything? His mom got to run away. His dad ran away years ago, never to return. He tried to run away. He went off to school to get away, but how did that work? When responsibility came, when he had to take care of his mom's stuff, his sister, and now his aunt, there he was. Why did it always have to fall onto his shoulders?

He hadn't realized just how much anger and hurt he was carrying until he stood there, his friend in the door, snarling at him. He just wanted to scream back. To lash out at his friend who didn't have to worry about anything. When Sully needed money, his parents, still married and living on the other side of town, were there to give it to him. He was the boy who never had to grow up. Why did Jason have to take care of everything, but Sullivan got to live without a care in the world? And Sullivan wanted to yell at him for trying to wake him up? He wanted to fight with him? Well, what about all the shit that had been thrown at him?

Oh yes. Those fires suddenly burned through him. The thoughts didn't fully race into his consciousness, but they hovered there on the fringes. He felt the heat, the rising flames in his chest, the burning sensation behind his eyes, and that annoying sense of just wanting to scream and hurl himself at this boy-man who was his friend.

He had to swallow and push it all back down. He couldn't let go. That wasn't him, and that couldn't be him. He would still leave. He would go back to school. He had to be the responsible one.

Reigning in his rage, he looked at his friend. "Man, come on. I really need you. Please, dude," Jason said, cutting into the rant Sullivan was still lost in.

Sullivan stopped and looked at him. It really didn't take much more than that. He didn't know what his friend saw there. He could only imagine how he looked…tears threatening, rugged, downtrodden, his voice soft and pleading, defeated. Whatever it was, he saw Sullivan's shoulders sag. He knew that his friend, as frustrated as he was, was still his friend.

CHAPTER 4

"Now I lay me down to sleep. I pray the Lord my soul
to keep. If I die before I wake, I pray the Lord my soul to take.
Now I lay me down to sleep. I pray the Lord my soul to keep…"

He didn't know how long he had been chanting. He was
sitting alone in one of the pews of his church. The sun was hot
against his skin as it attacked him through the multicolored
window depicting Jesus on the cross. His stump hurt, he was
warm, and the dry cottonmouth he was experiencing made him
realize he must have been sitting there for some time. Had it
been hours? He barely even remembered leaving his little
sleeping room in the back of the parish.

He remembered the fires that had flooded through his
nightmares, and the man that had been coming for him. The man
with the red eyes and the dark skin, but not black in the way of
natural skin color. This man's skin was pitch black, like burned
coal. He wore a black suit, and the only thing that was
discernible about him, as he had walked towards Father
Carpenter in his nightmare, had been those burning red eyes that
pierced deep down into his very soul. He felt them singe at his
heart, his blood burning its way through his veins. He tried to
stop looking, to turn away, but as he ripped his gaze away to
look down at the ash at his feet, the smell of the man attacked

him. The rotten meat, the burning flesh, all mingled to make his stomach turn. The smell grew stronger as the man approached.

Even awake, he couldn't help himself. He felt a tremor of fear run down his spine. He couldn't shake the feeling it was more than just a dream. He had never felt anything like that. This one was so vivid, it had felt real, the heat from the flames burning him.

Father Carpenter slowly stood up, his old knees shaking. He wasn't sure if it was from siting for too long or from fear. He wanted to believe it was his age, but the moisture at the edge of his eyes told him he was lying to himself. He could feel that tightness in his chest. That feeling like he was on the verge of a panic attack, that something inside him just wanted to drop down, roll up into a ball, and just cry and hide from everything.

He couldn't let it. He had to keep his composure. It was only a dream, and he couldn't let it paralyze him. He would have to use it, have to come up with a new sermon, using this fear when he spoke to his people.

A long breath escaped him. He took in another deep one and, closing his eyes, focused on pushing it all away as he exhaled. It was a trick he had learned from those hypnosis tapes he had used to quit smoking. Breathe in a long deep breath, hold it, count to ten, then visualize all that pent up frustration and pain, seeing it escape as you let it all out. Just breathe.

"Father, are you okay?"

He opened his eyes to see Cynthia standing at the end of the aisle. He hadn't heard her come in, and she had snuck up on him. He must have been deep in his trance to not notice because her shoes always echoed loudly in the large space of the expansive church.

"Yes, I'm fine."

"Are you sure?" She stepped closer to him, not coming into the row he stood in, but the one in front of him. He had to smile at how she kept her distance, not wanting to invade his space…or maybe it had more to do with her respect for the cloth.

Cynthia wasn't one of the oldest members of his parish, but she was in her late forties and he sometimes worried that maybe she had a thing for him. She seemed to like to hover around, and she was always there in case he ever needed anything. She had been there when his wife of twenty years had passed away. Was she there as a friend, or someone who wanted more? He would like to think that all she wanted was to be closer to God, and thought she could achieve that by being closer to him. But sometimes there was a heat that came off of her, a burning he could feel emanating from her when she was close. It made him question her intentions.

She was so much younger than him. Her golden blond hair was starting to turn a silvery white at the fringes, and her face was still untouched by wrinkles that would soon mark her years. The years were being much better to her than they were to him, and he briefly thought about their age difference. He was getting up there, as he was reminded of every morning by looking at the pale, wrinkled face in the mirror. It was an ancient face, but with the little fat that he carried, it had that slight chubbiness to it that showed he was not wanting. He felt that the roundness added a fatherly quality. He didn't have the hard lines, and he knew that his smile was warm.

He smiled at her now, his near perfect dentures glistening, and he watched as her expression softened, the look of concern disappearing as she smiled back at him.

"I told you, I'm fine." He reached out and took her arm, looking in her eyes. He wanted to make her believe him and not have to worry. After all, it had just been a dream, and he had to push it out of his mind. Just let it go, breathe it out, let all the negative energy release out of him.

Once again, he noticed how warm she was, but there was something else now. He could feel an energy. Her grip twisted, then she was holding his wrist. The warm sensation passing through her turned hot, and the iron grip she had on his wrist hurt. He winced in pain as he looked first at his wrist, then up into her eyes, pleading with her to let him go.

His mouth went slack, hanging open when he saw the dark man standing behind her, his arm touching her shoulder. The father felt a weight on his chest, and something gripped his heart. The air around him seemed thick and it was hard to breathe, and when he *did* pull in breath, he smelled that putrid scent. The large space of the church suddenly felt small and full of rotted meat.

"Father?" He saw her mouth say the words, but he heard the deep, gravelly voice of the man behind her. "Father, are you okay?"

"Get away, you demon! Get away! Go back to the fires of hell! Stay away!" He closed his eyes, lowering his head and starting to pray.

"The fires burn," the voice said. Cynthia's voice was no longer there and he knew if he opened his eyes, he wouldn't see her there, either. She would be gone, and that dark man, with those red, burning eyes, would be there looking at him. They would burn into him, tearing away his soul. He couldn't look at them. He couldn't open his eyes and look at that face.

"I saw the fires you bring, you demon. Get away. The Lord will stop you. The Lord will tear away your fires, bringing forth the light of heaven."

"Don't blame me for the fire. Blame your God," the voice rasped.

"Dear heavenly Father, we pray in your name. Your rod and your staff, they comfort me. Lead me through…" Tears fell down his cheeks. He could feel their coolness in the suddenly hot room. No, he had to push it away. He had to push that fire away and feel the cool breeze of heaven. His Father was there, his faith was behind him. He had to believe in it and push this demon away, opening himself to the light and the glory of heaven.

"Dear heavenly Father, your rod and staff, they comfort me." He felt as the grip on his wrist loosened. "Amen." He opened his eyes and looked up.

Cynthia was gone. He was alone in the church, but he still smelled the presence. The dark man had definitely been there.

Father Carpenter hurried out of the pew and rushed to the front doors of the church. Suddenly, it didn't feel so big in there, and he had the overriding sensation he needed to get out. Even under the watchful gaze of Jesus looking down from the cross, he no longer felt safe there. Somehow, evil had defiled the place. Even in the house of the Lord, the devil had made his presence known.

* * * *

"So is everything in place?!" Sarah yelled as she kept her head down while hurrying out from under the decelerating whirring helicopter blades that spun around above her. Her blazer jacket was billowing out behind her and she felt like she had to hold the jacket closed against the air being blown at her by the blades.

She was yelling to the man who was standing just outside the range of the blades. Eric Ranger stood there, tall and lean in his pressed suit. He was also holding his suit jacket closed against the force of the wind, although he looked like he would never be put out by any breeze. His hair was always so perfect, it looked like he could walk through a hurricane and not have a strand out of place.

Of course, he needed to be. Eric was a wannabe politician. He was the one who ran her department, which always seemed to make him feel like he ran her. At least that was how he sometimes made her feel. Like having her rush there by helicopter, knowing she didn't like to fly, meeting him on the tarmac of the Atlanta airport, rushing to a charter plane, and she *still* had no idea what was going on. She didn't like being left in the dark.

She could tell that he couldn't hear her as she neared. With the loud whirring of the blades, and the cry of the engine as it was winding itself down, she could barely hear her own thoughts.

Well, if they were in a rush and didn't give her any information, she could play the power game, too. Eric should know that women always win. Or was that why he never came to her place anymore? It didn't matter. He would learn that he was not the boss of her.

She walked past him. She already knew the plane sitting there was for her and her team, and maybe a few additional team members if Eric had thought they were needed, though she would have liked to have been able to choose her own team. She knew walking past him and just continuing to the plane was sure to agitate him, and that was good. Let him be frustrated with her. Maybe next time he would send some information ahead of time so she could at least look at it while she was on the helicopter.

"So, is everything in place?! What's going on and where?!" she yelled to him again as he hurried to catch up to her. She was glad they were starting to get farther away from that damned helicopter. The roar of those turbines no longer felt like they were pounding inside her ribcage.

"Wheels are in motion. Here," Eric said, handing her a case file.

She looked at the extremely thin folder. She opened it and stopped, staring at only five pages. The first was a bio of someone she already knew very well. Bryan. While he wasn't a part of her team, he was one hell of a scientist and worked on the same floor as she did at the CDC. He would often run his own teams, though he was never one to go into the field. Mosquitos terrified him, and an unsterile location would send him over the edge. In the lab, though, he was about the best there was in identifying pathogens.

She flipped past her coworker's dossier, and went to the next page. It was a breakdown of a town. There wasn't much detail, but it shocked her to see that it was on United States soil, and that this was a hot crisis incident. Had there been a terrorist attack? She didn't remember seeing anything on the news but, then again, there wouldn't be if it wasn't public.

The town was small and in the middle of nowhere. Why the hell would there be a terrorist strike there? Unless the terrorists were experimenting and something accidentally got loose.

"It started when I got a phone call from an old friend. A doctor with whom I went to school. Said he had something strange. It was only luck that Bryan was in the area. He had a wedding he was glad to get away from for a while. I guess it got him out of the rehearsal dinner."

She turned to the next page. There was the short transcript of Bryan's call. He said something about spiders, but he could have been delusional. If Bryan hadn't been heard from since, he must have contracted whatever it was. If he only had time to call in shortly after he arrived, then whatever it was moved fast. That was an incubation time of only an hour, maybe two. That wasn't good. There could be something to the spider comment, but that meant they were dealing with some venomous outbreak of some type of spider they had not seen before.

Either that, or Bryan, not being a field scientist, overreacted and all of this was being blown out of proportion. Part of her, the part that cared about a friend and colleague, hoped that wasn't the case. Yes, that would mean a lot of people's lives would be in danger, but Bryan's name would not be tarnished, and his career wouldn't be over. Of course, his life may have already ended.

"Bryan okay?" Sarah asked, not looking up from the file.

"Don't know. I listened to his call again. He hadn't been in the town too long. On his call, I heard banging in the background. Sounded like there was some kind of trouble. He didn't sound right, and he started to go on about spiders crawling all over him." He paused and Sarah looked at him. His face was grim. "He initiated the 'K' protocol."

Sarah had just turned to the next page. It gave a brief rundown of the quarantine they had established, then a minor notation at the bottom saying that the "Katharizo" protocol was being used. That didn't make her happy. She didn't know all the details of the "Katharizo" protocol, which she knew had been nicknamed by many in the military as the "K" or "Kilo" protocol because they couldn't pronounce the actual name, but she did know that once the military established the quarantine, they would cut off all communication into and out of the town. If they had already done that, there was very little chance that Bryan had been able to make a call out. Even if he made it to the inner perimeter, the military wouldn't believe him, and if he tried to push too hard, she knew that the military had orders to shoot anyone who was becoming aggressive towards them.

So her friend may still be alive and he just couldn't get the word out. Was she allowed to think that positively?

"K" protocol also meant that there were things already in place for her team. It was meant for biological terrorism, and was in place as a way for things to move quickly.

"K" protocol meant that while they were rushing to get her to the closest air strip where she could meet with the rest of her team, the lab would already be set to go into the infected zone. The "lab" was of a design that she, with the help of many others, had built to be customized and highly mobile. Since it was established, the politicians working with military and other scientists, as well as a budget committee of money-saving number crunchers, had all worked together to create this cost-effective, highly mobile plan.

While the scientists wanted high tech mobile labs with massive amounts of security, monitors, and fancy equipment in a large vehicle the government felt would cost nearly a half-million, it was not considered cost effective to have these vehicles all over the U.S. Sure, they could make a couple of them and have them near the major cities, and had that plan been approved, there would be one of those vehicles now coming from the Chicago area. She had never seen the final approved plans.

She really did not want to start thinking of the zone as a town. The fact that Bryan was there was already making it hard for her to have the emotional detachment she needed to stay focused on the job at hand.

Bryan.

"Anymore from Bryan?" she asked Eric, looking up from the documents. They had neared the plane and he was already stepping out of the way to let her climb up into it. She didn't think he would come with her. He served no purpose to the team, and with him still working on his political future, he wouldn't want his face anywhere near this.

Eric's face already told her what he was about to say, but she couldn't even hear him say it as the plane's turbines had already started to cycle up the moment her foot touched the stairs into the lush compartment. She wondered if it had been automatic, though she knew that someone must have been watching for her and the moment she was there, they had orders to hurry up and go.

She looked at Eric, and though she couldn't hear him, she saw him shake his head and mouth the word, *No.*

Sarah's heart sank a little as she walked the rest of the way into the compartment. Protocol "K" wasn't good. Sure, there were the problems with the mobile lab, and it was not the perfect solution, but she also knew what the worst case scenario was. That was what sent frightened chills down her back as she went to meet the rest of her team.

CHAPTER 5

Sullivan was at the bar, but Jason really didn't want to think about his friend back there because Sullivan was just as likely to drink the bar dry as much as serve it to any of the customers. How could he have ever trusted him? What would his mom say? She would kill him. She would throw him on a grill and cook him alive.

He shouldn't be thinking about that. That was not why he had left the bar, and he would not have left had it not been important. His mother would have to realize that. No matter how Sullivan handled the bar, she would have to realize that Jason needed to check on Lisa.

It wasn't like his mother never left the bar. She had occasionally rushed out for emergencies, so there would be no reason she should get so upset with him. She wouldn't, but that wasn't what was really bothering him.

What bothered him was thinking about what he was going to find when he got back to the house. He didn't want to think about it. Still, the images pushed their way in. The more he fought against them, the more he saw some monster standing over his little sister, and she was…she was…

He shook his head and brought himself back to pay attention to the road. He wouldn't allow that thought to finish.

No way could he think that she could possibly be dead. There was no way he would let that happen to his little sis.

No, she was going to be fine, but that didn't stop him thinking about what he was going to find. He did not want to go back to his parents' house and see what Tina had left there. Even worse, he was dreading finding it and had no idea what he was going to do about it. If she killed him, did that now make him an accessory even if he called the police? Because she ran away, could she still claim self-defense? How could he call the police when he knew that might mean his aunt would go to jail?

His head ached, all of his thoughts trying to pull him at once, trying to gain traction. It was like a whirlwind inside his head, blinding him from focus. He felt like he just wanted to lay down, close his eyes, and let all the thoughts explode in their own directions.

He had to struggle to focus on the world around him and pay attention to where he was driving. It was made harder by his familiarity with the roads and how he could drive home mindlessly. He didn't want to do that. It wouldn't be safe, not this time of day when there could be kids riding their bikes around the bustling town.

Looking around, he saw that he was only a block-and-a-half away from his house now. There was a slight turn to the left, a quick turn to the right, then he was on his block. The last block in town and one of the most deserted. There wasn't much at this end of town. To his left, there was a row of trees that ran along his street, ending in the old, abandoned house that was a strong wind gust away from falling down. To the right was the long stretch of property, one he knew well from having to mow it so often, then his house. The street wasn't long, only one block, and the house he had grown up in was a quarter of the way down. There were a couple more after that, neighbors who have come and gone over the years. He wasn't even sure who lived in the two houses near the other end of the street, but he knew somebody lived there as their yards had started to get mowed again. Then the street ended, and he would have to turn to the right to come around along the back side, or drive straight off into a cornfield.

He briefly looked over at the woods. He knew the woods so well and, while they didn't run too deep before they ended at the cornfield on the other side, there were paths through there, some he helped create. There were hidden bases that he and his friends had conquered growing up. There were little cement bunkers here and there, not visible from the road, ones that he had often imaged had been military stations. He had once had a childhood fantasy that there were military bases hidden underneath the town, a whole society doing military experiments. Somewhere, somehow, someday, he had always imagined he would find the entrance and sneak his way down to it.

How crazy that seemed as he got older. He tried to think about those memories. He tried to grab onto them, let them take possession of his mind, and not think about what was going to be in the house. Think about the happy thoughts, the times when he took the metal detector down the paths, trying to find secret doors.

It didn't work. He thought about the woods and walking through them, but then he saw a shadow memory, dark images of a man-shape dragging the body of a little girl through the woods. The little girl wasn't moving.

He closed his eyes and let the car slow to crawl, inching slowly towards the house. It didn't look all that menacing, but why should it? From what his aunt had told him, everything had happened inside the house, so nothing could really be seen from the outside. It still looked like that innocent little house he had grown up in, the one with never enough room so they always seemed to be tripping over each other. The warm place where he always thought he would feel safe and comfortable.

This house no longer seemed like that safe home he grew up in. There *was* a menace to it now. Some kind of evil seemed to be inside it, the two front windows looking like eyes that seemed to watch him. They continued to glare at him as he slowly passed by in front of them, and then he was looking at the large picture window of the living room. The sun glinted off of it and he couldn't see anything. He continued on until he reached the tip of the driveway.

He parked just off to the side of the driveway, that little patch of gravel where his grandmother parked, and then became his spot. The car sat there, him sitting inside as he let it idle. He really didn't want to get out of the car. Getting out of the car meant he had to deal with "it", and he really didn't want to.

Sweat was beading on his forehead, despite the air conditioning running full blast. His chest was aching as his lungs burned. He felt like his breathing wanted to race faster than he would let it. His palms were wet and he was gripping the steering wheel to the point that he wasn't sure he would be able to pull his hands away from it. He hoped it was his imagination that made him feel like the ridges on the steering wheel below his fingers were deepening.

He turned off the ignition. The car stopped rumbling, and he was left with the lonely sounds of a clicking noise coming from under the hood. It seemed like a clock was ticking, trying to push him into motion. He cursed under his breath, wishing he didn't have to do this. If he could just keep putting it off, maybe he wouldn't have to. Maybe the guy would just come walking out, he would be okay, and there would be nothing for Jason to worry about.

His heart was beating and threatening to force its way out of his body. Either it was going to work its way up into his throat, or it was going to pound its way out through his ribcage. No matter which way it chose, it wanted out.

Damn organs.

He let his hand slam down on the steering wheel and, to his surprise, a tear forced its way down his cheek and fell onto the grey, hard plastic. He let his head fall into it, bringing his arm around to cradle it. What the hell was he crying for?

"Come on, Jason. Get your shit together," he said to the wheel, having to fight with himself to keep the tears from flooding out of him.

He reached over and pushed open the door, nearly falling out of the car. He didn't want to do this. His body was fighting against him, his mind was telling him not to go.

Then his feet were on the ground and he found himself walking around the front of the house.

"Make sure you grab a cue stick from the pool table when you go into the house," he whispered to himself as he bolted past the bushes on his left and leapt onto the front cement steps. He took them two at a time, nearly tripping over the third step that, for some reason, was taller than the others. He caught himself and made it to the top.

The cement porch had posts like it was meant to be fenced in but, for someone reason, had never been finished. Other than the metal supports every four feet, there was nothing to hold up the roof overhead, and the cement itself had once been blue, but was now faded to a peeling dirty gray color. He quickly crossed it and made it to the front door, pulling back on the screen door, but not too hard. He still remembered breaking the door two years ago, and he didn't want to repeat that incident, especially since the door hadn't been completely fixed.

He was trying not to think about what he had to do. Thinking about everything else around him, the porch, and the door helped keep him from focusing on any of it. But reality came crashing back as some force on the other side of the door slammed into it. The screen door slammed shut as he had let it go, shocked and unconsciously taking a step back, amazed he hadn't screamed.

His heart started beating even faster, which he hadn't realized was even possible. His hand hovered over the doorknob. Someone was in there. Did they have his little sister? Vince had to have his sister in there. What was he doing to her? Was he hurting her? Had Tina's ex brought other guys with him, others that she hadn't known about who had come to his rescue? Were they fighting in there? Whatever was happening, what had hit against the door had sounded large and pissed.

And whoever was inside was getting pretty frustrated because he heard something thrashing around. He tried to identify if he heard one person throwing things, or if there were two people fighting. There was another loud thump, probably on the pool table, then the sound of shattering glass and another loud crash as something landed against the floor.

Jason wasn't sure what to think. His hand slipped off the doorknob, his breath catching in his throat and his weight shifting onto his back foot.

What was he doing? Instincts had started to kick in. Voices inside his head screamed at him to get the hell out of there. He wasn't a fighter. He wasn't really much of a lover, either, but definitely not a fighter. He was a college kid, not a scholar, not a sports kind of guy. He was a computer geek. So what was he planning on doing? Dropping a monitor on someone's head? That would be all well and good if it was an old CRT monitor that weighed fifty pounds, but he doubted the new slimmer flat screens would even do any good.

Focus.

Think.

He can't run. His sister was in there.

There had to be something that he could do. He couldn't allow himself to think about running away. He needed to think about helping his sister.

How would he fix a computer virus? Well, there are many types of viruses… No, he couldn't allow himself to think about the details. Okay, he's dealing with a virus. The computer's having a problem booting into normal mode, which would be the same as going in the front door. So he had to find a *new* way to get into the house. He had to deviate around the normal startup mode. Okay, so boot into safe mode then.

The window would be his safe mode. So far, thinking like this was working for him, as long as he didn't pay attention to that smashing glass.

Another loud bang came from inside, then what sounded like somebody doing a slow Godzilla stomp started to move to the door. He struggled not to think about Lucy. She was in there with whoever was slamming around. He hoped he wasn't too late and that they hadn't done something terrible to her.

Don't think about it. It's a virus. He was going to try going into safe mode. Safe mode would make everything okay.

He tried to walk as quietly as he could. Given the hardness of the cement, it wasn't too difficult to move with stealth. Then again, with how sensitive his ears seemed to be, even his breathing sounded too loud to him. Keep thinking about the virus. It wasn't something to worry about. It was only a computer virus.

He reached the window just as the pounding sound on the other side stopped. Out of curiosity, he wished he could see it, but he also was thankful for the thick curtain that kept him from looking in.

The air around him seemed to have stopped as he held his breath. Sound no longer seemed to exist. The world had fallen silent. The window was only inches away from him, and he knew it would be unlocked. He'd been locked out of the house too many times to count and he knew that he could always get back in that way. All he had to do was reach down to the base and push his hands flat against the glass to get suction. Then just lift and it would open.

His hands wouldn't move. They felt like they had become cement blocks, unable to be lifted.

His lungs burned, he wasn't breathing. His head was getting light and fuzzy. It was caught in his lungs as he tried to keep from opening the window. He didn't want to know what was on the other side. Not knowing made everything easy. He didn't need to think about anything. He could just stand there and close his eyes. When he did, it would all just go away.

Virus. Fix the virus. It was all just a virus, and he needed to go into safe mode. However, going through that window was anything but safe.

Suddenly, glass shattered and showered over him.

The air in his lungs burst out and he stumbled backwards. He didn't know what he was doing, and he barely saw the yellow, tangled mess bursting through the window and coming towards him.

When his foot stepped back into nothingness, he started falling backwards. "Shi-"

* * * *

Rob pulled on the screen door of the bar, the springs squeaking as it opened. The damn door was just as frustrated as he was. It wanted to be left alone, to stay closed and not let anyone into the little corner bar. Just let this damn day end and be over with. Was it even noon yet?

The mechanic had said they would be able to tow his car in and change the tire. Because he wasn't smart enough to write down the tire size, a tire he could barely afford was now going to also include the price of being dragged into town.

Right now, he wished he could drown himself in his own pain. Get away from all of the bullshit, order a bottle, and just fall into oblivion. He sure as hell deserved it. He felt like he needed it and he doubted that if Chief Renner found out, he would even care.

Okay, that wasn't true and he knew it. The chief would care. Not just because it would make their little police department look bad, but it would mean more than just a dereliction of duty. It would make him look like he had a problem. Rob, the man who barely touched any alcohol, except for an occasional beer on a Saturday afternoon. It would look like he couldn't stay away from the stuff, even while he was in uniform. If Rob couldn't be trusted now, what was he doing when he was alone at night?

This day couldn't end soon enough.

He stepped through the door and felt like he was disappearing into the darkness of the bar, the sunlight not reaching too deep into the cavernous room. He was relieved by the lack of light, and while the room wasn't much cooler than the hot day outside, the shadows were cool enough to be welcome. He was suddenly aware of the murmuring of the television as some news network was on in the background. There was the hum of the coolers, and the chatter of an argument that was in the heat of escalating to something more than rushed words.

As his eyes adjusted to the light, he saw Bruce sitting at the bar just ten feet in front of him. He was sitting back in his bar stool, filling it and threatening to spill over the sides, and was turned to the man at the left of him, a grease-covered man wearing a white tank top that was badly stained with sweat and grime. What Rob could see of the man's hair that fell down past his shoulders was covered in filth, but looked like it was blond at one time. The man was turned to face Bruce and was leaning in, pointing at the large man.

The bar was dark, lit by fluorescent lights accented in green and behind glass to keep them from being plain. It did help to give the place some atmosphere, but he felt like it wasn't enough light.

The bar was laid out with the long stretch of wood just ten feet in front him. To his right was a shuffleboard game with a sign hanging over it that said, "Every day I'm shufflin'", and a row of digital slot machines behind it. Thankfully, he noted that the sound was off.

Out of the corner of his eye, he saw a bit of movement and turned back to the bar. A stocky man, maybe in his late twenties, slightly unshaven with a hat that reminded Rob of the lead singer of AC/DC, was quickly taking a large bucket off the bar and placing it on the ground. As he did so, Rob saw him quickly sweeping the bar of what he guessed were tickets, putting them into the bucket. Rob pretended not to notice.

"He is a goddamn socialist who is tearing this country apart! He is takin' our jobs, and spyin' on every damn thang we are doin'," came from the grease-covered man. He didn't really have a southern drawl, but it was more of the Midwest southern that Rob had realized he had been hearing more and more. It was like an attempt to imitate the southern drawl, but mostly consisted of cutting off the "g" to everything.

"That may be so, but you can't be saying shit like you're going to drive down to Peoria and kill him. It's against the law." Bruce was trying to keep his voice level, but Rob could sense he was having a hard time keeping calm.

"He needs to be put in jail."

"That may be-"

"For what?" Rob said as he stepped deeper into the darkness.

"For breakin' our constitutional rights! For spying on us! Shit, what *hasn't* this president done? Hell, look at all them damn illegals he's bringing into the country. Soon, we're going to have to start speakin' Mexican just to order McDonalds." said the dirt-covered man who was sitting closest to the window. Rob noticed the tickets the AC/DC kid had been sweeping off the bar had been in front of the man. Now the man was glaring, his eyes fixed on Rob.

"And when have you been spied on?" the bartender said, stepping back. Now that Rob's eyes were adjusting to the darkness, he could see a slight smile at the corner of his lips. This guy liked egging on the man.

"I don't have to take this shit from you."

"When?"

"Just last week. Damn sheriff pulled me over. He heard I had drugs in the car. He HEARD! They've been listenin' in on my phone calls. That shit ain't right!" The man was easing back into his stool, taking a long drag off his beer before slamming it back down on the bar, pushing it to the edge so that the bartender had to get up to fill it.

Rob eased himself onto the stool just one down from Bruce, who smiled and saluted him with his can of Coca Cola. The other man seemed to growl at him and muttered under his breath, "Fuckin' pig."

Sullivan neared Rob. He could see that the man was tense, scared to the point that he seemed like he would rather be anywhere other than about to approach him. Rob knew it was because he was still partially in uniform, though he would guess that an officer on duty would look a lot cleaner and less sweaty than what Rob had to look like right now. After all, he had been standing at his car and sweating his butt off for most of the day.

"What can I do for you?" Sullivan asked.

"I'll take a Coke," Rob said.

"I'm buying," Bruce chimed in quickly, then turned to Rob. "So what did they say about your car?"

"Won't be able to get it towed until the afternoon. Their tow truck is already out and having some trouble getting back into town. Something about a road being closed. The driver is trying to come in from a different one, rather than waiting for the road to open. They're supposed to give me a call here when they have it at the shop."

"Oink, oink."

Rob lowered his head. He could feel the eyes of the room on him. His jaw hurt from the back of his teeth grinding, and he had to fight to keep from snapping back at the jerk. His skin was thick. His years on the Chicago PD had toughened it. He couldn't let it get to him. There was no way a small town pissant was going to draw him out.

It was easier said than done. He already wasn't having too good a day, and the idea of taking out some of that frustration on the scrawny little man seemed like a good way to let off some of that steam.

He looked up at the bartender and noticed that the man was still stiff, watching him. Bruce was watching him, too, and he began to realize that his posture was showing some of the frustration he had been feeling, as they both seemed to be holding their breath and waiting for him to do something.

The man called out to him, "You got a problem? We haven't done nothin' wrong in here, so why don't you just leave us alone?"

Rob looked down at the man, returning the glare. He let the words hang in the air for a minute. He was still having to fight back the quick retort that was on the tip of his tongue. He took another deep, relaxing breath. At least it was an attempt at a relaxing breath. It hadn't done much to relax him.

"Just here for a drink. Do *you* have a problem with that?"

"This ain't your place."

Rob smiled and turned away.

From somewhere in the back in the bar, there was a "pang", then a loud slamming sound, like a door being thrown closed. Rob looked to the other end of the bar and saw that just past where the counter stopped, there was a lighter area that must lead to a back room. An old man was walking up from back there. Rob couldn't make out too many details, the light behind him making him not much more than a shadow in the darkness of the bar, but Rob could see that he moved with a limp. The man made his way to the end of the bar and sat in the farthest stool. Rob noticed the cigarettes on the in front of him, then noticed there were ashtrays all along the bar, which implied that people were smoking illegally in there.

Rob turned to look back at the redneck and, sure enough, he had a pack of cigarettes open in front of him and the ashtray was nearly full of butts and ash. It suddenly explained another reason why the guy didn't want Rob in there. Then again, he really should get out of his uniform. Under his thick shirt, he had a plain white undershirt, which was probably soaked, but he thought about stripping down to it. He didn't like the idea of strutting around in just his sweaty undershirt, but was sure he would get less glares than by being in his uniform. If it got worse or if they had to be there for too long, he would think about it.

Sullivan quickly returned with the soda and a glass of ice. He poured part of the can over the ice and it fizzed up high. Rob watched it, then looked up at Sullivan.

"Thanks."

Sullivan just nodded.

Behind Sullivan, the TV sitting on top of the stand-up freezer started to hiss with static. It was followed by the same from the TV at the end of the bar and the big screen mounted in the opposite corner. Rob hadn't been paying attention to it, until all of the televisions had gone out at once.

"Turn them damn things off!" yelled the old man from the end of the bar. Rob didn't know who the man was, but could tell that he was one of those grumpy old men many people probably didn't like to deal with. Rob imagined him making phone calls about neighbors, complaining about music and parties when the neighbors just had a few friends over.

Rob grimaced and turned to watch the man behind the bar struggling with a large remote. It was one of five he had pulled out from underneath the bar, and Rob could see that the man obviously didn't know which one went to what. Finally, he was able to figure out one of the remotes and the big screen turned off. It had been the loudest of the televisions, and removing the booming sound of the static was a relief.

Sullivan set aside that remote, then started working on the other two televisions. They were identical, so the owner probably bought them at the same time. The same remote should operate both of them, or so Rob thought. However, instead of turning it off, he started to flick through the channels. Each of them was static.

"Just turn the damn things off. What kind of idiot do you have to be not to just turn them off?!" yelled the old man from the end of the bar.

"Must have forgotten to pay your cable bill," said the grease-covered man a couple seats down from Bruce. He had a nasty tone to his voice, almost as spiteful as the old man.

"Service is probably just out," Bruce said just before he took a gulp from his soda. Unlike Rob, Bruce was drinking it straight out of the can.

"I don't know. Don't even work here. I'm just helping out," Sullivan said, looking at the TV's, then grabbing the tangle of remotes and tossing them back under the counter.

Rob looked around the bar and tried to find a clock. He wasn't sure what time it was. The shop had told him they might know something this afternoon, but he wasn't even sure how long from now that was. What time had he left this morning? It had been a little past six, right? No, it had been past eight because the sun was already up and he was running late. He had wanted to leave earlier, but had slept in.

Robyn, his wife, wouldn't be expecting him home until early tomorrow morning because he had a shift tonight. He was supposed to go straight from the courthouse back to Standard, grabbing the squad car so he could go on patrol. Chief Renner was going to stay on duty until Rob got there. Of course, that meant the chief was just going to have the squad car sitting in his driveway, handling everything from his house.

Even though Robyn wasn't expecting him and she had no idea the day he was having, he figured he should still probably call her and give her an update. Besides, it would be nice to hear her voice, and he had to tell her that his cell phone was still at home so she wouldn't be able to call him. He wanted to ask if she could do some laundry. He hated asking her and knew that he was sure to get a rebuke. She would be upset, but he hoped she would understand. He would have to explain to her how he was covered in yuck from this morning and wanted to change out of his sweat-drenched uniform when he got home.

"Hey, can I use your phone for a minute?" Rob asked. Sullivan was filling a glass with a bright golden-colored beer. Rob glanced around quickly and, not seeing any empty glasses, figured the beer must have been for the bartender. When Sullivan took a huge swig out of it, he knew he was right.

"Local or long distance."

"Standard?"

"I'm not sure if that's long distance or not. Guess you can try it and see. There is a block on the phone for long distance. You'd have to use the pay phone at the end of the bar for that."

Rob hadn't noticed it before, but there was an old rotary-style phone at the end of the bar with a large slot on the top for quarters. He looked back when Sullivan hand him the cordless handset and he nodded his thanks as he grabbed it. He hoped that calling his wife would still be a local call, as the redneck who was enjoying making rude sounds his way was sitting one stool down from the pay phone. Rob didn't want to get any closer to him than he had to.

If it meant him either getting his way or avoiding the situation all together, Rob could be very diplomatic.

"Hey, after you're done, I need to give my wife a call."

Rob nodded to Bruce as he pressed the TALK button and the phone lit up, but as Rob started to press buttons, he noticed it wasn't making any sound. He held it to his ear and listened. He pulled it away and pressed the OFF button, then pressed the TALK button again. He held it up to his ear. Still nothing.

"Phone's dead," Rob said as he looked at Bruce. The man just looked back at him, a confused expression pinching his brows. The man went from being confused to red-faced as he reached over and held his palm up. Handing the phone over, he watched as Bruce repeated the motions Rob just went through. Then he watched as Bruce did it again and again.

"When's the last time this thing was charged?" Bruce bellowed, looking up at the kid behind the bar. Rob wondered if Bruce realized just how loud his voice had suddenly become. The quiet man Rob had met earlier had faded away to this new man who didn't react well to things that weren't happening how he wanted.

Rob looked at the televisions, both of them now just blank screens reflecting the sunlight coming in from outside. So the televisions had no reception. Looking at the receiver, it looked like they were both hooked up to a satellite, so that meant there was no satellite signal. Okay, he could see them having issues with that. DISH was known for having issues, especially in this area. A good strong wind could throw it off, then it would need to be recalibrated. It was a pain in the ass, but was known to happen.

But it wasn't windy outside. Hell, he would have loved a nice little breeze blowing when he had been stuck sitting out there by his car. There was barely even anything to rustle the leaves. There was no way in hell that anything was blowing strong enough to throw off the signal.

And the phones were out. Those would be coming through on the old traditional telephone wires. A system that hadn't been upgraded since…well, he didn't know when. Sure, internet companies were always boasting about putting in that fiber optic cable shit, but none of that had reached there yet. Had it? They were still telephone lines, so that had to be it. The old telephone cables.

What was he getting at? He wasn't too sure. It just seemed so strange…

"Hey, bud, what's got you thinking?" Bruce said. Rob looked over at him, seeing that the man was staring at him.

"Get the phone working?"

Bruce shook his head, then they both looked when they heard a loud "clang" come from further down the bar. The redneck had slammed the receiver down on the pay phone, as well.

"You need to tell your fuckin' boss to pay your fuckin' phone bill," the man said, looking disgusted as he went back to his beer. "They turn the fuckin' power off and I'm out of this shithole."

"So what's up?" Rob tuned his attention back to Bruce, who had turned back around and was refocused on him.

"Shit if I know. Just seems kinda funny both the television and phones are out."

"Yeah, it does."

"Hey, can I see your cell phone?" Rob looked over at the bartender. The man quickly reached into his pocket and pulled out his smartphone and handed it to Rob, who just looked at it. He had no idea how to use the damned thing. Why couldn't things stay simple? He had his nice little flip phone. You opened it up and dialed a number. Where the hell was the keypad on this thing?

"Yeah, um…I got no idea how to use this. How do I make a call?"

The bartender reached out to take his phone back. The kid took a quick look at it and shook his head. "Nope, no bars. Won't be able to."

"Huh," Bruce grunted, then looked over at Rob.

"Yeah, huh. Something's not right."

"Well, what are you going to do about it?"

"Do about what? It's just odd. No cell, satellite, and TV, but what could it be? Hell, far as I know, it's a nasty sunspot causing issues. Wouldn't be the first time."

"Yeah. Sunspot."

"Hey, hear anything in news about sunspots?" Rob asked, looking at the redneck, then the bartender. Travis just turned away, but Sullivan was shaking his head.

"Well, don't know what else it could be," Rob said.

"Yeah. When do they get your car towed in?"

"Soon."

"No offense, but I might not stick around to make sure you're okay. I don't have a good feeling about this," Bruce said as he reached for his soda.

Rob silently agreed with the man.

CHAPTER 6

Luke lifted his hand to the dashboard vents of the car and felt the muted cool air as it rushed in. The forced air was trying to fight against the heat of the midday sun, but it failed. It wasn't nearly cool enough, and he was silently cursing at how ineffective it was.

The day wasn't getting any cooler, and it wasn't even the hottest part of the day. He was sitting in an idling car so, of course, the air conditioning wasn't going to be blowing very cold air on him. They were designed to cool on the move, to keep the car nice and comfortable while a person was driving. When it wasn't in motion, the designers didn't care if the car kept cool or not.

He was in a damned European car. It doesn't get hot over there, so why would they design something to keep cool when the temperature outside exceeded tolerant levels and the day was scorching hot? Those damn Germans. It was just another way to torture us for kicking their ass in the past.

And why the hell did he have some expensive Euro-trash model rather than a good ol' American made car like he had growing up? Because Euro speaks success, especially when your clients and marks were expecting you to show that you were successful.

Yeah, and he was left to suffer.

He brought his hand back to the leather wheel of the car and started to impatiently tap on it.

He shouldn't even have had to sit there as long as he had. This was supposed to have been a quick run up here to pick up his son, Ryan, from his basketball game. Then drop the little rug rat at home to make a tee time with a new client. That was at four, and it was nearing one now. He still had plenty of time, but he didn't like to wait.

The damn basketball game was supposed to have been over a half-hour ago. His son knew he wasn't supposed to shower. He was to hurry out. Luke already had a towel draped over the passenger seat for his sweat-soaked son, and leather treatment for the seats once he dropped him off at home.

He didn't like to wait. Clients who made him wait got charged for it. His son making him wait, well…that punishment would come later tonight. He was sure Ryan would have an excuse just like he always did. Damn, when would the boy learn that excuses didn't do anything but get him into more trouble?

Luke heard the slamming of the large metal door and looked up in time to see a figure stumbling out the door of the gym.

It wasn't his son, but some people coming out meant the game was over, so his son should be following soon enough.

Little pissant better hurry his ass up, Luke thought as he reached forward, grabbing for his phone.

* * * *

Her breathing had slowed, and she no longer felt her heart trying to burst out of her chest. Denise guessed she must have been calming down, but it didn't feel like she should be. She was still paranoid about what she had just seen. She couldn't stop herself from looking in the rearview mirror. Were they back there, still following her? Had she driven far enough for them to give up?

Would she ever be able to run away far enough? She could still see the face of her husband…or what was left of it. Most the flesh had been ripped away, one eye hanging down and touching the bone that had been all that remained where his unshaved cheek once was. That face had been coming after her. That jerky, contorted corpse, covered in what had been his blood, forced its way through the back door of their general practice office.

She knew the others had been there…the ones who had infected her husband. There had also been that CDC guy, but she only remembered her husband. Her eyes had locked onto his one eye, and she had wanted to see him in there and know that some of him remained. There had been nothing, so she ran.

She knew she was lucky and had barely gotten away alive.

She looked in the rearview mirror again. In her mind, she saw him on the road, trying to walk towards her, coming after her. When she actually checked, though, the road behind her was empty. The day was quiet, the sun burning hot, and life seemed to have faded away from the town…as well as her husband.

She looked down at her phone laying on the floor on the passenger side. She wasn't one to typically give in to her anger, but after repeatedly trying to call her brother after he hung up on her and getting no signal was something she just couldn't handle. She had to take her frustration out on her phone so she threw it. She wanted to get out of the car and take a damn hammer to the thing for betraying her.

After all, how in the hell could her phone do this to her when she needed the damn thing the most?! She *needed* it. She needed to talk to someone. Even if her brother, whose help she needed so badly, would not talk to her, she could still call someone else, anyone else, who she knew wouldn't think she was crazy. She just needed to talk, needed to find someone who would listen to her and be there for her. Someone who would wrap her in his arms and tell her all of this was going to be okay.

She needed her husband.

She couldn't stop them this time. The fountain of tears she thought had already flowed through her and had dried up was coming again. She could feel it. She could feel the itch in her nose as the sadness tried to consume her again. He was gone. There were those things, and he was gone. He was infected. He was one of them…whatever the hell *they* were.

She wouldn't cry. She couldn't let herself cry, but why not? What else did she have now?

No, no, no, no, no.

She had to find her brother. She already knew where he was. She just needed to go there and find him.

Looking around, she hadn't even realized she had pulled into the parking lot of the middle school. There must have been something going on as the parking lot was nearly full. She absently tried to remember if she knew about it. She had some vague memory, something that Lucy girl mentioned this morning.

She thought it was odd to have a game at the school on a Saturday after school had already let out for the summer. She did remember reading somewhere about it being some special make-up game against their rivals. The previous game had been canceled due to bad weather or something.

Denise tried to focus on remembering. It helped get her mind off of what was really going on, but she couldn't quite remember the full reason as to why.

She passed a man sitting in his car, then she looked up and watched as the doors opened. A couple people were coming out… Wait, they weren't people. She noticed how they walked, staggering in that awkward motion of someone who didn't have complete control over their limbs. Their shirts were covered in a mass of gore, ripped and partially torn away to expose ripped skin underneath.

In disbelief, she nearly stopped the car to stare at them. How had the things gotten there, as well? Were they all over the town? Had it really spread that far, that fast? That couldn't be right. Whatever it was, there was no way it could spread like that.

Not that it mattered. There was no time to stop and think about it. She needed to get out of there and find Tom. He would have to know something about what was happening. She didn't stop when she hit the edge of the parking lot. She just barreled out into the street amidst a roar of horns from the traffic around her.

She hadn't cared if she got hit, and she didn't know how she hadn't. *Oh, well*, she thought. She had to find her brother. He had to know. He had to call someone because this was getting bad.

She looked again at her phone on the floor, giving it a dark glare, accusing it of being the evil traitor that it was. Damn it!

* * * *

Luke felt the car shake as something slammed into it and he finally looked up from his smartphone to see just what in the hell was going on. He had heard the metal doors slamming open, and people had been coming out of the gym. His son, the lazy slob, should have been one of them so that he could get the hell out of there. He had business to take care of, dammit.

Part of him figured the shaking of the car may have been his son, excitedly rushing because they had won the game. But even he wasn't that stupid. His son knew that this car and its appearance meant more than his life. He wouldn't dare run into it.

Luke looked around and saw that someone had, indeed, slammed into his car, and was now looking at him from the passenger side window.

"What the fuck?!" he yelled over at the woman. Luke could see she had a dazed look, as though she was staring at him, but not really seeing him. Her mouth was open and it looked like drool was running down in a dark streak along the ridges of her mouth.

Great, another fucking special ed to deal with, he thought as he looked at the woman. As if his son wasn't enough to deal with. And was that…? Was she *drooling* on his car?!

"Get the fuck away from my car!" he screamed. Part of him wanted to get out of his car, rush around to the woman and shove her away. However, public perception and sales were intertwined, and he couldn't afford to take a hit on his perception meter. He had too many "big fish" locally so he

80

couldn't afford nasty talk about him attacking some retarded woman just for drooling on his car.

Wait, was that ketchup on the front of her shirt. Great, she was going to rub up against his car and smudge that shit all fucking over. He bet Ryan had put the bitch up to it. There was no way someone could be this messy, and there she was, grinding up against his car. She lifted her head and it looked like she was trying to bite his window when he noticed… No, that couldn't be. There was *not* a large part of her throat exposed. It must be some kind of new, in-style tattoo. Like those guys who have parts of their lips and chin removed and rings put in so you could see their teeth. He tried to tell himself that, even as he knew he was looking straight into the trachea and saw that her vocal chords were just hanging by threads of flesh.

The gym must have had some excellent face painters. That's all it was. It was nothing more than make-up effects and face paint. In fact, he remembered when his son was at a church lock-in once, and this one guy made it look like he had been shot and part of the bullet was exposed. It was creepy for being at a church function, but it was fascinating how the guy did it. This was just another one of those make-up jobs.

"Get off the car!" he yelled again. He hadn't noticed that his hands had balled into fists and his knuckles were white, so he started to stretch them out. He was mad, but he wasn't afraid. This was all normal. It was just some nut that probably knew his son and was trying to play some bullshit prank on him since his son didn't have the guts.

Come on, Luke. Just breathe, he thought as he put his hands back on the wheel. He closed his eyes, blocking out the world around him…the sounds, the sun-filled schoolyard…and mentally started counting to ten.

He made it to five when his car shook again. His eyes shot open and he turned to look. It wasn't the woman, though. She was still standing there, looking at him, but now there was another person. This one had slammed against his passenger window and had his face pushed up against it. Both of them stood there, their hands on the glass, the dull eyes looking at him. Their eyes were blank… No, they weren't quite blank. They were hard to read, but there was *something* there. It was hard to tell what, though. Where these people stoned? His fingers twitched as he looked at them and he found himself nervously tapping his thighs.

Just past them, he saw that there were more people coming out of the gym. They were all walking strangely towards his car. They were unbalanced, staggering. Some of them nearly tripped over each other, and some actually fell into others.

There was another one at the front of his car, walking around towards the driver's side. When he came around the front of the car and was shuffling up to the driver's side, Luke could see the right half of his face was missing. Blood still oozed and dripped down the exposed cheekbone. His right eye was hanging outside the socket, held there by what looked like a thin piece of string.   Luke couldn't stop himself. His stomach suddenly lurched and before he could do more than turn his head, he felt the remnants of the morning's breakfast explode from him and onto the passenger seat. The acrid smell filled his nostrils and when he stopped, the smell made him cramp and vomit some more. Coffee, eggs and sausage… Their strong smells, combined with the smell of his stomach acids, and he couldn't stop himself from losing more and more of his breakfast.

More of them slammed into his car. He pulled himself back up, his stomach now only left with the ability to dry heave. The smell just made him want to continue to launch everything he had ever eaten. He had already lost all that he could, but the smell just made it so much worse.

He looked up at all the bodies that were now around the car. There were at least twenty out there now, slamming into the car. It wasn't like they were shaking it, like crowds did at riots, pushing to shake and rock the car to get it on its side. No, these things, were reaching their arms out towards him. The ones around the front of the car were hitting it with their bodies as they were trying to climb over to get him, but they seemed to have forgotten how to climb. They were slamming into the car as though they were trying to walk through it to get him. The ones on the sides were trying to reach through the glass, but they were still slamming their bodies into the car. It didn't seem to register to them that it was there. They just continued to try and grab him through the glass.

When he looked at the ones on the passenger side, he noticed that the doors were unlocked.

"Thank God," he mumbled as he turned back to the door panel to quickly lock the doors. These things weren't normal, and dumb as a box of rocks. They hadn't even tried to open the door. They just wanted to keep slamming against it. Well, they could slam into the door all day. It didn't matter if the door was locked or not. They weren't getting in.

He felt the door give way. That comfortable feeling of having the door closed was gone and the door was opening.

He looked over, but didn't get the chance to see what was happening before he felt the pull of hands tearing at him, pulling him in different directions. He was being pushed and pulled back and forth like a rag doll.   One hand had trailed downward across his face and gripped just below his chin. It was pulling hard. He could feel the nails of the hand dig into the soft flesh of his upper neck

He knew he was screaming. He felt his lungs exploding. It was hard to hear over the pounding on his car, but he felt the vibrations all over his body.

Then there was a sharp, searing pain on the side of his face, and he could feel hot liquid streak down his cheek. There was another sharp pain on his arm again, followed by the warm liquid. The nails under his chin moved, then he felt one last searing pain. He saw as one of them, one who looked like she had once been a woman, was moving down to bite his throat.

The last thing he saw before the darkness took over was her open mouth. Inside, there was a moving darkness. Pouring out of the darkness and crawling around the edge of her mouth were hundreds of little spiders. Then he felt her mouth touch his neck. The pain was almost pleasure as he felt the release of the flesh and the hot, gushing blood that left him.

Then there was nothing.

* * * *

The sergeant stood outside of his command tent and looked across the road at the high corn stalks surrounding them. It was too close to harvest time for this to be happening. The stalks were all too high. They stood there, reaching for the sunlight, basking in the summer heat. With the lack of rain, the corn was a yellowish-green, but it would still support and keep a family fed for another year.

He didn't like the problem the corn being so high caused, though. It took away so much of their view and it would be so easy for the very people they were trying to quarantine to just wait until night and sneak past them. He had patrols endlessly going through it, but people could still get through. It was like playing a game of hide-and-seek, but those playing were carrying automatic rifles with orders to shoot. Still, it was easy to get through. All he had to do was remember his childhood when his brother, sister, and himself would run through those cornfields, hiding from each other.

He turned to look back at the farmhouse that was on the "safe side" of their barrier. More than likely, the field belonged to that farmer, or he owned the house and rented out the land. Either way, the family that lived there was responsible for it. That also meant he probably either owned the equipment or housed the equipment on his land to take care of it. He hoped it didn't come to him having to-

He broke off the thought. He didn't want to think of having to take any drastic measures. Not yet. Not when they still had no idea as to why they were out there, what type of threat they were up against, and why they had to keep people in and away from Hammond.

The wind blew a subtle gust and he watched as the corn swayed. It was just starting, and he was grateful to feel it as the summer heat had been unbearable without it. He heard the corn as it rustled, and as it mingled amongst one another, he felt like he could hear faint childhood laughter. He heard them, his brother and sister, running away from him because he was "beca

It wasn't the first time that day he thought about his sister. Her and her family were in there. He wanted to call her. He wanted to see how she was, or to try and get her out before anything bad happened. The town was quiet so far, right? Nothing could be happening. There had to be parts of it that were safe. Maybe he could sneak in, leave the corporal to watch the barricade. It wouldn't take long. He could rush in, maybe take a private or two with him, and he could get them out. It would always be his duty to protect her. She was his little sister and it was up to him.

However, if he did, it would cost him more than just his position. He could easily get jail time, or worse. If something happened while he was in town, it would be even more on his head. Then there was also not knowing what was in there. He didn't know what possible danger he could be letting out, or why the town was being quarantined in the first place.

"Sergeant!" he heard his communications specialist yell. The man hurried to stand and to make his way out to him. The sergeant glowered at him, letting his glare be the command to speak.

"Sergeant, there is a bunch of chatter on the police band. There seems to be some kind of riot breaking out. Right now, the cops don't know much. They just know there is a madman killing people in a department store and, just now, there has been a new report of a bunch of people killing and going nuts during some sporting event at the local gym."

Wade knew it was a basketball game. He knew because his sister and her son were there. Her son, a pretty good basketball player, was on the team, but Wade thought he wasn't playing today. He knew about some trouble the kid had gotten into, and he had actually been the one to talk to the coach. Being old high school friends, Wade had talked Sam into keeping his nephew on the team, but making him sit out what would be the most talked about game in a long time. However, he'd only sit out the first three quarters of the game. There was no use in being completely cruel to the boy, but it would teach him a lesson about being a good team player and not torturing his teammates.

But his sister and Shane would both be at the gym. If there was something there, he had to go and get them out. Now he *knew* they were in trouble and needed him. He had to go and get them to safety.

He turned away from the young man and looked in the direction of town. While his eyes couldn't see too much beyond the corn and some of the trees, he could see the gym in his mind. He imagined the death, carnage, and violence. Most of those people had never seen violence, except on television. They had never experienced and been a part of it. His stomach knotted knowing his sister and her family were caught up in it. He had seen enough death in his time. It was easy to image the horrors that she had to fight her way through. What madness was going on in there? What was causing it?

"Sergeant? Sergeant, what should we do?"

He realized the young man was still talking to him. The specialist probably thought they should move in and try to restore order to the town. That was his first thought, too. He wanted to go in and help. He wanted to make sure that the people and the town were okay.

That was supposed to be their job. When things get out of hand, or additional help is needed…whether it be to support local police or helping the hungry…you called in the National Guard. Right now, they were doing the opposite of what they were supposed to do. They were cutting people off from the supplies they needed to survive, and staying away while it was getting out of control in there. Law would break down unless someone went in there and stopped it…namely, the National Guard.

"How are you getting these reports? Communication was to be locked down."

"Radio chatter. Police radio, as well as some civilian ham radios."

"Jam it."

He had to look away from the soldier. He could feel the wetness at the corner of his eyes. He was having to fight to keep it from escaping. He was a United States soldier in the line of duty. He would not be able to go in there and save his family. He had to save his country *from* his family. He had to push all that down.

"Sergeant?"

"You heard me!"

He was losing it. He knew by how the soldier looked at him that he had gone too far. Snapping for no reason wasn't right. He needed to keep his cool and calm down. Pushing down so much pain caused his tempter to flare, and he couldn't allow that. He had to stay calm.

But he knew what his men were really asking. They wanted to know what was going on. They wanted to know how far they would have to go. Their families were possibly at risk, too. How far was this going to go? Who was going to get hurt? They were the protectors. They should be in there restoring law and order, not allowing riots or whatever was happening. So, when the day was done, was the commander going to take the responsibility for it?

Did he really think they were worrying about who would take responsibility? No, he wasn't, either. Sure, it seemed like an obvious question, and had they been anywhere else, he was sure that might be on their minds. He needed to stay calm, and he needed to get their minds off of where they were. He needed to push them, keep them going, make it so they weren't thinking about it.

"Move! Get your asses moving and get it done. Keep the patrols moving through the corn. Rotate out with the barricades. Move!"

What the hell was this country coming to?

He turned to look toward the town again.

It truly was a nightmare scenario, but even in his worst nightmares, he had never thought anything as bad as this would happen. Locking down a town; no information as to what was going on; the idea that every potential person trying to leave that town, even his own family, could be a threat…

"Sergeant! Colonel Fey is on the line for you!"

And the day just keeps getting better, he thought sarcastically, having to bite back the words before he actually said them.

Between generals and colonels calling, he didn't know what was going on out there on the outer line, but he could tell there were too many cooks in the kitchen. Even though he wished they would give him some more information, they were just going to ignore his request. He knew they weren't calling to see how they could help him. They were too busy going back and forth, and he had to hear orders come down in triplicate. This day was only going to get worse before it had any chance to get better…*if* it could get any better.

CHAPTER 7

Travis inhaled deeply, relishing the soothing sensation that seemed to envelope him. The sensation seemed to flow like warm water around him before he let it out in a long exhale.

The cigarette felt good. The damned heat did not.

"Damned cop," Travis muttered under his breath again since he now had to walk outside to smoke his cigarette and would no longer be able to play the "8's". He had been muttering it a lot, even when the fucking pig could hear him. Travis really didn't give a shit. Let the bastard hear him. What the hell was he going to do about it? Nothing, that's what! Because the damn pig was just going to sit there and watch him, but wasn't going to do a damn thing about it. Well, yeah, because the damned bartender was too damned scared to let Travis continue doing anything.

It hadn't been going that well for him anyway, but the fucking pig didn't have to come in there and ruin it. Travis' luck had been about to change. He had felt it. He had that itch, the one on the back of his hand. It told him something was up, and with the shit that had been happening, it had to have been something good. He'd shoveled too much shit recently, so something good had to be coming. It had to be his time.

And why the hell did the son have to be there? Fuck that. Why did the son have to leave and put that damn imbecile behind the bar? Hell, that asshole didn't even know where the tub had been to play the "8's". That old man had to go back behind the bar and find the tub for the bastard. Why the fuck was that guy back there? It didn't matter, though. The son had been no luck, and that SOB was even worse. They had just been taking Travis' money. Don't they know he needed that? He needed that damn money. Where else was he going to get it?

And that fucking pig. Fuck the three of them. They could all just go straight to hell.

"Fuckin' pig," Travis said to the empty parking lot around him as he let out another twin line of smoke from his nostrils. He wasn't sure if it was the cigarette burning his lungs, or the anger he felt that made him want to slam his fist against the wall. He wanted to pound something, beat something, and feel it break.

At first, he had thought about going to one of the other bars closer to downtown. When he had stormed out to light up his smoke, he had meant to start walking. It was a ten block walk, but it would be away from there. Yeah, but what the hell were his choices? He was kicked out of the Diamond, and his damn ex-bitch was bartending during the afternoon at the Razorback, so that wasn't an option, either. He had a new wife now, but that pussy downtown still liked to spread stories about him. The lying whore was not one to let things go. Who gives a fuck about the damned child support? She had a damned job. Hell, *she* should be supporting *him*.

The other problem with going downtown was that they were all closer to downtown and right near the cop shop. He wouldn't be able to smoke in there, either, as they had problems with the police already keeping a watchful eye. None of them came close to taking chances with getting caught breaking the cigarette ban. Gambling, sure, but fuck. None of those places let him run a tab anymore. They all knew him, and most were still saying he owed them. Money hungry bastards, all of them.

"Motherfucker," Travis said, closing his eyes, letting himself fall back so that his back came into contact with the hot siding of the tan building. As his body settled back against it, he kicked back, slamming the heel of his steel-toed boot into the hard cement of the foundation. Nothing happened, but he hadn't really expected it to. He just needed to lash out against something, and the building behind him felt as good as any.

He knew he should be home. They didn't have the money for him to waste up there. His wife was pissed at him and wanted him home. "Save money and drink at home," she had said.

Yeah, like he wanted to be around her nagging all day. She wouldn't be leaving for work for at least another couple of hours, and the last thing he wanted to do was sit there, listening to her bitch and the baby scream. It was bad enough he had to spend all damn night at home, listening to the damn thing wail, but he was damn sure not going to waste all of his damn *day* listening to it.

Besides, maybe he could run into someone here who needed some odd jobs done. Then maybe he could earn some extra cash. What would sitting at home get him? More time to drink and just think about how he had lost his job in another layoff? How the fuck would that benefit him? How would that do them any good? As long as he was at the bar, he was looking for work.

"Fucking pig."

Exhale.

Travis felt the warmth in his fingers and knew the cigarette was close to burning him. It would taste like shit now, but he wasn't going to let anything like that disrupt it. He needed to get what he could out of every damn smoke. He had enough money for a few more beers and another pack, but that would have to last him all night. He couldn't be going about wasting them.

If the pig wasn't there, he could play a few more rounds of "8's". He had felt it right before the cop came in. His luck was changing. He was on the edge of it. He had just needed a few more fucking pulls.

Damn fucking pig.

That fucker was keeping him from his money. That cop was fucking stealing from him, that's what it was. He was stealing right out of his pocket, taking away money from his hard-working family. Not only that, but Travis *needed* that money. He would need cigarettes tomorrow, and if Laurie didn't make enough tips that night, he wouldn't have any drinking money until Wednesday when his unemployment check came in.

Travis took the last pull of the cigarette and tossed the butt with a flick of his fingers, not watching wherever it landed.

"Damn pig better leave soon," Travis said as he opened his eyes and pushed himself off the wall.

He stopped when he noticed that someone was walking down the middle of the street towards the bar. Travis normally wouldn't have paid much attention to the man. Hell, people often walked down the street because there weren't any sidewalks, and the middle was just as good as anywhere else. It was quiet enough so a car coming would be heard long before it ever reached the person.

But something was off with how the man was walking. He had seen many late night wobbles and staggers of drunks making their way to their cars. Who was he kidding? He was usually one of them. But it was only noon. It was way too early for anyone to be doing the late night shuffle. It just wasn't right. The man would stumble, jerk, nearly fall, catch his balance, then stumble again. Not like he was drunk, but like he had no control over what he was doing. It looked almost puppet-like, like there was an unseen master somewhere in the sky above, controlling the strings.

Yeah, he had seen a few people that bad off, but this was in broad daylight. Whoever was that wasted had one up on Travis, even in his worst days.

Whatever. It wasn't his damned problem. He had enough of his own problems to worry about rather than worrying about some other sorry S.O.B.

* * * *

Rob heard the loud clang of the spring against the cheap wooden door as it was slammed closed. He never knew why, but it always seemed like whatever bar he had ever been in always seemed to have cheap doors on the bathrooms. They either had that heavy spring on them, causing it to slam closed, or they just had no door at all. He never knew why bars always felt that having such a powerful spring on the door was something they all required, but it seemed to have been hidden somewhere in some secret bar owner's manual. Plus, they always kept the light dim so when you came in from outside you were blinded until your eyes adjusted.

Oh, well, he thought.

95

He was annoyed, a headache was looming just behind his temple, and he was trying his hardest not to show it as Bruce had been trying to make Rob feel like it was all going to be okay. He just wanted to get his car towed, fixed, and get the hell out of the little town and back home. Not that the town was bad, but something in his stomach was warning him. There was a flutter, and he had the growing feeling things were not right. He could see that Bruce was feeling the same way. When he heard the phones were out, he had planned to leave and get out of there. Rob wasn't sure why the truck driver stayed.

Rob had been looking out the open front door every couple of minutes or so to see if he could see his car finally being towed into the garage down the road. They had a nice view down the street and all he had to do was walk over and take a look. He had done it many times already and Bruce was starting to give him questioning glances, but Rob was more concerned about his car. He wanted it done.

He walked around from the back of the bar just as the tall, rough-looking man that had taken a walk outside, probably for a cigarette, was sitting back down. The man had been giving Rob nasty looks since he had come in, and had been making snide little comments. He obviously had some issues with the local law, and Rob was just another one in a uniform. It was probably just better to let it drop.

The last thing Rob needed was to have an altercation in a bar that he shouldn't even have been in, even if he was only in partial uniform. Rob had taken the shirt off while he had been in the bathroom. Now he was only wearing the black slacks, gun belt, and white undershirt. The shirt was near transparent from all the sweat, and he was sure his smell had to have been pretty ripe. He doubted he would want to sit next to himself.

The man gave him that long glare again, then he turned away and went back to studying his beer. Rob wondered if the man realized just how beaten down he seemed when he wasn't looking at Rob with all that hate. Whenever he looked away, it seemed like he just died a little more inside. His shoulders sagged; that lost, aimless look melted into a gaze looking at nothing but the shimmering gold of his beer.

Another jobless one. Rob had sensed it from the beginning. It was becoming a look he was getting used to seeing. More factories in the area were laying workers off, and that look was becoming a growing cancer of many residents in the towns. Plus, with the drought last year raising food prices, it was like adding a brain tumor to an already suffering man. It just made life that much harder to think about and live with.

Rob tried to tune into Bruce, who was going on about some story. It was something about how he had either been broken down or stuck in some traffic jam. Rob wasn't sure which. He had missed or just not paid any attention to that part of the story. The gist was that he had been sitting down in Arkansas in heat worse than this, his air conditioning was out, and he had to wait for five hours. Rob didn't know how many more trucker tales he could take.

"So, Bruce," he finally broke in as he saw the bartender bring Bruce another cola. "Thanks for all the help. I thought you were rushing home to get to your wife and little…girl, right?"

Bruce took the can of soda, took a drink from it, then set it down, a long look on his face. Rob wasn't sure what he had said, but he didn't mean to upset the older man.

"Yeah, it's going to be nice getting home. I miss 'em. I miss 'em way too often. It's going to be nice doing a local contract that gets me home most nights and on the weekend. It's going to be something." Rob heard a melancholy in the man's words that didn't seem to go with what he was saying.

"You don't sound too happy about that."

"I am, I guess. I mean, I am. Really. I love my family. They are my everything, and when I wake up in the morning, they are the reason I get behind that wheel and drive for those eleven hours. They are my heart and soul."

Poetic words, Rob thought as he put his empty soda at the end of the bar. There was a good heart in the large man. Rob could feel it. There was something else, though. Rob had this strange feeling there was a dark shadow hovering over the man, and a storm was threatening the horizon. He didn't know how he knew it or what it was. It only appeared to him when he looked at the man out of the corner of his eye, but he couldn't mistake it. It was there, a cloud of something vicious that was entangling the man.

Rob nodded to the bartender as he set down another soda, blinking away the visions of what he saw. The can was already open, and Rob listened to the fizz, pop, and sizzle in the silence as he waited for Bruce to continue. He thought it was best to wait the man out, and Rob had a sense that there was something he needed to get off his chest. He wondered if the man really had anyone he could talk to. He took a sip of the soda, felt the icy chill as it slid down his throat, then felt the soothing sensation as it hit his near-empty stomach. It reminded him that he was getting pretty hungry, but the Coke tasted so damn good. How long had it been since he had allowed himself to drink soda?

"Yeah. Starting Monday, I'll be home every night. You know what, though? I've been driving over-the-road for ten years. It's a lifestyle. I'm, well…I'm worried I won't last at home. As it is, whenever I'm home more than three or four days, me and my wife start to fight. I love her to death, but it just seems like we can't stand to be around each other too long. What if me being home every night is a bad thing?"

"I don't know, man. You love them. I know that isn't always enough, though."

"Yeah. My contract…actually, my lease, but I always call it a contract because it's felt like a noose around my neck since I signed it…will be done. I turn the truck in, then I'll be done with her."

"Well, that's a good thing."

"Yeah. I don't have to go local, though. That's what I keep thinking. I can always sign another lease, take on a new truck or, hell, I could go back to being just a company driver. I don't know how well I would do giving up my freedom, and going on them damn electronic logs, though. I don't know if I'd survive."

The man starred at his can, watching as the little droplets of condensation ran down the side, then dripped to the wood grain counter. He pushed in on the aluminum with his thumb and watched as the can popped back into shape.

"You gotta do what ya gotta do, what feels right." Rob knew he was just giving contrite answers. Bruce seemed like a good guy, one Rob could call a friend, but he didn't really know enough about the guy to give him real advice.

And this wasn't the conversation Rob wanted to be having. How had he steered it there? Bruce had said he was leaving earlier. It had nothing to do with his home life, but had to do with the phones. So why were they having a hard time talking about it?

"I think what I need to do is just take some time off. Hell, that's why I don't want to hurry home, even though I 'm 'hurrying' home. I want to get there, but the longer I can put it off, the longer it takes to think about it. Being tired as all hell isn't helping things. I was already driving my second log when I picked you up. I don't even know when my fourteen expired."

"I didn't hear that," Rob said, smiling, though his lips were tight and he was growing a little concerned. Rob now noticed the dark circles under the man's eyes. He did look tired. He just thought it had been the long hours on the road the man suffered through day in/day out. If he had just heard Bruce right, he had been up for about twenty hours already. He should be getting some sleep.

"How much farther you gotta go?"

"I'm just down the way about another hour, so not that far. I'll make it home for supper."

"That's good."

"Still nothing about the car, huh? Only been an hour, though."

"Yeah." Rob stood and made his obligatory look down the street. Right now, he would actually be shocked to see his car show up at the garage. He was getting so used to not seeing it, looking down the road to see the mechanic standing in front of the open garage doors for the occasional smoke break.

This time, though, something was different. His car still wasn't there, but there was a man walking, stumbling down the center of the road.

The man wasn't drunk, but there was something off to how the man moved. Rob had taken enough people to the drunk tank, watched enough late night brawls and people stumbling to their cars to recognize the walk. There was something different to how this man moved. It was like, well…he wasn't sure exactly what it was like. It was lurching and unsure. The man was trying to test his limbs and wasn't sure how to move on them. He would shuffle his feet forward…one, then the other…then he would lose his balance. Instead of a man who would pick up his feet and stumble forward to regain his balance, this man would just stop and sway.

"Huh, I hadn't heard anything about a Zombie Walk going on in town? Man, the guy seems to be lost."

Rob looked back at the larger man behind the bar. He was pretty sure he had introduced himself as Sullivan. He'd been decent, quiet, and had kept the soda's coming. Other than that, Rob had barely noticed the guy, but when he looked at him now, he saw more of the unkempt hair that trickled out from under the hat, and the few days of stubble. He wore glasses, but they didn't look right on his face, like they were slightly askew. The bartender was looking past Rob and out the door.

"A what?" Rob asked, surprised.

"A Zombie Walk. Get a bunch of people together, they dress up like zombies, and walk around a neighborhood. Jason and I went to one up in Chicago last year around Halloween. Lot of fun. Even had an officer pull up to us and warn the passing pedestrians to beware of zombies. Even they got into it." Sullivan was smiling, and Rob had a sense that the man was reliving past memories.

Rob found that the idea of people dressing up as zombies and walking around hard to believe. Just what was the world coming to? He remembered zombies as a part of late night television or some crappy movie in the theater. He turned back to look at the "zombie", his skepticism growing. He had been a Chicago officer for a number of years and had never even heard of anything like that. Maybe it had just not been a part of his beat, but he just couldn't see the appeal.

Was he really getting that old?

He tried to imagine what he would have done if he would have come upon the group back in his Chicago days. He probably wouldn't have done too much, as long as they weren't hurting anything or bothering anyone. He doubted he would have played into the fantasy, but if he was having a good day… Hell, why not.

And, sure enough, the guy outside was doing a good job of impersonating a zombie. That walk was definitely reminiscent of what he guessed it would look like if a dead man rose up and tried to figure out how to walk again. Now that Sullivan had said something, Rob realized what it was that had been bothering him about the person. The clothes the man wore looked rugged. Rob couldn't see the make-up the man was wearing, but what he could make out looked good, at least from a distance.

"I wonder why he's all by himself, unless he's lost," Sullivan said. He was now looking intently down the street.

Rob looked back at him, asking, "Why do you say that?"

Sullivan shrugged. "The whole point of doing a Zombie Walk is to do it with a group. Get some friends together or meet new people with similar interests, then do the walk."

"Probably some kids getting together and shooting their own film," Bruce said just before upending his can of soda and setting it back down on the edge of the bar.

Tina, who seemed to move out from the shadows of the hallway, grabbed the can to toss it in the recycling shoot that lead to the basement, then went to the cooler to grab another.

Rob only glanced at her briefly, but he could still see how messed up she was. There was clear indication of shock.

What the hell happened to her, he thought. He wasn't sure, but he thought he could just make out the start of a nasty set of bruises around her neck. It was the kind of bruising someone got from being choked. He had seen it too many times. He didn't like seeing it on her, but she wasn't talking.

Rob turned back to the man outside and saw that the people in the bar weren't the only ones who had seen the man walking down the street. The mechanic Rob had spoken to just about an hour ago had been coming out of his garage and had noticed the man. He was now walking over to him.

His instincts tugged at him, and before he realized what he was doing, he moved forward. His hands had a mind of their own as he reached out towards the door. Something was pushing him to go outside and get a closer look. A voice in the back of his head screamed that something was wrong. There was a growing growl pushing in, and a knocking of drums pounding behind his temples. There was a taint to the air. Darkness pushed in from the corner of his vision. Something was out there, and he had no other word for it. It was just a wrongness.

The growling grew louder, pausing Rob's hand on the door. Before he could back away from it, there was a roar of a loud engine. It barely had time to register before he saw it at the intersection. The car whipped around a turn, gravel flying and wheels squealing as they spun. The car was fishtailing and just barely missed hitting the telephone pole on the other side of the street. Then the wheels found some grip on the asphalt and it sped out of view, moving fast past the bar.

"Shit," the redneck muttered, standing behind Rob. Rob looked back and saw he was already walking towards the back door when a fiery redhead, one of the shortest Rob had ever seen, was coming in. She was a slightly larger woman when it compared to her height, but seeing the little package that she carried in one of her arms, Rob guessed it had more to do with recently giving birth. She was hot, fired up, and screaming as she came into the bar.

"What the hell do you think you are doin'?! This isn't some job. This isn't work. In fact, it looks more like you are spending money. Just what the hell do you think you are doing? We can't afford this! We can't afford you spending the money I'm making as fast as I make it. Until you get another damn job, you don't have a cent to waste up here in this shithole."

Rob winced from the tongue-lashing, and he could tell right away where it was aimed. He was glad it wasn't aimed at him, as just being near the target was hard to bare. She whipped those words around so fast and furious, the redneck had stopped in mid-step and now looked like he was ready to turn tail.

"Get home." He scowled back at her, somehow finding his backbone.

Damn. Rob knew *that* wasn't the right answer. He also knew that this wasn't going to be pretty.
The woman glared at him, then at the rest of the people in the bar.

Everyone, including Rob, went back to the bar, taking their seats and trying to act as though there weren't two rival nations about to have an all-out nuclear war right there in the bar. It was obvious they were all having a hard time not looking. Rob could feel heat radiating from the pair.

"Get home?" Her voice was booming off the wood paneling of the small bar, the room suddenly not feeling large enough for the two people standing in its center. "*Get home*?!

You get your own ass home. You need to get home, or get a damn job. I have worked all week, then I come home and have to clean up after you, clean up at night and all damn weekend, when *you are supposed to be there*!"

In the large mirror behind the bar, Rob could see the redneck clenching his fists and looking like he was just moments away from doing something that Rob didn't think he could just sit there and watch. He caught Bruce's eye and, in that second, he could see the concern on the trucker's face, and Rob had a feeling Bruce was about to do something, too.

The redneck started to shift, and his hand was coming up. " h-" he was saying, but his words were cut off by a scream from outside. It wasn't a normal afternoon funfilled scream from the days many cookouts or other outside events. Rob had heard this scream before. This was desperate, death at the end of it, and before it would get there, pain was its best friend.

* * * *

Hammond was a town like so many others in the Midwest. A town where the church to bar ratio was about the same, and the drunk that was falling down as they tried to find their way to their car would be standing next to you in church. That woman who had been with everyone in town, working her way from one guy to the next for sexual pleasure, would be singing soprano in the choir, and that guy who cheated you on some deal would be the usher passing around the collection plate. Hammond was a town where church was a place for the sinners to feel like they could get saved for taking an hour out of their time one day a week.

Was that all religion was, though? A place to feel like a person could get saved? Was there not any actual salvation out there? When the end came, when the rapture struck and pulled forth the righteous, was it the Sunday wannabes who would be a part of it and would that one day dedication truly be enough?

When the end came, what would happen? Who would be left? Who would be saved to fight the evil in the streets? If the righteous were called, would anyone remaining even try to fight the evil that would wash over the land, or would they see it for what it was?

They had to know. They had to be able to find their way to God. There had to be a way to help them, to make them see. There had to be a way to make them find the light. The stench of hell, the maggots that rotted the meat and ate the corpses was rising. Death was rising. There had to be a way to save them. There had to be a way into the light.

"Please, Lord, help me! Help them find the light!" Father Carpenter said. He was stumbling. He knew his feet and his legs were week below him. He walked on them, but they just didn't feel like they were his anymore. There was so much going on with his head, so many thoughts and images flowing through him, that he felt like his body couldn't control itself.

He remembered he had left the church and had taken to walking down the street. It was bright outside, and he relished being a part of the light. He knew the light was faint, though, as there was a darkness that tinted it. There was an evil growing. He had felt it. He had seen it when that creature had infected Cynthia and she had smelled of its foulness. It had tainted his church and he had known he had to get out of there. He wasn't yet sure where he needed to go, but he just had known that *he needed to go.*

He had to be a part of God's plan. He had to get clean. He needed to wash away his sins and get clean. God needed him, was calling to him, and the good father had many sins he needed to wash away. Cynthia had only been one of his sins, but what about all the ones that came before her? He needed to wash them all away.

"And some say the world will end in fire!" he heard himself call out. Fire! He had seen it in his nightmares. A fire was coming. It was going to burn them all away. It was going to cleanse the wicked. It was coming for them all. God had once washed away the wicked. He had been a more wrathful God then. He was supposed to be a God of peace and love now, of forgiveness. God forgave the sinners. He had given his son to them. He had saved them. All he needed was forgiveness.

Forgiveness for sin. Oh, how he sinned. The images of the forbidden flesh flashed before him. As he ran his hands along her smooth skin, he remembered that it was gentle and soft, and his hands had felt so rough against it. The bareness, the pink softness, the wetness as he had moved his hands along her different regions. He had broken his vows, but God forgives, and God had to forgive him.

"Some say the world will end in fire," he said again. He had seen it. The fire was coming. It would take them all, and they were all going to burn.

Around him, he heard screaming. It was a horrible sound, and his chest clenched tight as he knew that God's wrath had begun.

CHAPTER 8

His heart beat viciously inside him, pounding out a crescendo of agony. It pounded so hard and fierce, it felt like it was trying to break free, escape the torture around him. Its intensity pained him, burning through his body, and pushing his ragged breath out in gasps. His face was hot, and he felt his skin tingling and on fire.

He could feel he was still alive just in the amount of pain he was in, both from the scrapes and cuts from falling off the porch, and from the emotional pain he felt inside that threatened to lock him down into a ball. He was thankful for the physical pain because he knew if he wasn't feeling it, he would be feeling nothing but emptiness, and that would be worse. He would be left with the hollowness, his world falling into that of a gray void. One where he would just give up, roll into that ball, and let it trap him.

But if he allowed himself to fall into the black hole consuming his emotions, he knew he would never escape. If he just gave in, let himself be pulled into that pit, he would never break free. He would stay there, cocooned in his own pit of despair, and would let the dangers around him consume him. He would have been balled up, crying, and back to being that nine-year-old boy who would always lock himself in his room whenever his parents were fighting.

His tires screeched and he could feel the car shifting gears. As he took the turn, the right side pulled itself up and he knew the tires were nearly off the ground. He felt like he shouldn't have slowed for the turn, but knew if he had taken it any faster, he would have lost control. It was still threatening to roll over and he had to fight to keep control. Just breathe, calm down. He needed to get control of himself, just as much as he needed to keep control of his car. He was losing it.

That thing back there… That couldn't have been his sister.

He needed to get help.

What the hell was happening?

Too many thoughts and images of what had just happened were trying to storm through his mind. All of it was firing through him, and he couldn't figure out which he wanted or didn't want to see more. Images kept blinding him, as he would see them nearly as clear as the road he drove on. With each flash, another tear rolled down his cheek.

He was driving. He couldn't be thinking about any of them now.

He had to get help. He had to get the cops. He had seen one cop rushing into the Rowplex when he was driving back home, but he didn't know he would still be there. How long had he been at his house? It couldn't have been that long. Would the cop still be there? He *had* to still be there.

He saw the stop sign up ahead and knew he had to turn left. The street was a dead end, and directly across from the stop sign was a house.

Susan. It was Susan's house. Susan, his mind was spinning and it seemed like suddenly he could only think of her. He thought of when he had spent time there as a kid. He thought of them when they were just about to go into kindergarten. He had spent the night at her house. It was his first sleepover. They had played… What was that game? His mind tried to remember the name of it. Something with them spinning around on a disc, giggling.

Come on, Jason. Get it together. Focus on driving. Pull your head out of your ass before you end up in Susan's living room. What did it matter if she was still away at school or not? Damn, he needed to pay attention.

He didn't want to pay attention. Paying attention would mean having to remember that he was running from something, and if he was running from something, he would have to remember what it was. But he didn't want to remember what that was. He didn't want to remember *who* that was.

No! He wasn't running from her. He was running to get help *for* her.

The street quickly came to another stop sign. He would have to turn to the right and, again, he didn't wait to stop. He turned the wheel hard and felt the wheels slide as they hit the loose gravel in the center of the intersection. At least he wouldn't have to worry about flipping the car. He was good at maneuvering out of a fishtail. He could control this. If he just stayed and fought for control, he would eventually win, then he could focus.

The car straightened out and, this time, he couldn't avoid it. He saw her, his sister, in his memory.

* * * *

When she had come through the window, he hadn't been able to stop himself. He backpedaled. He didn't definitely know it was her. All he saw was a mop of wild hair breaking through the window to come for him. He had only a second to wonder how she had been able to break through it before his foot stepped back into nothingness.

As he fell back, he knew he was falling off the porch. As a kid, he had jumped and ran around that porch so many times, he knew every centimeter of it. He knew how much of it there was to run across and take a flying leap, and he knew he had stumbled backwards far enough to know that when he fell, he was going to land flat on his back. What he didn't know was if he was over far enough to crash into the rose bush, or if he was going to fall onto the hard ground.

He wasn't sure and he didn't care. He was still focused on his sister, his little baby sister, and her body as it broke through the glass. He hadn't wondered too much about how she broke through. The glass window had been thick and would be hard to break, but Jason remembered the BB holes that were hidden towards the edges. The ones he and his cousin had done years ago, the ones his mom still didn't know about. He was sure that if she ever found out, she would still put him over her knee and tan his ass. Well, not anymore. Not after all that was happening. It was nice to think she would get upset over something so small and, in a way, it was a comforting thought to get punished over something so superficial. However, he knew she would never find out about the window and, now, it paled in comparison to everything else. It paled in comparison to his failure as a big brother to protect his little sis.

The world around him came back. He remembered that face, what had once been his sister's face, tearing through the window. Then he landed hard into the side of the rose bushes. The thorns of the thick, stiff branches tore into his flesh, and he could feel his back as it was pricked from the side branches as the force from his fall was pushing him away from the bushes.

He didn't have time to register it, as he was past the bush and landing on the large rocks that made up the bedding around the front porch. His body rolled and continued down the little embankment until he could finally catch himself.

His back and arms had thousands of little fires of agony, and he could see the red lines already starting on his hands from the thorns. His head felt like a hammer had crushed into one side, and his cheek felt like it was swelling fast. He didn't think there was any part of him that didn't hurt.

He brought his knee up under him as he worked to stand. He needed to see just what the hell was going on. Up on the porch, he heard the scraping and shattering of glass and he knew that his sister was still pulling herself out of the window. He turned back and caught himself reaching for her. She must be trying to get away from someone. He must have gotten there at the right time. Maybe she would be okay.

She was lying on the cement just outside the window, her pale face looking at him. Her eyes were a dead gray and her mouth hung open, her tongue hanging out. He could see that, at some point, she had bitten through most of it and it was limply hanging there. There were scrapes and cuts on her face and along her arms, one cut jutting down from the right edge of her eye, exposing the side where her eye should have been.

He took a step back, noticing there was no blood coming out of any of her wounds. He could see the flesh was peeled back, and could see what looked like blood underneath, but it didn't pour out of her.

She reached an arm towards him, and he instinctively took a step back, then another, his hand dropping down to the bush around him, and he used it to push himself farther back. Her arm reached out for him, then it came down to the cement and she used it to push herself up and inched closer to him. He took another step back, freeing himself from the bush.

"Lisa?" he said. His voice sounded alien to himself. It was strained and he could hear that it was ready to crack and break into sobbing tears.

Oh, Lisa, what happened?

He heard rustling and saw another one, a man he vaguely remembered, rustling through the rose bushes and coming towards him.

The man was stumbling, looking like what Jason could only think of to describe as something from a zombie movie. They both did. He couldn't help but react and started moving away from both of these things. He needed to get away from them, to run and hide, do whatever it took. Those things weren't right.

But he couldn't leave his sister. He couldn't just leave her behind. He needed to do something, but what? She was messed up, maybe even sick. Maybe that was all it was. Some kind of virus. If it was, maybe she could get better. She just needed a doctor.

No, she was in no shape for a doctor to come for her. She was not mentally fit right now. Even if it was just a sickness, she was out of her mind.

He needed to get more than just a doctor. What other kind of help could he get? This was a small town. A small, *pissant town that barely even had any kind of decent cell service. What backwards place didn't allow for decent cell ser-*

Yes! That's what he needed to do! He needed to go and get help. He needed to run and get someone…or could he call them on his cell phone?

He probably could, right? Emergency services could help.

He reached down towards the pocket in his pants and was frustrated when he didn't feel the bulge of his phone.

Shit, it must still be in the car.

He turned and ran back to his car. It wasn't a long run, and it was in the opposite direction of both of them. He got in, and slammed the door, quickly hitting the locking mechanism. His eyes darted around. He felt like he couldn't breathe and wasn't getting enough oxygen. The windows around him were fogging up, and his chest heaved as it was trying to force air in and out faster than he could process it. Everything around him seemed to be shaking. No, he was shaking. Everything around him seemed like it was in a haze. He felt like there was a darkness threatening to push itself over him.

What was he going to do? Oh, that's right. He was going to call for help. He needed to call 911. He needed to get someone there to help his sister.

He saw his phone sitting in its cradle. He grabbed it and quickly started punching in numbers. He hit the SEND button, then looked in the rearview mirror. He could see his sister pulling herself to the edge of the porch. What was wrong with her, with them? They both didn't act right. Was it some form of shock from all the trauma they had experienced? They looked like they were torn up pretty badly and needed medical attention.

His phone was still silent. He looked down at it, wondering why it wasn't ringing on the other end. He saw the red icon up where the signal strength should be. No bars. Worse than no bars. Absolutely no signal! That was bad. He couldn't remember the last time he had absolutely no signal in Hammond. Sure, they weren't going to be getting 4G anytime soon, but they had always had at least some signal. Why was there no service now?

He looked back over his shoulder and watched as his sister fell off the side of the porch. She hadn't tried to climb down or go over to the stairs that were only a couple of feet from her. She had just continued straight on her path and, in the end, had fallen over at the same spot he had.

He couldn't see her too well now. She was partially hidden behind the cement stairs and the front bush. He could see the vague shape of her moving, though. She looked like a black mass as her dark-colored hair was all that he really saw. Then her hand emerged, and she was again pulling herself up, fighting to get free from the bush.

She pulled herself free, her head emerging. She looked up, lifting her head, and looked at him. Her dead, hungry eyes were staring, and he didn't see anything left of Lisa in them. His sister was gone.

No! No! He had to get help. If he couldn't call anybody, he would go find someone. The Rowplex! He had to go there. He didn't know why the cop had been there, but if he could get him, they could radio for an ambulance. Then they could come and help her.

I have to find a way to save Lisa, *he thought to himself as he threw the car into drive.*

* * * *

Denise slowly pulled herself out of the car. A stillness hung in the air. There was something not right, but she just couldn't put her finger on what it was. It wasn't something tangible. She didn't know how she knew, but she did. It was something else, like a menace. There was something wrong, and all her senses screamed at her, telling her she needed to run away.

Where would she go? She needed to find her brother, and his car was right there. There were a bunch of cars there. If she didn't know better, she would have thought the store was open. The only way she knew it wasn't was when she looked at the front door and saw the broken glass and the lack of people.

She stood outside her car, listening to the quiet idle of her little four-cylinder engine as it hummed. There should be *some* sound around her. It was the middle of the afternoon on a Saturday. There should be a lot more people around shopping, driving, or even trying to leave town to go fishing or camping. The town was nearly silent, like it was dead.

There were no people. How many times did she have to think about just how abandoned the town looked before it really dawned on her? How much did she have to listen to the silence before she admitted she needed to get out of there? If everyone else hadn't already left or are leaving, then something had already happened to them. She didn't know how it was spreading so fast, but she had seen it. She knew what was going on. When would she admit it to herself and get the hell out of there?

She didn't want to think about it.

She was parked in the parking lot of the largest department store in the Rowplex shopping complex. She didn't typically shop there, but she knew it was where many of the people in town went for their office supplies and computers. It should be open. She should see people there.

She counted fifteen cars. Five of them were police cars. There were the two local squad cars, the two "weekend warrior" officers who had driven their own cars, and then a state trooper who must have been in town at the time. The cop cars were all positioned in a line out in front of the store, blocking off a perimeter around the entrance. The rest of the cars were all parked in parking spaces.

Denise had stopped close to the nearest cop car that had been at an angle across the little entry road that was in front of all the stores. That little road people would always cross as they went in to spend away all their hard-earned money. She had no idea what to call it and didn't care. She also didn't care that she was stopped in the middle of it.

Where *was* everyone?

She looked around. She had seen maybe two cars pass by the shopping center. She couldn't hear any other car traffic on any of the neighboring streets. As she listened, she realized that some of the police cars were still running. Why wasn't there an officer out there? There should be at least one to two officers standing with the squad cars.

She shifted her weight to step around her open door and the sound of the little bit of loose stone was loud to her ears. When she closed it, the sound of the door echoed like a hand clapping in a canyon, then dying away.

She walked to the squad car, her stomach in knots as it tried to scream at her not to go. She ignored it and reached the closest car. Her footfalls were loud, and she stayed low. She only made it a couple of steps along the cars when she saw a leg sticking out from behind one of them. She hurried for it, stopping when she saw all the blood.

* * * *

The Rowplex had once been a strip mall packed with stores. Large chain stores would try to get in there because, even though it was a small town, Hammond was large in comparison to those towns around it. It had a large parking lot that would be full of cars as families would come in to do their grocery, gift, and whatever other shopping they would need. There were toy stores for the kids, clothing stores for the moms, and the general everything stores and hardware stores for the dads. It had something for the whole family. It even had an auto parts store, which was uncommon to see in a strip mall.

It was tucked back a little bit off the main street, having to take a little driveway back to it, but the wide open parking lot could be seen from the road. It wouldn't be strange to see a line of cars going in and out of the shopping complex, sometimes being held up by the traffic light.

However, over the last ten years, stores closed. Larger chains had invaded the towns to the north of Hammond, and as the factories started to go out of business, less people came there to do their shopping. The mall slowly became more and more desolate. After a while, it became a ghost town, with the exception of the one remaining office supply store and a few other smaller chains. Many questioned how they even kept in business with the very few customers they still received.

Around the corner on the side of the strip mall, there was the remaining auto parts store, kept in business probably because they were the only auto parts store still in town, and the

China Buffet. What would a strip mall be without a Chinese restaurant that didn't accept credit cards?

Jason wasn't thinking about it as he raced into the parking lot, but when he was a kid, his mom would often bring him there. He would be tortured by her taking him to the fashion place. Of course, his mom probably felt more like he was the one torturing her with how he would disappear while she shopped, only to later be found amongst the center of the large clothing racks.

That was back when he was not that much younger than what his sister was now. Lisa, his little sister, the one he played with whenever he came home from college. The one he could still lift up and swing around when he could get enough momentum. Not that he did that much with her anymore, but they still did other things. She loved to talk books with him. He still fancied the occasional young adult book, and he was so ecstatic over Lisa getting into reading. She would get so excited when she found a new series that she enjoyed and, when he came home, he would listen to her as she told him all the reasons he just had to start reading it. And he did the same for her when he came across a new series of books that he thought she would enjoy.

Just yesterday, he had been telling her how much he thought she would love the Scott Lynch series he had started reading. While it wasn't quite young adult, he couldn't think of anything in the books that was too questionable, and she would love the witty charm of the series.

That had been yesterday. Was it only just last night that he had been talking to her about it? It didn't seem like it. She had looked at him. Her eyes had always been such a beautiful brown. He often enjoyed how they were able to look on with so much wonder. Her eyes…

The cold, dead eyes that blankly looked in his direction flashed in his mind, not the eyes of the child who had looked up to him, a sparkle at the edge as she'd listen to him talk about the books. He saw the ones that somehow followed him, while not being completely there. That blank stare, a face that didn't register emotion, yet moved, jaw opening and closing as though seeking something to bite into.

Even when he closed his eyes, he still saw her looking at him…not as his baby sister, but as that sick girl. She was sick. He didn't know what had happened to her, but she needed help.

He nearly missed his turn because he was going too fast and hadn't realized he was at the light. If he wasn't careful, he was going to get into an accident. He hadn't seen any other cars around, but that could just be because he wasn't paying attention. There could have been in a crowd of people around and he wouldn't have noticed. That wasn't a good thing.

Why wasn't his cell phone working? Why couldn't he just call for help? Of all times for his damn carrier to be blocking his calls, now was *not* the time. He was certain he had paid the bill, so there should be no reason for his service to be cut off. He was sure he had paid it before he had come home, largely because he was afraid of his service getting turned off on his drive. He had a paranoia of driving large distances without cell service. He had been stranded too many times out on back roads while living around there, and he never went anywhere without his cell phone to call for help now because his car was not the most reliable.

Like many of the turns he had taken since he had run from his house, his tires squealed. This time, he felt the other side of the car rise up, threatening to roll over. There wasn't any gravel for him to slide onto, so the car kept its grip on the firm surface. It wobbled, trying to push him further up, the car wanting to finish spinning. He was turning the wheel, straightening it out and letting the vehicle come down on all four wheels. This wasn't the way he wanted to get the attention of the cops. The last thing he needed was to be fighting them over a reckless driving ticket when he was trying to get them to call for emergency services.

At least the cars were still there. In the back of his mind, he had been worried they would all be gone by the time he got there. He was grateful when he saw them still parked in front of the retail store, but why were they blocking it off? It would be just his luck if someone was robbing the damn place and taking hostages on a day like today. What the hell else could be going on? It sure did look like something out of a movie.

Yeah, there were the cars, but where were the people? Other than the main squad car in town, and a couple others that he knew belonged to the local part-timers, there was only a couple of other cars parked in the lot. The cop cars were in a block formation, but the rest of them were just in regular parking spots. There weren't any people, though. Where *was* everybody?

The Rowplex had long since developed a deserted feel to it. Even when there was a decent amount of cars in the lot, it still felt empty. Cars without people, parked in such an obvious, attention-grabbing way, made it feel even more isolated. He accelerated towards the group of cars in the center of the parking lot.

He neared them and barely saw a woman staggering out. She didn't look up. He swerved hard and eased down on the brake, somehow keeping enough control over himself to keep from slamming his foot down. The car fought against him, but he kept control. Too many years of driving too fast told him that if he had done it any differently, he would have lost it. The car just missed clipping her.

The car stopped, the engine ticking. He hadn't turned the key. It just decided to die on its own. The damned thing was complaining about all the abuse he had put it through for the last hour or so, but now was not the time for the damned beast to act up on him. She was a stubborn old pain in the ass that he often cursed at and accused of being alive because she had a personality all her own. Currently, that personality was pissed. He would have to deal with her later because he saw the woman he had nearly hit looking at him, her eyes locked on him through the side mirrors of his car.

Her eyes were wide, and he had a sense that he recognized her, although he couldn't remember from where. She was an older woman, thin, wearing a white blouse tucked into a pair of jeans. She had an attractiveness to her, even though her eyes were open wide with shock. It didn't take long before the look was gone and she was glaring at him. Why was she glaring at him? She was the one that had come out of nowhere. If anyone should be upset, he should be getting out of the car, walking back to her and yelling.

He was reaching for his door, pulling hard on the handle. He was halfway out of the car when the first shot went off. He wasn't sure what instinct kicked in, but he quickly found himself lying on the asphalt, his mouth stinging from hitting the ground. His teeth felt like he had knocked a few loose and his jaw felt like it rubbed the rough surface. He had to spit out the dirt.

He couldn't be certain it was a gunshot. No, it was probably just a car backfiring. Or, since it was July, just some firecrackers. Never mind the fact that he was parked by police cars, without any of the police officers around. It couldn't be gunfire.

Another shot rang out. It was muffled, but he heard glass shattering and guessed it was coming from the store. Then another shot not muffled by the glass doors. That was clearly gunfire. Someone in the store was shooting.

He looked over at the woman he had almost hit. She was crouched low. She hadn't been an idiot like him and dove down. She had the sense to just crouch down behind the cars. She had her hand out, using one of the squad cars to support her. He watched as she pushed herself up a little to peek over the car's hood.

Feeling like an idiot, he reached out, his palms on fire from the little scrapes he had gotten from the rose bush and the asphalt. If he survived today, he was going to look like he had his ass handed to him. He pushed against the ground, doing the best version of a push up that he could with his legs still tangled in his car. He pulled one leg free and heard it crunch on some gravel, causing the woman's head to quickly snap around to glare at him. She didn't have to motion for him to be quiet. He understood just by the heat of her eyes that she felt he was making too much noise. Even though he doubted anyone in the building could hear them, he understood that she was terrified. She may not have been showing it, and she sure as hell had a better head on her shoulders than he did.

As quietly as he could and staying low, which wasn't easy as his back was stiffening up and it was hard for him to stay slouched, he eased his other leg out. He actually found it easier, though it hurt more, to just stay on his knees and crawl over to her.

It felt like he was in a damned action film as he moved closer to her. However, he didn't get too close. He was curious about her, but her intensity scared him. He eased himself close before rising up and peeking over the trunk of the squad car.

The first thing he saw was all the blood. There were puddles of it in different spots, two large ones just in front of the cars. Those two puddles went into rugged patterns of lines that crisscrossed, some long and thick, while others were thin. It looked like there had been a massacre, then someone had dragged all the bodies inside. He followed where all the lines lead, which was to the shattered door; however, it didn't look like it had been shot out. It looked like something had been pushed through it. There were bullet holes, but most of those were on the outer panes around the door, and they were just spider webs of broken glass. It was amazing the glass hadn't shattered out with what little of it remained intact.

Then he looked at the broken door. There was a shape there, standing just beyond what he could see. With the sun peeking over the building, shining right into his eyes, it was hard to see anything. He heard it, though, the crunch of broken glass as the shape moved closer to them.

"We need to go," he heard a sniffling voice say, and his attention was pulled back to the woman crouched just a few feet away from him. She had taken an unsteady step back away from the car, no longer using it to steady herself. She was already turning to rise, moving towards his car.

They couldn't go, though. He still needed to get help for his sister. If he left, where would he go? He could go to the doctor's office in town, but hadn't they sent her sister away this morning?

Why had they sent his sister away? The doctor must have seen her getting sick. He should have known something was wrong. If Jason took her back there, would it do any good? The doctor obviously didn't know what he was doing. He wouldn't be any help.

He would have to drive to the hospital to get her help. Well, that wasn't going to do any good, either. If he took her to the hospital, that would be one thing, but to go there and come back with an ambulance? That was even *if* they would come with him. There was sure to be questions. Why hadn't he just brought her with him? How would he explain she had tried to attack him, and that his baby sister scared him? What rational man would believe him? They would think he was just pulling some prank.

He needed to find the cops. They had to help him.

"No."

"What do you mean, no?"

"I need their help."

"Help?" The woman stopped going towards his car and turned to look at him. She was obviously confused, and he could imagine why. He wasn't sure what her deal was, and if people were shooting at him, he was probably about to do something really dumb, but there had to be someone there he could talk to. Besides, it had to be safe in there because there weren't any cops outside to keep him out. The situation inside had to be under control.

The woman was reaching for him, but he was able to keep away from her as he sidestepped, then he started moving around the back of the car. She followed him, but he wasn't sure why. As he had an itch pulling at his spine with everything that was happening, he was happy she did.

"You're not going to find help there. We need to go," she said to him in a loud whisper. It sounded like she was trying to keep quiet, but was still speaking loud enough that he could hear her.

He was getting closer to the shape. The shape was small, but not as small as a child. It had to be a short woman.

"Hey!" he quietly called out to it.

He noticed the shape stumble to the side, like hearing him yell at it had caught it off-guard. Then it started moving forward again, noticeably faster this time. It emerged from the shadow of the building, and he could see he was right. It was a woman.

Or she *had* been a woman. He wasn't sure that was the right thing to say about her now. Now, it was just like his sister. Gashes covered her arms. Her clothes, once black slacks and some red-colored uniform shirt, were now in tatters. Pale skin was torn, exposing muscle fragments that were dangling from her.

Jason stopped. He couldn't move. He was watching as she was coming closer to him, but while his mind was screaming that he needed to run, he just watched. His body seemed like it was on a separate frequency and that what his mind was telling him he needed to do, he just couldn't bring himself to obey.

She stumbled closer, her pace quickening, though she was still staggering horribly. Her face was somewhat familiar. He wasn't sure if he actually knew her, or if it was just because he saw her around somewhere. Becky? Wait. Where had that name came from? Maybe he had gone to school with her?

"Come on!" he heard, and realized the voice was not inside his own head. Someone was actually yelling at him. Why was she yelling at him? Didn't she know that they needed to help this woman? She obviously needed medical help. His sister needed medical help. They had to find help!

He turned and looked at the woman standing by him. She was holding her hand out, reaching for him.

"We can't. We need to find the cops. My sister needs help." He heard the deadness in his voice. He should be panicked. Why was he talking so calmly?

"They're all dead," she said with exasperation. Her lips trembled and he saw that her cheeks were red, like she had been crying. She was pointing to where she had been coming from when he had almost hit her. "One of them is over there. We need to go. If you want to stay alive, we need to get out of here. Now!"

She reached forward and grabbed his arm. He tried to stay there, but was surprised at how much strength she had. He staggered forward, then was half-running behind her.

"Get outta here!" yelled a voice. Jason looked over his shoulder as a man emerged from inside the store. He was holding a shotgun and limping heavily. Even though he was far away, Jason could see the line of blood that was flowing down the man's leg. The man was aiming his gun at the thing that was staggering towards Jason.

It must have heard him yelling because it stopped and looked back at the man as he was working his way around it. He kept his distance, staggering to keep away while shuffling towards them.

Jason recognized the man. Dog. While large men with huge gun collections was not that uncommon there, you could always tell Dog by his hat. It was one of those that Jason thought of as a fisherman's hat. The center was straight, but not quite rigid, and the sides were uneven. It had been Dog's look, and with everyone knowing just how unstable Dog could be at times, no one ever thought to joke about it.

The man was scary. He was a common fixture at the bar, and Jason's mom had warned him about the man. Dog was known for trying to scam drinks out of the bartenders, paying for them two at a time so he could try to get a third one free, saying he already paid. Jason had never told his mom just how much Dog intimidated the hell out of him, so there had been many times he had gotten that third and sometimes fourth drink free.

Dog didn't look that scary right now, though. He looked panicked. He was gesturing with the shotgun in a "shooing" fashion, like he could physically push Jason away.

"Get the fuck outta here!" he yelled again. Dog was trying to move quickly, but the limp was bad. Jason could tell he was in a lot of pain. It was obvious that the leg was slowing him down more than he could handle. Behind Dog, Jason could see another shape as it was making its way into the store.

Jason turned to look back at the woman. She had stopped pulling on his arm and was also staring. She was watching Dog coming towards them. Her eyes were big, the whites visible as she watched him. He wondered if she was going to go after Dog instead. He was still bleeding, so they could help him, get him out there.

The thing turned towards Dog.

"We have to go," the woman whispered close to his ear. He turned to look at her. Her voice was trembling, her lip quivering. "There is no help here, and we can't help him. We need to go."

Jason took a step away from her and turned back towards Dog.

"No, no, no!" screamed Dog.

Jason heard more glass breaking. Dog had stopped hurrying towards them and had turned to look back at the front of the store. What had been one shape coming out of the store was now three, including that fat asshole, Tom. It didn't feel like any skin off his back seeing that son of a bitch, still as fat as the days when Jason used to work for him in high school, limping heavily on one side. Jason could see that, like many of them, Tom's shirt was covered in drying blood. Behind him, he could see the chief, in his torn uniform, shuffling behind the large bulk of his former boss.

Dog's shotgun must have been out of shells because instead of firing at the things coming towards him, he grabbed it by the barrel and brought it up like a baseball bat. He was turned towards the things that were coming towards him, but was still backing away.

The woman pulled at Jason's hand again, then stopped and let his arm go. When he turned, he saw that she wasn't looking at him anymore. She was looking past him, and he watched as something changed in her. The arm that had grabbed him let go and pulled back to her chest. There were fresh tears in her eyes and she looked like she wanted to scream. No, that wasn't it. He recognized that look. He had seen it just hours before. He had seen that look from his aunt as she had been falling apart.

"Thomas. Oh no, Thomas," she said, backing away from him, never taking her eyes away from the group coming out of the store.

There was a shuffling, and Jason looked up to see another shape moving from in between the squad cars. He started over to them, but she was back by his side again, grabbing at his arm and pulling.

"You can't. Don't get too close to them."

"What?" He looked at her, confusion showing on his face. What was she talking about? Why couldn't he get close? What if the guy needed his help?

"Come on. There's nothing we can do. We need to get out of here. Come *on*!" She tugged at him.

He heard a grunt, and something slammed nearby. He looked and saw that the person getting up from in between the cars had fallen back into the car for support. Looking closely, he could see why. The guy was big, looked like maybe he had once played football. He thought he recognized the guy as being another one of the local cops. This was the guy who'd often be called out to the bars to break up the fights, which would usually result in one or both of the fighters going home with probably more bruises than if the cops hadn't been called in the first place.

The guy was moving slow, and it was obvious as to why. There was a large part of his right leg missing! Just past the man's knee, a few sharp pieces of bone stuck out. Dragging behind him and hanging off of a few strands of what was maybe muscle and skin was the rest of the man's leg. The man should be dead, or lying on the ground in pain. Instead, he seemed to stumble, hop, and lean his way against the parked cars, moving towards them.

Yeah, there wasn't anything Jason was going to be able to do to help this poor son of a bitch out. The thought of running over to the man and giving him a nice right hook to the jaw did appeal to him. Not that Jason had much reason to. It had never directly been him that he had harassed, but the idea of hitting a cop just felt like it would be something he would enjoy.

A sharp tug from the woman quickly erased the fantasy, and he stumbled back, quickly following as she ran to the open driver's door of his car and climbed in.

"What the hell are you doing?" he asked as he hurried over to her.

She looked up at him, then looked away. He was struck again at how familiar she looked. He didn't think he really knew her, but he knew he had seen her around town. Not that it was a big town. It was always easy to see everyone, but impossible to meet everyone. He didn't know how small of a town you had to live in before you had that unbearable knowledge.

He tried to place her, but it didn't really matter. She was in his car, and he sure as hell needed her out of it.

"Come on, get out," he said to her as he grabbed the door and put his body in the way, preventing her from closing it, but she wasn't looking at him. She still had her head turned and was watching Dog through the passenger door.

Jason looked over the top of his car and watched as the group of the five things neared the large man. He hit the first one that came close to him, causing it to stagger away. It was odd to watch how it moved. Jason was actually surprised the thing didn't fall. Instead, it just continued to stumble away from the rest of the pack until it evened itself out. Then it stopped, turned to look back at Dog, and started to stagger towards him again.

Dog smacked a few more of them and, each time, they would stagger away to catch their balance, then come back after him.

"Oh shit!" Jason heard Dog scream out in a voice that was much higher than he thought the man could produce. He dropped the shotgun to stare at his arms. "Get them off of me!" he screamed as he started to swipe at his arms, growing more frantic. Then he started to scratch and tear at his skin. "The spiders! Get them off of me. They're in my skin. Get them the fuck off of me." Watching him, Jason cringed, then the things were on top of him.

"We need to go."

Jason looked down at the forceful voice he suddenly heard from below him. The woman was looking up at him, the tears wiped away so she no longer looked like the devastated woman he had seen.

"I said we need to go."

Jason nodded. "Yeah. Get over in the passenger seat. I'm driving."

She hurried out and he sat, closing his door. It didn't take her long until she was seated beside him. He didn't wait for her door to close as he slammed the car into drive and was flying towards the exit of the Rowplex.

* * * *

"Where are you going? We need to get out of town," the woman was saying as she struggled to get on her seat belt. She kept pulling on the strap, and it would start to come out to wrap around her, then stop until she tried pushing in and pulling out again. He was torn between wanting to tell her it was broken and enjoying watching her fight with it.

Who the hell was she, and why did he even pick her up? Why had she wanted to come with him?

"I'm going back to my mom's bar," he said. His aunt, his sister… No, he couldn't leave yet.

"No, no! We have to get out of town."

"My sister is sick, and my aunt needs me. I'm not leaving until I get help."

"There are more of those things. We need to go."

"More?"

"More! I don't know what the hell they are, but we need to get out of here. No heart beat or blood flowing. By all accounts, they shouldn't be up and walking around. I don't know what to call them. It's not-"

She didn't know what they were, but he did. "They're zombies," he said, finally admitting it to himself. He had been trying to ignore the thought, even though the realization had been building up since he had left his house. He had known it, but hadn't wanted to believe it. Even though there were many people out there that lived each day preparing themselves for the possibility of a zombie outbreak, he and Sullivan jokingly being two of them, they never really thought it would ever happen. It wasn't real. It was fiction. *Zombies…were…fictional.*

Yet, he couldn't have seen what he saw. Seeing was not believing.

The woman had blinked at him when he said it, and while she had been leaning towards him, giving up on the seat belt now that they were momentarily stopped, she now leaned back against the passenger door.

Jason didn't really think too much about it as he reached for the door locks, locking them in. He had seen too many zombie and other horror films to take for granted that something couldn't come along and pull open the doors.

"I need to get back to the bar. My aunt is there, and I'm, well… She needs my help right now. If you want, I can take you back to the Rowplex. Maybe someone else will come along, or maybe you can drive one of the other cars there, but I need to go back to the bar. I should also let the people there know what's going on. They should try and get out of town, too."

He hadn't thought about what they were going to do. He didn't know what he was thinking until he was already saying it, but it was a plan, or a partial one, and finally saying it helped him justify to himself that it was the right plan. The woman was right. They *did* need to get out of town, but he wasn't going to just run away and leave everyone else. He wasn't a hero, he wasn't going to fight for some great cause, but he wasn't going to abandon everyone, either.

Jason took a brief look around, making sure to check and see that the light was still red. Even though they were on one of the main streets in town, it was still a side street to the main highway that ran through town, so coming from the Rowplex always meant you had to sit at this particular light for what felt like an eternity.

He looked back at the woman who had picked up on his nervous look around and was now doing the same. However, she seemed to take more time. He figured she must have been lost in thought. She was probably wondering, since there was no traffic and all the police back there were probably dead, why in the hell was he stopped at a stoplight? He wondered that himself, but habits and paranoia of being pulled over again were hard to break.

Then he thought about it. There were no other cars. There were some parked at some of the businesses, but the town was quieter than he had ever seen.

"Where the hell is everyone?" he asked, thinking out loud.

"Yeah. I know there was the game at the school, the exhibition with Roanoke middle school, so there had been a lot of people there, and they had the summer festival scheduled behind the school for after the game." She didn't go on to say that she had never seen the town so dead, even while all that was going on, but she didn't have to. He had lived in the town long enough to know how much of a big deal the summer festival was to the town and when it was going on, much of the town did seem to die. It had never been like this, though.

"The light's green."

He looked up. When he started forward, he heard a distant humming. It was quickly growing louder, changing into a whining sound. Jason was halfway into the intersection when he turned and saw that a thin, black shape was coming at them fast.

He stopped the car and watched, knowing that there was no way the person on the bike could slow down enough to stop or do anything but go around them. He figured that not knowing which way the guy chose to go could cause a collision. By staying still, even though he was in the middle of the intersection, maybe the guy could adjust. Yeah, that's why he did it. It didn't have anything to do with the sudden shock that had taken his foot of the pedal and slammed it on the brake.

The bike roared past them, swerving around in front of them, just missing the front bumper of his car. Then it was gone.

Jason suddenly had the feeling that he needed to find a bathroom. His pants seemed a little moist.

CHAPTER 9

They crowded around him, their skin ablaze, the stench of their burning flesh suffocating him. The putrid fumes overwhelmed him and he had to fight down the nausea. He could taste the vile flavor in the back of his throat, and the biscuits and gravy from the morning weren't tasting as good as they wanted to come back up.

Everything was spinning, everything was moving faster and faster. He was losing control, lights flashing. The bodies rubbed up against him, and he could feel the heat. It was burning away at him, tearing away at his soul. Tears stung the edge of his eyes, and he felt their momentary wetness on his cheeks.

He heard the screaming, the cries of the dying. He knew the flames were tearing at them, scorching away their flesh, and he could feel their howls of agony as it worked its way deep down inside of him, stabbing at his heart. Screams he knew he could not save. They were the dying, the ones he had to watch die. The ones that no matter how many different ways he tried to save them, he never could. He would always have to stand there and watch them burn alive.

He watched them every night. Every time he closed his eyes, they were there, waiting. They were the ones he hadn't

saved, the ones who had burned to death the last night he served
as a Chicago police officer. Those were the ones who had been
killed in that drug lab because he hadn't been able to get in there
to save them. He had barely been able to save himself and
hadn't been conscious. He knew they were there beyond the
door. He hadn't seen them. He hadn't died with them, but they
were with him every time he tried to sleep. He was right there
beside them as they all died.

In the hot summer day, he heard the screaming and he
was right back there, caught in that room. His sweat was boiling
on him. The terror was threatening to overwhelm him. He didn't
know if he was ready to handle this again.

"You okay?"

He looked up to see Bruce staring at him. Rob hadn't
realized he was leaning against the shuffleboard table. He had
fallen into it, barely able to maneuver to keep himself from
passing out on the floor. The waking nightmare had pulled him
in so quickly, he had nearly lost himself completely and could
have slammed down onto the floor. As it was, he had been able
to reach out in time and had caught the side of the table to keep
from collapsing.

That night, the one when the drug bust had gone wrong,
he hadn't been the officer in charge. It was when he was still a
Chicago beat cop. He had been the lone survivor in the building.
All the other officers, the dealers, and the slaves they used to
cook their stuff had all died.

They called it "survivor's guilt", or so he was told. He
had only gone long enough to the therapist to get discharged,
allowed to wear a badge again. Maybe he should have gone
longer. Maybe then he wouldn't be plagued with the nightmares.
Every night, he was still with them, trapped with those people.

"Hey, buddy?"

Bruce was rising, and Rob first thought he was coming to check on him. When another scream came from outside, the large man turned away. Rob felt the tendrils of his memory pull back as he snapped back to the present. He pushed himself up, using the shuffleboard table to get his bearings, then he was following the trucker, surprised at how fast he moved. He still felt the pain of the images rattling around in his mind.

Bruce beat Rob to the door, causing him to have to reach in front of him to keep the screen door from slamming into his face. Then he nearly ran into the larger man when Bruce stopped midway down the steps.

Rob saw why, but he wasn't sure what it was he was seeing.

The mechanic had come into the street, probably to see if the man was playing or seriously screwed up. Whatever the reason was, it hadn't mattered. When he had gotten close enough, the thing had grabbed the mechanic. They were now both on the ground, blood flooding the street around them.

Rob didn't know what he was seeing, but that didn't matter. He still reacted. Quickly moving into action, he leapt over the side railing, instantly regretting it when he felt the jolt from landing on the ground. Pain shot up his bad side, but he ignored it as he rushed to get around the larger man. Then he was running.

He wasn't sure how fast his feet would carry him, his legs working to betray him as the old injury from his Chicago PD days tried to slow him down. He already knew he wasn't going to be able to get there in time to save the man's life. With how much blood he saw, he wasn't sure how he was still screaming. That thing-

Thing. Rob wasn't even sure if he wanted to think about what the thing was. Was it an undead corpse, reanimated like out of a horror film to devour the brains of unsuspecting people? Was it a zombie hell-bent on devouring the flesh of civilization? More than likely, he figured that *thing* was a deranged man, caught up on some drug that was a passing fad, dressed up in some elaborate costume. He didn't give a shit what that *thing* was, it was killing a man and needed to be put down.

Strangely, Rob knew he would rather it be either one of the first two options than having to deal with the third. He could shoot down and kill the undead zombies of the world, but what do you do to a living person, unarmed, who is out of their mind on some drug. With his training, he knew some self-defense moves he could use to fight the man.

More violence. More of the reason he moved away from Chicago.

His stomach was in knots.

Behind him, he heard Bruce calling back into the bar to call for 911. It made sense. Call local police and the hospital to send out its ambulance, but were the phones back up?

The phone lines were out, and *something* was devouring a living person. Something about that nagged at him, biting at him in the back of his mind, trying to gnaw his way into his active thoughts.

Think about it later, officer! commanded a voice in his head. It was his commanding officer's voice from back when he was still a Chicago beat cop, and it was right. He had to focus.

Rob was reaching down to his sidearm when he heard Bruce calling out from behind him. "Rob, stop! Look!"

He stopped and saw what Bruce must have been looking at. There wasn't just one of them. There was the one with the mechanic, but now Rob could see there were twenty to thirty of them coming down the street. They were still a little more than a block away. From where Bruce was, they were just barely in view. He probably couldn't even see all of them, but Rob could.

What the hell were they? Was that kid behind the bar right? Was this all just an elaborate event? Some Zombie Walk where people were all dressed up and this was their idea of a good time? Was the mechanic in on it and it was all some kind of an elaborate set-up for some movie? Were there cameras hidden somewhere and he was rushing into the middle of a movie set?

He looked back at the mechanic, who was falling harshly to the asphalt. His head hit the ground with an audible *smack*, and Rob didn't have to look closely at him to know the man was dead, his throat torn out and large amounts of blood still spreading in streams away from him. The thing that had been biting into him was now standing there, looking at Rob.

Rob quickly reached for his revolver. He knew in his mind, as he had already reached for it once to snap the little restraining strap, the gun wasn't there. However, he still reached for it on reflex.

He was supposed to have been at the courthouse all day. He was a witness, and hadn't worn it that morning. Some courthouses wanted officers in full uniform, some preferred them to dress in civilian clothes, but Judge Whitmore had already instructed him that she preferred partial uniform and didn't like guns in the hands of anyone, except security.

The thing in front of him took a stumbling, hard step forward towards Rob. It was still just over a hundred feet away, close enough now that Rob could see the gore of the things neck where it had been torn out. Its eyes were a dull grey, bloody cuts and gashes ran up and down its arms. The thing had been wearing a t-shirt and shorts. The shirt was now covered in blood and, in several places, was ripped like claws had been trying to tear through it.

This was *not* a man in makeup. Rob was sure there was some pretty elaborate make-up out there that could do some amazing things to people and make them look dead, but he doubted any of them could have faked that large hole in the side of the its neck.

The thing took another step forward and, this time, Rob could feel himself react, taking a step back.

The hazed over eyes continued to stare at him. They looked dead, but there was something about them that seemed to stare straight into him. Those dead eyes looked at him with such a hunger, but if the thing was hungry, why did it stop on the mechanic? Why didn't it just continue to eat him?

It took another step forward, Rob took another step back.

The mob of things behind it was spreading out. They seemed disorientated, but were still working their way towards him. Rob watched as one man came out of his house to see what was going on. The closest one to the man caught him on his stairs as he had been coming down to them.

Rob heard the man's screams as he took another step backward.

The thing in front of him made a noise. It sounded like it tried to say something, but it came out as more of a wet, gurgling moan.

"And the Lord striketh down and burned away the flesh, the evil of the world. For once he washed away the evil and sin with rain, now he brings plague. The dead rise, and only the righteous shall be saved. The sinful will be left. The rapture it is upon us," came a booming voice.

Rob looked over his shoulder and saw a priest walking past the bar. The man looked old and ragged, but was hurrying towards him.

"You have to get away! Get inside!" Rob yelled and started towards the priest. They had to get away from the things while they still could.

He was getting closer to the bar. It didn't seem like the safest place but, right now, it was better than any other option he could think of. Bruce was still standing at the door. Two others stood in the darkness beyond. He couldn't quite tell who it was, but someone inside was standing there, watching them. At least someone was smart enough to stay where it was safe.

Down the rest of the street, the town seemed dead. No cars were driving around, and no one was out dealing with yard work on such a hot day. As long as the people stayed in their houses, he reckoned they would stay safe until some kind of help showed up.

This wasn't his town, this wasn't his job. But he still felt like there was something he should be doing to help.

Like what? Get eaten? That really didn't seem like too good an option. Right now, the only option he could see was to get back to the bar. There was nothing more that he could do for the mechanic.

"These men are cursed, but even the cursed can be saved. I have seen the demon. He has come to me. Has shown me the fires that are coming, but the Lord has kept me safe. I am saved, and I must save others. I must save the wicked," the old man said. Rob grabbed him by the shoulders and held him, turning him so that he was forced to look at the off-duty cop.

"We have to get you to safety. Come on." Rob was already moving past the man, trying to force him to walk with him. The man turned and saw him and he stopped, his eyes widening.

"You! I see you!" the old man said, his voice full of wonder. "Have you been touched, or are you an angel?"

"I'm no angel. We need to get out of here."

"But you are blessed. I see the light surrounding you. You must know. They have to be saved. We have to save them." The man broke away from Rob's grip. "They must be saved." Rob tried to catch him again, but the old man had turned and was now running towards the things.

"You can't!" Rob yelled as he ran after the old man. He was amazed at how fast the priest was able to move and, once again, cursed his bum leg. It wasn't the first time the leg slowed him down, and now he cursed even harder at it, watching as the man moved farther and farther away.

The priest didn't look back. He moved towards the things, raising his hands. Rob could see the bible the man carried. "Dear Lord, save these men and bring back the souls that have been taken out of their bodies. Redeem them, save them, give them back the life that the demon claims, and show them the lighted path to heaven."

Rob stopped. There was no way he was going to be able to catch him. "Don't. You have to come with me. You can't save them!"

The priest didn't look back.

Rob turned away, hurrying to the bar as quickly as he could. It didn't take long before he heard the first of the priest's screams, but Rob didn't look back. He cringed as he heard the agonized cries, but he continued on. There was nothing he could do for him anyway. He should have kept hold of the man, forced him to come back to the bar with him. He should have-

But it was too late. He started to wonder just what was going on. What in the hell were they going to do next? Just down the street, he saw a car rounding the corner and coming towards him, racing down the street way too fast.

CHAPTER 10

Wade could hear the yelling outside his tent. It wasn't the first one of the day, but they were getting worse. More people were trying to get out of town, not knowing what was going on. He didn't know, either, but he couldn't tell them that. They were trapped, and there was nothing to do but keep sending them back. Send them back and just keep praying that none of them would push back. If they didn't go back… Lord, he hoped no one would put him in that position. If it was pushed too hard, he had his orders. He had to follow them.

The order had come directly from the colonel, so there was no room for argument. This area was to be treated like a hostile zone, unless new orders came in. They had no idea what they were up against, but they were told to fear the worst.

Hostile zone? Yeah, this wasn't some hostile zone. It was a town.

Sergeant Wade looked out the flap of his tent and towards the family that was now parked at the inner barrier of the blockade. The father was standing at the edge of the sawhorses, looking like he was going to cross over to walk the ten feet to the outer border and another set of sawhorses. The mother was standing behind her passenger door. And Wade could see a little girl sitting in the back seat. There were a couple of cars sitting behind them, but none of the people in those cars were getting out to cause trouble. It was either because they were just going to wait their turn, or because they figured there was no need to add to the guy who was already causing a scene.

The father had that look, one that Wade recognized. The man was thinking dangerous thoughts. He was on that threshold of walking forward, taking that one step. Wade heard the sound of multiple clicks, and knew that his men saw it, too. They were getting antsy, worried about what the man might try. They were letting him know that firearms were now aimed on him and prepared to fire. This was a train wreck getting ready to jump the rails and Wade knew there was little he could do.

"Sir, back away! Step away from the barricade!" one of the soldiers was yelling at him. Wade couldn't tell who was calling out, but he approved of the commanding tone that was firm, but also held a note of concern.

"What the hell is going on here?" the man called back, leaning forward.

So far, they had been lucky. There had been no shots fired and no one had tried to cross. So far, things were not escalating. However, he knew things were going to get bad soon. The later in the day they went, this powder keg would eventually blow. Thanks to the officers above him, they had ordered him to sit right on top of the fuse, holding a match.

At least he was lucky that no one was coming into town, as well. Of course, that was probably due to another barricade much farther out. There may even be an officer at that one, maybe even regular army, not just the weekend warriors that were all here in the inner circle. Of course, let's not expend the more valuable troops when there are ones not as well-trained and seasoned that we can use. Let us put the National Guard out there and let them be the ones closest to the blast.

God, how he hoped not. He hoped like hell he was just being cynical.

"Sergeant," a young voice said, sounding nervous. Wade looked up to see a young PFC, his communications operator, standing just outside the tent. This was the command tent so the young man could just come in, but Wade figured him to be too green to know that, so he was waiting for permission. It wasn't a surprise the sergeant didn't recognize him. There were a lot of newer faces that had been with him on active duty when they had gotten the call.

"Come in," he said in his clipped, commanding tone. The young man entered and came to attention, the sergeant returning the courtesy.

"Yes, soldier?" the sergeant asked.

"We've heard from HQ. They've set up their outer perimeter another five miles out."

So they've finally officially acknowledged to him where they were. At least that was a start. He knew they would be forming an outer perimeter but, so far, they hadn't allowed him any of that intel.

"Okay. Any word on the reinforcements for the barricades at the inner perimeter?"

"Yes and no, sergeant." The young man had a pained expression, and as he tried to stay tight in his "rest" stance, he still tried to squirm as much as he could without really moving. The news wasn't going to be good.

"Reinforcements have arrived; however, the outer perimeter is not letting them through. The reinforcements have been reassigned to positions at the outer barricades."

So they weren't going to let anyone else in or out? That wasn't good. So it probably was a biological problem in the town. Something had happened and they didn't want to take a chance with exposure. So what the hell had the town been exposed to? How? This was the Midwest. There weren't any hidden facilities here, or none that he knew. Though the whole point of a hidden facility is so that not everyone knows about it, they typically keep them away from people. There are only farmers, cornfields, and plenty of small towns and people, so there was no way they would endanger it with a top secret military project. Not around there.

So what the hell were they exposed to?

Anthrax? Sure, it was a possibility, but why the hell out here in the middle of nowhere? Unless a terrorist cell was trying to poison the food supply, maybe something with the corn? If so, they hadn't thought it out too well. Most of the corn around here wasn't used for food and went into bio fuels.

"Sergeant?" the PFC said, pulling him away from his thoughts.

"That's all, private," the sergeant said, turning away.

"Um... Actually, sergeant, there is something else."

Wade turned back and looked at him, his eyebrows going up as a signal for the man to continue.

"The regional law enforcement from the area that came to help us barricade the back roads is wondering when their relief will come. Some of them are long past the end of their shifts and want to get home. They're starting to have problems with people trying to get out of the town, and I think they just want to get out of here before it gets worse."

Worse?! Of course, they did. And now their reinforcements are being stopped at the outer perimeter. Even if he did relieve the police officers that they had called in as temporary aide, the officers had no way out. He would just have to keep them sated and try to keep them hopeful.

"Tell them their reinforcements will be here soon. Another two hours and they will be cleared through the outer barricades to replace them."

"Two hours?"

"Just tell them."

Yes, let us lie to them. Better to string them along now rather than having them become part of the problem and try to leave.

"You're excused. Go and find Marshall. Have him report to me," he said, excusing the soldier, who quickly scurried off.

"You can't do this! I have rights!" The sergeant stepped to the open tent flap and could now see the man was yelling at a row of troops. One soldier was in front of all the others, his rifle raised and pressing sideways against the chest of the man, trying to push him back. His men should never have let him get that close.

And, if this was biological, they could all be exposed to it. This wasn't going to get any better. In fact, he suddenly felt like it was about to get a lot worse.

* * * *

Syn felt the engine between her legs more than she heard it. The padding from her helmet kept a lot of the noise muffled, but it didn't matter. To her, she just loved to feel the bike beneath her as it roared down the road. It was hers, and speed was her ecstasy. She had lovers, guys from the towns around, but her only true excitement always seemed to come from the thrum of the motorcycle, the "crotch rocket", as it soared down long stretches of road.

Eighteen hour days, with the occasional day lasting for nearly thirty-six hours, had led to the power she now harnessed between her legs, but every hour of sleep lost was worth it. She had worked two and three jobs, sometimes four, going from one shift to another until she was done. Each day, she inched closer towards having the money. Every dish she washed, ass she kissed, high kick and spin around a pole was worth it. The bike was hers. All she had to do was twist on the throttle and the world fell into oblivion around her.

Was she trying to kill herself? Did she want to speed into a fiery inferno? No, she just wanted the speed, and if death came at her, she was ready for it. She wasn't afraid. *Fuck it, fuck the world and, for god's sake, fuck this town,* she thought.

But, yet, she was still there. She would still be there twenty years from now. If not here, she'd be in another town nearby. Her life was here.

Yeah, sure it was. She had a little crap of an apartment over in the "cardboard city", where the drugged up assholes had their parties into the wee hours of the night, and the creeps, who were lost in their own hate, lived. She guessed she could be considered one of the latter. She sure as hell had her share of hatred for the town and the dipshits who lived in it.

Still, it was her home, it was her life and, as much as she hated to admit it, it was very much a part of her. She had grown up there. It had been a small town, but her mother had been well-established in the PTA during daylight hours and, in the evening, was just as well-established in the bar scene. Most nights, her parents would be out together, and once Syn had become old enough, at the age of nine, she would go out with them. Her favorite had always been dart nights.

There was August Days, the July Summer Heat festival, the 5K runs, and the bike-a-thons. There were the people that she hated until she wanted to party, then they became her best friends. Most of her high school class still lived there, working in the factory just outside town.

It was a town that was easy to hate, as there seemed to be nothing to do but drink beer and get involved in all the drama, but it was also a town where you could have a lot of fun just hanging out with each other. Sure, when the town got together, there was plenty of beer involved, but they knew how to party.

The new bike, Syn's pride and joy, sped along the road. She had already rounded onto the main street, and she just wanted to get out of the shithole. She knew she wasn't going to be getting out for too long. Maybe a hundred miles or so along the interstate, down past Champaign and back, letting the wind blow her hair back from where it fell out from under her helmet. A hundred miles there should only take an hour once she made it to the interstate, then an hour back. Maybe she'd stay there for the night. She had a few friends in a band there. She could see if they were playing, or just hook up with the drummer.

She hadn't noticed that the streets were quiet. She had seen a patch of pedestrians walking down the street, but there might just be some parade. People were people, though she really had wished they would have blocked off the street if they were having a block party. She didn't like how close she had come to hitting a couple of them.

Then she was on Main Street. She had thought about going slow just to get out of town, but the thrum of the engine was speaking to her, and it screamed to gun it. She hadn't seen much traffic. Sure, there were red lights, but she saw a clear shot.

Then that damn car came out of nowhere. That had been the only green light she had. She ran all the damn red lights and didn't have a single issue, but as she neared the only green light, a damn car starts pulling out from the side street. *Un-fucking-believable*, she had thought for a second as her reflexes reacted.

She had made it, though. In front of her was just a couple of curves; the bridge with the little road that went down to the dollar store; then another curve, where she knew there was often a speed trap; then open highway. She knew there was often a speed trap because she had gotten speeding tickets there on a monthly basis, though she knew part of why she was always pulled over was because that prick of a cop just wanted her to work her way out of it.

Damn pigs never had anything better to do. It's not like there wasn't any drug abuse in the bars on the strip. No, they had to harass drivers like her. Well, today she was going to have a little fun with them. The bike was new, and they wouldn't know it was her yet. She was going to blow by there and just see if they had the balls to follow her.

Time to see what speed was really like, she thought to herself as she twisted the throttle farther, feeling the heat. Moistness grew between her legs.

"My god. This is better than sex."

* * * *

Wade was pretty sure that he would have to go over there and talk to the man. He could see his men getting fidgety. He did not want the situation to escalate because once that started, there was no going back. No matter what he did now, there was no right answer. One way or another, he would be the fall guy. Direct order or not, murder of United States citizens was still murder. The question of his orders being lawful was a nasty grey area.

"Yeah, well, don't follow down that pity party, Pete," he said to himself. After all, he knew when he took an NCO position, wanting that extra pay and responsibility, he was opening the door for something like this, and it was his own damn fault and decision that put him there. Sure, there were a lot of other people he could blame, but it always came back to himself.

Yeah, I don't think so. He could try to say the entire thing was his fault, but he wasn't the dipshit up the chain who threw this together.

Wade took a step towards the barricade and the man who was arguing with the soldiers. Yeah, this may not be his fault, but it could be if he didn't shut down this trouble now.

"Sergeant!" He turned to see that Marshall was hurrying to him. In the distance, he heard something. It was familiar, but he wasn't quite sure what it was. He could tell that it was coming from town and coming closer.

"Marshall," he said to the specialist as he came to attention in front of him. "Most of your platoon isn't here. I'm assuming they are on the outer perimeter. I need you to get a call to someone and see if you can find out what is going on."

Marshal looked at him, a troubled look in his already young and frightened eyes, but he also had that curious look as his eyebrows were raised. "Sergeant?"

"Do it and report b-"

Wade was cut off. That motor was getting louder. It sounded familiar. He had a Honda at home and knew the whine they made as they were approaching their top speed.

Most of the other troops were now looking, and the family who had been yelling was now getting ignored. The men were looking around at one another. He could see they were getting anxious, and he couldn't blame them. Wade was already hurrying over when one of the men turned and called out for him.

"Get in positions. Take appropriate action!"

He could see the motorcycle now. It was coming their way and it was coming fast, not showing any indication it was preparing to slow down. The man who had been arguing with the private backed away and stepped behind his own car door, his wife quickly sitting in the car. They didn't know what was going to happen, but were smart enough to get out of the way.

"Get that car out of here!" Wade yelled. He was done dealing with them, and they needed to leave. The private closest to them raised his M-16 and pointed it at the man. The sergeant, still thirty feet away, could see the eyes go wide on the man's face. Wade didn't care who the person at the other end was, but it was intimidating looking down the barrel of a gun that large.

The man slowly eased himself into the car. His hands were up, immediately raised when the rifle was pointed at him.

The sergeant couldn't see the man's pants, but could see the puddle where he was standing.

He looked back to see the bike getting closer, growing in size from a distant dot to a noticeable shape. It was coming in way too fast. It was already at the point that it was not going to be able to stop. They were going to run the barricade. Damn, he couldn't let that happen.

"Get into firing positions."

His men moved out of the direct line of the bike's path. They were now in a position that would allow them to shoot without being in the path once the shot was fired.

The sergeant knew he had to give the order because the longer he waited, the more there was a chance the bike would hit someone. He had to make the call. They had to put the person on the bike down.

He also knew what it meant. Right now, there was no violence, but once he gave that order, all their fates were sealed. There was no more chance of them just standing down and leaving with only minor inconveniences to the town. Shots would have been fired, and the town would officially be under quarantine with little chance of anyone ever being allowed out.

Something in his gut told him he was in that category, as well. He was one of the many trapped in, and he would be stuck there, too.

He sure as hell hoped it was all worth it.

"Fire!"

He heard the shots ring out, echoing into the afternoon. Birds in nearby trees took flight from the sudden loud burst of noise so close to their peaceful perch.

Wade looked at the bike as the rifles were fired. He watched as the person on the bike sat upright, then fell back.

The handlebars of the bike turned sharp left, then suddenly right. The driver, who had been falling back, was launched forward as the front tire caught on the cement, the back of the bike flying up into the air. He knew it didn't matter because the person was already dead. It was just an empty shell flying towards them.

Then the body landed to the ground with a *thump*. It didn't move. The bike skid past it, but the body had taken the blow and just lay on the ground.

The bike stopped a couple yards short of reaching the back bumper of the family's car. He heard the woman in the passenger seat gasp and he turned to look at them. If he allowed them to go back into town, they would cause a panic. He couldn't allow them to stay where they were, and they couldn't be held prisoners there. He had no place for them.

Damn.

The soldiers who had fired on the motorcycle had gone back to their positions, one going over to the father's door.

Sergeant Wade felt the wetness at the corner of his eyes. He did not want to do it. He did not want to give his next order. He couldn't let them just go back into town, but he also couldn't keep them there. He only had one option, but he couldn't. He couldn't give that order.

Then there was movement in the car. The man was reaching across to the passenger side, but his wife already had it in her hand. He knew what it was. The glint of metal was easy to see as the sun reflected on the silver barrel. They had made his decision for him and now he had no choice.

"Fire!" Wade called out, his own voice strong and alien to him. He was proud that it didn't betray the child crying inside of him.

"Sergeant?" the private asked.

"You heard me."

Marshall was still behind him, and Wade looked at him. The specialist's face was pale, his mouth hanging open. When the rifle fire erupted again, the sergeant watched the man flinch and look away. They had all seen combat before, but overseas combat was not the same as shooting families on U.S. soil. Sergeant Wade knew how the soldier felt.

"Get in touch with somebody. Find out just what the fuck is going on."

"O…out there?" the man said. Yeah, Wade knew just how the specialist felt.

"Then get a detail and start digging a pit. We'll need to burn the bodies."

"Shit," he heard the specialist say under his breath.

Wade wanted to correct him. It wasn't just shit they were walking in. They were in deep shit, the kind that was deep enough to bury them all…and none of them were ready for it.

How could they be?

CHAPTER 11

What is madness and where does it end? Where does it begin? The world is lost in insanity. Is it because we do things too quickly, or because the world moves too slowly? Decisions take forever to make, but when they *are* made, systems get put into place to make the process move faster. What happens when life becomes automated? When thought is taken out of the process and the wheels move on their own while the driver is asleep at the wheel? Isn't that how the worst accidents happen, when no one is awake at the controls? Or did we ever truly have control?

Not for the first time that morning, the general wondered if maybe that was what was happening. While he wasn't out on the line, he watched as the different reports came in to him…from the sergeant who was on the inner perimeter, to the colonel who manned the outer perimeter, to the satellite feeds that were updated every half-hour.

And why? Why was he watching a town being quarantined on American soil? A town they had cut off from the rest of the world and were treating its citizens as though they were prisoners. The people there had rights, and they were treated no better than if they were overseas.

No, that wasn't true. So far, they had only locked down the town. Soldiers weren't patrolling the streets and martial law hadn't been implemented…yet. Would it ever get to that point? What would make them do that? What would push them that far, and how much farther would they have to go? They were already to the point of inner and outer checkpoints. This was a military offensive against their own people. What would it take to get to that next level?

He shouldn't think that way. This wasn't them fighting an enemy. The troops weren't there to fight the townspeople. They were there for quarantine. It was for their own good and for the good of the rest of population. Why? They still didn't know.

The process was all too damned automated. No one knew what was going on. The process had taken control. Phone calls had been made, and the town had been locked off before the question "why" had even come up. The perimeter had already been established before he had even received that first phone call.

He was kept in the dark, his office hidden deep within a military bunker just south of Chicago. He was in Joliet, where the military had long ago established their hidden base beneath the public façade of the actual base. A base within a base, secrets within secrets. He was buried so far below that if a nuclear attack was to strike even the outer edge of the city, he would be safe.

Protocol K called for him to take up shelter there. It wasn't for all commanders across the country, it didn't stretch that far, but because he was well within the region the protocol was activated in, he had been moved there and put in direct communication feeds so he could coordinate the situation. He had direct feed to it all. Then he would process it, make what decisions needed to be made, and pass on what information needed to the commander-in-chief and the chief of staff. However, when the time for decisions came, he made them. They were his decisions, but on paper and no names were recorded. He was simply the general, and the president was to be kept in the dark.

Worst case scenarios had to be considered. The president had to be kept out of the loop so he had deniability, and the general had to be unknown so he had the ability to do what needed to be done without fear of repercussions. But so much was already done before he even decided on anything. So much in a no thought, wheels in motion, automated process.

He had the report still open on his desk. It was a small folder, and some of the papers that should have been included in it were strewn out over the top cover. He had the dossier on the doctor, Brian Thompson, the man who had called in the protocol. There was also a history on Dr. Samuel Wilson, the doctor who had originally called the CDC.

It didn't seem possible that a lonely town doctor could call the CDC, get someone out there the same morning, and that person would call in the quick lockdown protocol. It just didn't seem like that was possible. Katrina had been a disaster, largely because of how slow the National Guard had been to react, but here were two doctors able to move the United States military faster than the president had when there had been advance warning.

That just didn't seem possible, but there they were with a town cut off, and they still had no idea why or with what they were dealing. What had caused all of this? Was this Dr. Thompson some kind of idiot? Well, that seemed like it was a little harsh, and anyone who even knew about Protocol K had to have a significant amount of details about what, why, and how it would need to get called in.

The man wasn't a field agent. Would he be the best person to establish such a protocol? What if all of this came down to an over-reaction due to a doctor making a misdiagnosis? It's not like there are no other protocols. "K" just happened to be the most extreme. There were still all the "A" through "L" protocols, all of which were less drastic. No, "K" was the most severe. The protocol that had been established to move faster than thought.

The general looked at the picture of the man again. Some scrawny-looking doctor with glasses, just like he would expect to see. Nothing spectacular looked back at him…pinched eyes; long, thin nose. The man looked like he didn't interact well with people. Not that the general had ever met him, but he just had that sense. Then again, that could just be him stereotyping what he expected. There were many scientists out there, and not all of them were that way.

No, the general was pretty sure the picture gave off the sense that this man did not like being around people. It was probably one of the reasons the doctor was not out in the field.

What were they going to do, and how were they going to proceed? The team from Atlanta should be going in soon. He had heard that they had landed not too long ago, and their mobile lab was already en route to the town. One good thing about Protocol K moving so quickly was that those systems that moved without direction moved smoothly, and he just had to hear about the updates. He wasn't having to call, make plans, or give out orders. For the most part, they were just following off of a checklist, checking things off one by and one when they all locked into place.

Either way, this was going to be a mess. If the doctor had been right to call it in, they had the job of cleaning it all up. If the doctor was wrong, then they had a bigger mess. How would they handle the media once the news broke? If this went to hell, it was going to be a nasty black eye on the current administration. It was probably a good thing the president didn't have to worry about re-election, though he doubted there would be another democrat in there anytime soon after this mess.

Maybe he should just fuck it up.

Yeah, that would look good on his career, even though his retirement was only a few years away. No matter how it went, it wouldn't be the worst thing he had ever done. He had many nightmares locked away, hidden behind lost nights of little sleep. Generals don't become generals by making easy decisions. Nightmares of children screaming and burning babies were a part of his life now. He could never remember from when they were, but they always threatened him on the edges of his sanity.

Maybe he should just retire and be done with it. He had years left, but he could take early retirement. He shouldn't have to think about things like this. His time could be done. He didn't need any of this.

Yeah, but he could never walk away while the situation was still active. That was just not the way he was wired. No retreat, no surrender. Never walk away from a fight, even when it looked like you couldn't win. There was no way he could turn away from this now. Maybe lesser men could, but he was not a lesser man.

"Sir!"

The general looked up to see Lieutenant Evan standing in the door. Evan had been his assistant for the last six months, and he was glad the kid still had that straight edge to him. The general liked the "pop" to the stance. He hated to see how relaxed officers would usually become. There was nothing like seeing the newer officers still stand straight and have that "Gung Ho" spirit. Though, on bad days, sometimes the general just wanted to smack it out of him.

He was becoming a grumpy old man, and today was one of the bad days. Right then, he just wanted to bark at the kid, yell at him to go polish some brass or some other menial task just because he seemed too eager to please.

"Yes, lieutenant. What is it?"

"We have a report that there are casualties in the town."

The general lowered his head. He didn't want to hear it. He knew it was going to happen soon, but he had hoped he was wrong. He had hoped people would somehow be able to keep their calm so that it wouldn't escalate.

"What happened?" He heard the question croak out of him in a voice that he didn't recognize.

"I don't know, sir. We don't know how many yet. I just know that shots were fired. At least one woman is dead, but it sounded like that was an early estimate. Sergeant Wade hasn't reported in with official word. We just know that someone tried to run the blockade and they needed to be put down."

Put down. The lieutenant spoke of it like they had been putting down an animal that had gotten out of control. Maybe that was one way to look at it. Maybe that was even the *right way* to look at it as it would do no good for him to start thinking of any of them as people. That was a luxury that he just did not have.

"Thank you, lieutenant," said a familiar voice from the hallway. "That will be all."

The general looked up to see Major Samuel S. Burns standing in the doorway, returning the young man's salute, then waving him away. The major stood tall and straight, his silver hair high and tight in the military fashion. He had a handsome face, and it could easily be seen why he was often the "poster boy" for serving in today's military. However, his smile, spread widely as he looked at the general and made his way into the room to sit down, never touched his eyes. Those cold, dark eyes could look into the general's and see the sins hidden there. The general always had an uneasy feeling whenever he was dealing with the man, and he had a hard time suppressing the shudder that ran through him as they shook hands.

Just how much younger the man in front him was, the general couldn't say. His face always seemed like it never aged, and as long as he could remember, Sam had always been a major, was always around the Oval Office, no matter what president he served.

"Hey, Sam."

"Dale."

"You shouldn't be here."

"No? Why not. The president thought you might want someone here to whisper in your ear. I volunteered because I thought you might need a friend."

"Yeah? Is it getting that bad on the hill? Didn't even know the president had been briefed yet."

"Just that a town was under quarantine due to an unknown biological agent."

"Unknown biological? Do you have intel that I don't? We don't know what the hell is in there yet. The team hasn't gone in yet. We haven't heard from either doctor, the one who called it in or the CDC guy who called in the protocol, and we have now got the town cut off from the outside world. So we have no way of knowing what is going on in there."

"Really? I was lead to believe that it was a dirty bomb. That this was a terrorist action."

"And from where did you get this?"

"That's what is being said on the hill. The NSA caught some chatter that something was in the pipeline. They were quick to jump on it, saying this must be it."

"Yeah, in a small town, buried deep in the Midwest, someone launched a biological attack on the U.S."

"We don't know how bad this will spread. Dale, we can't afford to let some deadly strain of the flu or anthrax get out. All it would take would be one release in small town in Middle America. This could be an attack."

"Do you see anthrax in your sleep now?"

"Don't you?"

The general did, or similar attacks, but not for why the younger man envisioned. The general had been on the ground and had seen what chemical warfare was capable of. He had seen how it could melt away the skin, make organs explode inside the flesh, or make boils cover a child from head to toe, killing them within seconds of exposure. He had seen the horrors that had been ordered by the evil in men's hearts, and he had once been the man who would be there to cover it up so no one ever knew.

Over too many years of black ops, he had seen the worse that humanity was capable. He did have those nightmares.

"So what is the situation?"

"Like I said, unknown. The CDC should be going in soon."

"And we have dead bodies? People trying to run the blockades?"

"As far as I know, just one person is dead. Like I said, you shouldn't be here. The president needs deniability."

"The president can't take bad press, no matter what it is. As it stands, he is the most unpopular president in U.S. history. He can't take another hit and expect to get anything through Congress. Right now, he is having to fight just to keep his policies in place and not have them repealed. If this goes south, even his own party will be turning against him. Whether I am here or not, the president is going to get marked by this. It's a town in the United States. We can't go holding people against their will without good reason. And we can't be having loose cannons shooting at people."

"What do you expect me to do? We can't maintain the quarantine if we don't keep up the pressure. My people need to be able to defend themselves, even against the population."

"They need to find another way. This needs to be finished and covered up. It needs to happen quickly, before making it way too far in the press."

"How do you expect to do that?"

"How do *you* expect to do that?"

"Sam, you're not making this easy."

A short, clipped knock drew the general's attention and he quickly called out, "Come."

The lieutenant entered, another folder under his arm. "Sir."

"Yes?"

The lieutenant gave a quick look to the major and the general nodded for him to continue. "We have more reports. Sergeant Wade reports there are multiple people dead. They were trying to force their way through the blockade. He was able to push back some, but two families and one motorbike rider were killed. They are taking care of the bodies now, making sure to follow proper protocol."

Yeah, not that the proper protocol was going to do anything to save those men. The sergeant didn't know it yet, but the moment he had accepted his orders and had gotten his troops into that town to set up the perimeter, he had written his own death sentence. If this all went south, there was no way anyone from that close to the town would ever be able to get out of there…unless the CDC was able to get in there and either identify that it was just a false alarm, or was able to work out some kind of cure.

And if this all turned out to be a false alarm, there was no saving any of their careers. Damn, this protocol moved way too fast. Who approved such a thing? There were only ways to make this worse, and he couldn't see anyway for this to turn out favorable for anyone.

"Thank you, lieutenant."

"There's more, sir."

"Yes?"

"We have gotten the latest satellite feed." The young man stepped deeper into the room, the general noticing the little sidestep the man did to avoid getting to close to the major. Then he grabbed the images from inside the folder and put them on the general's desk. "From what we can make out, multiple riots have broken out in town. That falls in line with some of the earlier reports of violence." The man pointed to what looked like a parking lot around a strip of buildings. There was a large group of people surrounding one man.

"We also have these." The man set down another image, this one also in a parking lot. The picture showed a large group of people surrounding a car. It was a good image, better than the first. There was the group around the car, but then a smaller group off to the side. The car door was open, and there seemed to be a body being dragged from it, what was probably splatters of blood all over the ground, and a small group around where the body was probably lying.

"There are other images in the folder. Various streets that groups of people are walking down. It's not clear as to what they are doing, but looking at the evidence, it seems like these groups are looking for more people to attack."

The general's eyes were wide as he looked up to glare at the major sitting across from him. "It has to be biological. Some kind of nerve gas."

"Sounds like it."

"Get on the horn. Find out the ETA on the CDC. We need them in there. We need to know what this is, and what can be done about it. Tell them to get their asses moving!"

CHAPTER 12

"Tina!" Jason called out before he was even past the first door and into the back hallway of the bar. "Tina!" The door slammed behind him, shaking in its frame. The heavy spring attached to it sounded louder than usual, making his voice seem to be cut off by the sound. He rushed through the little hall and stepped out into the cool darkness of the bar.

"Tina!" He looked at the group that huddled around each other at the other end of the bar. They were craning their necks to look out the window, as though somehow changing that slight angle of their body would allow them to see a little better. He studied the group, looking for his aunt. He was hoping to find her, grab her, and get her… Get her where?

He and Denise had planned on getting Tina, then they would rush out of town. He had promised the woman that. It was the only way he had coaxed her into staying with him as he came back for his aunt. Now they were there and they would all get out of town.

Why, though? Now that he was in the bar, a place where he felt safe, a place that he had promised to watch after, why would he run? This was where he had grown up. Long before his mom had worked out a way to buy the bar and had only been a bartender there, this had been where she raised him. This was

175

where his mother brought him, her friends as his daycare, as she worked behind that long stretch of wood. It was where he had learned to throw darts and play pool. Video games had been the poker and the slot machines, and he had lost many quarters learning to play them. As much as he always said he wanted to get away from the place, to live a life outside these walls, this was much more a home than the house on the other side of town. He had known these walls much longer.

So why should he leave just because something strange was going on? Sure, some crazy stuff was happening out there, but was it strange enough to leave town? Who was to say it wasn't worse outside of town? To up and just abandon his mom's bar? And what about his sister? If they left town, would he really be able to get help for her? *Was* there any help for her?

"Tina!" He didn't see her in the group.

Sullivan had turned toward him, and Jason could now make out who was there. That one angry, dirty guy was still there, and now there was also a thin woman who looked like she had done too much of too many and only the shell was left. Of course, with her blond, bleached hair and her orange spray-on tan, she probably thought she looked good. There was the trucker who had shown up just as Jason had been about to leave to get his sister. Mr. Jones, of course, who had actually gotten up from his stool and made it all the way to the other end of the bar. Then there was another man he didn't recognize and couldn't really make out. He was kind of behind everyone else, and the sun was bright behind him.

It seemed like more people were showing up. Did they really want to leave? He thought briefly of what he had just seen at the Rowplex. The local cops… That had been them coming out and looking like those things, hadn't it? Were there more of them out there? There had to be. It made sense to get out of there, didn't it? But, again, he had that nagging feeling, the sagging in his shoulders that told him he was now safe.

"She's in the bathroom but, dude, you really need to come over here and check this out," Sullivan said. Jason stopped studying the walls and looked at him. It was hard to read the expression on Sullivan's face. Did his best friend actually seem to be excited?

"In just a second," Jason said as he turned to go towards the bathrooms.

"Dude," Sullivan said, rushing toward him, "you should really check this out, and I am going to have to kill you later over this shit."

The back door slammed again. The excitement Sullivan had shown quickly changed to panic and the big man was reaching under the bar and pulling out the fire extinguisher, holding up the bottom of it and getting ready to use it as a weapon.

Jason stopped rushing to the bathroom and looked at the man that had always been his closest friend. He watched him, his friend that had been a slacker now standing as though he was a warrior ready to fight. He looked over at the group, noticing how they were all nervously standing there. The truck driver was leaning against one of the slot machines, drumming his fingers across the top.

All of them had taken their eyes off of him and had turned their attention to Denise standing behind him. The strung out woman in the group was the first to show any recognition, then a guilty look and a downward glance let Jason know that she was trying to avoid the newcomer.

"Hello, Nurse Winston," the young woman said.

Denise looked in her direction. Her eyes were open wide but then squinted as she fought to get used to the dimness of the bar.

Once he confirmed she wasn't a threat, Sullivan gave a little nod to her, then looked away, turning back to Jason. "Dude, you really have to see-" He was cut off by the sound of gunshots outside.

Sullivan was already rushing back the length of the bar, but Jason hurried to catch up. The bar seemed darker than usual, and it seemed like the bright windows just pulled him over to them. He went there, and the rest of them parted, allowing him through. It was obvious they had had enough and didn't care to watch what was out there anymore.

He looked out and saw the people just under a block away. It looked like it was at least an eighth of the town right there, and they seemed to be storming into houses. There was something not right about them, and he immediately recognized what it was. He had seen enough of it to tell what they were.

He closed his eyes and counted his breaths, fighting to keep it together. He couldn't think about his sister anymore. He had to push it down, at least for now. He could think about her later. He could grieve about her later but, for now, they just had to get out of there.

Sullivan had been saying something to him. Sullivan was having the time of his life and was repeating himself. Jason opened his eyes and looked at him.

"Fucking zombies, man! I told you it would happen. Fucking zombies. Dude, there are fucking zombies out there."

Yeah, Sullivan was right. There *were* zombies out there. He realized that his life had turned into a horror movie, like the ones he had been watching all his life.

Night of the Living Dead, the Romero version, was vivid in his mind. He had already been thinking it. The quiet streets, his little sis… All of it had been building up to it. He just couldn't allow himself to believe it, not until someone started saying "We're coming to get you, Barbara", or unless someone actually put a name to it. Leave it to fucking Sullivan to put a name to it…to them. Zombies. They were real, and they were just outside.

Jason thought about the end of *Night of the Living Dead*. With the man… What was his name? Ben? He wasn't sure. He just remembered they had found him in the end. Jason could have sworn he had seen multiple versions of the movie, as that scene always played out differently in his head. In one memory of the ending, he saw the man as a zombie and they shot him, throwing his body on a pile of other zombies.

The other ending he remembered was similar. The body was still thrown on a truck. The difference was that when they found the man, he had never turned into a zombie, but they still shot him. Zombie or not, when the outside world came in, they just cleaned up everything and didn't wait to find out if you were dead or alive.

Shit, they were all fucked. They were probably all going to fucking die.

Sullivan was saying something else, but it wasn't until he felt the hand on his back that he finally pulled himself out of his thoughts. He turned and looked at him…his friend, who he had given the radio host name of "Sullivan, the Zombie Hunter" as a joke to how Sullivan always had wild theories on how he would survive the zombie apocalypse. Well, the zombies had arrived.

"Hey, man. You okay?" Sullivan asked.

Jason blinked, wiping away the last of his internal thoughts for a while. He nodded. "Yeah," he croaked out. He was sure if he said more, or put more effort into it, he would lose the battle of holding down the bile that was still trying to work its way out.

"You kinda went away from me there. I was saying that they started showing up shortly after you left. With how vicious these things are, and watching how they act, I wasn't sure you were going to make it back."

"Came in through the alley in the back. Didn't see them out front."

"We watched the first one attack a guy. Then there was this crazy priest. Other people came out of their houses to see what was going on. You know, a large group of your friends and neighbors are out in the street, you want to see what's up. Well, the zombies attacked the people, then went into their homes, going after families.

"The people that didn't come out, who just were ignoring things outside, well…they weren't too smart, either. We could see some of them watching out their windows, like we were, but they didn't close their front doors. They only had the screen doors closed. Screen doors don't do shit against zombies. I don't know how the zombies figured out to go into the houses. Maybe they have some of their former memories.

"Man, that's fucked up if they do, but they were trampling over each other and into the houses. Now, the ones that *did* have closed doors, well… enough zombies hitting the front door of a house, and most these houses were just built cheaply, it doesn't take too much pressure to force them in."

Sullivan was rambling on. Jason wasn't sure if he was stopping for short breaths, or if he could just talk in such a stream that after doing it for weeks during his broadcasts, he had built the ability to not need air. It was hard to catch everything the man was saying.

After a second, though, he did catch on to what he had said about the doors. The zombies had trampled through the screen doors?

Jason looked at the front door. When he had left, the large metal door had been open to have fresh air come in through the screen door. His mother hated to pay for air conditioning and always wanted the front door open. He breathed a sigh of relief when he saw that they had closed the door, put the large metal security bar across it, and had moved the shuffleboard table against it. It would take a damn tank to get through the steel door to begin with. He knew that just because of the scratches on the front of the door where burglars had tried crowbars and everything else, and the best they had been able to do was bend up a couple corners of the door.

Of course, there were the front windows, which were eight feet off the ground, but unless the zombies learned how to fly, they should be safe in there.

In fact, the more he thought about it, thanks to his mom's paranoia, the bar was probably one of the safest places in town. The damned place was the Fort Knox of Hammond. Every time someone had tried to break in, or there had been something strange happening that got her a late night phone call, she would take more security measures. When someone had tried to force their way in, and almost succeeded, two years ago, the large metal fire doors had been added. The new doors were damn near impenetrable.

A faint smile crossed his lips as he looked at the door, then back at Sullivan. "There ain't shit getting in here," he said in a mocking redneck accent. It was supposed to come up as Texas slang but, as soon as he said it, he knew it had just come out wrong. He could tell just how bad it was by how Sullivan rolled his eyes at him.

"You know, ya bastard, I got my guns and stockpile at fucking home. At fucking home! And here is the zombie invasion. The shit I've been preparing for, and you have me fucking watching your mom's bar when it happens? I fucking hate you," Sullivan said, but his smile betrayed any actual frustration. Jason knew that, in his own sadistic way, Sullivan was just too happy that he was proven right to actually be upset.

Jason looked at the rest of them standing in the bar. They weren't excited. They were scared, and he understood why. While he had been smiling at his insane friend, he felt their fear and shared it.

Then he remembered his sister, and he remembered why he felt it.

He looked back at Sullivan. "Lisa is one of them," Jason whispered.

There was a moment of confusion, then he saw it hit Sullivan. That eager look on his face fell and Jason saw his color drain. "Dude…"

It was amazing how one word always seemed to have so many meanings. Jason once saw a movie where they had a whole conversation with just using the word "dude". As Sullivan said it now, Jason saw and heard the sadness in it. The word conveyed "Hey, man. I'm sorry, and I'm here for you" Just one word, but Jason knew that in their friendship, all that was relayed.

"We're fucked," Jason said.

Something inside Jason just snapped, and he barely noticed as he felt himself fall away, the world around him spinning.

* * * *

Jaime had been watching the kid that had come in, followed by the nurse. The bartender had been calling him "Dude" so often, she almost thought it was his name. Now he was just a heap, crying on the floor. *What a damn baby*, she thought.

When she heard more crying, she remembered that she had a baby of her own there, and that damned thing was now wailing, as well. Nadine, the baby who had ruined their lives, was sitting on the table and one of these losers must have fucking woken her up. Now she would probably never get the screaming creature back to sleep.

Jaime tried to remember the last time her diaper had been changed, or when she had fed her. She thought it had been just a couple hours ago, but wasn't sure. She had done it when she got up this morning, right? She was pretty sure she had.

She turned from the adult sobbing behind the bar and started to walk towards her own little monster, but stopped when she saw Denise, the woman Jaime knew as Nurse Winston from her infrequent visits to the doctor's office, holding her baby. She was singing to the little child, and the beautiful voice had calmed her.

With trepidation in her step, Jaime walked up to the nurse. "I'm sorry for missing my appointment this week," Jaime said. She wasn't sorry. She hated going, unless she was in pain and wanted to get more Vicodin, but the nurse probably already knew that. Still, she thought she needed to say it, as the woman was holding her little beast in her arms.

"You actually got her to stop. That's amazing," Jaime said nervously. She still wasn't sure how to react to seeing the woman out of the doctor's office. Somewhere deep inside, and she wasn't sure why, this woman made her antsy, and she could feel the end of her fingers start to twitch a little.

Denise looked up at the woman and gave her a weak smile. Jaime saw something there, something she had never seen on the woman's face before. The woman seemed to have bags under eyes, and the darkness in the bar cast shadows across her expression to make it look both haunted and possessive. That smile, with the barest hint of Denise's teeth showing, seemed almost to claim Jaime's baby as her own.

Maybe it was that way. Maybe the woman *did* want to take her child. Most days, Jaime would wish for that, for the screaming monster to just disappear; however, with this woman holding her little girl and giving her that look, she wasn't sure anymore. She had the sudden overwhelming urge to grab her child and hold her.

It had to be the light. After all, this woman had cared for her child and had nursed her through fever and sickness. This was the doctor's wife, the one everyone trusted. There was nothing mischievous there. It was just all in the lighting of the dim bar. *It makes the woman look like a witch*, Jaime thought. Maybe that was what it was. The light made the woman look…evil.

Still, it made her uncomfortable.

"Go find a couple of towels," the woman was saying. "We need to set her down on the table so we can get her diaper changed, but I don't want to lay her down on the cold, hard table without something soft."

Jaime found herself turning away, while still keeping a wary gaze on the woman.

* * * *

Jaime had been walking back to the table when Travis, her "always great for fucking things up" husband, walked over to her and whispered, "We need to get out of here."

Jaime hadn't realized how much she was lost in her own thoughts until she heard his voice and jumped a little at the sound of it.

"What?" She turned and looked into his eyes.

"We need to get the fuck out of here." He was trying to whisper, but it was too harsh and she was sure everyone else had probably heard it. He grabbed her by the arm and pulled her away from everyone, giving them only a quick look as he did.

"What? Why?" she said, looking back over her shoulder towards the woman holding her baby. Her banshee was quiet now, and the woman was changing her like she had done it a thousand times.

"I think she's planning on keeping our baby," Jaime said in an astonished whisper.

Travis shook her, bringing her focus back to him. His eyes were drilling into her, and she found herself not able to look into them for too long. Was this really the man she had come up here to yell at? The man she had felt had lost his backbone just after he had lost his job? The man who would get mad at people, only to drink that madness away? He didn't look like that man now.

185

Was she glad about that? She wasn't sure.

What was happening to her? Was she losing it, as well? There were fucking zombies outside, but she had been fine. She had watched them tear apart people out in the street, but she had been fine. The rest of them had been nervous and scared, but she had been fine.

So why couldn't she be focused now?

She hadn't been thinking about Nadine, so when did that change? That little monster had done nothing but terrorize them, causing them nothing but grief. Their life would have been so much easier without the creature screaming through the night, her husband yelling at her for not shutting the damned thing up. How many nights had she gone into that room, thinking just how easy it would be to take a pillow and cover the monster's mouth for a few minutes?

So why did Nadine change things and make her start to lose it?

"Where would we go?" she finally heard herself asking. She surprised herself with how weak she sounded. Where had this mouse come from?

Her gaze turned back to the nurse, who was now finished putting on a new, makeshift diaper…a bar rag. Suddenly, she realized it was because of the nurse. She had always had that affect. The woman had always been nice to her, but she knew the woman always thought badly of her. She thought she was trash. The nurse thought Jaime was a terrible mother and didn't deserve to have kids. Every time she saw Nurse Winston look at her, it was in her eyes. She thought Jaime was just another piece of trash, and Nurse Winston was so much better than everyone else. She lived in that nice big house just behind the doctor's office, that lavish house that was so much nicer than most the other houses in the town, while they lived in a trailer.

Well, the trailer was paid for, and it was theirs, and that nurse was *not* better than them.

She could feel the fire she often had, that chip she always carried on her shoulder for those snobs around town that thought they were better…her boss, the doctor, the nurse. The ones who all had it so easy. That anger at how they always looked down at her rekindled and she could feel the heat spreading throughout her chest.

Travis was saying something, and she tried to focus on it.

"We'll go to Bobby's. We won't stay there, but he's got guns and I know he's out of town for the weekend. He, Cougar, and Idjit had all gone over to the state park to camp and go fishing. We'll grab some of his guns and then get out."

"And go where? How do we know there's not more of them outside of town?" she said.

"How do we know there are? We get out and find someplace they're not."

"Just us?" she asked. She wasn't sure what she was asking. She guessed she was asking if they were going to ask any of the others, but she knew that wasn't what she meant. They couldn't take a baby with them. What if she started crying?

But they couldn't just leave her.

Travis looked at the woman who was cradling their little Nadine. She thought she actually saw some pain. She really wished she could tell what he was thinking. How well did she really know her husband? Would he be there for her if she needed him?

"We should," he said. He wasn't sure, either.

Travis didn't stop her as she turned and walked back to the woman and their child.

Denise looked up, and Jaime held her hands out. At first Denise stood there, gently rocking the little girl, the chubby little face resting on her shoulder, eyes closed. Her soft skin looked like it wasn't real, and Nadine's thumb had made its way into her mouth.

"What's going on?" Denise finally asked as she started to hand the baby over.

Jaime gave a quick, scared glance back at her husband, then looked back at Denise. Why was she scared? What did they owe any of these people? They were getting out of there, so why should it matter to any of them?

"We're getting out of here," she said.

Denise looked at them, then at the little girl in her arms. Jaime thought she saw the wheels turning inside that head. She thought she saw the look that told her the woman was wondering how much of a fight Jaime would give if she was to suddenly reach out and snatch the baby. Jaime pulled Nadine to her a little tighter, getting ready for the woman's grab.

It never came.

"We probably all should," Denise said, "before things get really bad."

"Where are you going?" called out one of the men from the other end of the bar. Jaime turned and saw it was that perverted old man who would always just stare at her breasts whenever she came in. Just being around the guy always made her feel dirty. No matter how desperate she was for money, there were just some things she couldn't even fathom. The man's rough hands as they slapped her ass made her remember why she never came up there anymore. Yeah, because she was so much better than that, and that guy was so much less sleazy than her boss.

"None of your business," Travis called back to him.

"Sure that's smart?" Sullivan said, helping Jason to his feet. Jason didn't look like he was crying as much now. His eyes were red and he just continued to stare at some point in the darkness behind the bar.

"Why do you care?"

"Don't really give a shit about you. It's the kid I'm worried about," Sullivan said, nodding towards Nadine.

"You don't get to make that decision."

"He's right," the cop said, walking towards them. He kept his eyes on Travis, and it looked like he was trying to talk down a situation. Jaime wondered just what the hell his damned involvement was in this, and why the hell he cared.

The cop just kept walking towards them, keeping his words gentle and smooth as he approached. "The kid… A girl, right? She's only going to make it hard for you out there. What if she wakes up and starts screaming. They'll come after you. You really want to see her get hurt?"

Jaime kissed Nadine's forehead. Her little girl *was* one hell of a screamer. She was going to be a nasty bitch like her mama once she grew up. She had a set of lungs on her that would tear down any macho man and turn him into a drooling boy in his boxer shorts who did what she said.

But she had to live that long first.

Jaime looked back up at Rob, who was now standing only a couple feet away. He was looking at Nadine, and she could see the glint of wetness in the corner of his eye, just barely able to be seen from the little sunlight coming through the back window.

Something was wrong with her chest. She felt like there was a bowling ball on top of it, a knife stabbing through her gut. Her mind was reeling. She didn't know what she wanted to do. The more she thought about it, the more she *couldn't* think about it, making it hard to concentrate on what she should do.

She looked at Travis, who was staring daggers at the cop. Yeah, she knew what was going through his mind, and knew she didn't have to make the decision. It was already made. She saw the burning there and knew, inside, he thought about the three DUI's he had, the third one costing him his job. Sure, he had said they were downsizing, but she knew better. Hell, she knew his boss! She had talked to the foreman, and he had told her it was due to his drinking.

However, Travis didn't think so. It was the cop's fault. It was his foremen's fault. It was the company's fault. It was all the politicians' fault. It was never his fault. It was never going to *be* his fault.

She knew she felt the same way, but to her, it all started with him. It was always his fault. The damn piece of garbage that was her husband was always going to be the loser who blamed everyone else.

"She's coming with us," Travis said with a snarl. He wanted the cop to fight him on it so he could hit him. Even though that wasn't the cop who pulled him over, it didn't matter. Travis saw all of them as the same. That was the cop who had taken away the little dignity he had.

The old guy walked between them and was limping his way towards the back door. Travis had to step back from the man as he nearly stumbled into him.

At the door, he stopped and turned back to look at them. "Well, you coming or what? Let's get the fuck out of here," Mr. Jones said to them. He turned and continued towards the outer back door.

"Once you go out that door…," Jason said to them as he came around Sullivan. He looked at Nadine, and Jaime was pretty sure the kid was getting ready to break out crying again. "Once you go out there," Jason said, wiping away and sniffing the nose that was trying to run, "we can't let you back in. We need to bar up the back door."

Where they really going to go out there? She knew it made sense. There were zombies out there, and they needed to get the fuck as far away as possible. They had to leave.

"You guys coming or what?" Mr. Jones said from where he had disappeared into the back hallway.

"What are you all going to do? Just sit in here and hope someone comes?" Jaime said to them. She was glad her voice still sounded strong, and she even heard her tone still coming out in her bitchy manor. She wasn't going to allow this to crack her, but she hadn't been sure.

"Jaime, bundle the kid up and come on," Travis growled from behind her, walking towards Mr. Jones.

"I don't know yet, but I know we need to take some time, figure things out. We don't know what the hell is going on out there," the cop spoke up. He was still walking slowly toward them. She could tell what he was doing. He was trying to talk them down, get close, and take their daughter away from them. He had that feel to him.

"Fuck you," she said.

"At least leave your daughter here where she's safe," the nurse said.

Jaime looked at her, then down at her daughter. She looked back up at the nurse, her gaze hard. They didn't care about her or her husband. They only cared about their daughter. They wanted to take her from them. They all wanted her. Just like her neighbors, who kept calling CPS on them, they wanted to steal her. Everyone, all of them. They all wanted her.

Well, they couldn't have her, not as long as she was alive.

Jaime shook her head and started to walk backwards towards the door. She didn't trust any of them. They all wanted her. She didn't trust turning her back on them because she knew they would rush her. They were all monsters. They would attack her, tear her apart to get to the little girl.

She made it to the door where Travis and that pervert were waiting. Travis stepped around the smelly old man and opened the door, then tentatively looked out. He quickly stepped out and started running towards their car parked halfway between the front door and the back door. Mr. Jones hurried past them, and she followed.

As soon as she made it down the steps, she heard the door slam shut behind her.

CHAPTER 13

"Sergeant! You got a call from the outer perimeter!" yelled his communication specialist, hurrying up to him.

Great, he thought. *They probably found out about Marshall's attempts to extract information from his friends out on the outer perimeter.* When he had asked the PFC to do it, Wade had known they would probably get in trouble. He had no question they would get caught eventually, but had his superiors caught on already? It hadn't even been over an hour yet. He had hoped for at least some bit of information before they were shut down.

That's all he needed was to get his ass chewed out but, hey, what were they going to do? Relieve him of his command and send someone else in to take over? There wasn't anyone else that could do the job well enough to take over. None of these soldiers would even come close to being on his recommended list to be his replacement. In fact, other than Marshall and a few others, most of these guys were pretty green, and had only seen the slightest bit of combat. Something he was continually reminded of as he walked the makeshift camp and had to constantly ride their asses.

He was just on his way to the command tent after checking on the field clearing project. They had found a group of soldiers huddled in between two Hummers, sneaking a smoke. He had ripped them a new asshole, thanking them for being the latest volunteers to become latrine digging engineers or, as he liked to call them, "shit diggers".

Keep busy or make it look like you're busy, but never get caught just standing around. It was always the fastest way to get more work added to your list.

He neared the command tent and looked over at the blockade. His eyes lingered on the drying blood stains that he saw on the cement. He couldn't really see them from the distance and the different obstacles that blocked them, but he still saw them. The images burned more deeply in his mind than anything else he had seen, and he knew if he made it to sleep that night, they would be there, a new set of nightmares to keep him twisting and turning in his cot.

The bodies were gone, the shallow, unmarked graves in the cornfield near them. Men were now digging a mass grave in case they needed it. He hoped like hell they wouldn't, but he wanted to keep them busy so they didn't have time to stop and think about what they were doing, or what they had just done. Keep them busy and keep their minds occupied.

They had moved the bodies and the car was repositioned to be another part of the blockade. He hoped it would be the only one added to it.

"Sergeant!"

He turned to see Marshall hurrying up to him. "Yes?" he said, his voice tired and clipped. He motioned for the soldier to follow him. Avoiding the command tent, they stepped around to its side.

"Okay. I was only able to get ahold of Jacobs, Swanson, Jessie, and Runice. Jessie and Runice are on outer barricades on the far side of town, but they told me what their orders were. Jacobs and Swanson are close to command, which is another five miles up the road, and they know less. They haven't been given any orders yet. They are in reserve to rotate out in five hours to another outer perimeter station."

"So nothing?"

"I didn't say that, sergeant. Jessie and Runice told me their orders."

The sergeant gave him a dead look. He was tired, and he wasn't really in the mood for information being stretched out for dramatic effect. Just give it to him, quick and painless. Stop this bullshit of a little at a time.

"Their orders are to fire on anyone who gets too close to the barricade."

"Okay. So how's that different than our orders?

"Because it doesn't matter who the person is or from what direction they come. Whether or not it is one of us from the inside, or someone trying to get in with direct orders from General Mayfever, no one is to get in or out. Anyone trying to is to be shot…no warnings and no matter if they are wearing a uniform."

So they were trapping them in, as well? Wade had figured as much, but wasn't happy he now had confirmation. Most of his outer flanks weren't being covered by his own soldiers but by area law enforcement, people who had been called in without any idea of what they had gotten themselves into. Many of them already called to complain they needed to get home to their families, having been on duty all night. If any of them tried to leave now, they would be shot, and he doubted they would shoot anyone who was trying to get out. Like a family of fools who argued until it cost them their lives.

He remembered the wife's face as she looked to their child. He wasn't even sure if it had been a boy or a girl. It was just an "it" to him, which was a saving grace, but he still saw the mother…her face, her eyes…and it was enough.

Yeah, he really doubted any of those officers had the stomach for that. He hated himself because he knew he could.

"Okay. Keep trying for more intel."

The soldier nodded and hurried away.

The sergeant turned back to the entrance to command and walked inside.

* * * *

"Yes, sir!" Wade snapped. General Mayfever, who had taken command of the outer perimeter, had not taken long to start yelling as soon as he had gotten on the line. The general was not used to waiting. Wade had barely made it through getting to the communique and giving his command codes before the berating insults began.

"Now," said the clipped authoritative voice, "we have a team that will be coming up to your lines within an hour. You need to clear a path for it, allowing it entrance. And make sure your men know what they're doing! I want you to be able to tell if that truck lab thing they are bringing in gets breached. If it gets breached and they try to get out of there, stop it. Also, make sure the other perimeter teams know, as well."

"Yes, sir; however, I have many checkpoints which are covered by area authorities and not troops. I don't feel they would be able to make that call. Any chance of getting them rotated out?"

"No." It was a simple, hard answer, and the sergeant felt pretty sure there wasn't going to be an explanation. However, there was a pause, as though the commander on the other end wanted to say something else, but couldn't bring himself to.

"Make sure to let the team know about these checkpoints that are not manned by troops so they can avoid them. It wouldn't do for an incident like a misfire to happen. Not with these people. We need them."

"Yes, sir."

The line went dead.

* * * *

When Sarah stepped off the plane, she was already feeling like she had worked all day. Her joints were sore, she was tired, and all she wanted to do was find a nice place to disappear. The second she stepped off the private jet, she knew there had been no chance of that happening. General Mayfever was already standing there to greet her. He didn't even give her the false pretense of wanting to be there with her. It wasn't that they didn't like each other. They couldn't *stand* each other.

"General," she said as she walked by him, not stopping to let him catch up. She knew it would annoy him. He was military, a war monger. Why had they called him in? Were they already prepping the cleanse initiative? They sure as hell better not be. Her and her team still had no idea what they were up against.

"Ms. Demoin," he said coldly. She didn't have to turn to look at him to hear the grimace in his voice. General Mayfever was taller than her, but while she was thin and wiry, he was cold steel. He was hard; his face was chiseled, always in an unreadable mask; his hair, which may have had some color and been longer once, was now gone, without any fuzz of silver to make him look grandpa-like. He was bald, lean, and his uniform was tight to allow for the muscles to be noticed beneath the fabric.

He always had the air of authority.

It wasn't *her* authority, though, and she couldn't stand for others who thought they were better than her to get away with bossing her around.

"So, what do we know about this Einstein of yours who made the call and then disappeared?"

He was talking about Bryan. So they still didn't have any details as to what was going on inside the town?

"What do you need to know?"

"Was he stable?"

That made Sarah stop to look at the man. He kept walking until he was past her, then turned back, his eyebrows raised.

"Yes. Yes, he was," she stammered. She hoped he was anyway. She knew he was a smart man, able to do his job like very few could. He was one of the best, but he was a lab rat. He wasn't a field scientist. It was always different out in the field.

Could he have made a mistake and then, out of fear of being caught, taken off and disappeared? She couldn't see him doing that. Not Bryan.

"Was? Has something happened to make him seem different?" The general had been talking to her, and she hadn't realized she had stopped paying attention to him.

"No. *Is*. You…you had said was. I had assumed you were sure he was…was gone." She could barely say it, still not wanting to believe it could be true. How long had they been colleagues, working at the lab together?

"Oh. No, we don't have any evidence of that. No one has been able to get in or out."

"Communication has been cut, though, but that doesn't mean much, right?"

"True."

* * * *

Sarah hadn't liked the man, and still wouldn't like the man. She felt the lab he had arranged for her was a cruel joke. This wasn't a lab meant to be workable. It was a thrown together hodgepodge that, with the slightest turn, the test tubes, fine-tuned microscopes, and chemicals would shatter on the floor. That was if they didn't blow up from a chemical reaction. No, this wasn't a lab. It was a bomb meant to explode at 60 miles per hour on a freeway.

She watched as the semi-trailer in front of her swayed back and forth in the wind. She didn't know much about trucks, but she didn't think it should be doing that. How much damage was it causing, and was everything she had requested in there?

She had wanted time to check everything out, but the second they had hurried off the tarmac, two Hummers had been waiting for her, her small team, and the soldiers who had been assigned to them for security. Something told her they would also be their executioners had any of them tried to run at the last minute. She could tell that Thomas, another member of their team, had already put that together because he eyed them cautiously.

Lights flared on the truck in front of her and her eyes went back to watching it. She hadn't realized her gaze had drifted down to the driver's sidearm. She thought his name was Rick. He had introduced himself to her as Private First Class Riker but, as she couldn't help but giggle at the obvious Star Trek reference, she had finally coached his first name out of him.

God, how awful, she had thought. His parents had actually named him Rick Riker? Sure, his name was actually Richard, but no one probably called him that. So, yes, her driver was Rick Riker, and if any of them tried to back out, PFC Riker would be one of them who would shoot them down.

He probably wouldn't even think twice about it. Even with his short build, he had a stocky frame and looked like he was a hardened soldier. It was a huge difference from the nervous soldier sitting next to her in the back.

She watched as the truck in front of her, its lights ablaze, started to shift to the side of the road. Then she noticed that they were matching its speed and pulling off to the side of the road, as well.

"We're stopping?" she asked.

"We are at the outer perimeter. We need to get clearance, then put on the Level 1 Hazmat suits before we proceed any further."

"Oh, god. Are you going to be able to drive in that thing?" She knew how restrictive and bulky the suits were. She always wished someone would design a more practical, better-fitting suit. However, the fault in her logic was just one word…practical. Was it more practical to have tailored suits for everyone who ever might need one, or to have one size fits all? However, you have the one size fits all, they would never fit properly. Practicality at its worst and finest, and she was left to complain about it.

However, this time, she was complaining more for him than herself. She wasn't a soldier walking around with guns, having to drive in the thing. She just had to do research.

She looked at the semi-trailer again. How the hell had they made that thing sterile? How were they supposed to work in there? Couldn't they have used a RV or something more comfortable? How had they secured it so they could work in there without having to constantly be in the hazmat suits?

As the questions ran through her mind, so did the answers. Sterilizing it wasn't too hard. They probably set up a clean room within a clean room, and as for equipment, they probably made sure to secure it all down so any shaking wouldn't cause damage to the chemicals. How were they supposed to work in there, though? Why not an RV? Well, the semi-trailer had no restrictions in it, like couches and a kitchen. While the luxuries would have been nice to have, they weren't going there to relax. They were going there to find out what was wrong and why the town was under quarantine.

She even remembered her report mentioning something like this would work in a situation where one of the prefabbed labs wasn't available. In that instance, the trailer made the most sense because it was wide open space they could quickly customize to their needs, working it into a useable space.

Damn, that monstrosity in front of them was her own fucking design!

They came to a stop.

She watched as the men around her were suiting up, then helping their fellow soldiers. They looked like space suits. *Damn, the things are ugly.*

A knock at her window made her jump and she turned to look. The general was standing there. She opened the door to get out and he moved out of her way.

"Suit up. Your team is about to go in."

She looked around. "Yeah, I figured."

"When you get in, the soldiers have orders to take you to the doctor's office. They have radios on a special frequency that isn't being blocked. Get word out as to what is going on so we know if we have something serious, or if your man just started spouting flying butterflies out of his ass."

Sarah nodded, a soldier already working around her to get her into her hazmat pants. She thought the soldier was a woman, but in the camouflage and the baggy outfit they all wore, she couldn't tell.

She wanted to just scream at the soldier, tell her she could dress her own damn self, but the woman was moving quickly and didn't pay much attention to her.

"Get us fucking intel. Then do whatever the fuck you do. If this is as serious as your man has lead us to believe, fix it."

The soldier finished putting on her suit, securing it so there were no gaps. As the soldier was reaching for her helmet, she turned to look back at the general. His eyes were burrowing into her. He wasn't happy, but why should any of them be happy? This wasn't a small issue. They had quarantined a whole town. If this turned out to be nothing, heads were going to roll. If it *was* something, who knew how bad of an outbreak they were looking at?

"I don't need to tell you what happens if you can't control it," he said.

As she thought about that, her mouth went dry. As she fought back a tear, thinking about what *would* happen if she couldn't stop whatever was infesting the town, she lost the ability to speak. She could only nod. Then he turned around and was gone, leaving her to think about just how bad all of this could get.

CHAPTER 14

Travis rushed out from the back door, nearly stumbling off the side of the stairs as he tried to hurry. He heard the old man coming up behind him and figured Jaime must be coming out last. He kept his eyes moving, watching for any of those things. He looked back and saw that Jaime bringing up the rear, Nadine cradled in her arms.

"I parked over here," he called to them. He didn't give a shit if they really kept up with him. He hoped the sharpness in his voice kept them moving. It was keep up or get left behind. He saw what those things did and this was all about survival. *His* survival.

He shot a look of disapproval at Jaime. Yeah, he wanted his kid to be with them. Well, at least he wasn't about to leave it in a place like this where they already thought of him as shit. That stuck-up hoy-ty-toy-ty owner's kid, that cop, and that damn nurse bitch who had been looking down at his wife… He could see how they all were looking at them, how they had watched as his wife had been yelling at him. He knew it, he could see it in their eyes, and he sure as hell wasn't going to leave his kid with them.

However, looking back at his wife, he also didn't want to bring them. Either of them were trouble, and they were probably going to get him killed.

His plan was to get to Bobby's, get the guns, and find somewhere to hole up. If they survived, then they would see what needed to be done.

No, he couldn't be thinking about that yet. Focus on what they were doing. Focus on where they were right now.

He scanned the road. Some of the zombies were at the end of the street, but he couldn't see any near his truck. Damn, he was glad he has his truck and not the car. It was a large, diesel Dodge pick-up that he knew could handle running over a few zombie bad boys along the way. Once they got in there, they were safe.

And Mr. Jones, that annoying prick, was coming with them? Nah, he didn't feel that was really going to happen. He'd probably use him as bait. After all, what did they say? "You don't have to be a great runner. You just have to be able to run faster than the man behind you"?

He looked back at Jaime again, giving her that harsh gaze. She *had* to bring the fucking kid. Something was wrong about that, too. He noticed it the first time he looked back at her, and it still nagged at him. Something was missing, something that had his nerves tingling. What had they forgotten?

Jaime was hurrying behind Mr. Jones, Nadine nestled with her head onto Jaime's shoulder. The little angel was asleep, not knowing that the world around her was going to shit.

Why was Jaime carrying her? Why wasn't Nadine in the car seat? Travis had seen her bring it into… The damn bitch had left it in there?! The fucking bitch. It's not like this wasn't going to be hard enough getting over to Bobby's to get the guns, but the damn bitch had forgotten the damn car seat.

Fuck!

He looked to the door to the bar, knowing it was no use. The loud clang from the other side of the door could be heard from where they were. The door was locked now, and the damned bastard kid had put that railroad track across it. There was no going back.

* * * *

Jason had watched as the trio made it to the back door, his stomach twisting with conflicting emotions. In one sense, he was glad they were going. All of them were a pain in the ass. Mr. Jones… Damn, he couldn't really say he would ever be sorry to see that son of a bitch disappear, but the man had a right to live. The redneck… Hell, he was annoying and his wife seemed like a bitch, but out there, without knowing anything yet, was certain death. Where the hell would they go?

Then there was the baby. While the others made their choices, the little girl didn't have one. They were taking her to her death.

His chest felt tight, his stomach was turning from the acid trying to rise up, and a pounding started to form behind his temple. This was all pushing into him, and he wished he could just turn it off. Sullivan was happy, this was his wet dream, but Jason just wanted to keep the damn things on television where he could turn them off when he was sick or disgusted by them.

The back door clanged shut as the trio left the bar, the woman going out last.

They were gone…and the door was unlocked.

He rushed into the back hallway to bar it, lock the three dead bolts, and put the large metal pole in place. The back door had more security than the front. While they both had the large railway rail that was put across it and were both large metal fire doors that were nearly impossible to break through, the back door also had three large deadbolt locks and the metal pole that fastened to the door and the floor.

It would take a bomb to get in.

He was getting more and more thankful for his mother's paranoia.

* * * *

At the sound of the back door crashing shut, Rob hurried to the front window and watched the zombies continue to spread out in the street around them. They busted down doors, and tore into the people around him, tearing out their flesh. And here he stood, having no way of going out there and doing a dammed thing about it. His skin crawled, and he continually tried to reach for his sidearm when he saw a new victim being caught or a new house being invaded. He had no idea just how many of them there had been when they started, but their numbers were growing exponentially.

He wanted to go out there and help the people that were still alive, but he knew if he had he tried, he would only be going to his own death. That was his job, though. He should have been out there, putting his life on the line to save more people. He was a protector. That's what he had signed up for so many years ago when he had first become a cop. Sure, during those many years when he had been cruising the streets of

208

Chicago, he had grown jaded and wasn't sure what it had meant to him, but getting out of the city had helped.

He was part of the community now. Sure, this wasn't his town, but he had now lived in a small town of his own for just over a year, and had slowly started to remember that people were people. That when he had chosen to become a cop, there had been some reason behind it. He was a protector of people. He was there to keep them safe, even if it was from themselves.

So how was he supposed to protect them now?

The first victim, the auto mechanic, the one who he had talked to that morning about his car, was getting back up. Shortly after the things had attacked at him and had torn at his flesh, they had quickly stopped, moving onto their next victim. He wasn't sure what that meant yet, but knew it was curious. They had attacked him, but hadn't eaten him. Now the man was back up. He was unsteady, but they didn't seem to be paying attention to him anymore.

Rob watched the man as he fought his way to stand. He was twitching and looking around. He seemed confused and swayed back and forth, staggering when his weight went too far to the left and right, forward and back. The man seemed like he didn't know where he was or how to walk. When he stepped forward, he was staggered cautiously, as though he wasn't sure how it would feel when his foot came down onto the pavement.

It made Rob think of his son, Jake. When Jake had taken his first steps, they had been that way. It was the first step of a little child who still didn't possess full control over his motor skills. More steps continued, each one a little less rough. However, when Jake was learning, after about four steps, he had started to dash into that child run that always ended in a crashing fall.

Jake. Robyn. He should have been getting done with court right about now and should have been on his way home. He wasn't supposed to be there, and he wouldn't have been if he had taken his damn cell phone with him this morning, or if he had made sure the spare tire had been fixed. Then again, if he would have bought new tires when the first one had blown rather than just continuing to put on those cheap used ones, he probably would have been in better shape.

Anymore guilt you want to put onto yourself? he thought. He had made many mistakes so he was sure he could find more if he stopped to think about it.

Yeah, there was. He never should have let them take that baby out of there. He knew he had no legal right to stop them, but they were all going to go and get themselves killed. He should have stopped them. He should have tried harder to rip the child away from her. He should have-

He strained his neck, trying to see down the side of the building the best he could. It was hopeless. The windows faced towards the front, and there wasn't a single window that would allow him to see along the side.

He watched as another mass of those things tore through another door. They were now in the same block as the bar, working on the houses right across the street.

"Outside is full of zombies, and all my preparation for them is ruined by me being here," Sullivan was saying as he stood next to him. Rob wondered what he meant by that. Was the man just part-crazy or really crazy? Something inside him told him he probably didn't want to know. After all, what kind of preparations would you make for something like this? Guns, other types of weapons… Was it legal or illegal? Rob could never fathom having what he felt like he would need to be ready for something like this.

As Rob thought about it a little more, he realized that if there was any place ready for zombies, it sure felt like this place was. The front door was secured strong enough, so it would take a lot of force to get through it. The windows were high and hard to climb up to if someone wanted to get in. The place had food. While it wasn't great food, it was enough to last the small group of people for a couple of days. All in all, the place wasn't that bad to hole up in until help came.

He hadn't heard the couple screaming yet, but he hadn't seen their car come around the front, either. He guessed they could have gone around to the back of the building. Still, he hadn't heard anything. He hoped that was good news. Part of him hated the unease and the not knowing. The edginess in his arms craved for him to open the front door and just take a peek to see if they were okay.

If the front door opened, how long would it take for those things to come crashing through?

Something slammed against the front door and, as a surprised scream caught in his throat, he knew he had his answer.

* * * *

"Are we sure they're zombies? I mean, there ain't any military bases nearby that I know of. Could there be anything underground nearby? Some hidden lab? Fifty miles south of here is where I call home, so I'm not sure I'd have heard any scuttlebutt if there was one," Bruce said as he turned away from the front window and took a seat at the bar.

Jason walked behind the bar, turning the sink on to wash the grease from the back door metal bar off before walking back over to the larger man. The man was nervous. He was trying to hide it, but his hands shook and his face had lost its color.

"I'll take a 7 with sprite on ice," the large truck driver said, blowing out a long breath as he gripped the bar. The man closed his eyes and was concentrating on his breathing. Jason ignored him and grabbed the Seagram's bottle that was on the back wall.

"What is a zombie?" Denise asked. She was still at the table near the car seat left by the insane couple that had just decided to leave.

Hell, Jason thought, *at least it got Mr. Jones the hell out of here.*

Denise saw that Jason was looking at her. Then she seemed to have realized she had said something. Her arms quickly wrapped around herself, and she lowered herself back into the chair.

"Zombies? That's easy. They are reanimated corpses," Sullivan said, quick to answer from his place by the front window.

Getting ready to dig into an old argument, Jason said, "Really? That's funny because dead men just don't get up and walk. Dead men stay dead. Military experiments, the ones that create super soldiers and new kinds of viruses, spread and make people look dead, but all they are is infected."

"They don't have a pulse," Denise said absently. Jason stopped, about to put the drink on the counter in front of Bruce. Both of them turned and were watching her. She just looked down at her hands, speaking softly, barely audible, "They don't have a pulse. Their blood doesn't bleed from the wounds they inflict on themselves. They don't seem to eat, but when they come after you, they tear into your flesh. They aren't so much eating you as they are biting into you to-" Her voice trailed off and was quickly followed by her sobbing.

Jason set the drink down in front of Bruce. Neither one of them had moved while she was talking.

"They could just all be republicans. They have no souls and are pretty lifeless," Jason said dully. He knew his attempt to lighten things up wasn't going to work, but he felt like he had to try. The air had grown thick with despair and relying on his wit was not a saving grace, but it helped him release some of the nervousness he was feeling, at least.

He looked at Bruce, who was starring daggers into him.

Yeah, his joke definitely was not going over well. He knew that most the people who came to his mom's bar were probably republicans, and he had learned a long time ago to stay away from talking politics. Well, he had *thought* he had learned, but when he got nervous, that was his go-to subject. Make fun of the crazies. It always made him feel a little better.

However, the look on Bruce's face made him cringe and he knew just how wrong he was. "But them damn democrats who are cutting military spending that probably caused whatever this was to get out. If you don't pay the guards to the prison, the prisoners go free," Bruce retorted.

Yeah, but the chiefs don't always know what all their little Indians are doing, Jason had wanted to retort, but knew he had better let the matter drop. This wasn't an argument that anybody could win. In the end, neither side would be right or wrong.

Bruce did have a point. Was this something the government had allowed to get out?

"How do you know so much?"

Jason looked up to see that Rob had turned away from the front window and was looking at Denise.

"She's a nurse," Tina said. Having emerged from the bathroom, she now stood at the end of the bar. Her eyes were red and swollen, her cheeks puffy. The left side of her hair was matted to her forehead.

Tina turned to look at Jason, and he could feel a knife stab into his chest because he knew what was coming. "Where's Lucy?"

He closed his eyes and, for a moment, he wanted to wrap his arms around himself. He couldn't do this anymore. He couldn't stay out there with them. Too many people, too many strangers, and he didn't feel like he could deal with the one who *wasn't* a stranger right now.

He stepped back into the kitchen area. His chest was growing tighter. His heart was pounding, feeling like it was trying to lodge into his throat. It felt like a hundred pound weight had fallen on top of him and he felt like he couldn't move.

He made it to the kitchen, found the nearest counter that the people from the bar couldn't see, and rested against it. Before he knew it, he was sliding to the ground, his knees pulled into his chest. His teeth ground together, causing pain through his lower jaw, and his face was buried between his knees.

The tears felt like a tidal wave rushing out through him, down a narrow pipe.

He had been able to push it out of his mind for a little bit, and had hoped he had been strong enough to cope with it.

He *had* to cope with it. It was Lisa, his little sister, the one who he tried to get to no longer be afraid of the monsters under her bed. Now she one of them, one of the monsters.

Lucy.

Lucy…Lucy.

He heard screaming outside, but he didn't run towards it. He didn't care. He didn't want to see what was happening. Let them all go. Let them stay away from him. Let them all just go to their own private hell and leave him to stay in his.

He looked up at the two monitors sitting on the counter on the other side of the kitchen. There were four images on each screen updating to a constant feed. Two of the cameras were facing inside, one over the cash register, six of them were outside.

He could see the screaming, the zombies, what was happening. He couldn't stop himself. He didn't know why, but he started laughing and, in his madness and grief, it just felt good.

* * * *

His truck had been halfway up the side of the bar, not more than forty feet from the back door. When he was back in high school, he used to have to run hundred meter dashes and run for miles around a track when he was on the football team. Forty damn feet. Shit, he didn't know how many meters that was, but it was nowhere near a hundred.

Still, those forty damn feet seemed to take forever. It was harder to get through than any of the runs he ever did back in high school, and he didn't think it had anything to do with all the cigarettes and beer he had become accustomed to. No, it was

215

the pair of iron barbells he had attached to his feet. One barbell was named Mr. Jones; the other one, he just called "The Bitch".

He really didn't care if the zombie things caught the three behind him, but he sure as hell wasn't going to run ahead just to have himself alone and surrounded by the damn things. Stay in a group, and if trouble came, he could run and leave them behind. You only have to be faster than the ones you are with. That's all he had to do. Jaime had the kid with her, and Mr. Jones could barely walk on that peg leg of his.

At least the coast was clear…for the time being.

When they had left the bar, he had been trying to hurry them, to get them to run. It had only worked for a few steps before he realized how much damned noise that was making. Then that damn asshole inside made as much fucking noise as he could to slam down that big iron bar on the other side. After that, Travis didn't think it was a good idea to keep hurrying. If they were quiet, the things would never know they were over there. They could just sneak to his truck. There weren't really any around there yet, so they should be fine.

"Why don't we just take *my* damned car?" Mr. Jones said as they were stopped at the hood of his car. It was a nice car. The man certainly did have some money tucked away somewhere. Yeah, he had probably been putting coal up his ass for so long, it had all turned into diamonds. Travis wasn't a caddy person, so he had no idea how old the car was, but he knew old, and he could tell it was well-preserved. The engine probably ran like a pussy cat…nice and quiet. It would be quieter than his truck and would fit them all.

However, Travis was not a Cadillac man, and his truck was a big four-wheel drive, with the deer rails on the front for running down game. It was a man's truck. There was no way in hell he was getting into a caddy. If he was going to die, it would not be behind the wheel of an old man death mobile.

"We're not taking the car. If we get swamped by them damn things, we wouldn't have a chance."

"Son, my caddy is an '84. Made like a tank. Whatever your shit box can take, so can my car, and we can all fit in her. How the hell are we supposed to all fit in that thing of yours?" Mr. Jones pointed to his truck.

"You can take whatever the fuck car you want. You don't have to come. I'm taking my truck. If we need to go through fields and shit, I'd rather have four-wheel drive large ass truck tires under me."

"Just shut up and move. Get us out of here," Jaime said as she glared at them.

Travis looked back at his truck. There was an open gap between the two vehicles, but he thought they could make it. The closest zombie thing he could see was making its way up the front stairs of the bar. There weren't any others for what looked like a half-block down the street. He couldn't tell if any of them were around the front of the bar, but they would still be too far away. Once they were in and he was behind the wheel, they would be safe.

They were almost out of there.

Just take a deep breath, he thought to himself. He did, feeling the tension rattle its way through him. His right hand twitched a little. It was a nervous tick he had never had before and he hoped something new wasn't starting. Now was not the time for his body to start playing games with him.

He took another long breath, held it, then let it out. "Okay, let's go."

He didn't wait to see how close behind him they were. He wasn't running because he knew they couldn't keep up with him if he ran. He didn't even want to know where they were behind him or if they were attacked. He just needed to stay focused on getting to the truck.

Slow, quiet, and safe. Slow, quiet, and safe. Stay slow, stay quiet, and they would make it there safely.

He reached the hood of his truck and stayed low. He could hear them shuffling behind him. They were at the truck, and all they had to do was get inside. They were so close.

"Give me your keys so we can climb in the passenger side while you run around and get in," Mr. Jones demanded. Travis shook his head. "Don't be a fool. It would be faster."

"Passenger door don't work," Jaime said. She wasn't that far behind him. Mr. Jones must have hung back a little, expecting to grab the keys and run around quickly. Jaime had come up next to Travis.

"You mean we all gotta climb in through the driver's side?"

"Seat belts don't work, either. That a problem? You don't like it, just jump in the back," Travis said, leveling his eyes at him. He didn't liked this old twat, and he sure as hell didn't want to put up with his shit now. They were almost safe.

The man glared back, neither one of them looking away. He hadn't meant it to be a macho thing, but the old man seemed to have something to prove about being the grizzled big dog he thought Travis should listen to.

Travis wondered if the old man was weighing his options, thinking about running back to his own car. He knew he was right when the old man finally flinched and turned to look back at the old caddy. He *could* make it there, but he would be on his own. Travis really didn't think the old man wanted that. He tried to play tough, but the man had to know his limitations.

"Shit. Gimme the keys and I'll run first."

"No, Jamie and Nadine go first. That way, you don't try taking off without us, and I *know* they won't take off without me." He glared at her and said the rest to her with that silent gaze. He knew she wouldn't leave without him because if she did, she wouldn't have to fear those things. *He* would be coming after her, and he was a lot scarier than anything they would do to her.

The old man looked at the ground…or was he looking at his leg? Travis really couldn't be sure. Suddenly, the man started to sob. Then he saw his head bob up and down and witnessed the tear fall to the ground.

"Yeah, get the kid safe. I shouldn't have even come out here. I should've just stayed in there and died."

Travis wanted to agree with the old man. Instead, he just scowled, turned away, and took another deep breath. "Okay, well, it's too late for that shit. Now let's move."

Travis quickly moved to step around the front of the truck, but he wasn't looking and struck something hard. He wobbled back and was going down, something coming down with him. He barely saw the white flesh as he came down on top of it, but he felt it thrashing around. It growled, some form of noise like nothing he had ever heard before, and that smell… He could have sworn it reeked of someone shitting their pants. His little shit's diaper didn't smell as bad as whatever that was.

He quickly twisted, pulling himself away from the tangled arms trying to grab him. He could see its face. Goddamn, the thing had been an old woman. He watched as its mouth opened and closed, lunging to take a bite out of him. She didn't even have her ventures in. He just saw gums behind dried lips.

He didn't think about what he was doing. His arms were reacting, pushing himself away. His knees were alternating, kicking blows into the thing's stomach. He twisted his body left and right, trying to pull himself away and keep it from getting a good hold on him.

It slipped right and he finally landed a blow. Its head rocked back, and the loose flesh that had been in pieces of what had once been her cheek was pulled farther back. It slipped more to the side and its balance was off. He was able to push against it, its head slamming down to the hard cement.

The thing paused for a moment. He could feel its limbs going limp around him, and he quickly pulled himself free.

He felt more hands around him and was being jerked away. They were grabbing him from behind, pulling at him. He freed his left hand and it connected with the zombie below him, as the old woman was coming back up to bite him. The blow glanced just off the top of its head. The zombie fell back, and he fell with her.

He felt himself pull free from the ones behind him and quickly rolled off to the side, crawling his way underneath his truck. There wasn't much room, but he just made it.

He looked behind him. The zombie he had been fighting with was already turning to follow him. Her arms reached out, trying to grab at his ankles. He kicked back, not doing much damage. Her arms kept flailing for his boots, and he kept kicking his feet at her. It was making it hard for him to move forward as he kept having to move a couple of inches, then stop to kick back towards the thing.

He could hear Jamie screaming for him…or was she yelling *at* him? Hell, she was probably yelling at him since that's what she normally did. He didn't have time to worry about her right now. She should have fucking stayed inside. Fuck, why the hell had she come out with him?

He kicked back again. This one actually managed to catch the thing in the nose and he watched as it reeled back with the blow, then some kind of dark goo seemed to flow down the front of her face.

Shit, what the hell is that? Are zombies supposed to be oozing that shit?

He was beginning to think that if he ever got out of this shit, the first thing he was going to do was start watching a long stretch of horror films. He needed to study up on this crap. This thing behind him was taking one hell of a beating to the head, and he thought they were supposed to die with just a little tap. This shit just wasn't right.

"Yeah, and you ain't in no damn movie, either, dumbass," he mumbled to himself as he started hurrying to the other side of the truck. The thing was a little further behind him now, so he could make it without having to kick back.

He reached the expanse on the other side, pushing himself up the second he was clear of the truck. Jaime was there waiting for him, her face stricken with pain. She had her hand out, and they worked together to help him stand.

He was on his feet, looking around for the old man. He didn't see him, but could see there were more of them back on the driver's side of his truck. They weren't getting in over there, but the passenger door also wouldn't be opening any time soon, not until someone did some metal work and busted out the big ol' dent Bobby had put in it three weeks ago. *The damned jackass*, Travis thought briefly as he looked at the dent.

He turned and looked at the old man's car. It was there, and there weren't any of the things around it yet. They had to get moving. They could take the car, but they didn't have his keys.

"Where'd you park?" Travis asked Jaime. When she didn't answer, he turned to look at her. She was backing away from him.

He turned and saw three of the things on the ground, but one of them was walking around the truck toward them. He could see the three of them on the ground were tearing into something, and he couldn't see the old man.

"When the slow one goes down, run faster," he muttered as he was joining Jaime in backpedaling.

"What?"

He turned to her. "Where is your car?"

"Around back."

"Go!"

He turned around. She was in front of him, but wasn't moving fast enough. He needed to go. She needed to get out of his way before he moved her out of the way. He was glad when she started to move faster. Maybe he had a look to him that had gotten her moving. He didn't care. She was moving. It kept him from thinking about what he would have done.

They rounded the front of the caddy, and he was already hurrying to get past her. "Come on!" he growled.

He looked back. They were getting away from the thing. It walked slow and sloppy, and it seemed like chasing them made it even worse. Since it was trying to rush, but not having any balance, it stumbled more and kept having to fight to get some sort of balance.

* * * *

Travis' neck was starting to burn from looking back and forth, plus the jolt of when he fell. With the cuts and scrapes on his arms, it was all starting to wash over him. He was stiff and sore and was tired of continuing to move. Tired and sore, it was painful to look at Jaime when she screamed. A wave of pain from the center of his back up between his shoulder blades forced him to flinch. He saw that Jaime had beat him to the end of the building and had just turned to run around to the back, but had fallen to the ground. Holding onto Nadine, she had no way to cushion her fall, and had landed hard.

"Dammit," he cursed through clenched teeth as he rushed to her. As soon as could see the back of the building, he saw two things making their way to them.

She cried out again, which was mixed with another sound. Travis looked down to see that Jaime was screaming as more pain shot through her, and Nadine had woken up and joined in. Mother and daughter were lying on the ground, screaming, calling out for more of them damn things to come and get them.

He looked down at her, then reached out for her hand. He wanted to get her up off the damned ground so they could get out of there. The things were all coming towards them. He could see down the road was still clear, but then where would they go? That road was a dead end, so there was no way out that way. There was no place they could go.

223

They only had two options…her car or back into the bar.

He pulled her up and she screamed out, biting into his shoulder. A stab of panic raced through him, as he feared she had become one of them. But he had heard her scream, right? It was hard to tell as it was muffled into his shoulder. She was biting down with the pain, and he nearly dropped to his own knees as he was sure she was about to break skin. He pulled her face away from his shoulder and looked into her eyes.

Her blue eyes, though a little hazed over, stared into his own, tears running down her face. He looked around. There were more of them at his truck now. These things were multiplying fast, and the longer they stayed out in the open, the more chance they had that they were going to get eaten like the old man. They had to get inside *something*.

They could try for the car, or they could try for the bar. The car would get them out of there. They would be trapped in the bar for who knew how long. The military should be there soon, right? They had to know about this. Could they wait it out?

If they got in the car, he could just drive away. How long and how far would he have to go to get out of there? She wasn't going to help much. The damn bitch couldn't even cook, and the kid was only going to make it harder.

How far could they get? How far would they need to go to find help? How much gas was in the car? Shit, with how she ran the damn thing, the tank was probably empty and she was driving on fumes until he put some gas in it. She had that habit of trying to see how far she could drive the car until he would go and fill it. When *was* the last time he put gas in?

He wasn't sure. He'd taken his own damn truck here, knowing it had enough gas for at least one more trip to the bar and back.

How far would they need to go to get help? It didn't matter because they didn't have enough gas to get there.

He looked back to the bar and the locked door. The steel reinforced door that was a damn near brick wall when it came to breaking in. There was no way they were going to get through that, and he doubted the people inside even wanted them back in there. That damned pompous cop, that truck driver, the damn college kid… Not a single one of them wanted to let him back in that door.

They could all go fuck themselves. He was going to find a way to get his ass back in there, then he would be safe.

They only had to make it a couple of hours, then the military would swoop in, kill all those zombie assholes, and they would all be okay. They only had a couple of hours to go.

"Everything's going to be fine. Just hold on," he said as he looked at Jaime.

Everything *was* going to be fine. There was no way he was going to let himself die…not here, not now.

CHAPTER 15

"Jason!" He heard the word, but it didn't feel like it was meant for him. He heard it but, while it felt familiar, it just didn't seem like it was for him.

"*Jason*! *Dude*! *Come on*!" the voice said again.

* * * *

Rob watched as Sullivan reached down to the young man who was sitting on the floor, propped back against the kitchen counter, and started to shake him. Rob winced when he heard the loud crack as Jason's head hit the wood, and Rob instinctively started to reach forward to stop him. He didn't have to because Sullivan was already backing away.

"Dammit," he said as he raised himself up and turned back to look at Rob and Bruce, who were both standing in the doorway.

"What the fuck's wrong with him?" Bruce said.

Rob knew there was a tenderness there, but the years on the road had weathered the man, and he was hard to read. He only recognized it as it was. It was the same tenderness his dad had, and Rob had learned how to recognize it long ago. Bruce's warm smile that he had gotten used to had long since vanished, the cheeriness gone. The man that stood in the doorway was a caring man, but he was also a worried man.

Rob looked back at Sullivan. "Something happened to Lucy, I'm guessing. Who is she?" Rob asked.

Jason let out another laugh, this one deep. It turned into a coughing spasm, but then ended with him hunched over, laughing some more. Then he looked back up and was again watching the feed from the security cameras.

When he had seen the old man taken down by three of those things, Rob had stopped trying to watch what was happening outside. He had come back there when they had heard the kid laughing. When they found him, Rob saw what he had been looking at. If he hadn't had the years in Chicago as a hard-nosed beat cop, he didn't think he would have held it together.

One of the things had been at the old man's throat, another one had been biting into his arm. The third had started biting into the old man's good leg.

Rob was glad they were in the kitchen. He was sure that if they were in the other room, they would have been able to hear him screaming. It wasn't easy watching it on the little screen like a silent movie, but if they had to endure hearing it while seeing what was happening… At least with watching the video without the sound, there was a disconnection which made it possible to believe none of this was happening.

"His little sister. He called me up here to watch the bar while he went back to the house to check on her. Something happened to Tina earlier, and they were worried someone might be there to hurt her, I guess. That's what I've been able to figure out from his aunt. She's the other one out there."

"That's his aunt? She's no older than him," Bruce scoffed.

"She's a couple years older, but isn't the responsible one of the family." Sullivan pulled up Jason's face to look him in the eyes. "Come on, man. Wake your ass up before I have to beat the shit out of you. Don't be that guy. Don't be the one who loses it to this shit and gets everyone else killed. Come on, man. You know the story. Get your ass up."

Rob could see Sullivan clenching his fists. It seemed strange that Sullivan was more irritated than concerned by his friend's reaction. Was it because Jason was losing it, disappointing him, or was it that he couldn't seem to get through to the kid?

Rob heard the clinking of glass coming from the other room and turned around to see that Bruce was gone. He had seen the man already have one drink, and guessed he was probably grabbing another. They all had their vices. To be trapped in a bar with all this shit going down was both a blessing and a curse. It sure did make it easy to just want to sit there and drink while the world around them all went to hell.

He really couldn't fault the man for drinking it all away. A part of Rob kept telling him he should do the same. There wasn't any point in fighting it. If they were saved, they were saved. Until then, why not just drink his cares away? Get a drink and throw it back. Why worry about all this shit going down? He couldn't do anything about it anyway.

That was also how men lost themselves and never made it back home. He had his wife and his little boy, Jake, to think about, and he wanted to get back home to them. There was no way he was willing to just leave them without a husband or a father. He needed to get back there for them. If nothing else, he needed one last kiss from his wife. The little peck he gave her that morning was not enough, and he needed that one last hug and ruffle of his son's hair. He needed them, and he wasn't going to let himself fall into some bottle and run the risk that he would not make it back to them.

And this boy had already lost his loved one, the one he probably needed to make the world make sense.

Just what would I do, he thought, *if I didn't have the ones that I love and value so much in my life anymore?*

He would probably be on the floor, too, laughing and losing his mind as the world around him went completely crazy. When he thought about it that way, going crazy and giving up did seem to make sense. Could he see himself being that way? He liked to think of himself as the protector, but could he stay that way without his anchors?

* * * *

"And another one, and another, and another they go. Where they stop, nobody knows. What goes up, doesn't come down. The night is long, without a frown. And the story goes, and the story goes. And Jason couldn't stop laughing, so says the story."

Jason was sitting there, his laughter coming in droves and he just couldn't stop it. Nonsense came to him, then memories. His head was fogged with so many thoughts. It made his head hurt, but with the tumble of thoughts, he just couldn't keep hold of one for too long. They were there, then gone. However, once gone, he had only a fleeting sense of what the memory had been.

230

He thought about Lucy. He remembered watching as she had come out of that window. He didn't know why, but it just made him laugh harder. She had nearly fallen on her face. She, the graceful ballerina, just fell right through that window and straight down. He was surprised she had even been able to stop herself from breaking her nose, but her hand had caught her just in time.

Outside, Mr. Jones, that poor son of a bitch, was being ripped to shreds. Jason had always hated the bastard. He loved watching as they bit and tore right into him. And the three of them looked so funny on the security screens as they tried to get away. Too bad they were in color. Cheesy zombie movies should be watched in black-and-white.

Zombies… Who the fuck ever thought there would actually be zombies? Sullivan had been saying it for so long, but Jason didn't think even he had ever truly believed it would happen. Zombies, just like right out of a fucking horror movie.

Right now, they were in their own damn horror movie, and he knew that he was becoming the one who lost his mind. The one who grew weak, lost his mind, then those guys standing over him were either going to have to kill him or die. Eventually, he was probably going to do something stupid and they were all going to die. They should just kill him now.

That brought another round of laughter, and he could feel his stomach hurting from laughing so much. "One plus one plus two plus one means there are no bullets in the gun," he said and exploded in laughter at the shocked expressions looking down at him.

"Great. Now he's quoting Tim Curry," came a voice that tried to break through the fog. Jason thought he should know who said it. He saw the face that was looking down at him and it seemed so familiar. It was somebody he should know.

"Hey, Tim. How are you today? I'm Jason, and I'm going to get us all killed," Jason said, little giggles coming out between the words as he spoke them.

"Come on, Jason. Snap the fuck out of it," the voice said.

"One plus two plus one, and I'm a sweet transvestite." He heard his voice crackle with laughter. "I said I'm a transvestite."

"Here, son," a deep voice said.

It was more solid than the other voices he had been hearing, and he could actually feel the fog around him clear a little. He could clearly see that there was a new man standing over him. He was a large man, unshaven, and Jason was sure he didn't really know him, but the man was putting something in his hands. It was a small glass, and there was a liquid that swished around inside it. Little droplets splashed over the edge, and Jason could feel the coolness of it as it ran down his hand.

The big man reached out and grabbed both of Jason's hands, steadying them. Then he brought them up to Jason's mouth. He looked up from the glass and saw the man had gotten closer to him so that they were only six inches apart.

Jason had a brief fear the man was going to kiss him, and he giggled at the thought. Not because he wanted it, but because everything was so dreamlike and surreal, he knew none of it could be happening.

"Drink this. Let it clear out some of that darkness. Okay, son? Drink it and feel it burn that stuff away."

Jason just looked into his brown eyes as they looked down at him, and something about that deep voice helped push away more of the fog. He felt himself opening his mouth, and he let the brown liquid rush into him.

And the fire blossomed. It started with his throat, burning an acid trail. He felt the fire reach down into his stomach and his body was suddenly awash with sensation. He sensed the laughter inside of him come to a stop. The world around him became cold and he could feel the tile of the floor under him, the soreness of his ass from sitting there for so long. Pins and needles stabbed deeper into his butt as he started to move around.

Then he felt it in his mind, and it helped to slow the world and thoughts around him. He could feel the fog receding, and the painful thoughts were slowing. He remembered Lucy, and how much he loved her, but she was gone. She was gone, and he still had his mom and his aunt. As long as he stayed calm and smart, he would see his mom again one day. He was definitely smart, and he would make sure Tina made it through all this, as well.

He looked up at the security monitor and saw that the things still had Mr. Jones. Well, he couldn't bring himself to feel any different about that. He still hated that old bastard, but he tried to tell himself he should feel something about him. He *had* known the man.

And what about the baby and the couple. Had they gotten away? He couldn't see them on any of the screens. Where were they?

A loud crash came from the other room and a woman screamed. The things were getting in! He couldn't waste time thinking about what happened to the family. They had to take care of themselves. He had to take care of his *own* family.

Rob and Bruce left the room quickly, and Jason watched as they hurried out. He tried to stand, but he quickly realized that being on the floor like that had not been good. His muscles had turned to jelly and his head, while it had felt like the fog had lifted, had a pain shoot through it when he tried to move. It was a stabbing pain that tried to immobilize him, reminding him he had just been through a hellish battle in his mind and it was not yet ready to do much work. He knew the pain as the type of migraine that always seemed to happen after crying too much, or for taking too short a nap after being exhausted. Not that he had that too often. Oh no, not him, never after dealing with everything with his dad.

"You okay?" Sullivan asked. Jason looked up to see that the big man, his friend for nearly fifteen years and the man who was like a brother to him, was still standing there.

"Yeah, just give me a minute. You should go check and see if they need help."

"I will," Sullivan said, but he wasn't moving.

"Zombies."

"Yeah. Zombies."

"I'm sorry, man. Here was your big thing, and you're stuck here. I'm sorry. I'm just-" Jason let a couple tears fall down his cheek. He looked down to try and hide them.

"Dude, don't. I came to help a friend."

"Yeah," Jason croaked.

"You know, once this is all done…"

"Yeah?"

"We're going to have to do a z-day marathon. *Night of the Living Dead*, original and Savini remake; *Dawn* original; *Day* original; *Shaun of the Dead*. We'll finish it off with *28 Weeks Later*."

Jason looked up, giving Sullivan a glare. By his smile, he saw that Sullivan was teasing him, and it helped. "You know, *28 Weeks Later* is *not* a zombie film. It's an infected film. Zombies don't run."

"There's the horror junkie that I know. Let me help you up."

* * * *

When Jason appeared at the end of the bar and saw what the hell was happening, he could have sworn he had just stepped into a nightmare in motion, and that it just shouldn't be this way. They should be safe, but some fucking asshole had to fuck something up.

At least he wasn't that asshole. Take the win where you can find it.

The nurse, who was the closest to him, was holding the baby, and as Jason approached, he wondered how the baby had gotten back in. It had taken a couple more steps for him to see past the cooler so he could see the rest of the bar.

He could hear the yelling. Men screaming at each other, the grunts of fighting, the cursing. He rounded the corner and stopped short.

The back window, the one too tall for the things outside to have ever gotten close enough to climb through, was shattered. It didn't take long for Jason to figure out how it had happened. There was a large rock sitting in a fresh dent in the pool table. Glass was scattered in little shards all across the top of the table, and the floor was covered in the larger pieces.

Travis, who had thought he had been so damned smart, was trying to crawl through the window. Jason couldn't see how he was managing it, but he could see the asshole wasn't alone. Hands from inside *and* outside were around him, trying to pull him to one side or the other. He must have been standing on something, but whatever it was, it was wide enough that they didn't have a clear reach of him.

The hands reaching for him from the outside were pale and grey. The hands had deep, dark gashes, but there was no blood. They were dead hands.

Rob and Bruce were at the window, trying to pull the damned redneck into the bar. What the hell were they thinking? He had been out there. Who knows what kind of exposure he had. He could be changing. Had they never seen a zombie movie?

At least Sullivan had some sense. He had hurried out of the kitchen and was screaming at them to push him back out. He had grabbed one of the pool cues and was using it too swat away at the hands.

Then the redneck slid into the room. They had helped him in and were now helping him over to a corner and away from the things. Sullivan stayed at the window, slashing down at the hands, trying to keep them from getting any grip.

Jason turned and saw that Tina was in a dark corner away from the light that filtered in through the now broken window. She sat there, her knees pulled to her chest, crying.

He knew she was thinking about Lucy.

His aunt wasn't that much older than him and they had grown up almost as brother and sister. He had always been lapping at her heals, following her around. When she had been a teenager and had sleepovers, he would always "visit" his grandparents' house and just kind of hang out there until it was too late for him to ride his bike home and he would have to stay the night.

He remembered it was often during their sleepovers that he first started to watch horror films. Her and her girlfriends would rent a bunch of movies and take over the living room, spending all night with popcorn and horror flicks. They would try to scare each other with the lights off then, at the end of it all, they would all do each other's hair and call it a night. Of course, he would hide for most of it, then would leap out at them whenever it was a scary moment in the film. She would come screaming at him and chase him back to the kitchen where his grandparents would be playing cards or reading books.

They would just smile at him, give him some fresh popcorn, and send him back in there to make peace.

Before he and Sullivan had started watching horror films, it had been him, her, and her friends. They had never been much into zombie films. That would come later when he and Sullivan would watch movies together. No, the girls would watch slasher films. They had seen all the *Sleepaway Camp* movies, all the *Friday* movies, and would often find the B-movies that no one had ever heard of.

She was in her own horror movie now and, like him, she wasn't holding together well. He needed to go over to her and help her.

He knew he would always help her. She was his big sister. Maybe not by birth, but she was. Even though he was younger, he knew it would be up to him to help her. He had to take care of her now. He didn't have Lucy anymore. He had to take care of what he still *did* have.

Jason looked back to see Rob yelling at him. Jason hadn't even realized he had zoned out again, and the sounds of everything around him suddenly came screaming back.

* * * *

Rob had heard the crash, and he hadn't hesitated. Instinct pushed him past the large truck driver, who barely had enough time to turn to the side. He cringed at the rudeness of brushing the man into the door frame, and knew he would be apologizing for it later…if there *was* a later. Those things outside and the sounds of crashing glass didn't leave him with much hope.

His hand lingered at his left side, still hesitating over where his sidearm should be…if he was on duty.

Damn, he wished he had brought it, and damn the courthouse for not allowing it.

Yeah, and damn him for not getting that tire fixed and forgetting his cell phone. There were a lot of things that he sure wished he could change for the day.

As his hand lingered on his left hip, it twitched with the desire to be feeling the familiar cold steel. Not having it made him feel like he did when he took off his wedding ring to do housework. There was just something about not having it that made the weight in that hand feel off and his whole body feel off-center. He knew it was more about the feeling of going into a dangerous situation and not having the weapon he had gotten accustomed to.

When he first heard the sound, he had expected the front window to be broken. He had to stop himself as he had been turning to run in that direction. The front window was fine, though. No broken glass. As he scanned the bar, none of the windows or any of the bottles were broken.

He heard a scream from behind him, "You're not getting in here until the child is in here first. You fucking bastard. You're just leaving her to die!"

The sound was from the back of the bar. He hurried back there, dodging around the big man again as he had been trying to hurry back there. The truck driver moved quickly for his size, jumping back as he hurried past.

Rob moved past him and hurried to the end of the bar. He saw Travis forcing his baby through the window, nearly throwing her at the nurse. The woman was actually blocking Travis from getting in until he did, and with how he had to reach to get his body close to the frame, he had to have been standing on something.

Denise had the baby, and Rob quickly moved around her. He couldn't remember the last time he had felt this limber. Somehow he was moving as though he didn't have pain from his accident, although he was sure it would come back to pound at him later.

"You better fucking let me in there!" Travis snapped at them.

Rob reached out and grabbed the man's hands. He could see that Travis had somehow managed to climb into the dumpster and was swaying on bags of garbage to get the height he needed to reach the window, but it didn't allow him enough height to climb in on his own. The redneck had been trying. His hands were cut and there were droplets of blood all over his hands and the bottom window frame. He must have tried to pull himself in the window right after he broke it, and the nurse had obviously been preventing him.

"Where's your wife?" Rob asked. His grip was slick and it was hard to hold on. The man kept swaying and losing his balance, and Rob had to fight just to keep him from falling out of the dumpster. Rob wasn't sure he could pull the man in by himself, but he wasn't going to if there was a chance they could save the wife. They weren't just going to leave her out there.

Travis looked over his shoulder at what was the only car parked in the back lot of the bar. Rob wondered why. He guessed that must have been the guy's wife's car, but-

Then he saw the bloody handprint. It wasn't easy to read and, in the dim light of the late afternoon, it could barely be seen, but the glint around it made it visible once you stared at it. It was on the driver's side door, and now he could see another one on the windshield. Someone had been attacked as they had neared the car, and their blood-covered hands had tried to hold onto the smooth, ungraspable surface of the glass.

"I was holding the kid, and she had the keys. The things got her. Now, please, help me. You got the kid. Do you want to say 'I told you so'? Do I need to beg?" The man sounded like he was near tears.

Rob had the guys arm. He was trying to pull him in, but the man wasn't helping. What the hell was wrong with him? But the man wasn't looking at Rob. He was looking at Denise.

Rob turned to look at her, but her eyes were locked on the man outside. There was a cold fire that burned there, something he hadn't seen in her before, and something he didn't think she knew she could feel until just now. Her eyes were burning into the man's soul and she saw something there that Rob wasn't sure he would ever know. He felt the grip on his arm loosen.

Rob turned back and saw one of the things coming around from the side of the bar, around from where the man's wife had been. It was covered in blood and gore, and as it stumbled forward, he could see that fresh blood was still dripping down from what was left of its jaw. Half the man's face was missing, kind of like it was blown off with a shotgun.

Another one rounded the corner behind the first one, then another one followed.

Rob reached out and noticed another pair of hands joining his own. "Come on. Get your ass in here. Those things are getting closer," Rob yelled.

"Come on. We'll grab ya," Bruce said. They were both talking over each other, trying to soothe the man into trusting them.

When the redneck turned and saw what they were looking at, he had no reservations. He nearly jumped into their arms and, as soon as Rob could feel his weight leaning in, he pulled back. He didn't so much hear the crack as he felt it and his right side collapsed from under him. Pain stabbed through him, and he had to fight harder to not give into it. His leg was trying to buckle. Electricity ran in a torrent of constant pain and his toes curled and his shoulders collapsed in on him.

He didn't know how he kept from falling. It probably had more to do with his grip on Travis than him being able to stand on his own leg. He remained firm, and they were able to pull the man up until he put one foot on the windowsill, and the other on the glass-covered floor.

"No, get him out of here. He's been exposed. He's probably turning. You can't let him in here!" Rob heard the bartender yelling. He turned to see the man…what was his name? Rob was pretty sure it was Surly or Sandy, or something like that…come rushing over to them. He ran right up to the redneck and pushed him, forcing him back out the window.

Travis fell back, stumbling in the dumpster. His feet failed him, and he fell amongst the bags of garbage.

Rob heard the man sobbing and he tried to feel some form of compassion for him. It wasn't easy. He had seen how much of an asshole he was. He truly seemed to only care about himself. If Rob did help him in, would he just screw them all over to save himself? Look at what happened to both his wife and the old man. They were both dead out there because they had been dumb enough to listen to that idiot. Leaving like that without any real plan or fully evaluating the situation was just ignorant.

Rob didn't have to turn and look to hear the little soft sounds of the baby. The man had saved his baby, so maybe there was something in there was worth saving.

Travis pulled himself back up. He had struggled, slipping once and falling forward against the front of the dumpster before he was able to steady himself enough to get his hands out again. Rob could see he was about to grab the glass frame of the window, so he reached out and grabbed him. Bruce also reached out again and they heaved up and pulled him in.

"We need to get something to close this window," Bruce said as Rob eased Travis to the floor.

Rob stood and they both looked at the pool table. It was too big, too heavy, and there was no way to use it. Maybe they could use the felt cover, though. Was a pool table something they could break apart and just use the top? The damn thing was huge and it looked like it was pretty sturdy. Maybe they could get it taken apart with a screwdriver and a few hours' work, but would it be strong enough to hold? Rob didn't think so, and they didn't have hours to wait while they worked on it, either. The things outside weren't going to give them that much time.

There was a loud smashing sound, and Rob looked up to see hands at the window. They weren't tall enough to really reach inside, and they didn't seem to have figured out how to climb yet, but they were trying to pull themselves up. Who was to say that, eventually, they wouldn't just climb over each other, then climb through the window?

Out of the corner of his eye, Rob saw motion and turned to see that Jason had come around to the end of the bar. He was the owner's kid. He should know if they have anything they could use. Maybe there was an extra door in back, or maybe they could start taking down the bathroom doors and putting them across the back window. Those doors were light, though. He didn't think they would hold any better than the top of the pool table.

"Kid, do you have any wood? Anything we can use to cover the window?"

He didn't seem to notice him, though. He was turned away from Rob and was looking at his… Who was that? His sister? Rob knew the boy had lost his younger sister. This one was probably his older sister and she wasn't holding up that well, either. No, wait. Hadn't they said something about an aunt?

His heart wanted to calm himself and try to take it easy on the boy, but there just wasn't time. He quickly rushed across the room until he was close to the boy's face and yelled the question again.

"Yeah," he finally heard the boy's soft voice say. It was just a croak, but Rob was sure that with how the boy was just holding on, it was all he could manage. And here Rob was, treating him like shit.

But lives needed to be saved, and he had to save them. Right? That's what his job was. To play the hero and save everyone, to save humanity.

And he was ready to quit.

"Yeah, what?!"

"There are boards in back, by the cooler. We use them to set up the buffet over the pool table."

Rob rushed past him.

* * * *

"Hush, little baby, don't you cry. Momma's going away, so you don't die." Denise was singing in a low voice as she rocked the baby on her shoulder. The child had been screaming and wailing when the window had first broken, and that asshole was just going to leave her out there. Denise saw it in his eyes.

The damn man. She knew how bad he had always been. He was one of the many she suspected beat their wives, but she had never been able to prove it, and Jaime was always a firecracker. Between Travis and Jaime, Denise had always felt like the chances of Nadine growing up abused, beaten, and mentally scarred was a near certainty. That was if the child had even gotten a chance to grow up at all.

Something about the couple had Denise always thinking as though they were the type that would allow something bad to happen to their child, then claim someone had kidnapped her. She couldn't be sure of it, but it all fit. They were that type. Two parents who should never have had kids because they cared too much about their own skins to care about anyone else.

244

When Travis had been trying to come through the window, he hadn't been bringing the baby in first. The baby was at his feet, and Travis was trying to push himself up into the window. The precious child was barely kept from being trampled on as he kept shifting and changing position. She was nearly crushed by garbage bags and the man was only worried about his own skin and getting himself in through the window.

Denise had hurried over, grabbed a pool cue, and pointed it right at his face. "You're not getting in here without that baby coming in first."

How could she let him in? When she looked at him and the baby, the baby was barely awake and just reaching around in the cute way that baby's did. Her eyes weren't even open, and her mouth was opening and closing, as if she was looking for dinner.

How could this man really be that blind and that uncaring? It didn't matter. If the baby wasn't getting in there, she sure wasn't going to let *him* in, either.

The man looked at her with hateful eyes. She could see he wanted to hurt her. He was standing there, not reaching for the baby. No, he was actually *thinking* about it. He was trying to think about the chances of climbing in, overpowering her, and beating her with the pool cue. She could see the anger. The furrowing of his brow, the intensity in the gaze, the way his pupils dilated at just the thought of violence, and the set of his jaw. He was preparing himself for a fight.

Then something collapsed under him and his height to the window shortened considerably, nearly losing his balance. He was swaying, stepping back and forth, flailing as he tried to right himself. Denise watched as the dumpster swayed and she could see the child starting to slide. The little girl, the baby who had no idea of the danger around her, gave out a slight giggle as she started to slide down, closer to his feet.

Denise's heart flew into her throat and it hurt to swallow back the lump. She stepped forward, reaching out, but she knew it was no good. The farthest she could stretch without cutting her stomach on the large glass shards around the edge of the window was still a good three feet away, and even if she was to clear out the window or cut herself on it, she could see she would still be way too far away.

Travis recovered, and turned back to Denise. His eyes were wide and pleading. He must have realized that now, with whatever had broken under him, he couldn't get through the window on his own. Now he was going to need help.

She wasn't moving. Her glare stayed firm and she continued to hold the pool cue to the point where its tip was just reaching the tip of his nose. He could stare down its long shaft into her dark, cold green eyes.

She watched as he quickly bent down to grab the little angel and then extended his arms, the baby held out for her. Her glare didn't soften, but she reached out, careful to set the cue carefully to the side as she shifted her weight. She couldn't stand that this man had actually weighed the options before saving his own daughter. She gently took the baby, keeping herself at the edge of his reach. Then once she had her, she turned her back on him.

"Come on! Help me!" he cried out, but she didn't listen. She vaguely watched as Rob and Bruce ran to help the man in. Then she watched as they raced to fix something to put over the window.

None of that really mattered to her now. The baby was with her again. No one was going to harm her.

"Hush, little baby, don't you cry, and it will be all right," she sang.

CHAPTER 16

Hammond, Illinois, was a small stop far enough away from any of the interstates, it was lost in a tangled web of country highways. In its early days, it had been a thriving town which had grown quickly. While there was gold out west, Hammond quickly became known for its coal.

Originally known and christened as "Hardscrabble" because the ground was hard, it hadn't taken long after its founding to get railroad lines to reach there. First, a train station had been put in and, being just south of Chicago, it allowed quick access for the town to quickly grow. Railroad companies were quick to invest and built up the town and the railways, and the town quickly became a crossroads in the Midwest.

The town grew quickly, stores and houses were built, and families fled there in flocks. It was a little heaven so close to Chicago that someone who wanted to start a new life and get away from the big city could move to the promised prosperity. "Come to Hammond and mine for coal". In the time of the great depression, a town offering jobs was in short supply.

At first, the coal was plentiful, but it was soon discovered that the deposits were not as plentiful as people first thought. Within five years, the coal mines were running dry, which led to the industry dying away. As it left the town, another one rose in its place. Manufacturing plants that first opened to use the bi-products of the coal had flourished in the town. Once the coal was gone, the plants found new ways to continue. However, without their core source for cheap and readily available resources, many of them were shut down and abandoned.

Glass production quickly moved into the first of the abandoned factories. Soon, Hammond was known as the leading glass production town, with other available plants being taken over. As Hammond Glass expanded, named after the owner, John Hammond, the town was soon renamed, as he was thought of as the savior of what would have otherwise been a town lost to the crumbling coal industry.

Hammond was the "Little Chicago of the Midwest". It was much smaller, but to many of the small towns around it, it was just large enough for the title. Having a larger police force, due to more crime, rowdier crowds, more drugs, seedier bars, and the stoplights, people were used to thinking of it as a dangerous place. However, most city people, people not from small towns, would laugh at the nickname. Those that actually *were* from small towns would understand that the more crime-ridden towns were easy to associate with the larger ones.

Having fallen by the wayside of necessity, being that the glass industry was not as needed and not as dependent on one location, Hammond was never again popular enough to have major roads routed near or through there. It was left as the merging point for two old highways that, more often than not, seemed forgotten when it came time for upgrades and repairs.

* * * *

250

Bernard set his tablet down and looked at the two other scientists that were in the Hummer with them. Sarah was in the front seat, looking through documents of her own. Lindsey, a much older scientist, who often could be found hiding Hershey bars in the pockets of her lab coat and was always talking about how she was on a diet to lose the many extra pounds she carried, took up much of the seat next to him. He had worked with her before and, although it was hard to tell with her completely covered in the protective suit they were all wearing, he knew her hair was silver-streaked with a few strands of what her original hair color was. He was sure she still had it back in a ponytail.

He turned and looked out the window. The town was definitely not what he had expected. It was a small shithole. Yeah, there was a shopping complex that looked like there had once been a town trying to build itself up but, overall, most the buildings were old and falling down. They had put in a couple of fast food joints, but it seemed like the town was mainly bars and churches.

And where the hell were the people? It was the latter part of the afternoon, the sun was getting ready to set, and there was no one around? No one headed home from work, or was trying to race home to get ready to go out for the evening? He had seen a couple of churches, but no one had been on their way to a mass. The gas stations didn't have anyone getting gas.

It was like it a ghost town.

"Little Chicago, eh?" he said as he looked up at the stoplight they had stopped at. The light was red, but he looked down both side streets and didn't see anyone coming. *Yeah, because the traffic is so heavy we need to sit here*, he thought.

"Did you see the cars parked at the department store back there?" Lindsey commented, her voice bubbly, as she always had the tendency to become whenever she was nervous.

"No, why? Were there actually people shopping?"

"No. They were parked in front of the store…oddly. I think a couple of them were squad cars, but not at all how you would expect them to be parked."

"How so?"

"Well, it was like they were parked in front of the store, blocking off access."

Now that was interesting. Maybe there *was* something happening here. But why here? What could be happening?

This was BFE, so what could be here, and when had it started? Had something been spreading here for a while and it only just now got noticed? The military had been quick to act. Did they have some hidden base here? If so, he would have thought the general would have told them about something going on, would have given them information they needed to know. The general actually seemed to give the impression he thought all of this was nothing and they wouldn't even find anything. Was it possible it was something even *he* wasn't briefed on?

Could it be aliens? Holy shit! Some kind of alien infection? That's why the military responded so quickly. They had seen it come down. Once again, though, why hadn't the general been briefed?

"Dr. Demoin, how was it that the general was able to get his troops deployed so fast? Don't you find it funny we are here almost right after the initial call, but the troops are set up already?" Bernard asked.

Sarah looked up from her folder and looked back at him. He could see it was hard for her to move around in the large protective suit, but she was able to somehow turn and he could see her face through the plastic. Was that a tear in the corner of her eye? Was she crying? Why? Was there something else they weren't telling him?

"It just happened to be near an armory, I guess, and the National Guard was there on a week-long drill. Not all of them, just some. They were able to get here quickly."

"Really? No secret military base or testing?"

Bernard saw the driver snicker. Sarah saw it, too, then looked back at the scrawny little scientist sitting next to the larger one in the back.

"Not that I'm aware of. Doesn't mean no, but I haven't been told anything."

The light turned green and they started to move forward, making their way through town. Bernard wasn't sure why the troops were driving so damned slow, but it seemed like they almost enjoyed the slowest possible speed to get there. He guessed it could have something to do with the suits. He imagined it wasn't easy driving with all the additional plastic surrounding your already bulky uniform.

Still, he wished they would just hurry up.

* * * *

Corporal Thompson saw the brake lights light up on the rear of the trailer in front of him, and watched as the large vehicle started to ease itself to the right of the road. He could barely see around it, but could see the little parking lot the truck was working towards. It was such a small lot, and it didn't even

253

look like it was fully asphalted as there was as much gravel there as hard-packed rock.

"Shit," he muttered. He was glad the large suit he had on, plus his radio being muted, kept him from being heard by any of the scientists in the vehicle. He had been listening to them, though. They were making little comments, wondering if there was a military base around. Of course they would blame the military. It's *always* the military.

Was it the *military* who invented the science behind the nuclear bomb? Was it the *military* who invented biological weapons? It was always scientists behind it all. And what about all the projects that never started with military funding, but had some crazy scientist behind it? Sure, the military wasn't perfect, he was sure there were many things hidden and being worked on, but if anything was happening, it was probably scientists behind it.

Corporal Thompson had seen how the lead scientist kept her folder open to one particular page, how she kept looking down at the picture of a scrawny man in a lab coat. It was obvious the doctor knew him. He couldn't tell if she was close to him or not, but she still let a tear fall here and there.

Yeah, that doctor had probably been doing something, and now they all had to come in and clean it up, although the area really didn't look like an area some well-funded scientist would be doing some kind of experiments. He imagined a large block building with high security, but that also meant nice housing complexes. This town had none of that. He had seen a nice house here and there but, all in all, this town didn't have any of the signs of prosperity he would have expected to see. Instead, the town just looked normal, like any other Midwestern town…except for the fact there were no people running around.

So if it wasn't a scientist's experiment gone wrong, just what the hell was going on in this town?

Whatever it was, he had no damned clue. The town was dead, eerily dead, in the way that made him think of old westerns. Tumbleweeds should be drifting across the street, and it felt like he would be seeing a gunslinger coming out at any time to block their path.

Whoa, where did *that* mental image come from? He couldn't place it, though it still felt right. The town was empty and the air was still, not even a breeze bristled through the trees. All of it just wasn't right, and he felt like there was something behind what he could see, some presence that was getting ready to attack them.

He wasn't psychic, though he had once served with a man who had him question his own beliefs. He never would allow himself to believe in witchy mumbo jumbo, but this man just always seemed to know things. They had been on patrol in Afghanistan, and that man knew they were walking straight into an ambush. Thompson didn't know how, but he had just known the bomb was there. That soldier had saved all of them, except for himself.

Maybe it was a close to death thing. Thompson hadn't known the sergeant well because he had been new to serving overseas. He had heard stories about the man before they went on patrol, but had never known him. However, he had sacrificed himself to save them.

What had been his name? He remembered so much about him, like that long scar along his forehead. It was a deep, indented mark, greyed as though the skin around it had never quite healed properly. What was the man's name? He had those dark, piercing eyes that would stare into you, freezing your insides with a frosted glare. Dammit. What was his name?!

He couldn't remember. When he tried, all he saw were those eyes. They had been the last thing he had seen of the man as he had pleaded with Thompson to get out of there. Those eyes… Not the glaring, dark globes that chilled soldiers into submission, but fierce, pained eyes that pushed Thompson to listen. He had, and he had survived.

And now he felt something and it made him wonder if this was what that sergeant had? He couldn't be sure what it was. The feeling that festered at the back of his stomach and grew stronger as they drove through the town. He could feel it swim inside him like something had come alive. It squirmed inside of him and burned as it slithered, a fire coursing through his veins and setting his nerves on end, the snake of that presence worming, tunneling its way through him and leaving an icy chill in its wake.

The feeling in his stomach was starting to turn into a lead weight as he saw the semi pull into a tiny lot. He knew his vehicle couldn't fit in there with it so, while he didn't like it, he had to park on the street, leaving his vehicle exposed and leaving them a farther distance from the doctor's office than he would have liked. This wasn't a good tactical position, but they really didn't have much choice.

He parked the vehicle and looked at the small building that he had heard was the only doctor's office in town. It was small and quaint, and had that small town feel to it. It sure did fit in with being a small town doctor's office; however, as the spawn of some deadly evil virus, he just couldn't see it. Whatever they were there for, that couldn't be it, but maybe the point was that it was so unassuming. Who would ever expect the heart of evil to be found in the body of something seemingly so innocent?

The building seemed so homey and welcoming. He could see why the sick would feel comfortable going there. It didn't feel modern, but he didn't think those that came there really cared. It felt like a place to go when you needed to feel better. It was a little building, surrounded by bushes, with a large picture window in front. It had a nice amount of shade from the trees around it, and was tucked back and kept in the dark.

Maybe that was it. Maybe the whole damned town had turned into vampires, all hiding away from the sun. The rational part of him wanted to laugh at the idea. The setting sun made the other part, the part that was home to a person's irrational fears, want to grab every weapon he had available and prepare to fight their way out of there.

He didn't feel watched, though. He didn't feel like the presence was watching them, but that it was there, waiting. They were already in its web. It felt their vibrations as they traveled along the strands. It didn't have to watch them. It already knew they were there.

* * * *

Corporal Thompson climbed out of the vehicle just as the scientists were getting out. There were three scientists, him, and his small platoon. Not that many, but as they were just there to see if there was anything to the phone call, the general wasn't going to send too many. It shouldn't be needed. At the first sign of trouble, they were to clear out. They were only to establish what was going on and if the call was legitimate. Though, to

257

Thompson, that seemed damn foolish to be thinking that now, seeing as they had already quarantined the town. Establish, confirm, and report. The scientists would do their work, then the corporal was to make his report.

They would all go from there.

His troops started to form in a line in front of the building. Most were already doing their weapons check, and were checking their fellow team members for any suit malfunctions or other problems that could have happened in transport. He would check in with them in a minute.

He was glad to see the other Hummer had swung around the truck and parked on the other side of it, blocking that side street and preventing any traffic from coming through.

He walked over to the doctor in charge and clicked the little switch in his suit to unmute his radio. "Doctor Demoin?"

The woman turned from looking at the large semi to look at him. She didn't look happy, and every time he saw her look at the truck, he had a feeling it was a large reason as to why. He was again taken with how attractive she was under that suit. He had noticed her before she had put the large suit on. Now, as he could see her sparkling blue eyes, he saw the rest of her standing there, easily imagining the suit as not even being there. However, those eyes still looked like they wanted to drill daggers into his own.

From what he understood, it wasn't what was called for in their protocols. It had been thrown together rather hastily to facilitate their needs. The fact it had been put together quickly out at Fort Leonard Wood and they had driven straight there, with much of the prep-work being done en route, probably didn't fill the doctor with confidence.

He guessed he understood her disappointment. He would have assumed they would have had something better than this already prepared and ready to go. Maybe they do, just not in the area. Maybe it was already in use, and something else was happening somewhere else. Who the hell knows? He just knew that the truck and trailer were the best they had now, and it was what they had to work with.

"Yes. Hello, sergeant. We'll check inside and get everything set up. Check with your troops and we'll let you know when we get things online."

"Yes, ma'am, but it's corporal, ma'am. Once we get on the radio, you'll confuse everyone if you give me a promotion and start calling me sergeant."

She blinked at him for a second and then, as it seemed to register, she nodded. "Okay. We'll set up. Get your troops ready."

"Yes, ma'am."

He went over to his troops, starting to call out the orders for them to line up, breaking them into two teams of three. One was to establish the perimeter around the building, the other was to set up a basic base of operations outside of the semi to set up communication and report their progress to the outside. He knew it wouldn't take long. It was just going to be a simple camp with no tents, just equipment. He hoped the scientists would get their crap together fast so they could get into the building and find out what they were looking at.

He watched his men hurry off, quick to their tasks, then turned to watch the scientists. The semi was one of those used for moving, so it had two of what looked like standard-sized doors on the side of the trailer. Corporal Thompson wasn't sure how it looked inside, but he watched as the scientists walked up the ramp that lead to the rear side door and disappeared inside.

* * * *

Sarah entered the darkened lab and quickly went around to find the lights in the trailer that the army had so graciously put together for them based upon her specifications. She found a switch and flipped it on. In a stutter, fluorescent lights flickered, the cool green flare of light attacked along the walls and hummed to life. She saw the lab that, while she had participated in the design, she had not been part of building. Since she had seen the truck, she had been skeptical about it.

Surprise ran through her as the lights around her came up to full power. She stood there, her mouth threatening to drop to the trailer floor. No, wait. It wouldn't hit the wooden floor of the trailer because it was covered. The whole inside of the trailer was coated, but what was that? She quickly moved out of the way to allow her team into the small workspace. She had to hand it to the military. It was clean, put together well, and was a way for the lab to be set up in any trailer. No wonder it was able to be brought on site in so little time.

She looked around, thinking that it was not only practical, but beautiful. It was near seamless.

In front of her was a five foot long Plexiglas table on the far wall. Mounted onto the table was a laptop. She guessed it was a seventeen inch by the way it seemed to tower over the rest of the mounted racks. She guessed it was so large to allow them to monitor the soldiers outside and watch their live video feed.

Further down was the lab equipment, fastened onto the table. There were holes with fastenings for test tubes,

260

microscopes and the centrifuge were near each other. Everything was designed to be turned on and ready to go.

And what made it all work was that it was all a part of a portable shell, which made sense. She could see underneath the clear interior shell, how the struts were into the bottom so that it could be forklifted straight into the back of the trailer without any crafting. Everything, except the chairs, was attached to the shell, including the lights and table. Looking around, she noticed that the chairs seemed to be absent.

Well, seeing as she hadn't thought about that when she had developed the design, why should someone else have thought about it?

Still, it was clean, functional, and made her feel like she had just walked into an Apple store. It had such a high tech and futuristic feel to it that it put her lab back in Atlanta to shame.

She looked at the other room in the lab. The front room was separated from them by a short hallway. Both rooms were divided and, in a traditional lab, the equipment above the hallway would never have been seen. Though past it was what her eyes locked onto. The operating table was able to be seen from where she stood. There was no privacy, but everything was completely in the open. The table, like everything else, was mounted to a part of the structure around her. It was beautiful.

She could see that the top of the hallway contained a large collection of tubes and a large metal box-shaped machine. It didn't look anything like what it was. It looked so small and simple, almost like an industrial air conditioner. She felt a smile cross her lips. Who would have thought that this little machine, with all the tubes that ran down the hallway, was the key that allowed them to go from the other room and get sanitized and cleansed so they would be safe to enter back into this main lab area? She knew how it worked, but it was the first time she had seen it.

In a way, it was something ugly that marred the view of the beautiful lab she was standing in, but it was still beautiful in her eyes.

She heard the sound of keystrokes and turned to see that Bernard had already gone to the computer and was getting them online.

"We're online," the younger, scrawny-looking scientist said, loud through the headset incorporated into their suits. She nodded to him and walked over. It was time for the show to go live.

* * * *

"System is up, corporal. Whenever you're ready, you have the go," came the crackling female voice over his radio.

"Roger, doctor. Over and out."

Corporal Thompson clicked off his radio and looked at the set-up they had situated on the hood of the Hummer. The engine still clicked and, in the quiet of the town around him, it seemed loud. He had already checked in and the general hadn't been happy with how slow they were going. He wanted results and he wanted them fast. He didn't want to hear that they had only just now set up their initial base.

"Alpha team, parameter status?" he said through their local team channel.

"Perimeter secured. Back door is open. We think we can hear something inside, but cannot confirm until entry. Over."

"Affirmative. I'm on my way back. Over," Thompson said, then looked over his shoulder, having to turn slightly to see

262

the remaining three troops walking around the lab. The men stood there, keeping an eye on both directions of the main street.

"Beta team, keep the perimeter secure. Back us up if need be. Over."

"Corporal?" came a questioning voice.

He wasn't sure which one of his troops was coming through the channel, but he understood their fear. Most of these guys were still early recruits. It was not his first choice of a team, with only PFC Baldwin ever having seen even the slightest bit of action overseas. Even then, it barely counted as Baldwin had only been over there for a few weeks before he got called back.

"Come in only if we call for you. Over."

"Yes, corporal. Over."

Corporal Thompson hurried around to the back of the doctor's office.

* * * *

He reached his three men at the back of the doctor's office. One was near the door, crouched low, his rifle pointed into the dark office. The other two men were facing their rear, keeping any eye out for anything that might be coming from behind. It was a smart tactical move, but something a soldier would expect to see more of they were deployed, not on U.S. soil. It meant something had them spooked.

He hurried up to them and the two guards watching their back seemed to relax slightly in his presence.

"We keep hearing something pounding around inside, corporal. We've called out, but no one has answered. Everything's dark."

He could see how dark it was as he neared. The end of
the hallway, that fake wood paneling, drifted into a shadowed
darkness that seemed to grow into a black void the further it
went. With the sun getting lower behind him, and the house
behind them casting its long shadow over them, it made the
depths of the hallway disappear. And those damn suits they had
on didn't allow them to equip themselves with night vision.

Great design flaw, he thought.

He could hear the pounding coming from inside. It
wasn't regular, but there was definitely something thumping and
pounding into one of the walls. It sounded like somebody
pounding on a door, but he couldn't be sure. If they were lucky,
it was just someone trapped and pounding to get out. However,
they couldn't afford to think that way. Maybe they would get
lucky and find someone who could shed some light on just
where in the hell everyone was in this damn town.

A tendril of a chill slithered its way through his spine
and he could feel it reaching down to tie a small knot in his
stomach.

"Okay. Sidney, you stay here and watch our backs.
Christian and Westdale, you follow behind."

Thompson looked back into the hallway. He reached in
and flicked the light on, hoping it would illuminate their path.
Nothing.

"Lights on," he called back as he attached the flashlight
to the top of his rifle.

He looked back at his men. He hoped he wasn't
showing them how nervous he felt, but they knew he was
stalling.

Okay, well, there was no more putting this off.

"Time to go to work," he said through his radio, then he switched it over to the open channel so the doctor and the other team could listen in.

"We're going in."

"Okay, cameras are hot. If you see it, we'll see it," came the female voice through his radio.

"Roger."

* * * *

Thompson made it to the end of the hallway, listening as the pounding grew louder. His chest hurt from listening to it, and it painfully fluttered to match the beat of the growing song. The rhythm was growing even as they stepped down the hallway. It would pound, pause, then pound again. It was like whatever was pounding would stop briefly to listen, then it would pound again.

"Hello? Is anyone in here?" he called out as they reached the end of the hallway where it split into two pathways. It felt like the darkness just absorbed his voice. It just fell away, and he could imagine no one had heard it. But the hallway had gone quiet. The pounding had stopped. He checked quickly to make sure he had keyed on his external mic.

The hallway was quiet. He could only hear the sound of his air filter as it recycled his breaths. Then, every so often, there was the hiss as excess air emptied from the tanks and the air processing cycle started again.

They all stopped and stood there, listening.

"Okay. Christian and Westdale, you go to the left. I'll head to the right. Go to the end and turn up. Make visual contact with me before we start the sides."

265

He was going alone. He could have sent one of them, but a good leader didn't send a man alone, unless he was willing to go himself. *None* of them should be going alone, but they needed results and he didn't have any choice. That didn't mean he would blindly take them into danger, but he had to play a little fast and loose with caution to get the job done. It wasn't much worse than when he fought in Afghanistan, but he knew to always keep an eye on his six, as well as the other guys. Would his men really know to follow that here?

The tendril of worry that had worked its way into his stomach expanded and he could feel a twang of pain as it was twisting through his intestines. He wondered just what it would be like to puke into his own suit. How bad would that festering smell be? He wouldn't be able to open and release it or he would expose himself. He would be trapped with the stench of his own vomit. And that wouldn't be too great of an example for his troops, would it?

He took the first step down the right side. It didn't look like it went too far. It would only be about three long steps down the hallway, then it turned into another hallway to the left. There was a closed door leading off to the right.

He took another small step forward. Counting his steps, three long and six short, he cautiously eased his foot forward. Maybe it was habit, maybe it was his desire not to take too much for granted, but his movements were reminiscent of when he was deployed and had to move cautiously, looking for tripwires. He moved slowly, his eyes constantly moving. If it even looked like a shadow moved, he glared in that direction and watched until he was satisfied that it was nothing.

"Stay calm," he mumbled, trying to convince himself that his racing heart was just because of the excitement of seeing some action again.

"What, corporal?" he heard over the radio. He couldn't tell which one had asked, but he knew it was one of the ones in there with him. He hadn't meant to mumble on an open channel. Damn. He'd have to remember to keep his mic muted.

"Reminding you guys to stay calm. Don't get jumpy," he said, as much to himself as them. Maybe giving the order would allow him to follow it, as well.

"Yes, corporal."

He took another step forward. The little glow from his flashlight reached the end of the hallway, but was barely able to show him much. His feet were lost somewhere below him. Anything could be down there and reaching out to grab him.

Another chilled tendril ran down his spine, this one making him shiver.

He reached the end of the hallway, wishing the pounding would return because, somehow, the silence was worse. The silence allowed for his thoughts to run wild, thinking about everything that could be there which he couldn't see. The hands reaching for him from behind, the snake-like arms reaching from the darkness below… They were the soldiers he had killed in action, the enemy he had stared in the face, and the ones who returned from his nightmares each night as he watched the light fade from their eyes.

All his nightmares, all the people from his past were there. He could feel them in that darkness. The ghosts of his past were there. All of them were there for him. They all wanted to take him with them, to become a part of them.

He reached for the handle of the door and let his hand just hover over it.

Come on, Jake. Get your head in the game, he thought, trying to scream it at himself through the clutter. *Get those memories pushed back down. Take those nightmares from the recesses that they hide in and get rid of them.*

He wasn't supposed to see any more action. He was stateside. He was supposed to be done. He had served his terms, and had done his time. He wasn't supposed to be back in the mix of it.

His hand clenched down on the door handle and started to turn.

The door reverberated with a loud explosion as something from the other side slammed into it. A loud force was there, but now it wasn't the slow rhythmic pounding that had been with them as they walked in. Now it was an eager, desperate sound that shook the door, the frame, and the wall surrounding it. Something was in there, and it wanted out…now.

Come on. Stay rational, he thought to himself. He had to. He couldn't allow himself to lose his head.

"Corporal?" Christian shouted over the headset. "Corporal, are you all right?"

"Yeah," he called back, hearing the tremor in his voice. He hoped they would just ignore it or take it for radio feedback.

He hadn't realized he had pulled his hand back from the door, and wasn't sure if he wanted to reach back out for it. The pounding roared again, smashing against the other side of the door.

"Do you need help? Can I assist you? Are you trapped?" he called to the door. Even if the person on the other side wasn't out to get him, he doubted he could have been heard over the consistent pounding against the wood. He could see the wood was splintering from the top, giving way. Slivers of wood were sticking out like needles, pointing towards him.

"What's your progress?" he called out over the radio. He stepped back from the door, leveling his rifle at it.

"We are down the left hallway to the waiting area. All rooms are clear. We are about to go back down the right hallway towards your position. Do you want us to hurry down, or clear the doors along the way?"

"Clear the doors. Don't allow anyone to sneak up behind us. Turn on any lights you can."

"Um…" There was a pause. Thompson didn't know what that meant, but he wished they would just spit it out. He watched as the door pushed out a little bit more.

"Spit it out."

"Corporal, all the lights are shattered. We've been walking on the remnants of the fluorescent light the whole way. Something broke them all down the hallways."

Something must not like the light too much, he thought as he brought the rifle up to his shoulder and positioned his cheek to the rest, getting ready to fire. He was starting to see a gap in the door in front of him, but he still couldn't see beyond the door as it was even darker in there than in the hallway.

More pounding slammed at the door, more wood fell down the front. He continued to take another step back until he was just at the threshold of being able to see the door clearly. He figured he was just about three feet back. That should be safe enough distance from whatever was in there if they tried to reach out for him.

Then the pounding stopped again, leaving the last blast of aggression echoing into the darkness.

Corporal Thompson stood there, feeling his chest burning. He hadn't realized he was holding his breath, but he still didn't feel safe enough to let the air out. He was cautious of the silence. He didn't want to break it. He tried to force his senses beyond what he could see. It was a futile attempt, but he yearned to hear what was on the other side of the door.

There was someone back there. He didn't know what they wanted with him, but he could feel some kind of presence watching him. They were waiting for him to step forward so they could attack. They could even have others hiding, others that his team had not found, waiting to sneak up from behind. They were waiting for them to be all in one spot.

"Status?" he called through his headset.

"Westdale is working his way to you. I-I'm checking out one of the labs. It's pretty messed up in here. There's a lot of blood all over and what looks like someone's eye splatted near the door. I was giving the scientists a closer visual."

"Roger. Doctor Demoin, in the future, please let me know when you separate my team. Thank you."

"Understood, corporal." He could tell by her cold tone that she didn't care and she would do it again. *Damn scientists.*

He heard footsteps and turned to see Westdale coming up behind him. Westdale's faceplate made a sort of nodding motion to him as though to acknowledge him. Thompson nodded back.

Then the door exploded, the upper half sending shards of wood at them. Thompson turned back to see the shape of what was coming out at them, but he didn't have time to think. He didn't have time to question if the person was coming at them for their help, or was there to attack him. He opened fire, and the shots sounded like cannon fire in the enclosed hallway.

CHAPTER 17

Shadows stretched and reached across the ground outside, pushing back against the pale yellow of the remaining light. It had felt so hot throughout the day, but it was now giving away its heat as it felt soothingly cool against her forehead.

It had been a long day. It had started just as she had seen the early morning shadows. She had watched them, not knowing at the time if her husband was all right or what was going on. She had seen the shadows receding, giving way to the oncoming daylight, and how the day with that red glow slowly gave way to the orange tint that had burned so hot.

She knew that now, as the color had faded away and the shadows stretched, night was quickly coming. She wondered how much would change once it did. Something inside her, the rock that had formed a permanent worrisome weight, was now growing, icy fingertips touching at her nerves. She knew that, with night, there was still more to come.

The icy fingertips, the little tremors that coursed through her body, were a continuous reminder of where all this happened. She kept thinking about what those boys had screamed. They yelled about spiders no one else could see.

Her skin had been crawling all day, tingling as she had thought about them. "Invisible spiders" her grandma had always called them. That tingling sensation everyone gets now and then. That sensation where a person feels something that isn't there, but can't quite help scratching at it. There was nothing there, right?

Now there could very well be. That tingling feeling could always mean that a spider was there, you just couldn't see it. The spiders could be all around them, but until you were already infected with them, you wouldn't know. You wouldn't see them.

Was that true? If it was, there would be no way to tell what was happening to them. What would happen if they came across a bunch of real spiders? It's not like this place wasn't known for having their share of spiders crawling about. Between woods and cornfields, there were all kinds of different creepy-crawlies that lived around there.

"Mmmm," came the sweet little voice that rested on her shoulder. She knew that little Nadine would be waking.

"Hush, little baby, don't you cry…" she sang. *I really should try and think of a new song,* she thought. She figured it had to be the eighth or ninth time she had sung it to her and while the child was too young to notice, *she* was getting tired of it. She didn't know why. She always had an arsenal of songs that she used throughout the years. However, this morning, all she could sing was that one song.

She could feel as the little one rested her head back into the nook of Denise's shoulder and was drifting off to sleep again.

"We do need to think about getting out of here!" came a shout from the other end of the bar.

Denise looked up to see that the large fat man was pointing at something down one of the streets. The man had been nice enough at first, and had seemed like he was staying calm. Most of them agreed it was best if they stayed put until help came. Eventually, the military would have to come in. They just needed to survive until then.

But since Travis had broken the back window, she had seen the large man changing. He was growing more agitated. He had been pacing a lot and had started to look out the front window more and more. At one point, he had gotten pushy with the cop until the cop had finally hit him, knocking him down.

It bothered her. He was a pot of water getting ready to boil over. She could see the red in his face, the sharpness in his eyes. He would quickly look around when there was a noise outside, then he would keep pacing back and forth to the window, pointing out there and saying something heated to the little group.

They were in the front of the bar, so she stayed towards the back with Nadine and Tina, who was no longer balled up in the corner. Denise had been able to help coax her to sitting in a chair at a table.

There were things outside. Some called them zombies, but she didn't care what they called them. They were eating people, and her husband was one of them.

Were they really *eating* people, though? She had a hard time focusing her thoughts. She kept jumping around, thinking for a moment about her husband, then trying to think more about the things outside. What were they? What were they doing? If they were truly eating people, then the transformed would be, well…eaten. Hence, no more zombies.

No, they weren't eating them. In fact, while she had seen many with multiple bite marks, it seemed like once the initial few bites were delivered, the things would move on and find someone else. So they weren't eating them. It seemed like they were more inclined to just spread themselves out. They were building numbers.

Denise walked over to the pool table and looked at the man who they had tied up and put in the corner. He glared up at her, watching as she walked around, carrying his child. She bet he hated her for that. She saw nothing but some twisted and perverse hatred in his eyes for her. He probably saw her as a social worker who was there to steal his child.

Not like the child shouldn't have been taken away from them anyway. She wished she had more evidence in the past to have persisted with getting CPS involved.

Too late now.

She looked at the two slabs of thick plywood they had put over the window. Rob had fought to get it up to the frame of the window. The bartender, the biggest of the three, stood there holding the bottom of the wood. The large truck driver had been using a pool cue as a dagger and a club to keep the hands from reaching in too far.

Bruce had batted at the hands, but the things gnarled fingers were more like claws than hands. They had constantly been reaching for him, and she saw how one had almost grabbed his shirt. The big man could move, though. With that large stomach of his, he was much faster than she would have thought, and had quickly pulled from the thing's grasp and had nailed it with the pointy end of the cue. Of course, the cue wasn't sharp, but he had been able to find the empty eye socket of the thing, and with a hard push and a sideways tug, there had been a satisfying crack.

The large man smiled as he pulled back the cue and saw that the tip of it had been broken into the zombie's eye socket.

The smile was short-lived and the thing had only fallen back for a second before it had time to recover and was reaching through again. This time, it was more vicious and flailed its arms as it reached in. Bruce dropped his make-shift club, as it was now too short, and picked up another cue. He came back, swinging it like a club.

Rob called out for them to get out of the way and everyone stepped back as they rushed the board into place. Jason and Rob on the sides, the bartender holding the bottom, they pushed it against the window, Rob called over his shoulder for the large man to grab the electric drill someone had set down on the pool table.

The driver was quick to act, and before the things could push in on them again, the sheet of plywood was up and they were securing it.

Once Bruce was finished drilling it to the wall, Jason took the drill from him and went around the sides again and again until it looked like the outer frame of the wall would come down before that plywood would come off.

"Just want to be sure. No need to take chances," Jason said to the large truck driver.

"Good, then tighten the one in your head," said the bartender as he walked away from the back window. Denise still couldn't believe how cheery the man was. He actually seemed to be enjoying this.

Denise turned away from the plywood and looked back to the front of the bar. She hadn't seen when, but Bruce had gotten another drink. The cop was staring in the direction of the back corner. She knew he couldn't see the window from where he stood, but she had the feeling he was trying to. As though he was trying to look through the glass that was no longer there.

Denise rocked back and forth, feeling the warm breath of Nadine on her shoulder. She was so small and innocent, and was being so good. She had stayed quiet for much of the day. Denise couldn't believe something so small and precious came out of those two vicious people. They did not deserve her, were not good enough for her.

Burp, came a little sound from the tiny mouth.

Denise looked at her, a smile touching the corner of her lips. Those little blue eyes were open and were looking up at her with their sweet little innocence.

She felt the warm breath on her shoulder.

She felt the breath again…on the wrong shoulder.

Nadine was cradled onto her right shoulder, but she was feeling the warmth on her left. She looked over, trying to look at the area, but she couldn't see exactly where she felt the warming sensation.

Tingles ran up and down her spine, and her left side started to itch, like there were tiny things crawling up and down.

She looked down and saw a spider on the floor near her foot. She quickly stepped on it.

Was it…? Could it have been one of those spiders? Was she…? But she hadn't been bit. Could it have been one of those things? Was she imaging it? Were the spiders real?

She pulled her foot away and looked down, but it was too dark in the bar. With one of the key sources of light now covered up, there wasn't enough for her to see.

Burp.

If she was infected, there was no way she wanted to pass it on to the baby.

She felt more tingling along her arm. Sure, she had been feeling tingly all day, but the sensation was stronger. She had to really fight to keep herself from itching at it. She wanted to dig her fingernails in and just scratch viciously.

She looked over at the corner where the baby's father was. He had stopped glaring at her and had his head down, looking at the floor. He seemed to be in a daze. *Did he even realize that he was twitching*? she wondered. Were they both infected?

She felt another warm breath on her shoulder and tried to look again. This time, she thought she saw a slight movement as something small slipped underneath the neckline of her shirt and out of sight.

* * * *

Rob walked past the nurse and headed to the back alcove. He was glad she was there, and that she had chosen to look after the baby. Otherwise, he probably would have had to be the one to do it and, right now, he felt like there was enough on his plate. He wasn't happy with how much Bruce was drinking. The owner's kid, Jason, was unstable…fine one minute, breaking down the next. Sullivan, the kid's friend, seemed okay, but he was enjoying himself too much. He had been one of those zombie apocalypse nuts before any of this had even gone down, and was overly ecstatic that he was finally proven right.

He heard a thump on the floor and turned to look. Travis was still tied up in the corner. Sullivan was right. They should have left the bastard outside. He got his wife and that old man killed, exposed all of them, made the building accessible to get into by moving that damn dumpster closer to the back window, and could be infected. Even if only half of that was true, Rob still wanted to take the man by the throat and just squeeze. He had never felt so much hatred as he felt towards this man, and it burned inside his chest.

Yeah, this wasn't his pick of a dream team, unless it was for a quick one-way trip into hell.

He kept his distance from the redneck and moved to the other side. He bent over and pulled the thick cord out of the socket, then straightened to look up at the big machine it was connected to. It was just your standard dart machine, nothing special, but he had an idea of a way to use it to secure the back window even more. Sure, the kid had gone nuts with the screw gun, but Rob could see the frame around the window was weak.

He pushed and pulled, getting it into place in the center of the window. In and of itself, it wasn't much, but now he had the second part of his securing plan.

"What the fuck are you doing?" the redneck said from his corner.

Rob looked and saw the man staring at him. Something about that glare told him the man had justified in his mind how this was all Rob's fault. There was hatred there, but also accusation. Maybe it was just years as a cop in Chicago, but he knew this man blamed him for going out there and losing his wife.

Rob shook it off and hurried around to the other side of the pool table, making sure to go around the opposite side from the man secured in the corner.

"Blocking off the window you broke," Rob said. He looked down at the legs of the pool table, relieved to see that it wasn't bolted to the floor.

Rob looked back at the man to see that he was twitching, his left arm shaking a little, and he wondered if the redneck even noticed he held it in his right arm, his right hand continually finding different little places to scratch. He could see a lot of red marks and grooves in various places on the man's skin.

"That dart machine ain't gonna do shit."

"It will when this pool table is pushed against it to keep it in place."

"Bullshit."

Rob turned away and pushed against the table. From the layers of wax around the bottom of the legs, he knew it wasn't hardly ever moved. He guessed the wax itself had formed a sort of glue, but he continued to apply the force.

His legs burned, his bad leg ached and pushed a dull throb in his lower back. He was about to quit because of the burning sensation in his right side tingling to a point in his lower back where fire was exploding. It wanted him to quit. He needed to give into it and just collapse. He wanted to fall into a heap on the floor, curl up into a ball, let the pain take him, and give up.

Then the table broke loose and was quickly moving. He had to take lunging steps to keep from falling into it but within three steps, it was slamming against the dart machine.

He stood up, his back screaming. The pain in his right leg flashed, but when it reached his lower back, the pain burned so intense that the sensation in his leg seemed to just disappear. He knew it was still there, but the rest of the pain made it pale in comparison. He heard the little pops as he stood straight, and some of the pain lessened.

He'd definitely need to see his chiropractor tomorrow…if he lived to see tomorrow.

Now it was time to get down to business. They had to think through this so they could *get* through this.

He heard a stomping sound and turned to see the redneck looking at the ground. The man looked up at him, glared, then turned away.

Yeah, Rob thought, *we also needed to get out of here.*

He wanted to get out there and get home. His wife and son were waiting for him and they had no clue what was going on.

He hoped they were safe, that none of this was near them.

It had to be centralized to this area, right? After all, there had been that CDC guy. He had been there to see the doctor, then there was the phones being out, and his car hadn't been able to be towed in, probably because the roads were blocked. They were in a quarantine of some kind so, following that logic, it had to be centralized to the town. His family had to be safe.

He looked over at Denise. She had been about to say something when the kid had lost it. She knew more about what was going on here. He found out that her husband was the local doctor. It didn't take a detective to figure out that the CDC guy had been there to see her husband.

Okay, so where *was* her husband?

He watched as she handed the baby over to Tina. Then she turned, looked up, and caught him looking at her. She had a scared look on her face. He could see it in the raising of her eyebrows and that crease along her forehead. She looked like she had been caught doing something and was silently asking for forgiveness.

"Can we talk?" he said. He had that professional cop tone to his voice. It conveyed that he was being polite, but it was also a demand, not a request. He motioned towards one of the tables in between the back alcove and the main room of the bar. She walked towards it.

* * * *

She eased into the seat across from him, and he tried to size her up. After all, he hadn't really paid much attention to her. She had just kind of slipped in with the kid when he had gotten back, and had stayed pretty quiet since then. She was watching over the baby, but he got a sense she didn't have kids herself. No, she was used to watching over other people's kids. It's what allowed her to be so hard on the redneck couple before the wife had been, well…taken away.

Her hands were trembling. She was nervous. Not really a revelation as he was sure they were all a little high-strung right about then. It wasn't every day zombies were knocking at your front door. No. He still refused to think of them as zombies. They were just things, or maybe even infected people, but he wasn't going to start thinking of them as zombies. Not yet, and maybe not ever.

She wasn't meeting his eyes, which bothered him. Was she hiding something? Had she done something she was ashamed of? Was she afraid of him? She couldn't be afraid he was going to arrest her, could she? Where would he take her even if he *did* arrest her? Or was it just that she had a general distrust for cops? That was more common in the big cities, but in smaller towns, the town doctor and their wives didn't usually distrust the police.

"You know something about what's going on outside, don't you?" he said. He watched her face and saw a little twitch around the corner of her eye and a slight jerk of her head that

283

told him she had nearly looked up at him in surprise. "You were about to say something earlier, before the craziness started," he went on. He was lowering his head, trying to get her eyes to meet his.

She gave him a quick glance then looked down to the floor. "My husband is the town doctor. I don't know if you know that or not, but he is…was one of them…things." She had stuttered over the word. She wasn't comfortable calling them zombies, either.

"Okay. So he was the one who called in the CDC?"

Now she did look up at him. Her eyes were wide with shock, and he could see the red puffiness around the corners that he had missed earlier. She nodded at him, so Rob went on, "Yeah. The guy had run into us outside of town, asking where the doctor was."

Rob shifted in his chair. The hard seat hurt his already sore back, making it difficult to sit in one position for too long. When he did, his leg sent electric bolts of pain to his back.

"I guess I should have gotten us out of town then, but I'd been around enough false reports and near misses to get too spooked about it," he said.

He knew he was rambling on, but he was trying coax the information out of her. Get her feeling comfortable and start a conversation and, eventually, she would open up more. It was a tactic he used a lot when interviewing a suspect. He found it worked a lot better than threatening them, and he did not feel like she was somebody who could handle being threatened. And for what? Just because she knew something was going on and wasn't telling? It would have been like beating up an old lady just to take her cane.

She nodded. "Yeah, he came to the office. I had stayed outside, then I heard some pounding and a door slam. Before long, I saw my husband and the two boys coming out like…that." She nodded towards the window. They couldn't see out, but they both knew what was out there.

"Two boys?"

"Yeah, two boys woke us up this morning. Well, one of them. One of them was too sick to get out of the car without help. My husband had them meet him in his office and checked them out. He was with them about twenty minutes and I had gone into the office early to get some paperwork done."

"Okay."

"Well, after he looked them over a little bit, he had gone into his office. When he came back out, he told me to lock up and get out of there. I don't really know much more than that."

"Do you know how it got out so fast?"

"Well, it probably had something to do with Lucy."

Rob looked from the nurse's distraught face and over her shoulder at the woman who was now sitting at the table against the wall. She still didn't look like she was all there. Her dazed eyes looked into the distance. She was rocking the baby, but he wasn't sure she fully realized she was even *holding* the baby. He wondered if he was to take away the kid, would she still be rocking back and forth? It made him think of all those people in institutions. He knew there were just things people couldn't deal with sometimes, and looking at the young woman, he had a bad feeling this was something like that for her.

"Lucy. That's the sister, right?" Rob said as he looked back at Denise.

"Her niece. His sister," she said, nodding in each of their directions.

"Okay. They had been there?"

"Yeah. Lucy hadn't been feeling well, and her aunt didn't remember what time the office opened so they were already outside when we got there. The moment the lobby lights came on, they were at the door. I let them in and had them sitting in the waiting room."

Rob nodded. This wasn't telling him anything. Sure, he was starting to figure out why those two were losing it, but that didn't tell him anything about the things outside.

"Is there anything you can tell me about the 'things'?"

Rob watched her as she kept looking at the table. Her hands were out in front of her, tracing lines along the side of the table. Here and there, she would mash her thumb down, as though smashing a bug. Then she would pull her thumb away and look at it. She seemed to momentarily lose herself in the motion.

Then she looked back at him and caught his gaze. Her eyes seemed like they had gotten even redder in the short time they had been talking. He thought she was on the brink of letting loose a fresh bout of tears. Her bottom lip trembled and he could see the fear.

"They kept saying things about spiders. That there were spiders in them, and they were trying to claw the spiders out. My husband didn't see anything, but it was clear they could. They would scream about them and try to dig them out. They would gash deep into their skin. I think that really spooked Ray, so he hurried back to his office."

"So there is something with spiders?"

"Maybe."

"Okay."

"There was also no blood."

“What?”

“They would dig and claw deep into their own skin, but there was no blood. I had also heard Ray say something about them not having a heartbeat anymore. He thought he had made a mistake, but…”

“You don’t think so.”

She shook her head.

He watched as she again smashed her thumb down onto something on the table. It was too dark in there for him to see it, but he watched her pull her thumb away and look at it.

“Okay,” Rob said as he pulled himself back. “Anything else?”

“Watch out for the spiders,” she whispered.

CHAPTER 18

The body, or what was left of it, crashed onto the cold, smooth steel of the table with a wet, splattering *kachunk.* Westdale, the large man in the large alien-looking suit covered in pieces of human flesh and some other kind of dark gore, stood there huffing and puffing from carrying the thing back to the trailer.

He was looking at the thing, a sneer on his lips, disgust showing in his eyes. He knew no one else could see his expression under the mask, and he was glad for it. He didn't want them to see how scared the thing made him, how his stomach turned, and the hatred in his eyes as he thought about how hard the damn thing had been to take down.

"Thank you, private," he heard behind him. He knew she was from Atlanta, all the scientists they were escorting were, but he could still sense that while her words were educated and pronounced correctly, there was still that hint of a southern drawl just at the edge when she spoke.

He stepped back and let her and another scientist start looking at the body.

"You guys made a mess of him. You didn't have to do that."

"Yes, we did." Westdale said back to her. He knew he was supposed to be a lot more formal, but that was one of the benefits of being a private. Not only that, after taking that damn thing down, he just wasn't in the mood for proper etiquette.

* * * *

When the door had exploded out, Westdale had been partially behind the corporal. He had seen the corporal getting ready, training his rifle on the door. He didn't know why the man had suddenly tensed and was now cautiously edging towards the door. Westdale didn't hear or see anything, but wasn't surprised. He had lost part of his hearing long ago, with no great story behind it other than good ol' heavy metal and the high school saying "If it's too loud, you're too old". He hadn't heard the pounding on the door but, thankfully, he was good at reading visual cues.

Seeing that the corporal had moved into action, Westdale started do the same and brought his rifle up. The door exploded outward, wood shards shooting through the darkened hallway. The corporal took some of the shards in the suit, but Westdale didn't have time to notice. He continued to bring his rifle up and aimed on the center of the doorway.

Then he paused. "What the fuck?" he let slip out.

The thing had once been a black man, but the man's skin had lost so much of its color, it seemed that ash had formed over the top of it. There were long gashes in its outstretched arms, and its eyes had lost all of their color and had gone white. It had cuts along its cheeks, around its neck. Its lips were raw and peeled back, moisture having been sucked dry from them.

In fact, the whole body looked like it had all the moisture sucked out of it.

Westdale shook himself out of his trance, not realizing he had just been watching as the thing had fallen forward into his corporal, who was now wrestling with it. His rifle dropped to his feet and the pistol that had been holstered to his hip was now out and he was firing into the chest of the man.

The sound of the gun was excruciatingly loud in the enclosed hallway, but Westdale watched as his platoon leader emptied his chamber, firing into the chest of the man. However, he kept fighting, like the bullets were having no effect on him. It kept pulling at his leader's suit, trying to get in. If Westdale didn't do something soon, it was going to get in.

Westdale sidestepped, pulled his M16 up, looked down the long barrel, sighted on the thing's head and, when he was sure he wouldn't hit his platoon leader, softly squeezed the trigger.

The head rocked back and he watched as it fell away from the corporal. As soon as it let go of its grip on the man, Thompson stumbled back. He looked over his shoulder at Westdale, gave him a nod, then turned back to look at the thing.

Westdale had been able to see the corporal's face through the faceplate and saw the shock that he himself had been fighting against.

"What the fuck is that?" Westdale asked.

"Some sick ass person."

"Yeah, right."

"Christian, how you coming?" the corporal said over his radio.

"I heard gunfire. I'm on my way."

"Negative. Check the rooms in depth. We have this one under control."

The corporal looked back at Westdale. "Good shot."

"Corporal," came the clipped female voice. Westdale wished the doctor would figure out how to use the damn radio. There was a command circuit where she could talk to the corporal directly without the rest of them listening in. He felt like he was sometimes listening to his parents fighting.

"Yes, doctor?"

"Get that body to us. We want to do an autopsy."

"Understood."

The corporal stepped forward and reached for his rifle. "Westdale, help me get this body over there. Christian, as we pull out, I want you to meet up with the perimeter team. Get with Brady, and you two triple check everything in here with a fine-toothed comb. Make sure to get everything on video so the doctors can see..."

The corporal was cut off as the corpse he was reaching for grabbed him first, grasping around his wrist. The corporal had been bending over to pick the thing up, and it was probably just luck that he had already braced himself for the weight. Otherwise, Westdale felt sure he would have watched his corporal fall straight forward into what was left of the thing's mouth. Instead, he watched as his NCO was able to rip himself away from the thing and pull himself back, but as soon as the thing had lost its grip, Thompson had fallen back onto his ass.

Neither the thing nor Thompson took much time to think about what they were doing. Thompson was backpedalling quickly, pulling himself back to where Westdale was positioned. The thing fell into a crawling position and started after the corporal. Westdale couldn't believe that, even with a large gaping hole in the center of its head, the thing was still coming after them.

He flipped the switch with his thumb, switching the single shot rifle into a three shot burst automatic. He wasn't trying for accuracy anymore, and with the thing so close, it was going to be hard to miss. He pulled hard on the trigger, the sound exploding through the hallway.

Thompson had made it back to him, and Westdale could see that the corporal had reloaded his pistol and was shooting. Making sure he wasn't blocking his corporal's line of fire, Westdale positioned himself partially in front of the man, making sure to give cover enough for him to get back to his feet. Sure, the thing wasn't shooting back at them, but training and habits were just too ingrained, so it was hard for him not to do it.

His magazine emptied and the bolt locked back, waiting for the new magazine to be slid home. He popped out the empty cartridge, grabbed another one and, within less than a second, he had it cocked and loaded.

His eyes had never left his target.

How the hell could it still be coming after them? Most of his hits had been in the head and the upper body. The top of the head was gone, there were large chunks taken out of the man's face, skin was hanging and was ready to just fall off, and much of the exposed muscle had become pulp. However, the thing still continued. The bullets had gone straight though in some areas. Westdale could see behind the thing through a hole in the head, but it still came.

With the new magazine in place, he aimed straight for the eyes. The right one exploded in a small white cloud of gore, the ooze creating a river down the little part of his cheek that was left. He shot at the other eye, exploding it inward. He watched as more blood/brain/tissue matter splattered out from what was left of the back of the skull. The thing rocked back from the impact, then fell to the side.

"What the hell is going on over there?" Christian's voice came over the radio. His voice shook and Westdale knew how he felt. His stomach was trying to twist its way down, and he was sure it was about to come out of his ass if he didn't get some form of control over it. That would be great. His first real combat and he'd shit himself? He never would hear the end of it.

"This thing won't quit. Get over here!" Thompson barked into the radio.

Westdale looked back at the corporal. He was pulling himself up, but it looked like he hurt something on his way down. He looked to be in a lot of pain.

"It's not dead?" came the female scientist's voice.

"No. It keeps coming," Thompson said. He was finally standing up and was now looking past Westdale, watching the thing.

"On my way. Got tripped up on a desk I didn't see."

"Just move."

Westdale turned back to see that the thing wasn't moving as fast, but it was still coming towards them.

"Just what the hell *is* this thing?" Westdale said under his breath. He hadn't meant to ask the question out loud, but it just slipped out.

"I sure as hell don't know. Just keep shooting it."

"We need it for an autopsy," came the scientist's voice.

Westdale thought that if she wanted the damn thing so badly, why didn't she just come out there and get it?

"We'll try," said the corporal through gritted teeth. Westdale heard him reload his weapon. The thing was a couple feet away now.

Westdale dropped the empty magazine from his cartridge and popped in a fresh one, bringing his rifle back up to bear on the thing. Both of the men stood there, waiting. He took a step backward so that he was in line with the corporal, who was leaning against the wall and lifting his foot, experimentally rotating it. He couldn't see the man's face, but it didn't take a psychic to know he was in pain.

"Maybe if we shoot for the legs?" Westdale suggested.

"Yeah?"

"Take away the legs and it can't keep coming."

"We need to take it down. They want to study it." From his tone of voice, it was clear he wasn't happy with the order.

The thing was near them, crawling, reaching out.

Westdale opened fire as its hand reached out towards his suit. He blasted into the hand, pieces of flesh splattering back onto him. Fingers separated, the meat of the palm disintegrated, and the bone beneath was exposed. Westdale continued to fire. The bones just chipped away until, finally, there was barely anything left of the hand and lower arm.

The thing took another knee forward and reached out its other hand.

Westdale's rifle clicked on empty. He took a quick step backward, trying to get out of its reach, but it was still coming for him. He was too close to it. He couldn't get away in time.

"Come on, you bitch!" he said through gritted teeth. He swung the rifle around, moving it swiftly above his head and rotating it so the stock of the rifle was towards the thing. Then he brought it down, turning the weapon into a club.

The rifle slammed into what was left of the jaw. He heard a crunching sound, and quickly took a small step forward to prevent himself from toppling forward.

He pulled his rifle back and prepared to bring it down again. He could see that the little bit left of the bottom portion of its face was smashed in, the bone crushed into powder. A black ooze, which Westdale thought must have been blood at one time, fell. Teeth had been dislodged from its mouth, and the bottom jaw just seemed to melt to the floor.

Westdale felt his stomach clench in disgust, and he could feel his muscles already tightening, getting ready to gag. The thing reeled back from the blow, but then started moving forward again.

He had the rifle up, but it was too close and, as it wrapped its arms around him, he couldn't bring it down. He was shaking back and forth, wriggling as though doing some insane dance to get away from the thing. What was left of its mouth was trying to open and close, and that disgusting mass of gore that used to be its head was trying to get to him.

Finally, he had to admit it was a zombie. He had been refusing to call it that because to admit it seemed to lay some claim that fiction had somehow taken a nightmarish turn and ended up in his reality, but here he was. He knew the damn thing was a motherfucking, shit-eating, flesh ripping zombie. It was still trying to eat him, but why? Why the fuck did the thing want to eat him? It was dead. What the hell was it going to do once it fed on him? Where was it going to go? It didn't have a digestive system anymore. What the hell was it going to do with his flesh?

What was left of its right hand pulled at him, the stump of his left arm still reaching out, as though there were still fingers attached. It wrapped him up and was trying to pull him forward. He felt like he was a fly caught in a web because the thing seemed to want to smother him, to wrap him up.

He was finally able to get his rifle in between him and the zombie, and started to use it as a wedge against its face. He worked at prying it off and pushing it away, but it kept pushing forward. For a dead thing, Westdale was surprised at how strong it was. He was not that small of a guy and he worked out, but this thing kept pushing into him with enough force, it was hard for him to not only fight the thing off, but keep from falling back.

Westdale heard a shot from his corporal, but had no idea what he was firing at. He didn't see the thing react to the shot, and he hoped like hell there wasn't another one coming towards them.

"Shit!" he heard Christian cry out. Westdale could see movement out of the corner of his eye and he saw another pair of arms wrap around the zombie and start to pull him back.

He looked up as he pushed against its chest with the butt of his rifle and saw the grimace on the smaller man's face. Christian was one of those small, scrappy guys who didn't look like much when you saw him, but if you were to fight him you'd find out just how tough he really was Westdale had seen him take down a bear of a man in a little scrap they had on leave one time, and he had been amazed that the other man was the one on the ground when it was all said and done.

Christian was tough. He was a fighter, and he was a lot stronger than he looked.

Westdale looked up into the facemask of the smaller man and saw him tense his body, and Westdale could feel the release as the thing started to pull away. At first, it was taking him with it, but Westdale was able to get some leverage with his rifle, and pushed the thing back.

Christian stepped back, taking quick steps to keep from losing his balance. Westdale fell back onto the counter to the nursing station. It must have been the corner that caught him because he felt the edge stab into him like a dagger, and he could feel the icy touch of the pain shooting down his back and into his legs, making them threaten to go weak and give out under him. He fought to keep upright, leaning forward, then he was stumbling back into the hallway.

As he regained his balance, he looked back over at Christian. The smaller man was raising his rifle. "Clear!" Christian said into his radio.

"Shit," Westdale said. He knew he was right in the line of fire, and the corporal could still be hit with ricochets.

Westdale looked over and saw that the corporal was leaning into an open door. There was light in there from the rays of the setting sun outside. Westdale leapt for the corporal and grabbed him, both of them falling into the room. Their feet had barely cleared the entrance when the hallway behind him exploded in a fresh round of rifle fire as Christian started tearing into the thing.

He felt Corporal Thompson's body shift under him, hearing a few grunts. Remembering that the man had his pistol cocked and ready, and not sure if he had seen that it had been Westdale who had pulled him to the ground, he decided it was best to quickly get off.

Westdale rolled to the side and onto his back. He could see the flashes from the rifle fire in the hallway. He had already heard Christian empty one magazine hearing the sound of it falling to the floor, and then the slamming home of a fresh one.

All Westdale could see were the flashes from the rifle, gore that was splattering the room in front of him, and chips coming out of plastered walls.

Suddenly, all sound ceased.

"All clear," Christian mumbled, shakily.

* * * *

"There's not much left for us to even examine," the larger of the two female doctors was saying. They had put on their protective suits and were now leaning in to look at what was left of the zombie in front of them.

Westdale wasn't going to argue. The thing hadn't been pretty when it had first leapt out at them, but now it wasn't much more than a torso. Christian had fired at its legs until they were severed completely from the body. He had tried to shoot off the arms, but he had run out of ammo after only severing the arm they had already disabled.

So all that was left was a body with no legs; a head that was mostly gone to the point where if you looked down from the top, you could see the stump of the spinal column; there was still a little mouth left, though the bottom jaw had been decimated; one cheek still had some bone structure left, but the other was just a large hole; the eyes were gone, and so was the top of the skull where the forehead should have been.

In spite of all that, the body still did occasionally twitch. Even though the jaw was barely anything more than a vague shape, the remaining muscles there still tried to open and close it.

The damn thing still wasn't dead!

Maybe it wasn't a zombie because the zombies always seemed to die after a shot to the head in the movies. This thing had been shot to the head, its limbs removed, beaten, head nearly taken off, and it was still moving.

"Hey, do you guys want to hear something weird?" came Christian's voice over the radio. He and Corporal Thompson were still checking out the rest of the building. Westdale had no idea how the corporal was still walking with his injured ankle. He had seen the pain in the man's eyes, yet he was still working.

"What is it, private?" said the doctor. It sounded tired and came across very terse. She had straightened when he had called to them, and he could tell she was annoyed with the interruption.

"The body parts that are still in here are moving. The feet are rotating. Hell, even a finger is twitching. Do you want us to bag them and bring them back, as well?"

"Yes. Corporal, could you please make sure that we get all of those body parts," she said. It wasn't a question. The order was clear in her voice.

The corporal clicked into the conversation, "Yes, ma'am. We found some biohazard bags in the examination rooms. We'll bag 'em and tag 'em."

The doctor looked back down at the thing. Westdale watched her studying it. The other doctor, the larger female, stood near the head. He had no idea what her purpose was because she didn't say anything and seemed to always just stand there and watch the others. He didn't think he had heard her say a word since she had joined them.

Maybe it was because of that, but he couldn't get the image out of his mind as to her always just being the sidekick.

He could picture her in some movie, always being the one standing around eating a chocolate bar or some candy.

He knew that was mean. That it wasn't right to judge her by how large she was and how shy she seemed. Still, he just couldn't get the damn image out of his head.

He was thinking way too much about it.

He should be watching them, paying attention to what they were doing and making sure nothing happened to them.

"Damn, this crap is disgusting," came Christian's voice over the radio.

"Cut the chatter," the corporal said, sternly.

"Yes, corporal."

The corporal seemed like a decent guy. From what Westdale had heard around camp, he should have been a sergeant, but he never pushed for it. There was even a rumor that he had actually refused it a few times. From what others had said, he didn't want to take on the responsibility.

He could see that. He wouldn't want to be in charge of fresh young apes running around with machine guns, grenades, and assault rifles, either.

Westdale had no idea just why they would have put him in charge of this little squad.

"What the…"

Westdale looked at the doctor. He hadn't realized he had been staring at the larger of the two and had kind of zoned out. Now he saw that her eyes were wide, and she was looking at the body and the other doctor in a frozen expression of panic.

Westdale could see why. The things only working hand had reached out and grabbed the doctor's wrist as she leaned over it. She must have been coming across the center with the scalpel to cut down its chest. It held her there firmly, the hand stopped after just having cut into the pale white flesh.

"Soldier, get it off me," he heard her say in a high voice. He had the sense she wanted to scream, but something inside her was forcing her to keep control. That impressed him. Maybe this wasn't her first rodeo, and she wasn't all that uptight for no reason.

He hurried over to her, snapping into motion at the sound of her voice. His rifle was raised but, as he closed the three foot gap, he realized he was too close to shoot it.

If it was a human, alive or rational being he could point to its head and demanded it release her. If it was like a zombie from the movies, he could just fire into the head. However, he wasn't sure what the hell this thing was. No matter what they did, it just seemed like it never died. Its head was already a mass of gore, but it was wrestling with the tiny, frail-looking doctor.

In one swift, smooth motion, he rotated his rifle so the butt of it was forward. He wasn't aiming for the head this time. This time, he was going for its wrist. He couldn't really aim. The thing and the doctor were struggling and she was pulling, trying to shake free. It wasn't releasing her, and she was moving the torso around on the table. The thing was lighter than the amount of strength it seemed to possess, making the torso of the creature unable to get any leverage. However, that also made it a hard target.

He changed his grip. Now he held it more like a baseball bat, raising it over his head like a sledgehammer. Damn, he hoped like hell his drill sergeant never saw this. For that matter, he hoped none of his superior officers saw it, as he knew just how keen they were to bite his head off. Using the butt of the rifle was one thing, but to be swinging it down… Yeah, he knew it would not go over that well.

Who was he kidding? If he got through this shit, they sure as fuck better see there were extenuating circumstances.

Yeah, right, and pigs flew.

He brought the rifle down across its arm. He had been aiming for as close to the wrist as he could get without hitting the doctor's arm, but due to a sudden jerk of the zombie, he had missed and the rifle slammed down onto hers.

He heard her scream come from both within the room and his radio. It was like an echoing scream drilling into his head, loud and shrill. From the crack he had heard and how her hand was hanging at an angle, he knew it was broken.

"What the hell's going on in there?" came the loud, commanding voice of the corporal.

"It has the doctor. Your soldier has broken the doctor's arm trying to get her free. We need to get her away from it," came a rushed, panicked voice. He knew it couldn't have been from the other doctor in the room because she was still too shell-shocked and was backing away from the table. It had to have come from the male scientist who was still in the other part of the trailer.

"Fuck!" came Thompson's voice. "We are pulling out of the office sweep. Churchill, Redman, you two head back to command to assist. Randall, you stay on perimeter, and we'll meet up with you to secure, then we'll swoop back in towards the command in a sweep."

A chorus of "10-4" came over the radio.

Westdale didn't have time to respond. He had to react and keep reacting.

Once the pain had dulled in his head from the wailing scream, he saw that the doctor was collapsing to the floor, pulling the thing down with her. The rifle was useless so he quickly set it aside and reached forward, grabbing the thing around what used to be its chest.

Under the sensation of his gloves, he could feel the softness of the flesh. The thing was cold enough that it sent an icy chill through his fingertips, and it was squishy like he was grabbing soft hamburger after it had defrosted.

He put his foot against the table and pulled. The thing resisted and fought him with a strength that still surprised him. He was able to pull it back, but he could see he was pulling her with it.

He heard another scream. The thing was trying to gnaw at her neck with what was left of its jaw. There weren't enough teeth left to tear through the suit, and it really couldn't close what was left of its mouth, but he could see that it still pulled itself in close enough to hurt her.

The other doctor, bone cutters in hand, finally appeared. The thing was big and had ridges to it that made it look like it belonged in a *Saw* movie. It was nearly a foot long, the steel shining bright. He could only imagine it being used in morgues and horror movies.

The metal turned a dark black as she brought it down, starting to slice through its arm. The thing didn't react to it and the hand kept hold, even after the blade finished making its way through.

The torso fell back, Westdale releasing it and rolling in the opposite direction. He stopped, his breath heavy, quickly fogging his facemask. He could feel sweat beading across his brow. The suit seemed like it was growing hotter, burning him up. These suits were never meant to handle this kind of use and he was overheating.

He tried to look back over at the two doctors. He could hear the one still screaming, fighting against the hand. The other doctor, blurred in his vision, was bent over her, trying to pull the hand free.

"Westdale! Westdale! We need you out here. There are more of those things. They are all over the place," came over his radio. He thought it sounded like the corporal's voice, but it was too distorted. There had been too much gunfire in the background.

This whole situation was going to hell. They had to get out of there. The doctors needed to get away. *He* needed to get away. He realized there was no way they could take these things out. They had one in the lab which was just a torso, and they couldn't even stop *that*. It was like every part of the body was after them, out to kill them.

He needed a fucking flamethrower. Just how in the hell would the things like that? Burn the sons of bitches. He doubted any pieces of them would last against a fucking flamethrower.

Did they have one? He tried to think over their inventory. He didn't recall seeing one, but he sure as hell doubted they didn't have one. These guys seemed to have thought of everything. These were smart people. They had to have thought they might need to use a flamethrower for something, right? Fire was the best at cleansing a hostile infection. Isn't that why forests were put to the torch in some of those third world counties? To combat the spread of certain diseases?

Yeah, like he would know. Still, someone had to have thought of it. There had to be a flamethrower somewhere in there.

Westdale turned himself over, pushing himself to his knees, then reached out to the wall. He pushed off of it, but something slammed into his leg, causing him to stumble. He looked back and saw the stump of the arm hitting against his leg. It didn't have any stability, but it was flailing in a fashion to move it closer to him. It was somehow pushing its torso around so that the little of what was left of the skull was coming towards his leg. The damn thing was still trying to eat him!

"Fuck this!" Westdale slammed his large boot down, feeling the satisfying crunch beneath his heel as what was left of the skull shattered.

He had hoped it would finally stop moving, but it didn't. The stump of an arm continued to pound against his leg, and he fell back against the wall, letting it. It was only causing bruises at this point. He was just too damned tired of fighting with the thing.

He looked away from it to see that the hand was being pulled free from the doctor; however, as it pulled away, he saw it had somehow been able to rip a hole in the woman's suit. He could see that a trickle of blood starting to form. He doubted she even realized it yet, and he wondered what she would do when she did.

Then he had the fleeting, dismal thought of just how easy it was to become one of those damned things, and he had the feeling it was a hell of a lot easier to become one than kill one.

His leg took another hit. Who was he kidding? They *still* hadn't killed one. They had shot it, dismembered it, but it was still hitting him. It was dead as dead could be, but it was still trying to come after him.

"Westdale, get your ass out here! Churchill is down. Christian, behind you!"

Westdale hadn't heard any gunfire over the radio that time. He knew they were probably out of ammo. His squad was out there, while he was safe inside. They were all going to die. He knew it had taken much of their ammo just to bring *this* one down. They couldn't have had much left. How much did he have? Not much. Not much at all, and he doubted that if he had gone out there, he would even have been able to help them.

They were all dead, and they didn't even know it.

"Where are all these spiders coming from?" he heard the doctor ask.

He looked over at her, the fog in his visor beginning to fade as he was getting his breathing under control. He saw it, too. Not the spiders, but the male doctor looking down at the woman on the ground. He could see it in his eyes…fear.

Yeah, they both knew what that meant. Soon, it wasn't going to be much safer in there.

"Get them off me! Get them off! They're getting into my skin. Get them off!"

Westdale walked over to her, lowered his rifle so it was aimed at her facemask, and fired a single shot. The sound echoed in the small room, and he wondered if that had been the smart thing to do. After all, he was pretty sure that had been his last shot. He should have saved it for himself.

CHAPTER 19

They were still out there. Nothing had changed, but everything had. Minutes were dragging into hours. The sun was glowing, and the day was slowly passing by. The things were still outside. They had been moving along the street, more of the things joining the group, but there now seemed like there was an influx of more of them just mulling around out there.

At first, Sullivan and Jason watched them from the front windows, but over the course of the last hour, they seemed to just occasionally glance out in morbid curiosity.

In the bar, nothing had really changed. As it grew dimmer outside, inside seemed to become lighter. It was amazing at how perception could manipulate how the lighting was perceived. When the sun had been high, the bar had seemed like a dungeon, barely enough light to keep from tripping over their own two feet, but as the sunlight left, inside became lighter.

Rob looked at the ambient green glow coming from the lights behind the bar, then looked at his reflection in the bar mirror. That green light made him glow unworldly as he looked into his own eyes. If he had to describe them, he would say they were dark and sunken. He really hadn't gotten much sleep the night before because he had been having nightmares.

Bruce was the same way, as he had heard the trucker mentioning earlier that he had driven all night. Before he had picked up Rob, he had been hurrying home and had faked his logs so he wouldn't have to stop. It wasn't an uncommon practice, but it was highly illegal, and the truck driver was now showing just how tired he was. His head was slumped over the bar, just a few stools down from Rob, gazing into his glass of Coke. Rob wasn't sure when the man had switched back to just drinking soda. Or was he, as he didn't recall the bartender earlier just putting Coke into a glass. Not unless it had a little rum mixed in.

They were all getting tired, worrying when the things would try to get in again. It had been a couple of hours since that redneck and his wife had gone outside. The back window was broken, and while the things hadn't been able to get in, he had heard them try a few times.

He had no idea what they were going to do.

"Any ideas yet?" Bruce asked.

Rob looked at the reflection and saw Bruce was looking at him in the mirror, that green light catching the dark grease patches on his face and turning it into a hideous mask. Rob looked away to stare into his own darkness.

"I don't know."

"We can't just stay here, can we?" Denise asked. Both she and Tina had stayed quiet; however, Tina stayed by herself behind the bar, holding the baby. She was withdrawn, only focusing on the child in her arms. The world was a million miles away from her.

"I'm not sure we have too many other options."

"Why? What do you think is going on?" Bruce said as he glared at him.

"Don't know."

"So you've said. You've said that since we got here, but you *do* know something."

"What do you know?" Sullivan asked.

He stepped away from the front window to walk down to the cooler, pulling himself out a beer. He popped the top and started to drink. He didn't even put any money in the till for it, but Jason didn't push the subject. He hadn't been paying attention to any of their drinks for the last few hours. Probably a smart move, though Rob wasn't sure it had anything to do with money. The kid still seemed like he was more or less suffering from shock and was only really with them part of the time.

"I don't know anything. I can make some guesses, based off former military training and my experience as an officer, but I don't know if any of it's true."

"Cut the shit. What's going on out there?"

"With them?" He motions to the window. "I don't know. Is there a large military base around here? I don't know of any north of Marion. Then there's Fort Leonard Wood. Outside of that, I don't know of any, so I can't say military experiment gone wrong or some other conspiracy-related garbage."

"So what *do* you know?" Bruce was getting hostile.

"Phones are out. Cell towers are jammed. Television is jammed. That's what I know."

"You really think they're being jammed?" Sullivan asked.

Rob just nodded, then took another drink of soda. The Coke had started to taste sour to him. He thought he should switch over to water. He was probably getting wired up on the caffeine and sugar. Besides, it was now warm and had long since gone flat.

"But you're thinking something."

Rob swiveled, turning to look Bruce directly in the eyes. It seemed like there was some silent communication there, and the edge fell away. Bruce softened, nodded, then shrank back into himself. He brought his hands up and buried his face in them.

"What is it?"

"We're quarantined. Cut off from the outside world."

"How do you figure?"

"Okay, take what I've already said, but now add in the fact that my car still hasn't been towed in from out of town."

"But that could be because the tow truck driver got attacked."

"Could be, but add it up. Plus, take in the fact that the CDC was here before this escalated. How they got here so fast might be the biggest stroke of luck out there, or this thing might have gotten out faster. That's even thinking positive that it hasn't. But the CDC was here, they locked it down, cut us off, and now we're stuck here."

"So what do we do?" It was the kid asking. He still had that dead tone to his voice. Damn, Rob wished there was something he could do for him.

"Don't know."

"You don't think we can get out of here?"

"I think the military will have a blockade set up. Now, I don't think they would have been able to set up road blocks at all the roads, so they probably had to bring in area law enforcement to supplement their own, but the National Guard would have taken the main routes. If we could get out of here, it'd probably have to be on a side road so we could deal with law enforcement. Military will be under strict orders, and they won't let anyone through."

"So you think we should be trying to get out of here?" Sullivan asked.

"We could just stay put until help comes." Tina's voice was quiet as she squeaked her opinion from the back hallway.

"We could. We could just sit here and wait until help comes. That is, *if* help comes."

"Do you think it will?"

"I don't know."

"Well, fuck. Why don't you know? Come on, man. You're one of them," Bruce said as he stood up and started to pace the floor. "You're a fucking pig like the rest of them. You know this shit. You know what's going on."

"I'm in *here*. I'm in the *zone*. I've been cut off, same as you. How am I supposed to know anything?"

Bruce turned to look at him, the corner of his eyes wet with tears. "I want to get home to my little girl."

"I also have a wife and son to get home to. We both need to get out of here."

"The spiders! Get them off! Spiders! *Spiders! Get them off!*" came the redneck's booming voice from the back room. He had been so quiet back there, Rob had nearly forgotten about him.

They had tied him up around the back corner so none of them could see him…except for Denise, who was sitting at one of the tables at the back of the bar. Rob looked over at her and saw that she was standing and backing away.

He hurried back to her, motioning for her to stay against the wall. He took a quick glance her way and then turned away, rounding the corner so that he was in the back alcove.

It was brighter back there. The light that had been over the pool table was shining down in the center of the room. Travis had worked himself up so he was now on his feet and looked like he was doing some exotic dancing. He was lurching as though to some chaotic music in his own head, and was stomping his feet down at random times. Then he would stumble back, watch the light as it shook from his stomps before he would again bring his foot crashing down.

"I got to get them off me. They're all over me."

He was thrashing around, shaking as he moved. It struck Rob as to what he was doing. He was trying to shake the bugs off of him, then killing them as they fell to the floor.

The only problem was that Rob didn't see any bugs.

"It's okay. Just calm down. Everything is going to be okay." Rob held his hand out as he slowly moved forward. Travis didn't look up at him. He was lost in shaking vigorously around, trying to get them all off.

"They're getting into my skin. I can feel them. They're behind my eyes, I can feel them twitching. God, please! Help me!" He was nearly crying. Rob took another slow step forward. He didn't want to get close to the man, but he needed to get him calmed down. He couldn't have him spooking everyone else.

And then do what with him? He was becoming one of those things. Eventually, they were going to have to get him out of there. Why were they even delaying it? Because it was obvious there was still a person there. He wasn't one of those things yet.

"I wouldn't get any closer to him. In fact, I'd start stepping away from him."

Rob turned to look at Denise, who was still standing back against the wall. He was sure if she could become a part of the wall, she would if it meant getting further away from Travis.

"Get them off!" Travis screamed. He thrashed around, then ran back to slam against the wall, pounding the side of his head against it. "They're getting into my ears! Get them out. I can feel them crawling!"

"We need to get him out of here!" Bruce yelled. Rob looked at the truck driver. He was out of his barstool and was hurrying over. He came up next to him, his large frame rigid as he stopped and watched the insanity happening in front of them.

"How do we do that? We throw him out there, they'll tear him apart. You saw what happened to his wife and that old man."

"It's already too late for him," Denise said. They both turned to look at her.

"You know that for sure? Because if we throw him out there, that *is* a death sentence."

She just nodded, holding herself as she stood back against the wall. She looked down at herself, failing to hold their eyes.

Rob looked at Bruce. He saw the fear in the man's eyes. He felt the same way.

"I can't do it," Rob whispered.

"What do you mean you can't do it? You're the law. You've faced some serious shit. Weren't you from Chicago? You going to tell me you haven't ever killed a man."

"I've never shot anyone that wasn't trying to shoot me first. Throwing him outside is cold-blooded murder."

"He isn't a man no more."

Travis thrashed around in the corner, flailing back and forth, slamming his arms against the walls. He was safe from gouging at himself because his hands were duct taped behind his back. They probably should have taped his legs together because if the man truly wanted to, he could rush at them. However, it didn't strike Rob that they were his biggest concerns at the moment, as he was caught up heavily in what he was fighting against.

"I'm not saying I could, but if we did, how would we do it? We can't get close to him, can we?"

"No, you can't. Lisa never came in direct contact with the two boys, so if it spread to her, it had to have been through the air."

Rob turned to look at her. "Why didn't you get it?" Denise shrugged. "You think maybe you have an immunity to whatever virus it is?"

"I don't know if it's viral, but I don't think I'm immune."

"How do you know?"

"I just don't think I am."

Rob continued to look at her. He had a thought forming, something he was thinking they should do, but he wasn't quite ready to commit to it yet, and definitely not ready to say it out loud.

She watched him, probably seeing it on his face that he was thinking about something. He guessed with how she fidgeted, she must have known it was about her. She turned away from his gaze to look down the bar, back at the two young men who were watching them with avid curiosity. They stayed away, though. Probably smart of them to keep their distance.

"So what do we do?" Bruce asked.

Rob pulled himself from his thoughts to focus back on him. "We either get rid of him, or we try to get out of here before he completely changes."

"They already tried that. It didn't work."

"I know." He looked back at Denise. "But if this is spreading as fast as it is, the military will have checkpoints outside of town. We need to make it there. They might try to shoot us on sight, but she's been exposed and hasn't changed. She's immune. They need that. We need to get her to them."

Bruce looked at Rob, then Denise, who was now shaking her head vigorously. He could tell that if she had been able to melt deeper into the wall to get away from them, she would.

"I don't think it's a good idea to go back out there."

"You know any other options?"

"I have some guns in my truck. Sawed-off shotgun in a hidden compartment above the visor, and a semi-automatic underneath the driver's seat. I don't go to New Jersey much, but when I do, I like to be prepared. I've had people try to break into the truck before and had to send them off with 'Daddy's little helper'."

Rob was nodding at him. He turned and looked down the length of the bar at the two kids. "How's it look out there? Think we can make it to the semi?"

"They're spreading out, so maybe. Don't know, man. We got it secured in here pretty good. The windows are high enough, so they can't just climb in here. Back door is barred. Only access is the back loading door, which is barred, and the front door." Sullivan said, turning back from the front window to look at them.

"I thought you wanted to get back to your guns and hole up in the bullet," Jason said.

"Fuck. The bullet wouldn't last this shit. We need to get out of here if this shit spreads, but if the military can keep it contained, we might as well sit tight and wait for help."

"Think the military *will* contain it?"

Rob was walking closer to them. The two had been arguing back and forth, different scenarios about what to do in the wake of the zombie apocalypse. He had noticed that the conversation felt like it was an old argument, and they both went back and forth, changing views on what they should be doing. Neither could seem to keep it straight. Then again, Rob guessed that was probably the nerves, as neither one of them had ever actually believed it *would* happen. At least, he hoped neither one of them did.

Then again, it *was* happening. Was it really that crazy of a thing to believe in and plan for? The crazies no longer seemed so crazy when their conspiracy comes true.

"If the military does come in, I don't think they will be taking chances on saving too many people. It will probably be a firehouse incursion, burning out the infection. That is, unless they have already found a cure, but looking at how long it usually takes to research and find a cure to *established* viral infections, I doubt they will have anything for…" Sullivan stopped, thinking about it. Then he turned and looked down the bar towards Denise. "How long does it take for find a cure to a disease?"

"There isn't any set time frame to find a cure. Look at HIV and cancer. Both have spread judiciously, and have continued to spread. Millions on top of millions is spent a year on research to find a cure. HIV has been around a long time, hitting its stride in the eighties, spreading vigorously but, to this day, we still do not have a cure."

Sullivan looked from Denise to Jason, then to Rob. "Yeah. They're not going to be coming to help, are they?"

Rob shook his head. He didn't think they would, not with how many of the things were now out in the street. The numbers didn't add up. The military couldn't afford to send people in, other than to maybe take a few test subjects and then burn the rest.

Rob quickly looked over at Bruce, a sudden terrible thought making his gut wrench in pain. This could be bad. This could be very bad.

"They don't have to come in to burn them out. They don't have to send troops in."

"Who are you kidding? Of course they do. They can't bomb us on U.S. soil."

"No? Why risk troops?"

"There is no telling if those things have gotten that bad out there. We've only seen the one street. It might be isolated to just this part of town."

Rob nodded. Maybe it *wasn't* that bad out there.

Tina stepped out of the hallway, still holding the baby, which had been sleeping since they had gotten it back in from outside. It was so small and quiet, somehow able to live in its own peaceful world as the world around it was falling into a chaotic nightmare.

"That woman died out there. She doesn't have a mother now," Tina said as she looked at the baby. "I don't think it's safe out there."

Jason got off his stool and walked over to her. He put his arm around her and pulled her close. "Okay."

Rob nodded, put his hands on the bar, and lowered his head. "Back to square one. What do we do?"

"Do you really think it's a quarantine?" Bruce asked him. Rob looked into the eyes of the large man, a pained expression haunting his eyes.

He nodded slowly. "Just makes sense. My car should have been in town by now. Think about it. It's been more than just a few hours. There has been no tow truck. Have you seen any cars? Besides those things out there, have you seen anyone? And the television and the phones are all out. Can you think of any other explanation?"

"They got here pretty fast. Could they be doing some kind of experiment?"

Rob thought about that for a minute. He knew the government had done some truly evil things in the past, but he couldn't see this. Not in the Midwest, not on their own soil. He shook his head. He looked up to see that they were all looking at him.

A loud crash came from somewhere down the hallway behind the bar. Everyone jumped, and more pounding echoed down the hall. Tina quickly moved to look back that way, then turned to Rob. Her eyes were wide, like a deer caught in the headlights. He motioned for her to start backing away towards the end of the bar. He put a finger to his lips and she nodded, moving slow, backing away.

As she moved, Rob quietly climbed on top of the bar, the stiffness of his right leg working against him as he pulled it over, then hung both legs over on the other side. He tried to drop as quietly as possible. It wasn't far and there were mats on the floor to keep the bartenders from slipping on the floor when it got wet.

He looked around for a weapon. He caught motion out of the corner of his eye and saw Denise tentatively moving closer, coming from the back of the bar where she had been keeping her distance from everyone. He nodded to her, then looked around. His eyes fell on the fire extinguisher. From what he could see, it was about the only weapon he could see back there. He looked over at Jason.

"Do you have anything back here?"

"No, just the extinguisher."

Rob looked at it and grimaced. He didn't like the idea of how close he would have to get to hit anyone with it, and he doubted spraying the CO2 would do any good. But he guessed it was better than nothing. He grabbed it and pulled it from the hook it was hanging.

He turned back to the hallway. The pounding sound was getting more intense, sounding like something was slamming against the delivery door, trying to get in.

He took a step towards the hallway.

"Why are they trying to get in back there?" Bruce said in a loud whisper to Jason.

"How do they even know we're in here?"

Sullivan shrugged. "Who knows? They seemed to be going into random houses on the street, but it's like they just know where people are."

Rob turned to look back at the trio standing at the bar. He was glaring at them, mentally telling them to shut the hell up but, deep down, he wanted to know the same answers. They stared back at him, and all of them nodded. He nodded back and turned away.

There really wasn't much light in the little hallway that lead back into the cooler. Two doors off to the right lead to the bathrooms, and just beyond them was the back room that had the loading doors, then the small room that would lead straight into the cooler.

Rob stopped at the threshold, not wanting to go farther back, holding the fire extinguisher over his head to use as a weapon.

"Ahh!" he heard someone yell behind him, and he quickly ran back out of the hallway and looked down the length of the bar.

Travis had rushed at Tina as she had been coming around the edge of the bar, and Rob watched as she quickly backed away from him, holding his child tightly against her chest. She was trying not to stumble, but she also couldn't watch where she was going. Travis wasn't moving steadily, and was more like stumbling towards her.

"Help!" she screamed as she reached the tables and chairs near the wall, getting her legs tangled. She let out a scream, then she was falling back.

Rob was already hurrying over. The redneck was still moving towards her, and when she had fallen, had been there to fall with her. His arms were still fastened behind his back, but he was thrashing them, bobbing his head forward, his mouth opening and closing, trying to chomp down onto something invisible.

"Fuck! I told you the fucker was becoming one of them," he heard one of the kids saying from behind him, or maybe it was Bruce. He wasn't paying too much attention. Now they had to deal with this asshole. No, *they* didn't have to. *He* had to. It was obvious that none of the others were rushing over to help.

It was obvious when the man fell that he hadn't been under control. His feet were too far behind him to keep him from falling forward. He was close to Tina, who had fallen hard and was trying to protect the baby. While Tina was crying out from what had to be a bone-jarring landing, the redneck didn't seem like he was even phased by it.

As Rob rounded the edge of the bar, he stopped for a brief moment and noticed how the man wiggled like a worm, squirming his way towards her. Rob also noticed how the cut that had been on the man's leg was no longer bleeding. It had plenty of time to stop flowing, but Rob didn't really believe that was it. He was sure that if he looked at the man's face, into his eyes, he would see grey, lifeless orbs staring back at him.

He wasn't about to let it have the chance to get to Tina and the baby. He hurried behind it and grabbed one of its ankles, having to fight as the thing kept kicking. It wasn't actively trying to get away from him. It just didn't seem like it had full control over its body, and was concentrating on its goal, Tina.

He got a good grip and dragged the thing back, pulling it until it was back under the pool table light. He let go and moved away from it. It turned towards him, its lifeless eyes on him. There was no emotion in them, it was a dead look, but the mouth never quit moving.

It wriggled and writhed, working to twist its way around so it could start pushing itself towards him. Rob brought the extinguisher up and looked down at the mouth, the eyes, trying to remind himself that the thing was no longer alive. It wanted to bite into him, eat him, do whatever it was it wanted to do to him, and if he let it get too close, he would never see his wife or son again. He had to kill it.

Behind him, there was a loud pounding. Rob turned in time to see that the plywood was on the floor, and the pool table had been worked away from the broken window. The booming sound was the dart machine slamming against the ground, and four of the things were trying to get in the window. Somehow they were high enough that their arms were well inside the building and they were trying to pull themselves in.

Rob danced back, trying to keep Travis from biting into his ankles. Travis had managed to get close to him, and he barely kept his feet out of his reach. He tripped himself up and barely had time to get some semblance of balance to keep from falling to the ground. Instead, he slammed back against the bathroom door.

"They're getting in! Grab something to help. We need to push them back," he yelled to the rest of them. Travis was becoming more frantic, and Rob kicked him, sprawling the scrawny man back a few feet, but he quickly recovered and was turning to come back at him.

Rob looked at the little fire extinguisher in his hand and tossed it aside, hurrying over to the corner to grab a chair. Sure, he wasn't a lion tamer, and this wasn't Vegas, but he wanted to have the extra reach to push against them. He charged forward, slamming the legs of the chair into the first one trying to get through the window. It fell from the others, landing on the ground.

He aimed towards the next one and turned, slamming his chair into it, but the one next to it grabbed at the legs, and Rob had to wrestle with it. He was struggling, having to shake it back and forth. His grip was wet from his sweat-covered hands, and he could feel the chair starting to slip from his hands. He tried to jerk it back, to get it away from the thing.

For a moment, he was caught up in looking into its dead eyes looking at him. He saw the thing had gashes along its face, part of its jaw was missing, and skin was torn free from what was left of its face. Its arms and hands had claw marks up and down them, and there were nails stuck into its flesh. Probably from when it had still been human and had tried to claw the spiders out.

Rob wondered if the spiders were real. If so, where were they and why couldn't he see them? Denise had said all the infected things had claimed they had seen spiders before they had been transformed. Where were they? He wasn't seeing any, and he didn't see any coming after him.

He saw movement out of the corner of his eye. Travis was getting closer to him again. He kicked out at the man, slamming his shoe against his head, sending him back again. The chair slipped more out of his grip and he was holding onto it towards the top, not able to swing it anymore.

Bruce appeared next to him with another chair and slammed it into the thing that had been holding his chair. It fell to the ground, as did the other one that Rob had been trying to hit.

Three of them had fallen, and Rob and Bruce could see five more fighting to climb up and take their place. Twenty more were coming up behind them. The more the two men fought with them, the more excited the things seemed to be getting. They were making some weird groan-like sounds, fighting to push their way up.

Bruce looked at Rob, a look of sheer terror replacing that coolness the man had exerted for most of the morning. They both slammed chairs against the fourth thing, knocking it away, before they tossed their chairs to the side. They turned and saw Travis quickly trying to worm his way towards them.

"Quick!" Rob yelled.

They both hurried over to the thing on the floor and grabbed him by his ankles. Then they dragged him to the open window, working to fling the creature out and into the dumpster. He collided with the next wave of them that had been climbing up, and they all fell backwards.

"Get the board up!"

"It isn't going to last long."

"I know. Let's just get it up. We gotta get out of here."

"Where to?"

"Your truck. It has a sleeper. Think you can fit all of us in there?"

"It'll be a tight fight."

"Better than a beetle."

Bruce stopped as they had been lifting the board, giving him an odd look. Rob shrugged, knowing it was a bad time to make a joke, but he always had found humor his best defense in the worst of situations. Though his jokes were never funny, he enjoyed them.

"You know, a clown car."

Bruce nodded, though it showed either he still didn't get it, or just felt it wasn't funny. Then again, it could be he was questioning just how optimistic it was to think they were all going to get out of there.

* * * *

Jason watched as the two men hurried in from the back alcove, then turned to look at Tina. She was watching them wearily, holding the baby, unconsciously rocking to keep her asleep. It was amazing how the little one could stay asleep through so much yelling and racket. Every baby he had ever known had been a noise machine. This one seemed content to stay quiet and sleep.

Jason found himself smiling as he turned away, coming face-to-face with Rob. "We need to get out of here. That isn't going to hold them." He was talking to all of them, and Jason realized it was something the two of them had already talked about. They were now just letting everyone else know what their plan was. Jason nodded, though he wasn't too sure he wanted to go out there.

He looked over to see that Tina had also backed away from the cop and was holding the child protectively, her hand coming up to hold up the back of its head. Something was happening in her. She was standing up a little straighter. He wasn't sure if it had anything to do with the baby, but it might have. No one else was around to take care of the little one now, and Tina seemed to have taken it on. It had somehow transformed her. He couldn't help but look at her a little differently. She looked like she was…older.

"I'm not going out there, not with the baby. She could wake up, then they would be on us. I'm not leaving her here, either," Tina was saying as she backed away.

Jason hadn't realized she had been backing towards the front door. The hairs on the back of his neck stood up and something told him that wasn't the best idea. They should be staying away from the front door. If they were breaking through the barricade in the back, the front door wasn't going to hold. He didn't care if it did have the large rail across it. It was still fastened to bolts on either side of the frame. Those screws, as big as they were, didn't seem to be the most secure.

He twisted around and eyed the table next to the front door. Most days, it was just an empty table in the corner. It was really only there for Sunday's when they did the "Make your own Bloody Mary" day. It was the condiment table where they put out all the fixings. He looked at it and wondered how well it would wedge under the handle of the door, and if it would actually keep out the horde that was growing outside.

He just had time to think about it before there was a loud crash against the front door. While the locks held, a large crack formed down the wall along the side of the door. It was quickly followed by another pounding, then smaller slams.

Jason sprang into action and slammed the table under the handle, wedging it in as tight as he could. He didn't think it would hold long, but doubted it would matter. If the wall around the door gave way, the last thing they had to worry about was the lock. They needed something more to secure it.

He looked around, and saw that Rob and Bruce had already been thinking the same thing. Both of them were bringing over barstools and slamming them against the door.

"One of these won't do much good, but we pile a shit ton up, that should work," Bruce said. Sullivan had quickly joined them, and the four of them were rushing back and forth, grabbing and piling stools by the door until it was a large mound.

Now they had the zombies pounding at the front door, against the back window, and by the loading dock. He knew they had to stay put now, but where could they hide? Where was the one place they would be safe?

He looked over at Tina behind the bar. She must have scurried back there while they were fighting with the door. Good. Probably the best place for her. The only place left to get in or out was the large front window. He didn't think it would take them too long before they were trying to get in there, too.

"We have to get out of here before they completely get us penned in," Rob said.

Jason turned to look at him. "We need to get in the cooler. They can't get us in there." Rob looked at him. He was tired of this guy telling them what they needed to do. If they listened to him, he was going to get them all killed. Before Rob could stop him, he continued, "We can wait until help comes in there. We'll have food and water, and they won't be able to get in there. We can lock it from the inside. No one will be able to get us."

"Kid, think about it. Wait for how long?" Bruce asked.

"Dude, we can't stay here," Sullivan said.

"Sullivan, you're the one that always said when the zombie apocalypse happens, we get somewhere safe and wait it out. We talked about this shit," Jason reminded him.

"Yeah, and your mom's bar was not even in the top fifty places we considered a safe place to wait it out. We got to get out of here."

The two glared at each other. Neither was giving in.

"I'm not going out there," Tina said again. Jason could see she was already making her way towards the cooler. The pounding was getting louder back there. She was eyeing it hesitantly, but was still easing her way back.

"So how do we get out of here?" Sullivan asked.

He was standing in the center of the bar, looking around. They had blocked up nearly all the exits. There was only the front window, which they would have to break to get out. When they did that, this place was done. If they didn't go with the ones that left, they wouldn't be able to stay in there. They would have to get to the cooler.

Jason looked over at Sullivan. His expression was grim and his face pale. He didn't like it, either. As excited as they both had been about the zombie apocalypse finally happening and being in the center of it all, the reality was also starting to slip in. They just might not live through all of this. No matter what they had talked about and how much Sullivan had actually planned for it, they were still caught by surprise.

The best laid plans were for nothing, and they might be next on the menu because of it.

Sullivan was looking past Jason, studying the front window, as Denise was coming up behind him. She was becoming more distant and quiet.

He remembered when he had first picked her up at the strip mall. She had been so persistent and eager for them to get out of there. He was sure once the ones who were going would escape, she would be one of them. She was trapped in there with the rest of them. It was because of him that she was there. There had been a chance she could have gotten out, but now she was just another mouse in a cage.

They all were. They were all going to die in there. How long would it be before help came? They could hold out in the cooler for probably a week, maybe more. It would be a long week, and they would have to survive off of beer, peanuts, and whatever else his mother had been weird enough to store in there. She had always been the "Everything gets stored in the cooler" type of person, and he never understood it. Now he was thankful for it.

Denise was reaching out for Sullivan's shoulder. Did they know each other? Jason couldn't recall Sullivan ever saying anything about her, and he had always referred to the town's doctor as that "Not illegal foreigner", as though it was just a good thing the man wasn't from Mexico. He couldn't recall a time he had ever talked about the nurse as though he knew her, and they hadn't really said too much to each other since she had been there.

Then Jason noticed the long, deep gashes on her arms. He recalled seeing her scratching, but hadn't thought anything about it. However, now he could see just how deep they were. They dug down into the muscle fibers and there were strands of loose muscle hanging free, but there was no blood.

"Sully! Loo—" he had just started to say when she had him by the arm, biting down. Sullivan let out a loud scream, cutting through the bar, and turned, slamming his fist into the woman's pale face.

Rob and Bruce had been looking out the window, but turned. It took them a minute to register what was happening.

Rob was first to respond, grabbing the fire extinguisher that he had put on the counter and bringing it down on Denise's head. It hit home with a dull thud, and Sullivan screamed louder, his scream turning to that of a higher pitch because instead of Denise releasing him, she seemed to bite down harder.

The pain must have been unbearable, and Sullivan was trying to fight to get her off. Rob continued to pound at her head as Sully was trying to pull his arm away, screaming at each hit of the extinguisher.

It didn't take long. Sullivan's knees just seemed to give away, and he dropped hard on them. Denise came down with him and pushed forward, covering more of him with her body.

Rob kept slamming the extinguisher down on her, and Jason was grabbing one of the bar stools to use as a weapon when Bruce yelled for him to stop. Jason looked over at him. "There's nothing you can do for him. We need to get out of here."

Jason looked up and around. His gaze settled on Tina, who was down the hallway. She had the baby and was looking back at him. "I'm not going."

"We *need* to go," Bruce pleaded.

Jason looked at Tina again, the back at Bruce. "You guys go. We're staying."

"You realize once the…"

"Go!" Jason said as he brushed past Bruce and brought the stool down on the back of Denise.

Rob backed away, letting Jason through. The two of them stared at each other briefly, then Rob turned towards the window.

Jason heard glass crash, but didn't turn to look. He slammed the stool down on the corpse one, two, three more times before he was out of breath and backing away.

"Go. Get out of here," Sullivan was saying through gagging breaths.

Jason wasn't ready to go yet. He bent over Denise, grabbed her by the shoulders, and started to pull. He had to get her away from him. His friend was going to be okay. It was only a light bite on the arm. They could amputate it. There was still time. He would be okay. Everything would be fine.

Jason gave one more pull, putting all his strength into it, more strength than he thought he had. He felt his stomach muscles pull, his back started to ache. Now he wished all those hours he had spent playing video games that he had spent maybe a little of that time in the gym. Why couldn't he have worked out just a little bit? Would that really have been too much to ask? The thing never let go. She continued to bite into Sullivan. The little frame of a woman was stronger than him.

Jason's grip gave away and he was stumbling back. He hadn't realized he had stopped breathing until he felt faint. What was he going to do? His friend…

"Dude," came the labored breath blow him, "what the fuck?"

Jason looked down. He heard the gasping, gurgling breath and saw she had moved from just biting into his arm to biting into his neck.

There was no hope for Sullivan. His eyes were already losing their focus as they just stared up at the ceiling.

Jason had to get out of there. He knew that Tina and he had to get to back to the cooler. He could feel the breeze from the open window and didn't have to look to know that it was completely busted out. They were exposed now, and it wouldn't be long before the things started coming in.

He glanced in that direction and saw the first of the zombies crunching against the glass and trying to pull their way in. It was an old man wearing a plain pastel blue shirt and some kind of tan khaki shorts. Jason had a brief moment to wonder if the guy had been on the golf course this morning

Tina and the baby were in front of him, already moving down the hall. He made sure they had a clear path, then turned to look back. Sullivan and Denise were now out of view, but the one that had been coming in the window was now crawling its way onto the bar with two more behind it, pulling their way into the window.

Jason didn't know if Rob and Bruce were okay and if they had made it out. He couldn't see them. The three zombies were already inside, and more were on their way. He couldn't believe how many of them there already were. How had this spread so fast? The front window was quickly filling with them, and one was on the bar, working his way over it and falling to the floor.

Jason quickly woke up from his daze and stepped back. They had to go.

He turned to see that Tina was all the way in the back room already, holding open the cooler. The soft light from inside gave her a glow that seemed to halo around her, and the cool gushing air created a surreal fog. She had that heavenly look, and maybe it was because he felt like once they were in there, it was their first step towards salvation. He didn't know, but knew it was where they needed to go. They just had to lock themselves in and they were safe.

He rushed down the hallway.

He crossed over the threshold, realizing his mistake. How many times had he gone into that back room, tripped over that little step down, then hit his head on the low ceiling? No matter how many times it had been, he still always did it. Now, he did it again. However, he was running towards it this time, and when he hit the drop in the ceiling, he felt the white flash of pain shoot through his head.

He didn't have time to try and force it down. His teeth clenched together, and he tried to reach out to keep himself from collapsing. He could hear the things behind him. They were pounding louder and louder against the walls. His head was pounding. The world around him was spinning. The ground seemed like it was getting closer, then falling away.

He felt arms reach around him, and he spun away, quickly grabbing at the tentacles that tried to ensnare him. He could feel a bite on his neck, then another tearing into the top of his head.

"Jason!"

He opened his eyes with sudden realization, and saw that Tina had him. She was trying to pull him into the cooler. The baby was inside, lying on her blanket in a box that Tina had found. The pain in his head was subsiding a little, the pounding relaxing to a dull thud.

No, there was still pounding. He turned to see that the loading door was still getting pounded into. The door was pushed in about a foot, well off its hinges. There were now large gaps along each side and hands were reaching in, but when he had fallen forward, he had stayed just out of reach. The gap was growing wider, and it wouldn't be long before they would be inside.

"Jason, we have to get in the cooler. Come on."

He looked at her and nodded.

A hand reached out through the door and just caught his sleeve. For a moment, he thought they were actually about to get him. He could feel himself losing his balance and falling backwards. He could see down the hall. An old guy had gotten up and was stumbling down the hall towards them.

Tina quickly came around and pulled on Jason's arm. The hand felt like it had him in an iron grip, but they pulled, and it finally slipped free.

The hand tried to grab at Jason again, but they were already backing into the open door of the cooler.

CHAPTER 20

"Sergeant, General Mayfever is on the line, demanding an update."

Wade turned to look at McCormick, who had come up behind him. He hadn't even heard the young corporal walk up. He had been standing there, thinking, and wasn't really aware of his surroundings.

He was dead inside, he knew that now, and he really didn't even care. He didn't think he had long to worry about it anyway. None of them were going to get out of this. If he was honest with himself, he realized that fact once he had heard they were setting up the outer perimeter, but he had still done his job and he would continue to do his job.

He could no longer stand there and think about his sister, his family. They were already lost. If he had gone for them like his brain had been nagging him to do, they would probably still be lost. Even if he had been able to get them back out, they would never have gotten past the outer perimeter.

Now it was too late. Something was happening in the town. He just wasn't sure what. He had been getting reports from the inner roadblocks and had heard that shots had been fired. There were things, human-shaped things, attacking them every so often. He didn't have full reports, only that the things were hard to kill, and it took near dismemberment to stop even just one of them.

Over the course of the last few hours, they had stopped having any people try to get out. They had one family try to get out after the CDC team went in. Thankfully, that family had turned back without incident. There had been no others since then.

He turned around and followed the corporal towards their communication post. It was better not to think about what they already had to do.

What was happening in the town? The CDC was in there, people weren't coming out anymore, and now there were these "things".

"Stop where you are!" he heard one of his soldiers yell. He looked over to see a couple more soldiers hurry over, all raising their rifles. Wade could just see where they were pointing them and watched as five people were walking towards the checkpoint. No, that wasn't right. They weren't really walking. They were more like shuffling, staggering.

He walked over towards his men, calling out to McCormick, "Tell the major he will have to wait. We have a situation developing."

McCormick nodded to him and hurried off.

"What's happening? Why didn't you call me over?"

"Sergeant, they had been making their way closer, but had stopped for a while. We really hadn't known what to make of it."

They were still a couple hundred feet away, but were slowly walking towards them.

"What should we do?"

"Get yourselves in position. Jones, Krist, take up the corner positions. Then rest of you know where to go."

Jones and Krist walked off, working to the fringes of the barricade. Each one took a corner. That way, they could fire into a "V".

He could feel that something was happening, although he didn't know if that was because of this, or just because the day had been getting worse. The sun was low, and it would only be an hour until darkness. They weren't set up to stay out there for too much longer, and they were not prepared to be out there at night.

"They are not stopping," one soldier pointed out. He had to look at the name on the uniform. Tims. It sounded familiar, though he wasn't sure why. He thought maybe it had something to do with some discipline he had doled out. It didn't matter.

Wade stepped forward. "By order of the United States Army, you are hereby ordered to turn around and head back into town. You cannot leave. There is an incident, and you are ordered to return home and stay there. It is not safe. You must return home," he yelled out to them, his voice booming.

They kept coming, were only a hundred feet away now, and he could see there was something seriously wrong with them. Their clothing was ripped, exposing their skin. One of them, a man who looked to be in his late thirties, had a long rip down the side of his pants. It looked like part of his flesh was white and pale, but then there were dark spots.

As they continued to get closer, he could see that one of them was missing a hand, leaving only a bloody stump. The hand was gone, the bone exposed, and there was just a red mess where the hand should have been. When he looked closer, he realized that the hand wasn't completely gone. There was a finger remaining, dangling from flesh that just barely held it.

One of them, one he had thought had been wearing tight yoga pants, was not wearing anything. That wasn't a dark, workout garment. It was like she was coated in something. As she got closer, he could see where it had faded in a few places and there was pale flesh underneath.

He could see their faces in the remaining light. He saw the deep gashes in their skin, and the massive amount of disfiguration. He should have seen it before they had even gotten that close, but he hadn't been looking there. He had been watching their forms.

"Sergeant…?"

They were getting closer and he knew his men were awaiting his orders. He had given the order once already, but it seemed harder to take his eyes away this time. Just what was going on?

"Fire!" he yelled.

The first shot tore into the face of the woman covered in blood. The shot ripped through her cheek, and he watched as the back of her head exploded outwards. The woman stumbled back, falling. One down. The soldier who had fired was already turning to fire at the next one, but the sergeant didn't watch. He was watching the woman he had shot. She had fallen back, landed, and should have been dead. Instead, she turned over and stumbled to get up.

These were the things. These were the things the other barricades had reported about. They sure did look human.

What was going on in that town? These things didn't just *look* human. They had to have *been* human at some point. There was nothing that could copy humanity to that degree.

There was no imitation to that kind of carnage as it walked toward them. He was amazed and horrified by it. This was a horror film come alive. Would his sister be a part of it? Would he have to shoot her as she stumbled forward?

Just what the hell was going on in there?! He watched as the woman got back to her feet, the back of her head gone, the grey matter of her brain oozing out. The woman should not be moving. How was she moving?!

Wade looked to see the next man the soldier had shot…the one missing the hand. The soldier had made another head shot and the man had stumbled back, but didn't even fall to the ground. The right side of his head was completely gone, but he was still coming forward.

"Ah!" he heard the scream from one of his men, and he turned to see that Jones, who had been positioned at the outer leg of their "V", had a dark shape appear behind him and start pulling him back into the tall corn. Then there were more dark shapes emerging from the corn, staggering in from the sides, stumbling as they walked down the embankment of the ditch, moving towards his men.

He quickly pulled his sidearm and was hurrying towards Jones. Behind him, he heard more shouting and shots ringing out. He heard himself screaming, "Fire! Take them out! Fire!"

He didn't have to look around to know that all his men, who had been standing around most of the day, were now amidst a flurry of activity.

He heard another scream from behind him. He didn't need to turn to know that another one of his men was getting attacked.

Wade fired his sidearm into the first one he neared and watched the face disappear as his bullet tore through it, just to have the thing keep stumbling towards him. He fired again and again, the bullets slamming into the skull, exploding out the back, but the thing kept coming, barely slowing down.

He stopped before he got too close to the thing, realizing he had emptied his clip. He grabbed another from his belt and in a smooth, well-practiced motion, slammed the new clip into his revolver. As he did, he took a moment to stop and look around.

His men had formed a line at the barricade and were firing into the five coming down the street. The things weren't moving fast, but they were getting closer, and the bullets tearing through them barely seemed to slow them down. It made them stagger, but not stop. The five coming down the street now had more that had joined them, ones that had been in the cornfield. More dark shapes were still emerging, stumbling forward.

Jones was gone, and there was no way he could go in after him. Where Jones had disappeared into the corn, dark shapes continued to flow out. On the other side, Krist was staggering away from the field. He had his hand to his neck, but it wasn't stopping the flow of blood flooding out of him. His gaze was lost, he was going into shock, and he staggered as though he was one of those things. Behind him, there were three coming for him. Within seconds, they had overtaken him, and they all fallen to a heap on the ground.

"Fall back!" he yelled.

Where would they fall back to? He knew they couldn't make it to the outer perimeter, and even if they did, they would be shot on sight. Their only option was to hold. They needed to form up and get a strong line of fire that can wipe these things out.

Just ignore that there was probably even more of the things in the corn. He couldn't worry about that now. They had to get this taken care of. Get these things put down, then they could get patrols formed up and go hunting for more.

"Fall back! Form up!" He watched as his men were moving to fall back to his position, getting into a line of fire.

"McCormick!" he yelled.

He looked over and saw the little man was already near him, his face pale. The kid had probably shit himself when he had seen the first one get back up. He could see puke all down the front of his uniform.

"Get on the horn. Let command know we are taking fire and falling back. Tell them we're trying to hold, but may be overrun. Go!"

The corporal stood there, watching as the things continued to take fire. He wasn't even looking at the sergeant. He rushed over to him and harshly shook the man. Slowly, the man's eyes seemed to focus on him.

"Go! Get on the horn! Let them know we are being overrun!"

"Yes, sergeant," he said, but he still wasn't moving.

"Go!"

He had to forcefully push the man, causing him to stumble back. He caught himself, again looking at the things coming towards them. Then he was gone, running towards his little communication tent.

Wade turned back around and emptied his clip into the closest one, watching as its head continued to explode until it was nothing more than a bottom jaw on top of a body. The thing kept coming, its tongue barely fastened to whatever it was connected to inside its head, flopping as it continued to come. Those things were not stopping.

* * * *

On the bank of monitors in his office, the general watched the video feed. There were ten screens, various shots of different views inside and out of the trailer, rotating through as the situation was developing. All of the screens were randomly changing, but he had locked the one directly in front of him on a view of the operating area of the trailer.

He watched as the body had first been thrown down onto the table, then saw as the thing had leaped up and attacked the doctor.

The general had watched as part of a corpse came to life and attacked their scientist. It was vicious, and the soldier in the room with them seemed to have a hard time fighting it.

The general had also watched the soldiers inside the doctor's office, thanks to the cameras built into the helmets. He had watched as the three soldiers had fought against the same corpse and had barely been able to stop it.

Whatever the thing was, whether it was dead or not, it was not easy to kill. If it could be controlled, it would be one hell of a weapon. If they could find out what created it, find out how to tame it, it would be unstoppable. They would have the perfect weapon. There wouldn't be anybody out there who could stop them. Even fighting terrorists, they could just drop a few of these things in the general area of the insurgents and just let it go. There would be collateral damage, but that was easy to hide. The things couldn't be killed, and when the incursion was over, he'd just pick up the pieces.

He couldn't help but appreciate the pure beauty of how deadly just one undead corpse could be. It would revolutionize warfare, and it had just fallen into his lap.

"Sir?"

The general looked up and saw Captain Davis standing in the doorway.

"Yes, captain?"

"We are getting reports back. The soldiers outside the trailer are getting attacked."

The general looked over at another screen as it flipped back to the outer corner of the trailer. He saw three soldiers there. Two of them were fighting against the things surrounding them, while they tried to drag the third one towards the trailer. They still had quite a distance to go, but it was hard to tell just how far from the perspective of the camera.

He could see there were a lot more of the things out there now. They disappeared beyond where the camera could see. More were staggering into frame, surrounding his troops.

"Thank you, captain." He kept the commanding tone in his voice, hiding the exasperation he was feeling. He just couldn't believe how amazing these things were as killing machines. It was fascinating to watch as they surrounded their targets, attacked, then moved on. Whatever was in their way, they would just overcome. No matter what it was, they just swarmed over it.

It almost reminded him of ants. Wasn't it fire ants that did that? When there was food or danger, they would swarm over it, the workers attacking, then returning to their queen. He didn't watch television so he had never watched those animal shows, but he thought he had seen or heard something like that.

This was how he imagined they worked…surrounding, devouring, moving on.

Nothing seemed to really slow them down, so how could they control it? These weapons were too good to let go. They needed to find a way to prevent this from spreading, and they needed to get it contained.

"Knock, knock." He turned from the monitors to see that the captain had left, and Major Burns was standing there.

"Not good news?" the major asked as he stepped into the office.

"They are overtaking our CDC team and their support," the general said as he went back to watching the monitors. Not liking the man, he really didn't want to have to deal with him, although he knew as much as he wanted to ignore him, he wasn't going to go away. The major was like an annoying fly that, as much as you swatted at it, just would not fly away. Though a fly might leave a person alone if they ignored it long enough. He doubted the major would.

The major took a seat and just sat there quietly.

The general continued to watch the carnage on the screen. "Do you ever wonder why we do what we do?" the general asked.

"What do you mean?"

"I'm watching men die. Soldiers, somebody's husband or wife. People are dying, and for what reason? It's easy to contain the threat here, but we send these same men and women overseas to other countries to fight. We always look to find new weapons to make killing the enemy more effective. Kill the enemy while incurring the least amount of collateral damage. So we're always looking for that new weapon.

"So…here I am, watching those things kill people, and I'm watching it…"

The general turned, looking into the major's eyes. He could feel the bags under his own, and hadn't realized how tired he felt. The day was wearing on him. It was becoming a long one and he didn't think he was going to get rest anytime soon. Not until this mess was over.

"Here I am, watching this, and I don't care about the lives lost. I'm thinking about how great a weapon these things are. I want to find a way to control them. Why? Why do we do the things we do? Why do we do this?"

"We do this because it has to be done. We do this because others can't. And we do this because we love the look on the innocent's face right before we put a bullet through their skull."

The general's forehead creased in disapproval, his eyebrows raised as he glared into the other man's dark eyes. Those eyes just burned into him, not relenting.

"Have you ever actually been in the field? What do you know about it?" the general growled.

"I've done my time."

"Yeah. I'm sure you have. I can see it in your scars."

The smile returned to the major's face, but it still never seemed to be truly genuine. It stayed there as the major seemed to be studying him. It unnerved him, but he tried to hold the man's glare. However, those dark eyes burrowed into him, and he could feel a pounding grow behind his temple. The world was thudding a tune, and everything else had gone silent, except for the humming of the monitors behind him.

The general turned to look back at the monitors, grimacing as he watched the things tearing into his men. The three who had been out of the trailer were now on the ground. His view was mostly obscured, but he could still see the dark liquid oozing out from under them. The parts of the bodies he could see were no longer moving.

"Did you know any of them?"

The general shook his head. Did he really know any of the soldiers under him anymore? He couldn't remember the last time he had really talked to any of his subordinates and learned anything about them.

These troops who were dying hadn't even been in his command. He learned long ago that it was not beneficial for him to even know their names. It was always harder to send someone off to die when you knew how many kids they had back home.

"Yeah. It's good not to know the ones you kill."

"Yeah."

"That's not what you're thinking about, though, is it?"

"Look at those things. They just keep coming. We've shot the hell out of them. Three of my men barely took down one of them. You get two of those things together and they are damn near unstoppable."

"You want to make more of them?"

"I want to know how to control them."

"To control them, you have to learn what they want. What are they after?"

"Looks like they're feeding."

"Are they?"

"Well, just look at them."

"Yeah, watch them. Look at that one. He doesn't even have a body anymore, but he's still eating."

The general looked at Burns, then looked back at the monitor he was pointing at. He saw one of the things without a head. It was still clawing at one of the men, but he couldn't really see what it was trying to do. It looked like it was trying to bite them, but there wasn't any head! It was pulling itself forward, the exposed spine moving forward and back.

"It doesn't know," the general mumbled.

"Maybe."

"You're right. If we could contain them, find a way to control them, it would be a great weapon for the U.S. military. It looks like we could just drop one of these into a terrorist camp… Hell, drop one into China and use their over-crowded cities against them. And it wouldn't even technically be biological warfare. I don't even know *what* you would call it."

The general turned to look back at the screen. His soldiers were dying. Actually, he hoped they were already dead. With no sound, he couldn't hear if they were screaming. At least that was a blessing. To control such a powerful weapon, releasing these things on their enemies… All they had to do was learn how to control them, and it would be a landfall of a weapon. These things were unstoppable, and he had found them.

"So what are you going to do? What should I tell the president?"

"Sir?" The captain had hurried back to the door. He was carrying a stack of photos under his arm.

"Yes, captain?"

"The zombies are taking over the inner perimeter. The men are trying to hold, but they are having to fall back."

"Zombies?"

"Sir?"

"Who the hell started calling the biological entities zombies?"

"I don't know, sir."

"Well, tell everyone to stop," the general snapped. "We don't need that shit spreading. Get back with the sergeant. Tell him he needs to hold. Also, get with the outer perimeter and set up some back-up for them. Tell them to be ready to shoot anyone on sight, no matter who they are."

"Sir, there's more."

"What?"

"We have the latest satellite feed. It's spreading. It looks like it has spread through most of the town. The zom-, *biological entities* are nearly filling the main streets and starting to head towards the outer areas."

The captain came in, spreading out the images of the satellite pictures across the general's desk. Each of the pictures depicted different people in the streets, masses of the biological entities surrounding them.

The general looked down at the images, each one showing carnage. It was primal and he couldn't help but think of predators tearing apart their prey. They were in a jungle…that was it…and man was no longer at the top of the food chain. Whatever these things were, they were taking over. They couldn't be stopped and they couldn't be controlled.

They needed something bigger.

The general looked up to see Burns looking at him like he was his own predator, sitting there licking his lips and ready to chomp at his running prey.

"The president needs to prepare his statement," the major said.

"And that is?"

"You tell me? These things make an excellent weapon. If we send a mass of troops in to contain them, then we have time to study them, learn how to control them."

The general looked at the pictures again, then turned to look at his display. More of them came in from the outer reaches of the frame, filling it as they went to the downed soldiers. Yes, these things would make a great weapon. Control. They needed control.

But people were dying, his troops were getting pushed back. He had to face the reality of it. If he let this go on, it would get further out of control.

He knew he was about to let the greatest weapon the United States had ever seen slip through his fingers, but he couldn't handle the fallout if he were wrong.

The general looked down at the images. "Captain, get me an ETA on when we will have the M.O.A.B ready."

"That seems drastic," Major Burns said as he looked at him, his smile not even touching the corner of his eyes.

"The bird is already in the air. It can reach the nest in twenty minutes," the captain responded

"They have a go. Launch code, AN3DND, Protocol Pompeii," the general said.

"Yes, sir," the captain said, then disappeared out of the office.

"You going to go watch the fireworks?" the major asked as he stood, straightening his uniform, then walking towards the door.

"No. When the world ends, I plan on drowning myself in ice, rather than the fire." The general walked over to the large liquor bar and poured himself a drink, then dropped in three large ice cubes.

"Farewell, my friend."

The general nodded to him as the man stood in the doorway. For the briefest of moments, the general swore he could smell raw sewage, the heavy stench filling the room and trying to gag him. He tried to ignore it, but he felt his face crinkle as it overtook him. Something must have died in the air conditioning vents and he must be smelling it now that the air had kicked on. Quick as he had smelled it, the foul odor was gone, and the major had left the room.

The general turned and looked at his drink. He watched as the ice cracked, splintering into different fractures. It seemed like the world was cracking, breaking apart. Everything was ripping at the seams and, right now, he was at the epicenter of it all. It was right were the person could fall the farthest, and he saw his future swirling around in that rich brown liquid. He knew the whiskey would burn on its way down, and the idea of sinking into it nagged at the corner of his mind.

He had never turned away from his responsibility and he wouldn't start now. However, and not for the first time, he wondered why he had ever joined the military. He could have done so many other things with his life, and none of them would have brought him there. Maybe he could be off somewhere right then, married, happy, living another life. He could have been doing so many other things

"I should have been a watchmaker."

CHAPTER 21

Westdale was not a scientist. He had not studied to be one, nor did he ever care much about the sciences. In high school, he had barely graduated. To him, a clear liquid was water. He didn't need to test it. If it was clear, you drank it. Thankfully, in his lab work in high school, he never put his theory to the test, but he didn't pay much attention to what the teacher had been saying, either. It wasn't only because his teacher had been one of the driest individuals to have ever walked the planet, making the class very painful to sit through, but it was also just something he had never been able to wrap his brain around.

So as he was now surrounded in the mobile lab, he really couldn't care less about its construction, about how the different sections and parts of the lab worked. He was in one part with chaos erupting around him, and he wanted out. His two options were to either go straight outside through the side door of the lab, or go through the inner door to the other section. There was a third scientist there, but that one hadn't been exposed to any of this. Westdale assumed that if he made it there, he would be safe. Well, at least safer until he could find another way out.

Westdale stepped over the thinner of the female scientists, the one who had been giving him orders since he had first gotten there, and rushed to the side airlock door. The larger scientist was still fighting with the torso. He didn't think her suit had been broken yet, but he was not about to take any more chances. Not for these people who had gotten them into this mess. These people were nuts. They could deal with their own problems.

He made it to the door and pounded. The glass…or whatever it was because he couldn't tell through the plastic of his own suit…made no sound. It didn't matter, though, because the third scientist was standing on the other side, his scared expression obvious through the little visor on his face.

"Let me in!" Westdale yelled. He knew that, through the radio transmitter in his suit, the man could hear him, even if he couldn't hear the pounding on the glass. They had all been sharing a frequency, and it was what had allowed them to have taken orders from the scientists when they had been in the doctor's office. That seemed like it was a lifetime ago, when it had only really been an hour. The radio was still working, so the man could definitely hear him.

However, it seemed like he wasn't going to pay attention to him. Instead, he was too caught up in what was going on behind Westdale. Westdale turned, having to use his whole body to see what was happening. The thin scientist was still on the floor; however, the other one was back against the other wall. Her suit was torn open now, and the woman was digging at her own skin. "Get them off of me. Get the spiders out of me! Please! Get them off!"

He didn't know what she was talking about. He didn't see anything. She was clawing deep gouges into her cheeks, then her neck. The veins were popping as she was struggling with herself. He knew that with how she was tearing away at the flesh, she would soon be tearing away at her carotid artery, and then she *really* wouldn't have much longer. At least he knew that much of basic medicine.

He turned back to the door. He had to scream to be heard over the scientist's yelling. "Get me out of here! Open the door."

The doctor seemed to wake a little from his trance and looked at the soldier as though it was the first time really seeing him there. Then he started to shake his head. It was barely a visible motion inside the suit. "No."

"You have to. They are both infected. I'm the only one left."

"How do I know *you* aren't infected?"

"Look at them, then look at me."

The doctor looked at the two other scientists, then back at the soldier. He knew the man must be weighing his options. Westdale thought he was going to have to get harsh with the man, figuring if he ordered him, he would open the door before he thought more about it. Then he saw the man cave in. Even through the large protective suit, he could register a slump to the shoulders, and the scientist started pressing some buttons near the door.

"You'll enter the air lock. There will be a few minutes of sanitation to your suit to make sure nothing biological comes through, then the inner door will open."

With a loud hiss, the outer door opened, and Westdale quickly stepped in.

* * * *

355

Westdale stepped out into the other side of the lab and looked at the smaller man. His suit read "Bernard". He nodded an acknowledgement to the man as he stepped into the inner sanctum. He wished he could take off his damned suit, but as the other scientist had his on, he felt safer doing the same. However, according to the flashing light out of the corner of his eye, he knew he needed to get a new oxygen tank hooked to it because his was running low.

"Thank you."

The scientist nodded, then looked back into the other room. Westdale followed his gaze. He watched as both scientists were moving. The thinner one was still on the ground, flailing as she was trying to get turned over to stand. She reminded him of a turtle that was stuck on its back. He knew these suits were hard to get turned over in, but knew right away that it wasn't her problem. He didn't have to see inside the suit to know she had become one of those things.

"They're both dead."

Westdale turned to look at Bernard. "What?"

"Look at their vitals. They are both dead. They shouldn't be moving. Neither one of them has a pulse. They're both dead."

"That's not possible."

"I know it's not, but they *are* both dead."

Westdale watched. The larger scientist was stumbling towards the glass wall. It was one of the two walls that separated them, but he still took a step back. She slammed into the wall as though she didn't see it there, then reached out to try and push through it. He noticed that, at some point, she had found her artery and blood should have been gushing out of her. It wasn't, and now the flow had stopped, leaving a puddle of red liquid all over the floor and down the front of her suit.

He turned away, and saw that the other scientist had done the same. Bernard was working to keep his eyes diverted to the monitors. There was the status monitor that had everyone's vitals. Of all the names listed, his and Bernard's were the only two that weren't flatline. Then there was the surveillance monitor, which showed multiple feeds from multiple cameras. In every view, those things were surrounding the trailer. There were so many of them out there. So many of the indestructible killing machines. Just one of them had killed two scientists and had nearly taken out his whole squad.

"We have to get out of here."

"Yeah? How?" Bernard asked, his dry tone thick with sarcasm. They both watched the monitors. They knew how hopeless their situation was. "There's nowhere to go. We have to wait for help. They have to send more troops in, right? They have to send in help."

Westdale saw the things out there. Were they really zombies? He had seen enough horror films to think the term fit, but zombies were supposed to die with a shot to the head, weren't they? These things just kept coming. Those weren't movie zombies. These were the real thing.

Yeah, that logic made sense on some level, but he sure wished he could be facing off against some of those movie zombies right about then. He wasn't a great shot but, if it would put these things down, he was sure he could score a few head shots. Shoot these things in the head, though, and they just kept coming at you. Hell, they'd even come at you without a head, arm, leg, whatever. Every piece of these things wanted to take you out. It was like every piece was alive, and not having a head no longer mattered.

"I don't think there is going to be anyone coming for us."

"They have to. We're not soldiers. They need us."

"Look at that out there. Do you think they are going to send troops into that? For what? One damn scientist and a private? You may not have noticed, but everything you see in here is sure as hell being broadcast out to command somewhere. They don't need you. They'll have other scientists studying this shit. No. If we are going to live, we need to get the hell out of here."

The doctor looked at him, then back at the monitors. Westdale could tell he wasn't getting through to the man, so he was going to have to think of something on his own. He turned and started to look around the small, cramped area. Just how the hell were the doctors supposed to work in there? His studio apartment in Chicago was bigger than that, and that sometimes felt like it was no bigger than a closet.

His eyes were drawn to the liquids stored on different shelves, locked into place for transport. There were different bottles, all of them having small, detailed labels.

He looked back at the parts of the thing in that room. Something was coming to him. What was it? He had wanted something. He had been thinking of something before. What was it?

That damn thing had taken bullets, had been torn apart, but the pieces were all still fighting. It didn't matter what the hell they did to it. It still came after them. They could blow its head clean off, and it would still come after them. The thing was unstoppable.

But what would happen if they burned it. Not just burned it, but completely incinerated it? That's right. He wanted to find a damn flamethrower. Of course, he wasn't going to find one in there. They wouldn't have stored one in a lab. The place didn't have an armory. It wasn't set up for soldiers. It was set up for scientists.

"What do you have in here that is flammable?"

"Um, well…" The doctor turned his questioning look to the soldier, then looked around. "Well, we have some ether and some other things. I'm not completely sure what we have. Su-" The man gulped when he tried to say her name, then looked into the lab at what had once been his boss. He turned back to the soldier. "Dr. Demoin had been in charge of organizing the list of what would be in here, but I'm sure we have ether."

The doctor turned around, looking at the bottles. The man seemed like he was starting to pull himself together, though it was still obvious he was very nervous as he continued rambling on, "Yeah, I had been making jokes about it. Talking about how we really felt like we were all going to start cooking up some meth. Of course, Beth, who had been on a scholarship through school and was from a bad neighborhood, hadn't found it too funny. I still say this place feels like we're in some TV cop show and need to be cooking something. That's what they call it, right? Cooking?"

"How would I know?" Westdale mumbled, continuing to look around, wishing the man would stop talking. It was probably good, as it meant his mind was working again, but it grated on Westdale's skull, and he really couldn't care less. The less he knew about the former people in the other room, the better he would be able to put them out of his mind. He just wanted to scream at the guy to shut the hell up and find some flammable shit. He had an idea. He wasn't sure if it would work, but he had one. At least it was something better than they had thought of so far.

"Found it!" the doctor exclaimed, and Westdale whirled around to see the man holding up a large glass jar with the printed label, *(C2H5)2O.*

"What's that?"

"Ether. Ethoxyethane, to be precise. Highly flammable."

"Okay. Anything else in here flammable? And we're going to need jars, a lighter, and some cloth."

"Um…" The doctor looked around again.

Westdale had the opinion that the doctor seemed to be getting where he was going with his shopping list, so maybe they would be able to get out of there. He didn't feel like they would need to get very far. They just needed to clear a path to the armored Humvee parked behind the trailer. If they could get there, then they could race to get out of there.

"I'll gather up the flammables. There are some we shouldn't mix."

"So you get what I want?"

"Yeah. Molotov's. Good idea to see if these things burn. They seem to move slowly, so they make easy targets. Just don't get too close with this stuff. These liquids, if they get on you, will make you go up just as fast."

The doctor was grabbing jars, looking at them. Some he put back, others he thought about and then set down on the work table. "In those overnight bags over there, you'll find clothes. You should be able to rip up some of the shirts. Then soak them in this bowl. We'll have to wash our hands before we actually use these things."

The doctor finished putting glass bottles of liquid on the work table, and had taken out a large bowl. Now the man was pulling out smaller glass bottles that were like large beakers, with long necks and large rounded out bottoms. The man kept placing more and more of them onto the table until they had ten of them. Then he stopped and looked around.

"Only ten? I would have liked to have had more. The other beakers wouldn't hold the rag well, so I don't think they would work."

"Ten should be fine. The Humvee isn't that far. We get to that, we can get out of here."

"And go where?"

"From what I saw of the map, that side road should take us out to one of the smaller roads, where we'll probably meet county law enforcement. They will be less likely to shoot on sight when they see us coming, and I may be able to talk us through."

"Yes, but they will have more people at the outer perimeter. They'll be regular army with orders not to let anyone through."

"Let's make it there first. Then we'll worry about it."

The doctor nodded and went to work on creating the cocktails.

* * * *

"Are you sure you're ready for this? Once we open the door, there is no turning back," Westdale said as he looked at the back trailer door, then to the scientist standing behind him. The man was fidgeting back and forth, obviously nervous.

"Yes. We need to go."

361

They both knew they needed to get out of there quickly, and once that door was open, they needed to make sure they were right about their plan. It was their lives they were risking, but they couldn't stay there and hope for reinforcements because Westdale knew none were coming. He had known it when he realized how many of those things were now surrounding them, and more were coming. Thankfully, from what they could see on the cameras, the things seemed to be concentrating on the other side of the truck, where the other door was…where *he* had come into the trailer. Did the things remember that? He wasn't sure, but it seemed strange they chose to gather around there, rather than around the whole trailer.

It was another question, something else he would have to try and remember to note down if they got out of there.

Westdale stopped studying the smaller man standing there with one of the overnight bags slung onto his back. It wasn't easy with the suits, and it was going to be hard if he was going to grab the cocktails, but that wasn't the plan. They both had bags on their backs, and had cut open small holes, just large enough to easily fit a gloved hand into. They were set up that way so they could grab a cocktail from the other person and vice versa.

Westdale hoped the doctor's idea of doing it that way worked. It was a good teamwork solution, but he would feel a hell of a lot more comfortable not having to rely on the doctor. He could see him running off at the first sign of trouble. Westdale didn't know him, didn't know if he trusted him, but was now having to trust the guy with his life…like his platoon had relied on him. They had relied on his being there to have their back and when that time had come, where had he been? He had stayed there, safe in the lab. He had listened to their pleading for him, his commander ordering him to come out there and help. Where had he been? But that was unfair. What could he have done? Gone out there, only to die with them?

"I wasn't even supposed to be here today," Westdale groaned as he took a deep breath and raised his hand up to the door lock.

"What?"

"Nothing. Just a line from a movie. Seemed appropriate."

"Oh."

No, he *was* supposed to be there. He wasn't from there, he didn't know these people, but he had felt something that morning, even before he had gotten the call. Something had been pulling him there. He didn't know what it was, just some guiding force. In the back of his mind, he had felt the urge. He was supposed to be there. Why? So he could die? He didn't know, but he was in the right place at the right time.

"Ready?"

"Ready."

"Fire ready?"

"Yes."

"Light it up."

The doctor had been holding the first cocktail in his hand, a little butane torch in his other. They were thankful they had found it because neither one of them were smokers and carried a lighter. With a click and then a puff, Westdale heard the torch light up as he reached for the latch and started to lift up.

Time to go to war, he thought, as he yanked up, then turned the handle. He grabbed the cocktail and turned, the dim light barely showing anything in the growing darkness outside.

The bright light from inside had made him night-blind. As he cursed himself for not thinking about that, he heard the first of the things, then saw the pale arm reaching for his feet. He stepped back, barely keeping his balance in the large suit, then caught himself and stomped down. He knew the thing wouldn't flail back from the pain, but it was more instinct than anything else.

"Get back!" Bernard yelled from behind him. He knew what the doctor wanted to do, but they were still too close to the truck. If they threw their first cocktail there, they would be trapped back inside the trailer.

"Not yet!" Westdale yelled. It didn't matter that he didn't have to yell, that the radio headsets between their suits would clearly transmit their voices.

His foot slammed down. He was missing the things hand, but it was also not able to grab onto his suit. He wasn't sure which he was trying for more…to stomp on the thing, or to just keep it from grabbing him.

His eyes adjusted and he could see it was grabbing for him while trying to pull itself into the trailer. It was bending over, trying to wriggle its way up there. It wasn't trying to climb, didn't seem to have figured that out yet, but it seemed to know how to writhe and work its way forward.

Westdale took another step back, getting out of the reach of the thing, studying around him. The armored Humvee was twenty paces away, not really that far, so they could easily run for it once they got out the trailer. There was only three of the things between here and there.

However, now that the door was open, he saw those three were coming their way, and he wasn't sure if he was imagining it, but he thought he could hear scuttling sounds, like dragging feet on gravel. He was afraid the others from around the front of the truck were already coming around.

"We're getting boxed in," he said.

"Well, what are you going to do?"

What was *he* going to do? Damn, why did it come down to what *he* was going to do? He didn't want to call the shots; he didn't want to make the decisions. How the hell had he ever gotten in the position where he was in charge?

Well, if there was ever a time to take a stupid risk, he guessed it was now. Damn, this was going to be stupid. If he ever made it through this, when he told his kids about it, at least he could say he fought zombies and kicked their asses.

Yeah, Don, you got to make it out of this and have *kids first, dumbass,* he thought.

With that thought running through his head, and hoping like hell it wasn't going to be the last thing he ever thought, he ran forward and jumped off the edge of the trailer.

He landed hard and made sure to try and roll with it. He had jumped away from the largest group of the things, jumping to the right of the back of the trailer, but there had been only gravel to soften his fall. As he rolled with it, that large oxygen regulator on his back caught on the ground. He tried to continue rolling, feeling the pain pushing in on his back. His knees felt like he had taken a hammer to them. Then he was on his stomach, using his gloved hands to push himself up.

Now it was time to see just how stupid he really was.

He stood and turned around, already backing away. Bernard was still standing in the back of the trailer. Westdale couldn't see the expression on his face, but he was sure the blood had rushed from it and the man was looking at him in exasperation. He had already learned it really didn't take too much to rattle him. The man was smart and was doing a good job under the pressure, but he always seemed to have that moment when he'd get caught by surprise.

The things had all turned and were now looking at him. They didn't seem to react too quickly to change, either. Good. That meant he should be able to outmaneuver them. Right now, he was only thinking about getting them far enough away from the Humvee and the trailer that he would be able to take out a few of them with one of the cocktails.

"You ready with one of them?"

"What?!"

"You ready with the cocktail?"

"You want *me* to throw it?"

He heard the voice, obviously surprised. Westdale had also thought he would have been the one to throw the damn things, but there wouldn't have been a way for him to make that jump and still hold onto one. Did the scientist not realize that was why he had handed the thing back to him beforehand?

Well, actually, he had probably thought he had handed it back to him to light it. Westdale hadn't thought about that. He had just gone and done it, then jumped out the back. He didn't think they had time to think about it too much.

"Yes! Throw it!"

Westdale saw that the three were now fully coming towards him, completely having forgotten about Bernard in the trailer. Good, he was luring them away. He was working his way towards the streetlight, stepping backward so he was getting closer and closer to the light. Bernard, on the other hand, was kind of hidden by the bright light of the trailer behind him. He also wasn't moving that much.

He had a brief thought and wondered just how well these things saw. Their eyes were completely white. Could they really see him, or did they just sense him? How were they identifying he was the one to follow?

He took another step back, the gravel crunching under his boot. He could see them as they came closer to him. He was making it farther and farther away from the Humvee, but he still knew he could get around them easily enough and get to the vehicle. They moved so slow, he could easily run around them.

There was more coming, though. He could see about ten of them at the side of the trailer. They had all been along the side and near the front of the truck, but were now facing him and stumbling towards him. He wouldn't want to make it around these three just to run straight into them. He would want to go around and to the right side. There was that wooded border of the parking lot, so he had no way to know if there were any over there, but even if some emerged, he was sure he would see them in time to avoid them.

He was still studying the situation when a loud *whoosh* of air seemed to warm up suddenly in front of him, then he felt like he was engulfed in the flame. Fire was showering up in the path between him and the Humvee, the intensity nearly pushing him back. His vision was gone, and all he could see was white, black stars, and shifting shapes.

Then he felt the ground make sudden compact with his ass. He hadn't been pushed back by the explosion, but had been so blinded, he had just fallen back and had not even tried to catch himself. The impact sent shockwaves up his spine. His teeth ground together, and he could feel a wetness at the corner of his eyes as he fought down the pain.

"Are you okay?" He heard Bernard's voice crackle with worry over the radio.

"Yeah," Westdale grit out through clenched teeth. Just how close had the bastard gotten to him? He really didn't want to think about it. He could feel the flames, and his vision was still just shapes. The whiteness had faded away, but everything was dark with vague shapes now, and he didn't even know if he could trust that those were really there. "Did you get one?"

"No. I missed."

"We can't be wasting them."

"Well, I'm sorry. I was never any good with sports."

"Really?" The sarcasm was rich in Westdale's voice as he forced himself back up, trying to blink away the blindness. "I can't see. Are any of them close to me?"

He knew he was staggering nearly as bad as one of them now.

"Um, not really. I missed the zombies, but I got it between them and you. They have to go through quite a bit of it to get to you."

"And they're not?"

"No. They are just kind of staggering around, not getting any closer."

Westdale's vision cleared enough that he could make out more of the shapes. With how bright the flame was, night had become day, and he wasn't sure if he was getting his vision back because his eyes were getting better, or because the flame was starting to die down. He wasn't sure what had been in that bottle. He knew Bernard had made cocktails out of different chemicals he had found, and had told him different ones would have different results. This one had been a bright white flame, and had been hot enough that even through the suit, Westdale had thought his face would burn off. He didn't want to know what would have happened if he hadn't been in the suit.

He could see that the things were on the other side of the flames. They couldn't get to him or, at least, they weren't willing to risk it. That was good for him, but he could already see that one of them was turning back around to Bernard.

"Get out of there! Get to the Humvee and get in!"

"Wh-," he had started to say, but then the private saw him moving. He must have seen that the things were turning back towards him.

"All units, prepare for inbound. M.O.A.B. is en route. E.T.A is twenty minutes. All units, prepare for inbound," Westdale heard over his radio. It was quiet, and he doubted it had been intended for him. It had probably been a mistake sending it out to all military channels, but that didn't matter. He knew what it meant. He knew they had to get out of there *now*. If they didn't, there would be no help coming for them.

"What does that mean? What's M.O.A.B?" Bernard asked.

Westdale had been watching as the man climbed down from the back of the truck. He hadn't even tried to jump, but just gingerly worked his way down, using the back step to come down as gently as he could. Even with the things coming back at him, he wasn't going to risk hurting himself.

"Trouble. We need to go," Westdale said, already breaking into a run to the Humvee. As soon as he did, the three things turned towards him. He was sidestepping around the flame, keeping his distance by a couple feet. The doctor had warned him the chemicals, if they got on him, would turn him into a human torch, suit or not. He wasn't willing to risk that.

The heat from the blaze was dying down. As he ran, he saw that a fourth one was turning back to him. He was running towards the Humvee as fast as he could in the suit. They seemed to be ignoring Bernard again. Why the hell were the things so damned focused on him? What did he have that they wanted? Unless they knew something he didn't.

Westdale took a second to look back over at the scientist, who was slowly moving towards the Humvee. The man acted like he was trying to stalk over to it, like he was a cat burglar. He was hunched over, taking each step slowly and gingerly. The man was a scientist. He had been with them, but hadn't gone into that other room. Whatever the hell these things were, they had to have been created by something. It was kind of strange that, all of a sudden, these things were just there.

Just what did the man know, and why were the things not going after him?

Westdale pushed the thought out of his mind. He couldn't be wasting his time thinking about anything like that now. Even if the doctor did have something to do with this, it just meant Westdale should stay close to him. It was a sense that if the doctor was involved with this shit, he would have a way of making it out alive. The closer Westdale stayed with him, the more likely he would get out, too.

He made it to the Humvee first and quickly pulled open the heavy armor of the door, sliding into the seat. The darkness inside was comforting, and the little bit of coolness in there was a soft feeling of relief. Something about being in an armored vehicle filled him with a sense of security. They weren't out yet, but they were one step closer.

The engine roared to life in a diesel-fueled fury. He was checking the gauges when the passenger door opened and the doctor was fumbling to get in. The man was maneuvering, trying to squirm and wiggle, but between the tank and the bag of cocktails on his back, he was making it more difficult for himself than it had to be.

Grabbing a knife he knew was kept by the seat, he reached out and quickly cut off the bag from the scientist's back. It came free, and he pushed it into the back seat. Then he reached out and pulled the man in, making him land roughly.

"Watch out! Don't break those. Some of them would react badly if they got mixed."

"Close the door!"

Westdale was already putting the large vehicle into gear and enjoying the feel as it shot forward. The first two zombies in its way quickly slammed against the front of the Humvee. As the heavy vehicle bounced over them, Westdale felt a wave of exhilaration at knowing that was two less they had to worry about.

The doctor was still fighting with his door as Westdale pulled the vehicle onto the street. Okay. They were in, they were moving, but he had to figure out which way was the way out. He knew the map of the place. He had looked it over before they had come into town, but looking at everything now, in the dark with only the limited streetlights illuminating their way, he just wasn't sure where they were going.

"Do you know where you're going?" Bernard asked him as he finally pulled his door closed.

"I have a rough idea of the streets."

"So that would be a no."

No, you damned asshole. I do know where I'm going, but I just don't know where to find the road to start out on. It should be just up here on the left, and then we'll be shooting out through one of the minor roads that just the locals are watching. Westdale wanted to scream it at the man, but just bit down the comment and took a deep breath. "We just have to find Walnut Street. It leads straight out of town."

"Okay." It was weak. He knew the doctor wanted to say more.

The small roads raced by, the tiny street signs flying by faster than either one of them could read them. He wanted to slow down, but there were just more and more of the things around him. He saw them coming from the streets, some stumbling out of houses, some just in the middle of the street. He slowed down just enough to be able to either hit them without tearing into the armor of the vehicle, not that it would do any damage, or maneuver around the things.

The town was lost. There were too many of them. It must have spread quickly. Why hadn't they seen any of them when they had come into town? They had just seemed to let them in and then, now, there they were. How had they missed all of this?

Because they hadn't been looking for it. They hadn't known what they *had* been looking for. They would have looked past the people walking in the streets because they wouldn't have looked out of place. Not when you were only glancing at them as you prepared for a mission report.

The road seemed like it was getting smaller. It seemed like it was a main road, but the businesses had faded away to houses. There were stop signs that he just blew through, not paying them any attention. Trees cut out the little bit of moonlight, and large, leaf-covered branches canopied overhead. There were streetlights, but the world around them seemed to have crept into a darker night as so much light was being taken away. They were relying more and more on the headlights of the Humvee, which were not all that good to begin with. They had spotlights and additional lights that could be turned on, if needed. If Westdale wanted to look around for the switches, he could but, right now, he was trying to just focus on seeing what he could.

"Watch out!" Bernard yelled at him. Before Westdale could react, Bernard was reaching across and grabbing at the wheel.

"What are you doing?" Westdale growled at him as he fought with the scientist. The man wasn't that strong, but he was fighting to pull the Humvee to the right, which would take them into some yard.

"You're going to hit those people!"

People? What people? There were only those things out there.

Westdale continued to try and turn the wheel to get them back onto the road, but the tires were spinning in the grass of someone's yard. They were losing control as the vehicle twisted and turned. Westdale fought to turn the wheel back, but it was too much of an adjustment. They were quickly fishtailing back in the other direction, turning onto another side street.

Westdale barely had time to see the rising of the road and the large metal arms of the railroad crossing. With how they had turned, they were heading right towards them. He tried to fight the wheel to the right. They were still going too fast, and the Humvee was fighting to turn away from him, the wheel pulling in his hands. The whole vehicle was shaking, trying and go in so many directions at once.

This wasn't going to be good. Westdale knew it as soon as they were twisted in that direction. He tried to straighten out the vehicle so he would hit it square on. They hit the dip at the railroad crossing, then they were airborne.

The wheel had twisted from him, this time pulling itself completely from his hands as the vehicle had hit the side of the rut. They had hit it at a bad angle, and Westdale felt his stomach lurch. He knew that when they came down, it would be bad. With luck, they wouldn't roll.

However, he didn't really feel as though luck would land with them.

CHAPTER 22

Rob didn't need to look back. In that brief second, he had seen enough to know that they needed to get out of the bar. As he watched the woman he thought had been immune to the virus attack the bartender, he realized it wasn't just the world around them that was shattering. He had started to get used to the bar. It had been a wall of security between them and the things, but he knew they had to leave it eventually. He just hadn't wanted it to be with so much chaos, and he didn't want to leave anyone behind. He wanted all of them to go. They were all supposed to leave and get out safely. It was his own promise to himself that he would make sure to get them all out, but he had failed.

He always failed, didn't he? He had failed all those people in Chicago, seeing them die in that meth lab fire. So many women died because he failed them. He was the protector. He took his oath to protect and serve seriously. He failed that oath, and had promised when he got out of the hospital, he would not allow himself to fail again. Now, people were again relying on him to save them, and he couldn't. It was all falling apart and he couldn't save them. He had to save himself and get out of there. If he was to see his son and wife again, he needed to go.

Rob turned, bringing up the closest heavy object he could find, a stool they hadn't used against the door, and flung it through the front window. Then he was through it, landing on the large metal storm cellar door of the basement. The door was slanted downwards, so he slipped a little. His balance was thrown off, and he felt his bad leg trying to buckle. He thought he was going down because he could feel it bending. His weight shifted, his foot found solid ground, and he was able to stumble forward until he caught itself.

"Motherfuck!" he heard Bruce grumbling behind him. Rob turned to see him on the ledge of the window, easing himself down.

Rob didn't want to think about the yelling he still heard inside, the calls for help. Those two had chosen to stay behind, so he wasn't leaving them. This was what they chose to do, and they really wouldn't have been safe if they had taken the baby. If it woke up, it would have called attention to them. The things would have swarmed to them like flies. They would have had to leave the child.

Yeah, and he would have nightmares about *that* tonight. He would see babies around him. They would probably add to the fires that invaded his nightmares, add to the women who danced naked through his dreams, their skin burning off. He still saw the smiling face, the old man's face that had the tooth-filled smile that went from ear-to-ear.

Tina said she would take the baby into the cooler with her. They would all be safe in there. He just had to send in help. He could get help, get the military to come in after them.

But no one would be coming in. No one would ever come into the town. He knew that just as well as Bruce did. There would be no one getting in there. He should have tried harder to get them out of the bar. He should have *forced* them to come. He could have grabbed the baby and brought her with him. They could have kept her safe.

"Come on. We gotta get to my truck," Bruce was saying as he climbed down the metal door, his steps booming. *The sound echoes like a dinner bell,* Rob thought as he tried to make his way down behind the big man, but trying not to make as much noise.

He looked around and saw there were about twenty of the things around them. They weren't on top of them, yet, but they would be. They were surrounding them. While it wasn't a closed circle, it would be enough.

"Keep moving!" Rob called out to the man as he saw an open path and started running towards it.

Bruce pointed, calling out after him "My truck's over there. Where are you going?"

Why couldn't the man see? If they ran to his truck, there were more of them there. Sometimes you have to run away from something to get there. The best way between points A and B was not always to go straight. Sometimes it was better to go around the lake to make it to the beach.

Yeah, the beach…where he should have been. It was summer. He should have taken his wife and son to the beach. It had been a nice day. He should have taken them swimming, maybe have done some fishing. When was the last time he had taken Jake fishing? He really couldn't remember.

"Look at all them. There's a path here. We make it over to that road, there are less of them down that street. None of them seem to be by the tracks over there. We can cut up on the railroad tracks and come back to the crossing. We can't just run straight through them," Rob was saying as he rushed towards the gap. He was trying to keep as much of a distance from those things as he could.

These things were something more than what they saw. He had figured it out in the bar. He had a feeling there was something to the spiders that each of them claimed to have seen. It didn't make sense they couldn't see the things, but the infected always seemed to see them. If there were spiders, maybe they needed to avoid just getting bitten, but Denise had never been bitten. They needed to stay far enough away that something couldn't crawl on them.

"We can run faster than those things."

"Not if they gang up. Come on."

Rob wasn't waiting around for him. He made it past one that looked like it had lost most of his arm, the skin torn away down to bone. He wasn't sure if the things had been eating if off the man, or if the man had done it to himself. If seemed like, in the transition stages, the people had become very self-destructive trying to claw out the spiders. Every one of the things around them looked like, at some point, there had been some kind of self-mutilation. Even the ones who had been mostly eaten showed some kinds of claw marks around the face and eyes. He wasn't sure what that meant.

He came near one woman who was missing her leg. He could see the stump as she crawled towards them. What was left of her mouth was opening and closing, her teeth exposed, and part of her cheek was clawed through. She reached out another hand and pulled on the cement, making her way closer. Rob could see that three of her fingernails were gone, the tips gnawed off.

He made his way clear of her and was across the road and into the yard. He was just beyond the edge of that glow of the streetlight, and could see that Bruce was quickly coming behind him. Rob turned and took a minute to study the world around them. It had changed so much in a day, but if you took away those things, you could almost not see it. The lights came on in the houses that were set on timers, the streetlights came on as if life still existed. In the darkness sweeping through the town, the night sky could almost not even been seen in the horror that had invaded.

He knew that if he closed his eyes, he would smell the barbecues. In the house behind him, the small ranch house with the large window, he could imagine a forty-something cooking steaks; kids were playing in the yard, screaming and yelling at each other, collecting the fireflies as they flew in the twilight; a song was playing on the mp3 player they had hooked up to a speaker outside; the smell of dinner would float out from an open kitchen window; and the wife would be sitting in a lounge chair, just watching the peacefulness of the kids' chaos.

That world was gone, and he couldn't close his eyes to think about it. The world had changed in the course of a day. Nothing would ever be the same again.

It had all happened so fast. Change wasn't supposed to be like that. It was supposed to be gradual, not in the course of one day. This wasn't supposed to happen.

He could almost hear the sounds of the distant highway, although he knew it must have just been his mind playing tricks. There was a distant roar as something tore down the street blocks away. Back in his own town, he often heard that sound five to six times a night when one of the locals had decided it was time to try and race down the main drag, knowing that the chief was, more than likely, out of town patrolling one of the neighboring communities that paid for him to check on them.

Sometimes the kids would get caught, or sometimes he would just happen to come up there to have a talk with them when they would park their cars outside the sweet shop afterwards.

That sound had become comforting. It was a sound he recognized, and it had somehow become one he associated with home.

"Do you hear that?" Bruce asked as he came up behind Rob. The man was already puffing a little, but not because of the exertion. Rob turned and looked at him, seeing that the things behind him were working their way up onto the grass. It did seem like they had lucked out when they had come out of the bar. Most of the ones that had been towards the front had been more of the slow, maimed ones, ones that had maimed legs and would chase after them slower than many of the others.

Rob could still see the bar. It was only a little down the street because they really hadn't come that far yet, and he saw about ten of the things had stayed there, still pounding on the front loading door. Looking closer, he realized they weren't pounding on the door. It looked like they had gotten part of the door twisted and were climbing in the building. If the kids hadn't made it to the cooler, it was too late.

They still had to get across the next street and climb the fence that followed along the side of the railroad tracks. He figured they could run along it. If they were inside the fence, they could avoid the things and run straight down the tracks. Of course, he couldn't see any of the things caught in between the fences that bordered the tracks, but if any of them were in there, they would be trapped.

And they still had to climb the fence. That was beyond the streetlight, but there was still enough light for him to see, so he didn't think there were any there. There weren't any trees by the tracks, so everything should be clear. They just had to make sure not to get hit by any trains.

But no trains had come though that he could remember hearing. They must be rerouted or blocked. Maybe it was a dead track. He was too far away from it to know. It made sense, though, that they would have stopped the trains. Why let a train through when you had quarantined everything else?

"It's getting closer. Listen," Bruce said. Rob had heard it, but kept pushing it to the back of his mind. Still, that roar of the engine *was* getting closer. Very close. In fact, most of the things had turned away from them, starting towards the side street parallel to the tracks. Only the crawler seemed to still be noticing them, working her way one outstretched hand at a time.

He rushed into the streetlight, hurrying across, wanting to make his way to the tracks as soon as he could. They had to climb that fence while the things weren't noticing.

"Rob!"

Rob turned to see Bruce still standing there, then he looked to see where Bruce was pointing It was an Army Humvee rushing down the road. They were saved. The army had arrived!

Before thinking, he took a step towards it, holding up his arms and flailing them. "Hey!"

The things seemed to be too caught up in the sound of the engine that they didn't notice him. As they started to stumble towards it, it plowed through them, the heavy armor high enough that it forced the things to either get flung out of the way, or fall underneath and get crunched under the large tires.

Then Rob saw as the vehicle lost control. At first, it fishtailed towards them, but then it started going wildly back

and forth. It didn't take long. It had been going too fast, then it
had raced into that dip of the railroad tracks, going airborne.

* * * *

Rob was the first to reach the vehicle, surprising himself
with being able to push back the pain biting through his lower
back. Ever since the accident, whenever he had tried to run, he
had fought against the limp. It always pulled at him. It slowed
him down and he would often curse at it. Damn his leg. Dammit
to hell for keeping him from being able to help, for reminding
him of how he *couldn't* help. He wasn't young and healthy
anymore, and his body loved to send painful reminders to him
whenever he tried to push himself beyond his limits.

"I'll get the driver. You check to see if there is anyone
in the passenger seat," Rob called to Bruce, who was laboring to
keep up. He could hear the man's hard breathing, but knew it
meant he was still behind him. The things hadn't gotten to them
yet, which was good because they had rushed to the vehicle
without focusing or being too careful. The large vehicle had
done a decent job of clearing the way, so it hadn't been that hard
to follow its path.

He could hear slow, dragging steps on gravel and didn't
have to turn to know that the things were coming.

The Humvee was upside-down, and Rob ran to the
driver's door. The door looked like it had been crumpled on its
outer edges, but was still closed. Rob reached for the handle and
pulled. He was worried the rolling of the vehicle had maybe
wedged the door closed. He was thankful when, with a slight
groan, the door actually opened, revealing a man in what looked

382

more like a space suit than anything Rob had ever seen before. It was obviously some kind of hazmat suit.

These men were part of the team that had come into town. Something biological was going on. That made everything worse, and Rob even had to wonder if it was smart to get out of there. He wasn't a scientist and didn't know how something like that spread. What if they did make it out, only to carry it somewhere else? What if he took it home and gave it to his family? Could he live with seeing his wife or Jacob as they slowly tried to claw their eyes out, then tried to eat him?

But if he didn't try to get out, he would never see them again. He would know if he was infected long before he got home, right? He didn't need a doctor's degree to see what happened to these things as they changed. He would be able to tell if he was getting that way. He would know. He could stop himself.

Rob reached in to pull the person, he wasn't sure if it was a man or a woman, out of the vehicle. The man hadn't been wearing a seat belt, and had taken a good tumble while they had been flying through the air. He was heavy, and Rob had to put in a lot of effort to get him out. He heard something inside him pop, his right side suddenly feeling like it was lower and there was a numbness flooding through his lower back, but the thing inside the vehicle was moving. Then Rob dragged him out and onto the grass. The Humvee had landed in a large open field just beyond the tracks. Bruce's truck was parked in a gravel lot in the far corner. They were almost there.

Rob eased the person to the ground. He could hear a groan from the other side of the Hummer. When he heard pounding, he looked up to see Bruce fighting with the door. When he couldn't get it open, he pounded on it, kicked it, then

Rob watched as the man spat on it in disgust. Finally giving up on it, he had come around to the driver's side and eased the other man out that door.

So far, it didn't seem like either one of them was stirring. They must have been knocked out, but they still didn't know if either was alive. Rob didn't like it, but they were probably going to have to get these men out of their suits.

He reached down and grabbed the zipper along the chest of the first man's suit.

"What are you doing?" Bruce asked, eyes wide.

"We need to see if they're okay."

He ripped the zipper down the length of the suit, pulling it off his upper body. Bruce reached past him and grabbed the man inside the suit. Rob heard him grunt as he struggled to pull, then saw as they pulled out a man in a camouflaged uniform. As Bruce lowered him down, Rob bent over him, reaching to the man's neck to check for a pulse.

Bruce hurried over to the other man. "Be quick. We gotta get moving."

"Get him out of there. This one's still alive," Rob said. The pulse was strong and the man had only minimal marks on him. He had a bloody nose, but it wasn't gushing too badly, and there were already signs of what would be a puffy, bruised face later but, overall, the man seemed like he was in good health.

"This one's suit is covered in something," Bruce said as he pulled the much smaller man out of his own suit. This one wasn't wearing camo, and Rob though he must have been some kind of doctor. Why else would he be there? That, combined with the pale complexion and the scrawniness, Rob couldn't imagine him being anyone other than a lab rat. This guy didn't look like he ever made it out into the sun.

"Ether…," the man gasped. He was barely awake, but Bruce heard it and quickly looked down at the man. "The bottles broke. It's all filled with-"

"Uh, Rob, I think we better get going. I don't think we want to be around this thing much longer."

Bruce was glaring at the vehicle, a worried look creasing his brow. White smoke was already coming from inside. Then Rob noticed some kind of liquid dripping from inside the vehicle, pooling on the grass, then starting to smoke.

"Yeah, let's get out of here. Can you carry one of them?

"Can you?" Bruce shot back. He already had the scrawny guy tossed over his shoulder. Damn bastard must have noticed his limp, not that he was able to hide it. Rob grimaced at the man, but he bent down and hefted the soldier up. He couldn't carry him the same way Bruce was carrying the doctor, but he thought he could walk the man as best he could.

"Come on. This would go a hell of a lot easier if you would just wake up," Rob said through clenched teeth. To his surprise, the man's head shook a little, and he could feel his feet actually trying to match Rob's steps. "Come on. Just a little bit farther."

Rob looked around. Bruce had moved past him and was hurrying towards the truck. There was only one of the things between him and the large eighteen-wheeler. Bruce was easily keeping his distance from it as he made it around to the passenger seat.

"Spiders…," Rob heard the man gasp. His heart nearly beat out of his chest, then stopped. He nearly let the guy fall right there. There was no way he had gone through all of that just to save someone who was already infected. He had not come this far to go down now. He had not done everything he had to have some soldier get him infected with the things.

"Spiders… Do you see them?" the man gasped under his arm.

"No. Do you?"

He actually felt him relax a little, then the man started working his way out from his grip to hurry alongside Rob.

"No, thank god," Westdale said, his breathing a little more relaxed. They both rushed to the truck, making it to the passenger door. As Rob pulled himself up, a large fireball erupted from the Humvee.

"I thought those things only exploded in the movies," Bruce said as he pulled himself over into the driver's seat. Rob felt the warm blaze slam against his back, and when he closed the door it only gave him some relief. The flame seemed to be spreading around the large vehicle.

"Vehicles don't. However, all the flammable liquids we used *do* explode," the scientist said from the back of the truck.

Rob turned to face the man as he went into a coughing fit, finding some paper towels in the sleeper. Rob noticed it wasn't that bad of a set-up back there. The soldier and the scientist were sitting next to each other on the mattress.

"You okay?" Rob asked.

He heard a buzz and some loud beeping sounds, then an alarm ringing through the front of the truck. All three of them turned to Bruce, who was reaching down and cranking the key.

"What the hell is that?" Rob said, alarmed that their ride might not be able to get them out of there. The buzzing continued and the beeping seemed like it was getting louder, but Rob really couldn't tell.

"What?" Bruce looked over at him in surprise, then back to the two in the back. Suddenly, the alarm registered with him, and a huge smile spread across his face. He had to force himself not to laugh. "Oh, that. This trailer has been giving me air leak issues since I picked it up. Nah, it's fine. We just have to build up air. Give it a minute."

"We don't have much time," the soldier said. He leaned forward, draping his massive arms over the back of the seats.

"Why do you say that?" Rob said. He looked around, trying to see what they didn't know. He saw that the things were still near the bar, but they had stopped coming their way. It seemed like the fire kept them from coming closer.

He prayed that the girl, the baby, and the owner's kid were going to be okay. They had been good people. None of them deserved any of this, and he sure hoped they had made it to the cooler.

"Incoming air strike. Tactical nuke. This town won't be here in about ten minutes."

"What?!" Rob swung his head to look back at the soldier. He couldn't be serious. There was no way they would launch an attack on United States soil, would they? They couldn't get away with that. The press would be all over it. It would be a disaster for the president. There was just no way. It could not be done, not in this day and age. If not the president, there was no way somebody would actually follow those orders.

Though, in this day and age, they didn't need people to follow those orders. That's what military drones were for. People were inconsistent and not reliable, but a machine would always follow your command.

"Okay, so let's get out of here. Time to put the moose guard to the test."

"Moose guard?" the scientist said. "What the hell is that?"

"You saw those large metal bars up at the front, covering the grill? That, my boy, is a fucking moose guard. This bad boy can fucking take out a moose at sixty miles per hour and barely get a scratch. What do you think it'll do to these motherfuckers?"

Rob didn't want to say anything, but he had a bad feeling Bruce was actually about to enjoy this. He thought he saw a trace of a smile at the corner of his lips.

"Well, let's go."

"Still building air. Got about another thirty seconds."

Bruce revved up the engine, watching as the gauge on the dash slowly worked its way up to 50 psi.

"We got visitors. Three of the things trying to climb up the passenger side," Rob called out as he heard the first slam from the thing outside.

"Do you think they can get in?" the scientist said in a high-pitched voice.

"Not sure. Here, this'll help," Bruce said as he pulled down his visor. Rob didn't know what he was reaching for. All he saw was some paperwork and pens clamped up there. Then the large man slammed his fist to the upper area, an unexposed door popped open, and a sawed off twelve gauge shotgun seemed to fall into his arms. He quickly handed it over to the cop.

"Better not bust my balls over that later."

Rob wasn't even thinking about it as he turned and looked at the three things trying to break the window. Zombies.

He didn't know if he could ever really accept that the damn things were zombies.

"Okay, fine, but why do you even have the thing?" Rob asked as he started to roll down the window. He lifted himself up, putting his knee on the truck seat, and leveraged himself so that as the top of the window came down, he could poke the tip of the gun out and shoot at the first of them.

"You ever drive in Jersey? You do it once or twice, and then the third time, you carry a shotgun and whatever else you can hide."

Rob didn't want to think about that. He also didn't want to think about how loud this was going to be in the closed cab.

"Here."

He barely turned around to see that Bruce had forced a set of earplugs into his hands. The man really had thought of everything. He put the earplugs in. It was time to get these things down. They were already trying to get their fingers into the window and pull it farther down.

Rob fired the first shot. Even with the earplugs, the sound was like an explosion in the truck, reverberating through his skull. He was sure a few of his teeth had just come loose. The shot had hit one straight in the face, and the other two had both gotten a heavy part of the shot, as well. The middle one fell, taking one with him. The third one somehow hung on.

"Okay, let's move it, people," Bruce called out, then Rob heard a loud hissing behind him. Oh no, please let the brakes just not completely give out. That just would be how everything else was going today.

He felt his hope slip, continuing to fall into a darkness he had never known before, when the truck slowly inched forward.

"Okay, we can't go forward, so hang on. I gotta try to turn this thing around in the grass. If we're lucky, we won't get stuck," Bruce called out to all of them as the third zombie was back. It had steadied itself outside the window and was grabbing onto it with both hands.

Now that they were moving, Rob decided to try and just roll up the window. He doubted just one of them would be able to break through it. It was thick glass, and these things, while they were strong as a pack, didn't seem like they were too strong alone. Not that he had actually had much time with any of them, but he just had to have faith.

He rolled up the window as far as he could with the thing still holding on. Its fingers kept it from going all the way up. It wasn't going to let go.

"You have to get it away from us. It doesn't have to bite you to infect us. It just has to get close."

Rob looked back at the doctor. He had thought as much, but the doctor had just confirmed it. Just how much did he know? Once they got out of there, he was going to sit the man down and they were going to have a nice long talk. Depending on how Rob felt at the time, the shotgun may or may not be invited to the conversation.

Rob felt the truck picking up speed. He hoped Bruce had a plan on where they were going. He just had to trust him.

He rolled down the window just a little more, just so the thing's fingers weren't trapped. It could now pull away if it wanted to.

He was face-to-face with it. The grey eyes stared at him blankly, showing nothing. They were completely dead. The mouth that moved, opening and closing, trying to always bite down onto something. Only a part of the nose remained. The cheeks were gashed open. One ear was completely gone, obviously ripped off. It once had brown hair, although much of the scalp was exposed now, the hair and skin just ripped away.

He looked and saw that the person was wearing a name badge. It was barely fastened onto the torn shirt, just hanging on the strand, but he could see the name Billy. It had once been what looked like a younger man, probably the same age as the bartender and his friend.

Had it gone to school with them? That morning, it had still been just a kid, maybe a year or two out of high school. Who knows what it had been doing before this whole thing started. Was it going to college?

He could imagine how this boy had woken up that morning, enjoying that it was Saturday and that he didn't have to drive the fifteen miles to the junior college. The boy may have been studying physics, or engineering, or computer programming. However, if he was from the area, he was probably studying at the trade center in the junior college and maybe learning about plumbing or air conditioning repair.

It didn't matter because when the kid woke up that morning, he wasn't worrying about school. He had been going to work. Maybe he had plans to go to a party afterwards. Maybe he would see a girl there that he liked, and they would have gone and gotten drunk, screwed, and enjoyed themselves.

When the kid had woken up that morning, he had been alive. He had a life. He had been living it, working towards a future.

"Shoot it!" the soldier yelled from the back.

It brought Rob back and he was looking at those dead eyes, no longer showing any sign of life. This thing wasn't that kid anymore, and it sure as hell wasn't *alive* anymore. Whatever happened today, everything had changed. This boy would never be able to go back to what he was, and all that was left of him was to be this thing that killed. That morning, the thing had been a man. Now it was just another one of the things trying to kill them.

He pulled the trigger. With another loud explosion, the window shattered outward, the massive buckshot of the twelve gauge hitting the thing full in the face, then it was gone. It hadn't had anything to hold onto anymore, and it didn't react fast enough to grab anything else. It rolled away, tumbling into the night.

EPILOGUE
(PART 1)

He could hear them out there. It hadn't been loud at first, just one single pound against the door. He assumed it was a fist, but it could have been the zombies just slamming into it with their bodies. Of the ones he had seen so far, none had exhibited much control of their limbs. Either way, it had started with just one sporadic pounding. Still, that one pounding had told him what he needed to know. They had gotten in through the loading door. They were now in the little dock area, which meant they were now trapped in the cooler.

It was what he had meant to happen. They had run to the cooler. It should be safe for them to be in there. He couldn't imagine those things being able to get in, and because of the broken door handle, they wouldn't be able to accidentally open it. It took a special tool shoved into the door to open it, and Tina had grabbed it when she had first came in with the baby. They should be safe.

It was cold in the cooler, though. Not that he minded it, compared to how hot the day had been and how the bar had been stifling. When that cold air had hit his sweat-soaked body, it had felt like he was in an ice cooler. Like he was a fish that had been caught and thrown in, waiting to be carved up and served for dinner.

And they *were* dinner if those things got in there. They had the appetizer, the baby, then they could choose who they wanted to eat next.

They were sitting ducks until the military came in to save them.

"How ya feeling?" he asked Tina, seeing that she was shivering. He was trying to keep his own shivers down, refusing to take his eyes off the door.

"I'll be okay," she said in a quiet voice. She really hadn't been saying too much since she had gotten back to the bar after fending off her ex-boyfriend at his mom's house.

"Yeah, don't worry. They'll be here soon. We just have to wait."

"How long do you think?"

"Not sure. They won't want this to spread too far, but I can't see them coming in at night. They'll probably come in early in the morning." He didn't know why they hadn't come in already, although he guessed maybe they needed to evaluate the situation first. There was probably some scientist out there who had been in control of whatever experiment that had gone haywire, and he was trying to fight to get it back. Either that, or the doctor had died and the military guys had to figure out what they were up against. He guessed that made sense, although he wished they would hurry the fuck up.

At least his mom was on vacation and didn't have to deal with any of this. However, when she came back, he'd have to tell her Lucy was gone.

Lucy was gone. She was truly gone. He didn't know if he was going to be able to tell his mom that. He didn't know how he was going to be able to cope with it. Right now, it had gotten easy to push it out of his head. They had to get through this, so he couldn't allow himself to focus on it. However, once all this was done and they were saved, how would he be able to function?

He had also lost his best friend, watching as a zombie ate him. In a fucked up, funny way, that was the way Sullivan would have wanted to go. He would have wanted to have gotten in a few spectacular kills first, though. Something worthy of a zombie movie.

Now Jason didn't have anybody close. He wasn't a social person. He had his little sis, and he had his zombie-hunting, dumb ass best friend. Today, he had lost both of them.

He felt another shiver run through him, and ran his hands along his arms to warm them up. He could feel the hairs rising on his skin, and they itched a little. He dug slightly, tearing away at the sensation.

The room around him seemed to warm a little, or that could just have been him trying to heat himself up. It was a cold floor and wall, and both he and Tina were sitting against the back wall, keeping an eye on the door. The things were still pounding against it.

No, the room definitely felt like it was getting warmer. The air seemed different, like it was getting thicker. Overhead, he heard the fan of the cooler whine, and a smell filtered in. It was a rotten smell. He knew his mother was never one to keep meat in the cooler because they didn't serve food there on a regular basis. The little supplies they did have in the cooler were chips and crackers, candy bars, stuff like that. None of it would explain why the room suddenly had the stench of rotten meat.

"Do you smell that?" he said, looking briefly at Tina. She wasn't looking at him. Her head had lowered, and it looked like she had fallen asleep. Her hands still twitched, running along her arms. He had thought she had been shivering, but she wasn't. She was scratching, and the marks were getting deeper.

No, it couldn't be…

He thought he saw a spider, but he couldn't be sure. He blinked and turned to look away, focusing his gaze back on the door.

Movement caught his attention and he looked back at Tina. It wasn't her, though. It was past her. A little hand was reaching out of the box they had put Nadine in. She was reaching up, her hand reaching past the lip of the box to a man standing over her.

How had a man gotten in there?

But he wasn't really a man. He didn't look right. He looked like he was clothed, but Jason couldn't describe them and couldn't focus on them. Everything about the man was dark, and Jason could only make out his faint shape from the light behind him.

The man was stooped over the baby and had reached down. Jason could see the outline of a finger reaching out, allowing little Nadine's hand to grab him by the finger. It was kind of cute, as it reminded him of when Lucy used to grab his little finger when she had been small.

Push the thought down, Jason. Push it down. What the hell was this man doing in there and how had he gotten in?

"Who are you?"

The man stood, pulling his hand away from the baby. Jason could see Nadine had what looked like ash on the inside part of her hand, like whatever covered the man remained on her.

Jason looked up to stare into the man's eyes. He saw fire there, the flame burning where the man's eyes should have been.

Jason felt their heat. He felt it all through his body. It ran through his veins, and he knew the faster his blood pumped through him, the faster he'd be burned from the inside out. It felt like it was going to eat its way out of him just to have him spontaneously combust right there, his inner life force working against him, but then it centered on his own eyes. A throbbing formed and he had to force them closed.

Everything around him cooled back to what he had felt before he had seen the man. He could hear the hum of the cooler kick back on, no longer whining against some unnatural heat.

He counted his breaths, waiting until he reached a hundred. Then he opened his eyes, but wished he hadn't. Spiders. They were crawling from under the door of the cooler, from out of the vent of the refrigeration unit. Any crack in the wall, spiders flooded out of it then over him. He was covered in hundreds of them.

He opened his mouth to yell, but spiders ran inside before he could. They filled his lungs as he tried to breathe. He could feel them wiggling and squirming to make their way into his ears, climbing up his nose. They were everywhere, their little legs on his skin. He was infested with them.

He realized that if he was seeing them, it was already too late.

He wished like hell he hadn't been able to see them. He liked it when he didn't know they were already taking over.

Someone in the room, he couldn't see who because there were too many on top of him, was laughing. He didn't know when he had lay down, but he could feel a layer of spiders covering him. Even with them in his ears, he still heard the laughing. He knew it was that thing. He didn't know how he knew, but he did. The thing had won, and it was laughing.

EPILOGUE
(PART 2)

The general watched the camera feeds, watching as the five survivors each sat in their own isolation room. Five survivors… That had been all that had made it out. Of everyone…the townspeople, the soldiers at the inner perimeter and the outer perimeter…only five people made it out.

Four of them had escaped through one of the blockades just seconds before the M.O.A.B. had taken out the area. The fifth, Sergeant Wade, who had been commanding the inner perimeter, had also been found, though no one, not even the sergeant, could explain how he had made it just a mile from the outside perimeter.

Five people. That was it. All of them were now sitting there. He wasn't sure how long he would keep them in isolation. It was a mess outside. The biological entities were contained, although no one knew for sure what the hell they were, but they had to nuke a town to do so. The political aftermath was a nightmare. The president had tried to deny any knowledge of it. He really did act like his shit didn't stink, and it seemed like the fool actually thought none of this would blow back on him.

Now, the general thought they might actually have had the first U.S. President to be arrested on murder charges, but there would never be any hints at orders so nothing could ever get back to the president. That had been the reason for all the secrecy in the first place but, somehow, it seemed like that might not matter. The American people were crying bloody murder, and they wanted his head. It didn't matter if he had anything to do with it or not. Hell, most of the U.S. wanted his head after they heard about the Snowden leaks. This just gave them more justification for it.

Not that any of that mattered to the general. None of it would trickle down to him. He was in a special part of the country now, a special base, tucked away from everyone and everything. He was given one mandate and that was to find out what had happened in the town, then see what he could do to weaponize it. After all, there was just too much potential to let it go.

And all he had were five people who didn't know a thing. He wasn't sure how long he would keep them there. There wasn't much use as long as they weren't a threat. They couldn't politically harm anything more than what was already out, so he just needed to make sure they weren't dangerous.

A part of him wished he could just dig a big hole somewhere out in the Nevada desert and drop them all straight down into it. Just bury it all away so it would disappear. His name wasn't a part of it yet, which was good. How everything had been set up, his name shouldn't *ever* be a part of it. With all the backlash though, he didn't know if that would stay true. The truth always had a nasty way of coming out, usually when it could hurt him the most.

Someday, the truth would come back to bite him on the ass.

And the biological entities were all gone. Every single one of them was destroyed. No matter how much he wished he could have kept at least one for them to study, all of them had been burned. The necessity of it negated any possible way he could keep one for his people to study. They just spread too damned fast, were too hard to kill, and just too dangerous to keep around. If he hadn't killed them all, they would have eventually wiped everybody out.

It was over and they all had just barely survived.

* * * *

Sergeant Wade didn't know how he had survived. He was on the line with his men. He had stayed with them. No matter how much the brass was trying to come after him for abandoning his post, he knew he hadn't. He had been with them, fighting next to them. Long after he ran out of rounds, he was still there. He would take a rifle from a wounded soldier and would continue firing. Soldiers who ran would drop their weapons, and he would pick it up. He had *not* abandoned his post.

His post had abandoned him. Many of the men had fallen around him, getting overrun with the things. They didn't move too fast, but he wasn't backing away fast, either. They continued to move back, backpedaling to stay facing their enemy. No matter how many times they fired, how many bullets were shot into the things, they just kept coming.

McCormick had somehow gotten to his side. The kid had been smart. Get close to the guy who seemed to be surviving. It hadn't helped him, though. While Wade had been focusing on a group of the things coming from their left, one had come up on their right. By the time Wade had seen it, it was already too late. One of their soldiers, a private who must have gotten attacked early, had grabbed his communications man, pulling him to the ground.

Almost everyone was down. It was chaos. The war between life and death was battling all around him. He knew he didn't have a chance, but he was *not* going down until he had taken as many of the things with him.

Of course, none of the things were really going down. They just kept taking the hits, falling down, and getting right back up. Bullets riddled their bodies and they just kept getting right back up. It didn't matter how many times they were shot. They still came. It didn't matter if they had heads. They still got up and came forward.

After a while, he noticed that he was the last man and the things were surrounding him, but they weren't coming quickly. Instead, they seemed to stop a few paces away. The ones with mouths, were just opening and closing them, looking at him in that hungry, dead way, but they didn't come any closer.

Then he heard the inbound overhead and looked up to see the bird coming in. He knew it was a drone, and knew what must have finally been happening. He wasn't surprised. At some point, he knew they would have to drop a tactical nuke because there was no way they could ever allow any of this to get out. It had to be contained.

He let the rifle fall to the ground, hearing it land with a distinguishable sound of metal on asphalt. Then he just waited for the things to attack him as he watched the metal object fall from the sky.

They never attacked, and he saw a bright white flash surround him.

Then he woke up in the white room, not sure how he had gotten there. He was found miles outside the outer perimeter. It just didn't make sense, so the brass didn't believe him. Instead, he was labeled a traitor and someone who ran in the face of battle.

None of it made any sense.

* * * *

Bruce felt so relieved when they had made it out. There had been many times he didn't think they would. But they had, and here they were. They were alive. How the fuck did that happen?

He knew that moose guard on the front of his truck had taken one hell of a beating. Hell, his whole truck did. They had been lucky at that first blockade. The police were so overrun with those things, they didn't even care about the truck flying right past them. They had been damn lucky the cops hadn't had their cars across the road. Rob had actually been pissed at the negligence of the officers, even though it had saved their lives.

At the outer perimeter, they had even more luck. The soldiers out there had been in the process of pulling out. Bruce hadn't known why, the private in the back had said something about a M.O.A.B or something, but they just barreled through, passing the soldiers, who then chased after them.

Then something exploded, and Bruce had just stopped.

The soldiers had quickly caught up with them and, the next thing he knew, he was here…wherever the hell here was.

403

White room, the whole place reeking of sterilization. They had escaped from one quarantine to another.

And here he was in a small room with white walls that he stared at every day. No matter how much he slept, he felt like it was never enough. He was always tired, and the lights seemed like they were always on. And, occasionally, he thought he saw a spider. He would see one, then he would blink and it would be gone.

He had to be imagining things. Hell, with what they had all been through, he was sure he would be seeing spiders for the rest of his life.

And then there was the man, that foul-smelling man he had met at the truck stop. He couldn't remember anything about him, just that he smelled really bad. Bruce would wake up and see the man sitting in the corner, watching him. Sometimes Bruce would wake up and he wouldn't see the man, but he would smell him. The stench would be gagging him, and he would find it hard to breathe. He would have to toss himself over, so that he was on his side, and start dry-heaving. He would hear his horrible laughter, and it would rake inside his skull like nails on a chalkboard. It would echo on and on, and no one who came to check on him could hear it.

He wondered at just what point he had lost his sanity in that town. But hadn't he met the man *before* he went into town? In fact, hadn't the man been the one to tell him the interstate was backed up, sending him down 23 and through Hammond.

Maybe the man had never been real. Maybe *none* of this had ever been real.

And there was another spider crawling along his wrist. It was a small, black spider that he felt as its legs danced upon his hairs. It was feeling its way up along his arm. Was it real?

And, again, he heard that dark man. As much as he had looked around for him, he never could see him, but he always heard him laughing.

Hello,

I hope you enjoyed "Caught in the Web" which is book 2 of the "Invisible Spiders" series and that I haven't given too many nightmares. Who am I kidding, of course I wanted to give you nightmares.

Caught in the Web and the Invisible Spiders series as a whole came from an interesting idea and the more I build on the universe and work with these characters, the more they come to life. I truly love writing this series and hope to continue to find new ways to make it a scary experience to read each new chapter as it develops.

When I started writing "Hatched" the first book in the series, I had the idea that I wanted to extend the initial transformation into a zombie and that was my initial concept. I feel that zombies in themselves are not that scary of a subject, but the idea of becoming one is. So I took that idea and started to develop the concept.

As I was developing "Hatched" at some point I felt that while that was a book I really wanted to write, it would be a hard book to have people enjoy. I felt that the slow build didn't have much of a pay off in the "action" element of something in the zombie genre. So that was when I started developing the military aspect and was when the book started to become more a piece of a series and not a standalone story.

"Caught in the Web" is the pay off for the first book. It is the finale to that part of the story and it does end with one helluva bang. Though some might feel it ended a little clipped,

I felt to add on more action to the end would have been pushing the limits of enjoyment. There was a certain amount of closure and to continue with that one more chapter would not have been that entertaining.

So now we prepare for book 3, "Weaving the Webs." I will warn, when thinking in the aspect of the larger story, this was just the opening scene. Book 3 will be starting the series over again. It will be a departure from the story so far, as things are reset. Whereas one chapter of the story has ended, the next chapter begins almost anew, and the long story will start to build.

I hope all of you will enjoy and take this journey with me. It will be a bumpy road and there will be a lot of heart break, zombies, and of course, spiders…